— BOOK 4 —
TARAN EMPIRE SAGA

EMPIRE UNITIED

A K DUBOFF

Published by Dawnrunner Press
Cover Copyright © 2022 A.K. DuBoff

ISBN-10: 1954344309
ISBN-13: 978-1954344303
Copyright Registration Number: TXu2333804

0 9 8 7 6 5 4 3 2 1

Produced in the United States of America

TABLE OF CONTENTS

KEY TERMS, CAST & LOCATIONS.............................I
CHAPTER 1...1
CHAPTER 2...13
CHAPTER 3...28
CHAPTER 4...42
CHAPTER 5...56
CHAPTER 6...66
CHAPTER 7...78
CHAPTER 8...93
CHAPTER 9...107
CHAPTER 10..119
CHAPTER 11..132
CHAPTER 12..153
CHAPTER 13..174
CHAPTER 14..185
CHAPTER 15..200
CHAPTER 16..215
CHAPTER 17..231
CHAPTER 18..251
CHAPTER 19..258
CHAPTER 20..268
CHAPTER 21..280
CHAPTER 22..290
CHAPTER 23..303
CHAPTER 24..316
CHAPTER 25..327
CHAPTER 26..338
CHAPTER 27..350
CHAPTER 28..364
CHAPTER 29..372
ADDITIONAL READING...................................387

AUTHORS' NOTES 388
GLOSSARY 391
ABOUT THE AUTHOR..............................401

THE CADICLE UNIVERSE

Tarans are the predominant race in the Cadicle Universe; humans are a Taran genetic offshoot. Most of the Taran sphere falls within the purview of the Taran Empire, governed from the planet Tararia by a council of High Dynasty families. Earth is one of several rogue colonies on the outskirts of the Empire, separated so long ago that they have forgotten their Taran ancestry.

The Tararian Guard is the primary military force for the Taran Empire. Its counterpart, the Tararian Selective Service, includes a specialty branch with Agents gifted in telekinetic and telepathic abilities. The TSS is headquartered at a base inside Earth's moon, and its iconic Agents are known in Earth lore as the mysterious 'men in black'.

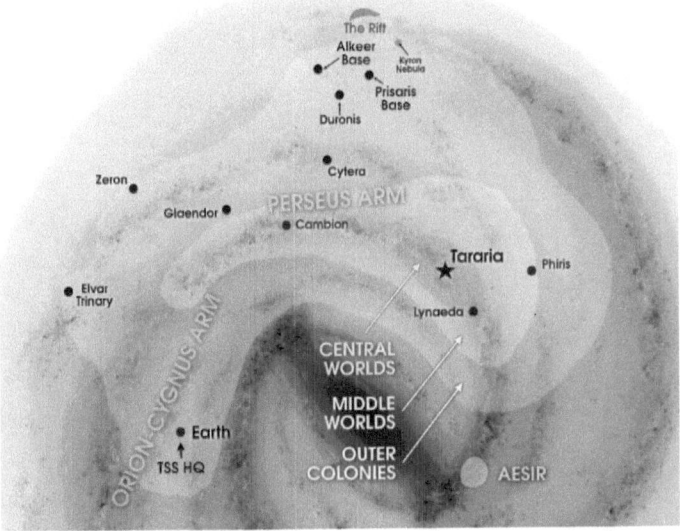

KEY TERMS, CAST & LOCATIONS

KEY TERMS

Taran – The race of all people in the Taran Empire; synonymous with human

Aesen – The foundational energy of the universe; pure energy capable of being shaped into any form

Erebus – The nickname for a race of high-dimensional aliens with exceptionally strong control of *aesen* energy

Jump – Faster-than-light travel through subspace using the SiNavTech beacon network

Beacon Network – The navigation method for subspace jumps, maintained by SiNavTech

Independent Jump Drive – A jump drive that does not rely on the SiNavTech beacon network for navigation

High Dynasties – The seven ruling families of the Taran Empire, collectively a governing council

Lower Dynasties – Influential families throughout the Taran worlds, second only in power to the High Dynasties

ORGANIZATIONS

Tararian Guard – The primary military force for the Taran Empire

Tararian Selective Service (TSS) – A quasi-military organization with Agents specializing in telekinesis; a complement to the Tararian Guard

Taran United Force (TUF) – A new unified branch of the Taran military

Coalition – A shadow faction operating in the shadows of the Taran Empire, known to have multiple arms including the Alliance and SPEAR

Priesthood – The former governing body of the Taran Empire

Aesir – A reclusive group of technologically advanced Tarans

CAST

TSS

Jason Sietinen – TSS Primus Elite Agent; son of Wil and Saera; twin brother to Raena

Wil Sietinen – TSS High Commander; Jason's father

Saera Alexri – TSS Lead Agent and head of Primus Division; Jason's mother

Michael Andres – Primus Elite Agent / Head of TSS Operations and lead Primus Division trainer; Wil's close friend

Lexi Karis – Head of Civilian Training; Jason's partner

Gina – TSS Agent on the Coalition task force

Ron – TSS Agent on the Coalition task force

Laura – TSS Militia officer on the Coalition task force

Pyra – TSS Militia officer and undercover operative

Kali Wietris – TSS Agent and undercover operative

Tararian Guard

Jakob Mathaen – Admiral of the Tararian Guard

Taran United Force (TUF)

Kira Elsar – Head of the recently formed TUF; former Major in the Tararian Guard

Leon Caletti – Civilian consultant, geneticist/scientist; Kira's fiancé

Taran Government

Raena Sietinen – Sietinen Dynasty heiress; twin sister to Jason; Ryan's wife

Ryan Dainetris – Head of the Dainetris Dynasty; Raena's husband

Cris Sietinen – Head of the Sietinen Dynasty and SiNavTech executive; Wil's father

Kate Vaenetri – Cris' wife and Wil's mother; member of the Vaenetri Dynasty

Celine Monsari – Head of the Monsari Dynasty and MPS executive

Other Key Characters

Dahl – Oracle with the Aesir; Wil's main point-of-contact and long-time friend

Melisa – Lexi's friend, who disappeared after joining the Alliance

Pesta – A sentient transdimensional weapon tethered to a Taran 'handler'

Ships

Conquest – TSS flagship with a unique telekinetic energy weapon

Horizon – Coalition command ship (captured by TSS)

LOCATIONS

TSS Headquarters – Base inside Earth's moon

Earth – A 'lost colony' of the Taran Empire, located in the remote Outer Colonies

Tararia – The capital planet of the Taran Empire

Duronis – A developed planet in the Outer Colonies, base of operations for the Alliance

Antaris – A developed planet in the Outer Colonies, former TSS outpost

Lynaeda – Technologically advanced central world, specializing in AI and cybernetics

Zeron – Remote Taran world known for its underground excavations

CHAPTER 1

JASON NEVER EXPECTED to find himself on a Tararian Guard ship, but he had to admit that their stealth tech was unlike anything in the TSS fleet. "It's kinda fun being able to sneak around like this," he said to Kira.

She smiled at him from across the small vessel's flight deck, where the two of them were observing the operation along with several members of Jason's Coalition task force team. "Pays to have friends with cool toys."

The TSS didn't have stealth ships of its own, as the perceived presence of the organization was almost as powerful as having a visible Agent; therefore, all TSS ships were a symbol, meant to be seen. By contrast, the Guard had dedicated special operations teams whose primary functions were to gather information without anyone knowing they were there. Kira had previously been attached to one of those units, and her former commander still captained one of the preeminent vessels, the *Raven*.

The ship had enabled Jason's team to covertly approach several of Monsari Power Solutions' facilities to gather information about their operations and assess how best to seize the assets. While the other sites they'd visited thus far had matched the specs stated in MPS' public records, this latest facility had exhibited several irregularities, observable even from a distance.

Located on an out-of-the-way asteroid, it was the kind of place no one would stumble across unless they had reason to be there. It would seem, for that reason, MPS hadn't gone to much effort to conceal the fact that they were up to more than the expected business operations.

Robotic soldiers standing three meters tall, complete with shoulder-mounted guns, paced in front of the door. At least a dozen additional guards of the flesh and blood variety were positioned in lookouts above and around the entrance. The transport ships at the dock were equally guarded, with an armed escort accompanying a series of crates being transferred to one of the waiting vessels.

Jason reviewed the scan data displayed as a holographic overlay on the front viewscreen, which supported his visual assessment. "We have a problem, don't we?"

Gina, one of his fellow TSS Agents on his task force, scowled at the scene. "That certainly doesn't look like a typical parts supply warehouse."

"Funny, I was thinking the same thing." Despite the levity in his tone, Jason was concerned about what it all might mean.

On paper, this MPS warehouse should hold standard repair equipment to maintain systems connected to power cores. While valuable and worthy of security, this operation had the appearance of a military installation. He could have justified it as MPS simply being cautious, but there were other facilities with the same specs on paper which hadn't had a fraction of this kind of security, indicating that something was different here—a clandestine aspect of the operation that they were intent to keep secret.

"Sir, we're picking up some strange readings in the GP scan," Anya said, looking over the shoulder of the *Raven*'s helm officer. As the team's tech specialist, she'd been tasked with verifying the ground-penetrating scan data gathered during the recon mission.

The scans could only paint a partial picture of what was going on inside the facility, but it was the best information they had at their disposal without sending in a team to look around. The imaging results were indeed unexpected.

"Ateron?" Jason stared at the scan data with interest. "What are they doing with high concentrations of ateron out here?"

"Technically, it appears to be an alloy, of sorts," Anya chimed in. "Which is strange, since ateron *has* no known alloys—but this definitely isn't pure."

"Has there been any sign of something like this before?" Jason asked.

"Yes, in the Gatekeeper tech," Gina said, crossing her arms. "But why does the Coalition have it?"

The element was not only rare but also extraordinarily expensive. The Lynaedans had control of the largest known deposits, but they were known for closely regulating the material they supplied to others. Even the TSS had difficulty getting enough to service the ships equipped with bioelectronic interfaces; ateron was necessary for those systems, and the limited supply meant the TSS had never been able to construct as many ships with those features as they would have liked. The fact that the Coalition had somehow gained access to the material was both annoying and confounding.

"Can we get any estimates of quantity based on this scan data?" Jason asked.

"We'll have to get closer," Kira said. "Even then, I don't know. There's some weird interference."

"Is it reasonable to get closer?"

She evaluated the information on the screen. "I can't guarantee they won't be able to spot us, but I will say we've gotten closer under more difficult circumstances without detection."

"Good enough for me," Jason said. "Let's see if we can find out more."

Kira gave a nod of agreement to the pilot, who then directed the ship closer to the asteroid.

Jason watched the information display, waiting for the scan data to update.

"All right, it looks like there's a significant deposit of the ateron alloy underground in this area here," Anya said, pointing at the relevant area on the screen.

To Jason's eye, it appeared to be a large storehouse. The material was showing up as a singular blob rather than individual items, but the general shape of it gave him the impression it was in stacked crates. The format didn't matter, though; the point was that MPS had ateron, and they should have no reason to possess it.

"What about voydite?" he asked. Now *that* material was central to all power cores. Granted, this wasn't a core manufacturing facility, but there should be at least trace amounts from repair components.

Anya's expression remained neutral, but Jason picked up the concern in her eyes. "None, beyond the power cores running the facility."

This whole thing is definitely a front. Coalition? There were so many unknowns. They already had enough evidence to justify a legal search of the facility; however, this wasn't the time to go in.

"Okay, let's head back to—" Jason cut off as several red warnings flashed across the screen.

Anya swore under her breath. "They're sending out directional pulses to check for objects in the area. The stealth tech won't hide us from that."

"Jump us out of here," Jason instructed.

"Can't from this range without making our presence obvious."

"I'll try to avoid the pulses," the helm officer said.

Jason nodded. "Do it."

The ship backed away from the asteroid with irregular movements as the helm officer tried to avoid the detection range of the random pulses. It was impossible to know what had tipped the facility off to the fact that they were being watched, but they were clearly equipped with security monitoring systems well beyond most civilian operations.

A projected course appeared on the front display, indicating a path that would take them to a jump point far enough away to avoid detection. It was much further than Jason would have liked.

He stayed quiet, watching their progress. *If they see us, they'll know for certain they're under investigation and that the military is involved.* While the Coalition no doubt had suspicions already, confirmation would change the situation. The TSS needed to act fast before Monsari had the chance to make a countermove.

A new red warning flashed, accompanied by an audible chirp.

"That was a direct ping. They spotted us," the helm officer confirmed, managing to maintain a smooth, professional tone despite the rising tension.

Shite, so much for stealth. If their presence was known, there was no sense trying to tiptoe away. "That's our cue to exit. Get us out of here," Jason instructed.

He caught Kira's gaze, and he saw the concern in her eyes. Getting caught was bad any way he looked at it. If Monsari wasn't on high alert before, they would be now.

How are they going to retaliate? It was a matter of when, not if.

The ship slipped into subspace, casting a shifting blue-green glow to the flight deck as the view outside changed to the ethereal ribbons of colored light.

"Where to next?" the helm officer asked.

"Scrub the rest," Jason said. "No sense drawing further suspicion by going anywhere else right now."

"Back to Overlook Station, then?" Kira asked.

He nodded. "I'll check in with Headquarters, and we'll decide how to proceed."

There had been half a dozen other facilities on Jason's investigation list, but those would have to wait. Considering the trouble someone had gone to in arming the asteroid, any other sites hiding similar secrets would no doubt be on the lookout for spies. They'd need to use a different tactic to gather the remaining information.

What are they hiding? It was a mystery he intended to solve.

— — —

Even after six years, Ryan Dainetris didn't feel like he belonged on the Taran High Council. Everyone else was a career politician—eager to hear themselves talk and flaunt their own importance. As much as Ryan loved his grandfather-in-law, Cris wasn't above the displays, either.

Consequently, Ryan found himself sitting quietly through most of the meetings, speaking only when asked a direct question about his opinion. This gave him time to study the others on the holoconference, learning their ticks and tells. He hadn't had many opportunities to put those observations to use, but the mental library grew every day they met.

This meeting was no different, stretching on longer than necessary while the heads of Baellas and Makaris argued over a proposed change to the tariff structure for goods sold on space stations versus planetside. Since the modification would create an incentive for space-based sales—and since Dainetris Galactic Enterprises was in the spaceship business—that seemed like a good thing. Baellas and Makaris were already making more impassioned arguments than Ryan would have, so he was content to sit back and let them do the talking.

"It's time to adjust for those changes in population centers," Eduard Baellas was saying. "If no one has anything else to add, I propose we put it to a vote."

"No objection," Kaiden Vaenetri said.

Cris Sietinen looked around the room. "All right. Those in favor of adopting the new—"

Across the holoconference table, Celine Monsari looked down—apparently reading a message on her handheld, based on her position. Whatever information had come across it,

Ryan's observations of her tells pointed to it being bad news.

"I'm sorry, I must attend to an urgent matter," she said.

"We're almost finished with business for the day," Cris protested.

"It can't wait." She dropped off the holoconference, leaving an empty seat in her place.

"Apparently, we'll vote on the tariffs next session," Cris said, not bothering to hide his annoyance.

The representatives of Baellas and Makaris both audibly sighed, and the rest of the councilmembers shook their heads.

"That concludes our business for today," Kaiden said. "Meeting adjourned."

As the High Dynasty representatives began dropping off the call, Ryan addressed his grandfather-in-law.

"Cris, do you have a few minutes to go over something?" Ryan asked. It wasn't unusual for them to speak after the council meetings, so there wasn't any reason for the others to be suspicious.

"Sure."

Ryan transferred their avatars into a private virtual conference space. "That was an abrupt end to the vote."

"Celine is self-absorbed and doesn't care about issues that don't directly impact her or MPS," Cris replied.

"I think she'd just gotten bad news."

"What makes you say that?"

Didn't he notice? Ryan hadn't thought his observation skills were anything special, but perhaps the other people in the meeting just had their attention elsewhere. "Celine's expression. She's normally so guarded, but I was watching her, and I could have sworn I saw a hint of fear."

The older man didn't reply at first. "Hmm."

"Do you know something?"

"I believe the TSS and Guard were doing that joint op today to check out several MPS facilities."

The TSS hadn't given out any details, but Jason had tipped them off that the investigation was happening. Except, it was supposed to be covert.

"Monsari shouldn't know anything about that," Ryan said.

"Which means either there's a leak, or the investigation wasn't as stealthy as planned."

Ryan's heart dropped. "What does that mean for us?"

"That we should be ready for anything."

— — —

Jason used the ride to Overlook Station to get his thoughts in order. They had decided on the location as common ground between the Guard and TSS; docking the *Raven* at Headquarters would invite questions they didn't want to answer.

Unfortunately, that might become unavoidable since the ship had been spotted near the asteroid. The only benefit was that MPS would only know it was a Guard ship. That made it all the more important to distance the TSS' involvement.

Jason and his team transferred to a TSS transport ship and quickly departed the station. By the time they made it back to Headquarters, Jason had completed his field report and was ready to debrief with his father.

He made his way into the base and headed straight for the High Commander's office. Wil beckoned him in when he arrived.

"Well, that went to shite," Jason began, taking his usual seat.

"What happened?"

Jason gave his prepared account of the event, highlighting the relevant details. He brought up a holographic map of the facility locations and used it to guide the discussion.

"So, two-thirds of the sites shouldn't pose much of a problem," he concluded, then adjusted the map to show the questionable locations in red, in contrast to the blue denoting the others. "These, however—the visual assessment and scan data don't match up with their documented specifications. I don't know what they're hiding, but my guess is those sites are a key aspect of those secrets."

"Then they're the priority in the seizure."

Jason nodded. Since Monsari was linked with the Coalition, they had effectively been funding terrorists and were open to prosecution. However, their breadth of influence meant that a formal move against Monsari could backfire if it wasn't handled well. "We need to make a clean sweep, simultaneously, across all of Monsari's and MPS' assets, as well as those of their strategic subsidiaries. We need to cripple them in one blow—no chance to run or regroup."

"Agreed." Wil leaned back, studying the map. "Every time we learn something new, there's another wrinkle."

"I never imagined the conspiracy would run this deep."

"Neither did I."

"I wish I knew what they were planning." Jason sank deeper into his seat. "I'm clearly missing something. We've been at this for well over a year, and the enemy keeps getting away. That's a failure any way you look at it."

His father shrugged. "I don't think I'd have made any more headway if it was my full-time assignment."

"You'd already ended a centuries-long war by the time you

were my age."

"That's not a fair comparison."

"Isn't it? You gave me the same CR designation as you. I know there's an expectation about my performance, whether you admit it or not."

Wil looked down at that assertion. He didn't reply at first. "You've faced more than many Agents, Jason, but you've never really been tested the way I was. I'd already lived a lifetime by twenty-five, and I wouldn't wish that concentrated education on my enemy, let alone my son. Do you have areas for improvement? Yes. And I offer guidance whenever I think it will be beneficial. Even without that intervention, I see you learning and growing every day. In the end, that's what's important. Eventually, you'll find yourself in a situation that will fundamentally change the way you see the universe, and from that moment on, you'll know you can face anything else life throws at you. But that's a journey of discovery you need to experience for yourself."

Jason listened in silence, recognizing the truth in his father's words. "I won't let you down."

"I have every confidence that you'll come out of this experience a strong and capable leader."

"Thank you."

"That said, you're not alone," his father assured him. "I'm here if you ever need a sounding board or just need to vent."

"I know, and I appreciate it. I think there's going to be a lot of that coming up. We need to make a decisive move against Monsari—soon."

Wil nodded. "Definitely."

"Going in there will be messy no matter what approach we take."

"Nothing about this situation is ideal. A mess is to be expected."

"But we need to go about it in a way that won't collapse the Empire."

"That is the key."

Jason crossed his arms. "Any ideas about how to do that?"

"That's what we're going to figure out."

CHAPTER 2

GIVEN THE UTTER failure of the covert probe into Monsari's holdings, Jason was eager to get back on track with other areas of the investigation. Following the debrief with his father, he called Ron and Gina to a meeting in his office so they could strategize about next steps.

The other Agents got settled in the visitor seats, looking as glum as Jason felt.

"I'll just say it, because I know what you're probably thinking: did we mess up, or do they have tech they shouldn't have?" Jason said to start things off.

"Well, they're sitting on a mountain of an ateron alloy they *definitely* shouldn't have, so possessing stealth-detection tech that can thwart top military engineering shouldn't come as a surprise, either," Gina replied, crossing her arms.

Ron nodded. "I agree. Under normal circumstances, the ship should have been un-spot-able."

Jason had been over the *Raven*'s technical specs ahead of time, and his instruction to go closer to get better scan data had been informed and reasonable. Nonetheless, getting confirmation from the other Agents made him feel better. *I need to stop doubting myself.*

He'd been struggling for months now and hadn't quite been able to regain his command confidence after the incident on Quel. He knew he had to move past it—and there were moments where it had slipped into the background of his memory—but it was still too present for him to be a fully effective Agent. There were people counting on him, and he needed to get it out of his head and get down to business.

"Okay, this is what we're going to do," Jason said. "We'll do a deep-dive into Zeron. Figure out what they're hiding." The information Kali had uncovered about the strange memory wipes of the workers was just too strange and had Coalition wrongdoing written all over it.

"Since nothing came up in the research, that will require sending in someone undercover," Gina said.

"Who?" Ron asked.

"Kira is who comes to mind," Jason replied. "Given past experiences, they'd be on the lookout for someone traditionally Gifted."

"Kira was on Duronis, as well as the raid on the *Horizon,*" Ron pointed out. "She might be on their watchlist now."

Jason nodded. "I've already thought of that. We'll alter her appearance. Pyra is also interested in continuing the investigation. A telepath and a null would make a good undercover team." As a TSS Militia officer, Pyra had previously been undercover as an assistant to Andrei Steyn. With his rare trait of being a null, making him immune to telepathic reading and control, he was uniquely equipped for this assignment to investigate alleged mental manipulation.

The two other Agents were quiet as they mulled over the

suggestion.

"Okay," Gina said at last. "But I think there's another area of investigation we should revisit."

"Which is?" Jason asked.

"The drugs the Steyns were peddling."

Jason's team had previously looked into the various business dealings of the Steyns, from the illegal drug sales to legitimate research through SPEAR Tec and had come up short on all fronts. "We didn't find anything unusual about the drugs when we looked into it before."

"We also didn't on Zeron," she pointed out. "I just keep replaying what happened to Andrei, with that weird mist-drug. Pyra attested that's what made him... well, whatever it was that happened to him. Ascend. Become Erebus. Whatever." She looked distinctly uncomfortable talking about it, pulling her arms tighter across her stomach and scowling.

Jason couldn't blame her for the apprehension; nothing about Andrei's fate felt right, especially Pesta's assertion, 'he is Erebus'. There had been no residual traces of the mist in his drug vial, so testing the substance had been one of the many dead ends in their investigation. Nonetheless, he agreed with Gina's logic. If Andrei had access to a drug that produced such strange results, what else may the Steyns have been placing in their drugs sold to others?

"It's been difficult to draw a clear line between the Steyns and the street drugs on Glaendor and the other worlds," he said. "The testing we've done so far hasn't revealed anything significant. And new products aren't entering the market. Seems like they stopped distribution."

Gina shook her head. "Then we're not looking at it right. Think about it. Why would the Steyns invest all that time and effort into building a drug empire only to walk away?"

"Marco and Andrei both died," Ron said. "Maybe the operation fell apart without them?"

"No, an operation like that has lieutenants who'd jump at the opportunity to take over in a power vacuum," Gina said. "They stopped."

Jason had to admit, it didn't make sense. "Either it wasn't lucrative—and what drug operation isn't?—or they ran out of product and were forced to quit."

"There's one other option," Gina continued. "They'd achieved whatever they set out to do, so they closed up shop."

Jason raised an eyebrow. "What illegal drug cartel has clear goals and a sunset plan for the business?"

"Exactly. Like you said, it's unlikely that they couldn't turn a profit. Which means it was either an issue of being unable to get more product, or they stopped for other reasons." Gina brought up some information on her handheld. "Now, until this morning, I'd just assumed all the survivors related to the business operation scrapped everything and went underground when their 'big demonstration' went to shite on Glaendor. But something wasn't sitting right, so I called in a favor with a friend who's a Captain in the Enforcers for a territory near Glaendor. She got me a copy of the records related to drug crimes for the past several months, and it was quite interesting."

"In what way…?" Jason prompted when it became clear she was teasing out the drama.

"I'm glad you asked." She flicked her hand over her handheld's screen to cast the information onto Jason's desktop.

A holoprojection appeared, detailing citations and arrests for several different drugs. Notably, there was one noted only as 'Vapr', which had spiked for a one-month period and then quickly trailed off two weeks prior to the incident on Glaendor.

"I'll admit," Jason began, "something called 'Vapr' is an intriguing parallel to Andrei's mystery substance."

"The consumption of which allegedly prompted a higher-dimensional sentient weapon to say, 'he is Erebus'," Ron added.

"It's a leap to say this drug came from the Erebus," Jason cautioned. Even so, it somehow felt right.

The Erebus had given the 'gift' of the power cell to the TSS while they had gone behind the TSS' authority and made separate deals with the people behind the Coalition. It made sense that they would have offered other miracle solutions to suit their collaborator's business needs. Everything was tailored for the audience, and pairing up with drug dealers... well, they'd get offered the next great drug.

"I recall something in one of Kali's field reports—a side comment about there being a drug with a high mortality rate. Is that this Vapr thing?" Ron asked.

Gina nodded. "Based on what my Enforcer friend told me, yes. The local Enforcers were gearing up for it to be a major epidemic, and then—poof. The drugs disappeared from the streets."

"Hence your assertion that a goal was achieved," Jason surmised.

"Yes. Which leads me to the biggest leap of all," she said. "Transdimensional nanotech."

Jason wanted to laugh at the suggestion, but he'd seen enough weird stuff over the past couple of years to know it was unwise to dismiss anything out of hand. Moreover, Gina had proven herself to be a smart and analytical Agent, and she wouldn't bring up an outlandish suggestion without reason. "Go on."

"We know there was a real drug. We know it was only available for a short time. We also know the Coalition was working with the Erebus and Gatekeepers. We know those aliens have been playing a long game to weaken Tarans in preparation for an all-out invasion. Agreed?" she asked.

Jason and Ron nodded.

"Given all those established points, a mysterious drug disseminated by the Coalition most likely plays toward the long game," she continued. "And I got to thinking, why would anything with long-term intentions only be available for a short time? The only reasonable answer is that it would be self-replicating and transmissible. They'd just need to hit a certain threshold for distribution before it would propagate itself."

"A drug that kills its users doesn't make for a good delivery method," Jason pointed out.

"No, but a virus is the same. I don't have medical records for the people who died after taking Vapr, but I'm willing to bet serious credits that all of them were from latent Gifted bloodlines on a dormant Generation."

Jason traced her logic. "And this drug activated the higher-dimensional energy link on the cellular level, and they died from the shock."

Ron exchanged glances with Jason and Gina. "If what you're suggesting is true, it would be a total game-changer. Forget about drug side effects, the tech could provide a path toward solving the Generation Cycle issue."

The multitude of implications ran through Jason's mind. Despite being high up in the TSS hierarchy, it was still way above his paygrade. "I'll need to bring this up with the High Commander."

"Yeah, I figured as much," Gina said. "I'll forward those Enforcer records to you."

"Thanks." Jason took a deep breath, considering what to do next. "All right, so we need to see if we can track down any users of the drug and check for potential nanotech of some sort, but we still need to figure out what's going on with the Coalition's leadership and try to determine what they're planning next."

"Agreed," Ron said. "The Taran element of the Coalition has been forced out. Now, it would seem the Gatekeeper hybrids and the Erebus are running the show."

Gina leaned forward in her chair. "Except, they can't be working completely alone. In all past instances, they've needed Taran minions. Just because the organization gave up Magdalena and the *Horizon* doesn't mean they're not still working with other Tarans."

"That's what I'm thinking," Jason said. "And given how cagey everyone got when Zeron was brought up, I think it might be as close to a planetary base of operations that they may have."

Gina pursed her lips, thinking. "Let's assume it *is* all related. We know the Coalition has kept a lot hidden. They have aliens in their leadership. So, what kind of thing would they have a vested interest in hiding?"

"This might be wishful thinking, but I can't help wondering if it's related to what my dad learned from the device on Earth. It said that there were other devices like that one, but it didn't say where those were located."

"So, Zeron could be another one?"

Jason shrugged. "I can't think of anything else that would be important enough for them to go to such great lengths to hide."

"True. *Someone* has been visiting the device on Earth every hundred years for millennia. It wasn't Tarans or humans, so aliens who have a preoccupation with Taran worlds make the most sense."

"*How* they were interfacing with it is another question," Jason said. From what he'd seen of the Earth research and excavation records, the device was buried and completely inaccessible from the surface. Unless there was some sort of TSD-style transport, he couldn't image how the aliens would be able to get underground to the device.

"Maybe Zeron will offer clues about that," Ron suggested. "All that stuff is underground, too."

"Good point."

"Has my vote," Gina said. "Hopefully Kira and Pyra can get answers."

—   —   —

Raena was itching for the next phase of the plan to begin. After Ryan filled her in on the abrupt end to the High Council meeting, she knew the time to act had almost arrived.

"I can't wait to put Monsari in their place," she murmured to Ryan as they prepared for a holoconference with her grandparents in her office.

"We can't make this move on emotions," her husband countered.

"Oh, there's plenty of logic behind it. They're a danger to us and everyone else who values autonomy."

"I can't argue with that."

The political pressure had been building for years, and something would have to give. What had become clear to Raena in her short political life was that it was better to lead a revolution than to be swept up in a wave driven by others.

There had been plenty of changes within the Taran Empire over the past several decades, but not all that much had changed, when it came down to it. Sure, the High Council now governed unilaterally rather than having oversight from the Priesthood. Yet, those were still a handful of representatives, born into their positions, and the same voices which had been exerting their influence for centuries. It was an oligarchy, plain and simple. The planets outside the Central Worlds didn't have a voice, and the people had stated their dissatisfaction with the arrangement loud and clear.

The only way forward was to grant representation where there was none before. That meant the High Council would need to give up some of its power—but giving a voice to others didn't mean stepping aside entirely. Raena saw it as an opportunity for a partnership with the neglected citizens of the Outer Colonies. However, she doubted everyone on the High Council would see it that way.

Before tackling that conversation, she needed to meet with her grandparents. If they couldn't be convinced that it was the best path forward, there was no hope to garner support from anyone else.

When she and Ryan were settled, she initiated the holoconference. Lifelike images of her grandparents appeared in the empty visitor chairs around her desk, almost like they were in the room.

"Thank you for meeting with us," she began. "I figured it

was past time we conclude the conversation about what to do regarding Monsari and the general civil unrest."

Kate nodded. "We've been mulling over the issues and have some ideas."

"Me too," Raena said.

Cris tilted his head. "I'd love to hear your thoughts before we share ours."

A flutter of nerves burned in her chest. While she fully trusted her grandparents, the proposal she was about to make went against everything that had been the norm in their lives. *They could love it, or they might think I'm a foolish idiot.*

She took a deep breath. There was nothing else to do but go for it. "The Taran Empire has become divided. The disparity between worlds is growing, and we need to get ahead of that imbalance before it becomes too great to overcome." She paused, glancing over at Ryan for support. With his nod, she continued. "I propose a political change—that we become a democratic republic."

Cris and Kate both stirred in their seats, but their expressions remained neutral.

She smiled when they didn't immediately object. "There's a reason you see some form of a galactic senate in so many sci-fi movies."

"I wouldn't know anything about that," Cris said, "but this kind of representative government is something we've seriously considered. The approval voting we rolled out when we ousted the Priesthood was intended to pave the way for including citizens in decision-making."

"This is more than decision-making," Raena said. "We need stability. We have to find a way to be united while each planet can stand strong on its own."

"Agreed," Kate said. "However, doing so is easier said than done."

"Well, now is the time to make it happen," Ryan chimed in. "If we don't do anything, there are dozens of planets that are ready to withdraw from the Empire, and that wouldn't be good for anyone."

Raena picked up that thread. "Someone out on their own is an easy target for bullies. And when times inevitably get tough, help isn't always an easy call away. We *will* find ourselves alone at one point or another, and we need to be strong enough to stand up for ourselves when that happens. It's no different on a planetary scale. Except, we've been focusing on centralizing resources to share across the Taran worlds—and that doesn't happen in reality. Instead, we should help the people of those worlds prepare to face their own bullies so they can fight for themselves. Strong individuals make for a stronger team.

"The Coalition gained so much support because people loved the message about strengthening local communities and building up from there. The organization went about it all wrong and was espousing those principles for misguided reasons, but the core of their message has merit. It's not only what the people want, but it's what I think we need right now."

Cris nodded. "The decision to centralize production of key goods was driven by finances, which isn't the wisest metric. It's designed to maximize profit, little else."

"The trouble is that decentralization would be messy work," Kate said.

"We'd have to carve up the galactic corporations into their local subsidiary components," Cris continued. "Except, many of those lines are blurred."

Ryan frowned. "Right. What about a company like SiNavTech that by its nature *is* galaxy-spanning? You can't sell off the beacon network into zones."

Cris shook his head. "SiNavTech is different. VComm would be, too. You need a unified transportation and communications system."

"Keep central control of those, then?" Raena asked.

"No. Those would need to become truly public entities, no restricted access."

Raena had come to the same conclusion, but she wasn't sure her grandfather would share that vision. "Would you give it up like that?"

"I didn't want it in the first place." He flashed a sad smile. "But the truth is, the old model for SiNavTech is on its way out. Autonomous jump technology changed that. Your father personally holds the patent to that, which can be renewed for hundreds of years to come. That's your real business."

"Likewise, VComm has always made more money from the sale of communication consoles and handhelds rather than anything related to connectivity," Kate added. "Making the communications grid open-access just means more opportunities to sell devices, and those manufacturing arms would be easy to carve up."

"Meanwhile, it makes much more sense to produce food, power, and sundries at the local level," Cris went on. "Ship manufacturing yards are perhaps not something for every planet, but maybe by sector. In any case, there's a way to help the Taran worlds become more independent while still being connected."

Raena brightened. "So, you're on board with the plan?"

"I wouldn't say it's a *plan* yet," her grandfather said. "But the *concept*? Yes."

"Okay." Raena nodded, folding her hands on her desktop. "What are the next steps to make it happen?"

—   —   —

Wil sensed a vise closing around him. The Erebus and their rogue Gatekeeper collaborators had been cornered in a challenging position, and one day soon they would be forced to act. The TSS needed to be ready for that—or better yet—make the first move.

It wasn't a question of 'if' but 'when' they'd need to make a bid for the survival of the Taran race. Trillions of lives were under Wil's care, and the events to come would be the defining moment for whether he'd be able to see them safely through.

He'd been spending his time thinking about the different scenarios, preparing for every contingency. Just like the Bakzen War, this was a matter of resource management and strategy. They were at the disadvantage now, just like they'd been then. And they'd won those battles, so they could come out victorious this time, too—it was just a matter of how much would have to be sacrificed in the process.

A chime sounded on Wil's desk, indicating an incoming vidcall. He checked the credentials to see that it was from his father.

"Hey, Dad," he greeted as Cris' image appeared above his desk.

"Hi, Wil. Is this a good time?"

"Those don't exist anymore. What's up?"

His father's brows drew together with concern. "Are you okay?"

"The fate of the universe has a way of weighing on a person. Nothing I haven't been through before."

Cris looked like he wanted to say more but thankfully let it go. While Wil appreciated his father's concern, it wouldn't help him in this matter.

"What can I do for you?" Wil said to move things along.

"We talked," Cris replied.

Wil immediately knew it was about Monsari and how to handle the tenuous political situation. "And?"

"There's too strong an argument to ignore."

Wil nodded. "Okay. What's the plan?"

"We still need to work out the details, but we're strategizing. I'll keep you apprised."

"Okay. I've been in touch with Admiral Mathaen, and we're ready to take joint action as required."

"Good." His father sighed. "I'm sorry, Wil. I never expected to be going through this again."

"Neither did I."

"I wish so much didn't fall on us—I don't like it. Never have."

"If you weren't leading this effort, I'd probably have walked away, if I'm being honest," Wil admitted.

"Likewise. A person can only go through so many revolutions."

Wil nodded. "This will be my last, one way or another."

"Mine, too. I've already done a lot for someone who swore he'd stay far away from Taran politics."

"That you have." Wil cracked a smile. "I'll be standing by. We're following a couple new leads over here."

"Anything promising?"

"We'll see."

"Okay. Talk soon."

Cris ended the vidcall, leaving Wil to his thoughts.

The conversation was confirmation that the Taran Empire was about to forever change. Every choice mattered. *This isn't just a fight for peace—it's about survival.*

CHAPTER 3

ACCURATE INFORMATION WAS the most valuable resource Jason could imagine right now. Unfortunately, it was also the scarcest.

Sending Kira on another undercover assignment was risky, but he trusted her. And trust was another resource in short supply, given how the Coalition always seemed to be two steps ahead. It was difficult to know if there was a leak somewhere, or if the aliens' extrasensory abilities simply gave them an edge. Either way, Jason knew the TSS wouldn't get anywhere by sitting on their hands. Even one tidbit about what was going on behind the scenes on Zeron might offer the breakthrough clue they needed to understand the Coalition's master plan.

Given the nature of the request, Jason thought it best to ask Kira in person. After checking that she was available, he went down to meet her in the section of Level 6 that had been designated for TUF activities. As the leader of the new military branch, she deserved far more than a hallway and handful of offices in the middle of TSS Headquarters, but it was helpful to have her close by for his present needs.

To his surprise, the TUF wing was more built out than the last time he'd visited. A colored metal sign was now mounted above the entry hallway from the central elevator lobby, indicating it was the operational headquarters for the Taran United Force, with the division's emblem prominently displayed. The hallway beyond had been refinished with a combination of light-gray, black, and chrome materials to differentiate it from the warm tones and wood found throughout the rest of TSS Headquarters. Though a small change, it did help distinguish the TUF area and make it feel more official.

Kira's office was toward the back of the hallway, past a row of other offices and research labs under Leon's supervision. Her door was open when Jason arrived, and she beckoned him inside.

"Hey, I like what you've done with the place," he said with a smile.

Kira smiled back. "Yeah? It's coming together. We still have a long way to go."

"Well, if we can figure out this Coalition problem, we'll all have a lot more time and energy to put into workplace renovations."

Her expression turned serious. "Right. What did you want to discuss?"

Jason took a seat in one of the visitor chairs. "How would you feel about spending a little time in the field?"

She shrugged. "You know, I was just thinking this desk was getting a little cramped."

"Good, well, we'd like to get to Zeron. However, I suspect the rogue Gatekeeper hybrids will be on the lookout for Agents, so…"

Kira smiled. "I'm your go-to telepath undercover girl, got it."

He nodded. "I don't like the idea of you going in alone, though. Pyra has agreed to accompany you, if you're amenable."

"He was the one undercover with the Steyns, right?"

"Yes."

"His face isn't known?" she asked.

"We were thinking that for this op, it might be prudent to alter both of your appearances, just to be safe." It wasn't a common tactic within the TSS, but the technology to make semi-permanent cosmetic modifications was widespread throughout the Empire. An engineered second-skin and pair of specialized contacts could convincingly trick even the most sophisticated facial recognition tools, only detectable under a surgical microscope.

Kira considered the suggestion. "I rather like my face, but I don't mind being someone else for a bit."

"Okay. We'll make the arrangements, and we'll get you out there as soon as possible."

— — —

With the word from his parents that the plan to take out Monsari was moving ahead, Wil decided another conversation with Admiral Mathaen was in order. They'd agreed to work together, so keeping him in the loop would reaffirm the trust they'd been working to build.

"I haven't figured out a clean way to do this," Mathaen said after they'd exchanged pleasantries and a general update.

"There isn't, really," Wil agreed. "We can't just strike the Monsari estate on Tararia. The only choice is to simultaneously seize Monsari's direct assets and as many of their subsidiaries' as we can link to illegal enterprises."

"The local Enforcers can swoop in on a moment's notice, and we'll have other backup standing by," the admiral said.

"Good. I hope there won't be much resistance, but we need to be ready for anything."

Mathaen nodded. "Should we involve the TUF in this?"

Wil shook his head. "I considered it, but I'd like to leave them out of the initial seizure in case it goes sideways. The TUF stands on the side of the people, so it can remain neutral."

The older man raised a dark eyebrow. "And yet, its leader is about to go undercover again on behalf of the TSS?"

"An operation no one else should know is happening if we all do our jobs." Wil did have reservations about Kira's involvement in the forthcoming field op, but the fact remained that her unique skills were needed. It was a risk they had to take.

Mathaen nodded. "Very well. I trust your judgment on the matter."

"I'll finish the tactical plan and get it to you soon."

"Speak with you then." He ended the vidcall.

Wil leaned back in his chair and let out a long breath. While he appreciated the other military leader's faith in him, he could sense Mathaen had concerns. *We can't second-guess these moves.*

The tactical plan to take out all of Monsari's assets in one sweep was going to be tricky, and he knew he'd need other eyes on it who'd seen firsthand what they were up against. Wil sent a text message to Jason and Saera requesting to meet.

While he waited for their arrival, Wil brought up the available data, including the reports from Jason's recent time in the field.

When Jason entered the office, he immediately noticed the information on the holoprojector. "Does that mean we're a go?" he asked.

"Not yet, but soon."

Saera was only a few steps behind him, and the two of them got situated in the guest chairs across from Wil's desk.

"What did you want to discuss?" Jason asked.

"How to best seize Monsari's properties. It definitely needs to be a simultaneous hit, but I wanted to go through the thought exercise of how it would play out."

"I've been looking forward to this for a long time," Saera said, getting comfortable.

Jason smiled. "Likewise."

"For starters," Wil continued, "you've identified these facilities as containing tech that by all accounts they shouldn't have." He highlighted the locations on the map.

"Yep, they're a big variable," Jason said. "However, I don't think we can go after those first, because that would tip off all the other sites that something was going down."

"Right, which means going after the established targets as well as these other places with unknown defensive and offensive capabilities. It makes distributing our forces a bit of a guessing game."

"Not necessarily…" Jason said slowly.

"What are you thinking?"

"What if we did our own recon? You know, astral projection style."

"I'm all for gathering details for planning purposes, but those observations aren't enough to justify military action," Saera cautioned.

"Yes, we need hard, verifiable evidence," Wil agreed.

Jason's shoulders slumped with disappointment, but he nodded his understanding. "In that case, let's hope Kira gets us what we need."

"She's come through for us before," Saera said.

Wil nodded. "Indeed. In the meantime, let's make sure we know what else we're dealing with."

— — —

Kira hadn't expected to be going undercover again so soon, let alone that her new mission would require changing her appearance.

She'd always felt like the odd one out in the Guard, petite and with hair in a vibrant shade that was impossible to miss. Her appearance had led to people regularly underestimating her, and she'd often thought about what it would be like to look different.

Kira examined her new face in a mirror offered by the surgical tech. She had to admit, she wouldn't even have recognized herself.

Gone were her hazel eyes, replaced with a rich brown from the contact lenses. Her red, pixie-cut hair was now shoulder-length dirty-blonde, affixed to her scalp with some form of technological wizardry that blended in seamlessly with her skin. Subtle prosthetics on her nose, cheeks, and chin completed the illusion.

"Nice work," she said.

"You can wear these for up to a month," the medical tech said, "but we generally recommend keeping it to a week to avoid irritation."

"Well within the planned window for our op," she said. "None of this will show up on scan?"

"It will be indistinguishable from your natural features, unless you find yourself on a surgical operating table."

"If I do, I'll have bigger problems." Kira hopped off the medical bed.

<Then we'd both be in trouble,> Jasmine said in Kira's mind. The embedded AI had a strong sense of self-preservation, which Kira had found quite useful for keeping them both alive since their pairing.

<How will this disguise play with my transformations?> Kira asked. The alien nanotech within her allowed the deployment of an armored second-skin. But since it was stored within her tissues and flooded to the surface, it seemed like it would interfere with the prosthetics.

<I can't imagine it would go well,> Jasmine confirmed. *<But we won't know for certain until it's done.>*

<In all fairness, if I have to transform, our cover would be blown, anyway.>

<A very good point.>

In their years together, Kira had grown fond of having Jasmine as her constant companion. Aside from the practical benefits of having Jasmine control the alien tech for her transformations, the AI was also great with code-cracking, research, and other tasks flesh and blood beings often found difficult or tedious. They made a good team, and it was also nice never being truly alone.

<I think we should put your new appearance to the test and visit Leon,> Jasmine suggested.

Kira also appreciated the AI's mischievous side and was always game for her antics. *<A brilliant idea.>*

She left the medical wing on Level 1 and headed toward the central elevator lobby. Since she was still wearing her TUF uniform, she got several strange looks from the passersby; the TUF was so small in numbers that every member was known, but they were regularly adding new staff, so she pretended like she was seeing Headquarters for the first time.

Fooling her coworkers was a great first experiment, but Leon would be the real test. They'd known each other since they were little kids, so if anyone could identify her, it would be him.

She exited the elevator on Level 6 and headed into the TUF wing. Leon's main lab was midway down the corridor on the right.

Kira knocked on the door.

"Come in."

She hit the door controls to slide it open.

Inside, Leon was seated at one of the workstations toward the back of the room. He did a double-take when he saw her, no hint of recognition in his expression. "Hi, are you new here? How can I help you?"

Kira did her best to disguise her voice. "Yes, just got assigned. I was told to see you about the…" She floundered for what to ask.

<Exhaust samples> Jasmine supplied.

<Oh, my stars, now we're just being mean.> She hid her smile. "…exhaust samples," she completed.

Leon's brows drew together. "I'm not sure I'm the right person to ask about that." Astoundingly, he was able to keep a straight face.

"Are you sure? I heard you're the best." Kira sauntered for him, looking around the lab like it was all new to her.

"Sorry, who are you, exactly?" he asked.

"Someone who'd like to get to know you better." She was only three meters from him now.

Leon still didn't seem to recognize her. "I need to ask you to leave." He reached for his console to alert security.

"That won't be necessary," Kira said in her normal voice.

He gaped at her with confusion. "Wait… Kira?"

She grinned. "All right, I'd call that a successful test."

"What… What happened to you?"

Kira closed the remaining distance between them and patted him on his arm. "Sorry, I had to have a little fun with it. I'm going undercover on Zeron for a bit."

His shoulder slumped. "Again?"

"It won't be for an extended time like before—just a few days to look around."

"That's what you said last time."

"I promise."

He searched her face, having difficulty making eye contact with her altered features. "It's weird seeing you like this."

"Not to worry, it's temporary."

"When are you leaving?"

"In a few hours. I know it's short notice, but other things have started to move, and we needed to react quickly."

Leon nodded his understanding. "Please be careful."

"Always." She leaned in to give him a kiss.

He pulled back slightly before returning the gesture. When they parted, he scowled. "I know it's you, but…"

"Just a different face and a fancy wig. It's all me underneath." She kissed him again, without receiving any hesitation this time. "I love you, and I'll see you soon."

"Love you, too. Good hunting."

They were no strangers to being apart. Her position in the Guard and now the TUF necessitated travel where he couldn't accompany her, so they'd had to get used to being out of touch while she was in dangerous situations. While this mission was less risky than some, anything involving the Coalition needed to be approached with caution.

The only remaining task was to pack a few travel items before heading to the spaceport. She swung by the quarters she shared with Leon and then went up the central elevator to the surface port.

A man was waiting by the shuttles when she arrived. He was on the shorter side with dark features and a slightly awkward bearing.

"Kira?" he asked tentatively.

"Pyra?" she replied.

He smiled. "You look nothing like your picture. Unlike some circumstances, that's a good thing."

She returned a smile. "Nice to meet you. Ready to go on an adventure?"

— — —

Lexi had been close to everything in her life falling into place, but now her new career in the TSS was once again in a state of transition.

Her suggestion to switch the primary training facility for the civilian training initiative from a planetary base to a converted freighter had been approved, and the renovations were almost complete. However, that meant they'd needed to rethink the social and housing aspect of the program, which had created more unexpected work on top of the curriculum considerations.

A large part of the issue was that there were legitimate safety concerns for the program's participants going forward. The Coalition's attack on Antaris was meant to be a deterrent, which was precisely why they couldn't give in. Lexi had expected many of the students to back out of the program, but to her surprise, they had, apparently, been messaging their instructors with pleas to resume their lessons.

With the sessions resuming, Lexi felt it was her responsibility to foster an environment where the students would be safe and secure. *We need to capitalize on that passion. Invested people will look out for their fellow trainees.*

She'd considered the security issue with TSS Agents and outside advisors alike, and they'd concluded that there simply was no guarantee that someone couldn't act against them from the inside. No amount of screening could root out every possible adversary, and the only surefire solution was invasive mindreading—a line the TSS refused to cross, no matter the risks.

The best answer was for the students to be their own security force, keeping an eye on each other, looking for anyone who wasn't invested in the program. A subversive would only be able to hide their true feelings for so long.

Beyond that, she'd need instructors and other helpers to foster a feeling of shared community within the program. The more they felt like a 'found family', the easier it would be to identify someone who was just going through the motions.

There was one person who she knew would be perfect for that support role, but she'd been hesitant to broach the topic again after a lukewarm reaction to her first offhand comment about it. Nonetheless, she'd seen Melisa recovering well and felt that offering her friend a new career path would be beneficial.

Why am I putting it off? Just talk to her already!

Truthfully, they hadn't been talking a lot about anything. It was weird to go from being *so close* to distant, but her relationship with Jason had changed their dynamic. Add in Melisa's missing time from while she was in stasis, and their lives were now in drastically different places than they had been before the events on Duronis. While Lexi wanted to rebuild their friendship, she wasn't sure things could ever be the same.

Avoiding talking to her won't help.

Her mind made up, Lexi left her office to go meet up with Melisa. She sent her a text message on the way, suggesting they meet up in the mess hall on Level 7, where Melisa's quarters were located.

When she arrived, Melisa was waiting by the buffet line. Since it was the end of lunchtime, there was no one else in the area.

"Hey," Lexi greeted. "Glad you were hungry, too."

"I was surprised to get your text. I figured you'd be busy." The accusation that Lexi had been a bad friend slipped through in her tone.

Lexi elected to ignore it; she *had* pulled away, and it wasn't fair. "I'm sorry I haven't spent more time with you. There's been a lot going on."

"Yeah, I know." Melisa started dishing up lunch onto her tray.

Lexi followed her through the line, grabbing her favorites from the serving dishes. "What have you been up to?"

"Therapy and catching up on news reports."

"Is it helping?"

Melisa shrugged. "How do you deal with something you

don't remember?"

Lexi didn't know how to respond. She'd had her own troubles processing everything that she'd been through, but it was different dealing with clear memories. She suspected that trying to come to terms with a year-long gap in her memory would be much worse.

They took seats at one of the booths toward the back of the room, still maintaining awkward silence.

"You know I'll always be here for you," Lexi said at last.

"That's nice of you to say."

"I mean it."

Melisa focused on her food tray, shaking her head. "You have higher priorities now."

"Having other people in my life doesn't mean I've forgotten about you."

Her friend was silent for several seconds. "I don't know why I'm still here."

Lexi saw that was her opening. "What is it you see yourself doing in the future?"

"I don't know."

"Would you consider being a part of my training initiative?"

"Doing what?"

"An instructor. Advisor. Advocate. We'd have to define your specific role, but the idea is that you could be someone to help make the students feel comfortable."

She scoffed. "When I don't even feel like I fit in myself?"

Lexi took a bite of food to give herself time to frame a response. "Finding other people who feel lost is another way to belong. You can help each other."

"Is this a grand plan to get rid of me?"

"No," Lexi hastily replied. "I just want you to be happy, and I get the sense that you're not happy here the way things are now."

Melisa stared at her plate. "You're right."

"I don't have all the answers, but this is something different for you. If it doesn't work out, fine. We'll figure out something else. Together."

Their eyes met, and Melisa nodded. "Okay, I'll think about it."

CHAPTER 4

KIRA HAD GOTTEN used to solo missions, but her favorite was still being part of a team. Partnering with Pyra wasn't quite the dynamic she would have chosen, but it was better than being on her own.

The ride from TSS Headquarters to Redstar Station, where they'd transferred to a civilian transport ship, had given them time to get to know each other a little and start working out a backstory for their relationship. To her relief, the conversation had flowed smoothly, and she found that Pyra was much more eloquent and poised than the persona he'd portrayed while working for Andrei, based on the field reports she'd reviewed.

"We're probably both a little crazy for going back in with the Coalition," Kira said while they watched the final approach to Zeron out their transport ship's viewport.

"Definitely. It almost killed me last time."

"I had a couple of close calls, myself."

"Yeah, there's something wrong with us for sure," he said, grinning.

The transport ship entered the atmosphere and docked at

a surface port, which was connected to the underground cavern systems where everyone on the planet lived and worked. At first glance, it bore little resemblance to the other Taran worlds Kira had visited throughout her military career—which wasn't surprising, since the people on Zeron tended to keep to themselves.

Upon exiting the transport ship, the first thing she noticed were the distinctive colored jumpsuits worn by everyone around the port, covering a broad spectrum of hues.

"Kali and Andy talked about this in their writeups," Pyra said. "The colors denote different classes."

"That's right. We need to sign up as offworlders—gray jumpsuits."

"There should be kiosks somewhere around here."

They looked around the reception area and eventually spotted a series of small booths. Kira entered and made a garment selection from an interface, and the jumpsuit was deposited out a chute in front of her.

<*This is a weird place, no doubt about it,*> she commented to Jasmine.

<*The rigidity and rituals are along the lines of a cult,*> the AI replied in her mind. <*There are surprisingly few records related to the customs on this planet.*>

<*Anyone that dedicated to secrets is usually hiding something good.*>

Kira knew all about that, given her homeworld. Valta was a one-of-a-kind, imbued with a unique substance in the natural environment which granted a small percentage of the population her unique form of telepathy. She'd since learned that it was a byproduct of alien interference and was a nanotech of sorts, but that didn't make the impact on her world any less miraculous. The entire planet was a nature preserve catering to tourists looking to be entertained by the abundant wildlife and mind-readers.

Kira had held greater ambitions for her own life, so she'd run off at eighteen to join the Guard. It was only when she'd returned for an undercover assignment that she'd reconnected with Leon—her teenage love—and gained the perspective to appreciate everything she'd left behind.

Worlds like that, with unique resources and small populations, were special. Its people needed to look after each other. Looking around Zeron, she saw empty expressions and apathy. These people weren't connected with their planet, and that didn't sit right. Her own people had gotten the same way when MTech had moved in with its fancy biotech lab and started illegal experimentations. There was no doubt in her mind that something similar was happening here on Zeron under the Coalition's direction.

<Are there any computer networks you can access for info?> Kira asked her embedded companion.

<Not beyond the port's transit comm channel. There should be something *here, even if it was encrypted. But there's not.>*

The mission wasn't off to a great start. Not that Kira was surprised; it had been a given that they were walking into a nasty situation.

She emerged from the changing hut wearing the new colored uniform, feeling like a frumpy servant. Pyra came out from his stall soon after.

"We're supposed to register," Kira said.

He nodded his understanding, and they headed for the registration area. They'd prepared digital fake IDs for that very purpose, which Jasmine would be able to alter on the fly if they ran into any trouble.

Kira went up to the attendant first. "Maxine Renwald," she introduced herself using the established alias.

The purple jump-suited attendant looked from his screen to Kira's face and back again. "Mechanic?"

"Yes," she confirmed, venturing a smile. "A trade that's always in demand, right?"

He didn't seem interested in friendly banter. "Go on through. Next."

Pyra stepped up and completed the process for his janitorial alias. They figured that dividing their personas between a skilled trade and basic labor that they'd have the greatest potential access throughout the city. While a higher-up diplomatic position could hypothetically open more doors, it would likely only be what they *wanted* outsiders to see. Lowly grunts always got the most unfiltered picture of a place.

"Let's look around and see if we can find any job openings," Kira said.

Though they had no intention of sticking around long-term, getting into a job for a day or two might allow a deeper dive than if they kept up the appearance of being strictly tourists—especially since there wasn't much of a tourist scene on the planet.

They wandered deeper into the underground city. It was carved directly from the red-hued stone of the planet, with many sections of the wall crafted into ornate scenes.

Kira tried to make sense of the images, looking for any clue about the culture or what might be going on in the less visible parts of the city. However, it seemed mostly like random landscapes and the occasional scenes of people. Perhaps there was some deeper meaning there, but it would take longer to determine than the casual observation she could afford right now.

<*Jasmine, can you save snapshots of the scenes and see if you can find any pattern to them?*>

<*Already working on it.*>

<*You're the best.*>

She roamed down a broad walkway with Pyra. There were storefronts on both sides of the walkway but few other features. A singular fountain in a rotunda area offered the only decoration beyond the carvings on the rock walls.

Most of the other foot traffic seemed to be heading in one particular direction, so they went with the flow. After half a kilometer, they arrived at the entrance of a structure. Well, a cavern, really.

Though the entire city was carved into the bedrock, it appeared to be a series of large caves. Within those caves were standard buildings, mostly of the formed concrete variety. The place where everyone was headed from and to, however, was carved into the bedrock itself so she couldn't begin to guess how large it might be.

"That looks worth checking out," Kira said in a low voice to Pyra.

"Any place with that many people coming and going is probably in need of more workers."

"My thoughts exactly."

Kira looked around for any sign of a reception area where they might be able to inquire about employment. There was nothing aside from a guard shack out front.

<*What kind of large operation doesn't have a reception area for visitors?*> she wondered, sharing the thought with Jasmine.

<*The sort that doesn't want strangers snooping around.*>

<Too bad for them.>

Kira wasn't about to give up so easily. If she couldn't speak with a receptionist to glean information, perhaps one of the workers could give her a clue about what was going on inside.

She spotted a woman coming out from the cavern entrance, heading in her general direction. She wore a rust-color jumpsuit, identical to most of the other people leaving the facility.

"I'm going to see what I can find out," she said to Pyra. "I'll meet you over by that fountain we passed."

"See you there."

Kira set an intercept course with the woman. When she was a few strides away, she put on a friendly smile. "Hi, I'm new here. Could you help me out with some directions?"

The woman looked at her with a completely blank expression, as though responding to the signal of words but not grasping their meaning.

Kira looked into the worker's eyes, initiating a direct telepathic link. Unlike the form of telepathy used by Agents and other Gifted, Kira's ability required eye contact to initiate and regular contact to maintain. Though limiting and inconvenient, her style had the distinct benefit of being undetectable by Gifted people, unless they were familiar with the telepaths of Valta and knew what to look for—and few had heard of her remote planet.

This worker had no mental guards up and seemed completely untrained, so Kira had no fear of detection. What surprised her, though, was the woman's mind was almost blank. Had she not been walking around performing tasks, Kira would have suspected she was in a comatose state. It didn't make sense.

Kira delved deeper, curious as to what might be going on. Her probe revealed there were significant gaps in the woman's memory—like large lengths of time had been erased. It went back years, and the woman didn't even seem consciously aware that she was missing those things. By Kira's estimation, it must seem like the poor woman would occasionally feel like she'd forgotten something, but then when she tried to remember what, she'd realize there wasn't a before-time to forget.

The only memories that seemed to have been committed were mundane tasks of going shopping for necessities and taking care of domestic duties. There was absolutely nothing related to work or the very facility Kira had just witnessed the woman exit.

<What the fok?> she commented to Jasmine.

<I was going to put it more elegantly, but yeah.> The AI had as much concern in her tone as she ever exhibited.

Kira severed the telepathic connection. "Sorry, I'll ask someone else."

The woman continued on her way like nothing had happened.

Unnerved, Kira watched her go. <What could cause this kind of memory manipulation? >

<I don't know of any such device, but that doesn't mean it couldn't exist.>

<A person did it, then?>

<That's more likely,> Jasmine replied. <However, we're on this planet to investigate potentially hidden technology, so this might be a clue to those ends.>

Kira really wasn't liking the direction the investigation was headed. However, she loved a good challenge and stopping evil sociopaths, so it was looking like she'd have plenty of opportunities in that regard.

The most pressing question was whether this woman was a one-off or if there were others with the same bizarre memory alterations. Kira picked another random passerby and looked into his eyes. Sure enough, he had the same memory gaps. She checked three more just to be sure, finding the same thing.

<It's just like Kali said in her report,> Jasmine said, processing Kira's observations through their mental link.

<That write-up didn't do it justice.> Kira's chest tightened. *These people were robbed of their lives.*

She wasn't an Agent, but she grew up regarding telepathy as a sacred thing. To glimpse another person's mind was a privilege, and it wasn't right to take advantage of that intimate connection. She'd had to manipulate people and forcibly extract information in the official line of duty, but she was always careful to leave a person's core being intact. What had been done to these people wasn't delicate or surgical—causing damage well beyond the impacted memories to affect the person's fundamental sense of self.

Memories weren't a linear thing. A given experience would trigger associations with past events, smells, or sensations, which created a complex web. That was why any kind of memory manipulation took a lot of skill, since each of those connected threads needed to be redirected.

Whoever had done these erasures hadn't cared about that. It'd left a bunch of loose ends to former associations floating around in the victim's minds, leaving them in a perpetual fog. It was barbaric.

Anger swelled in her chest, traveling up to heat her cheeks. <I have to stop whoever did this.>

<Keep a level head,> Jasmine told her. There was no doubt

that the AI would manually adjust Kira's brain chemistry if she detected she was getting too worked up.

Kira took a deep, calming breath. *<I need to chat with Pyra and see if he found anything.>*

She wandered back to their rendezvous place, making a concerted effort to walk like the locals and not seem too interested in anything. The last thing she needed was the creepy overlords singling her out as a troublemaker.

Pyra was waiting for her when she arrived. His eyes were downcast and his posture was rigid, clearly uncomfortable but trying to hide it.

"Everything okay?" Kira whispered as she approached, keeping her back to him as she pretended to read a sign.

"I get a weird feeling from this place," he replied.

"With good reason. These workers all have gaps in their memories—like, a *lot*."

"So, what Kali noticed is widespread."

"Yeah. And I think it's messed with their cognition. It seems like they're all kind of in a trance, just going through the motions."

Pyra glanced at the people around them, all with glazed expressions. "I was thinking the same thing—that they're all kinda… zombie-like."

"I've never seen minds this heavily damaged and have the person still be conscious."

"What memories have been erased?" Pyra asked.

"I don't know. Whoever did the mental manipulation left no trace of what used to be there."

"How is it possible to overwrite a memory that completely?"

"This was a daily practice," Kira said. "It appears the

memories were purged while they were still only in short-term memory. It's much harder to tamper with memories once they've been committed to long-term storage. That usually happens while a person sleeps."

"So, they do it to them as soon as they finish work each day…"

"Exactly." Kira crossed her arms. "The kind of harm I'm seeing only happens if you mess with someone's mind too often. Whoever did this didn't care about the long-term effects."

'Devastating' was the word that came to Kira's mind. She'd have to spend more time with the workers to be sure, but her initial impression was that the cognitive effects might be permanent. *It's like some sort of telepathic lobotomy.*

Pyra watched a group of glazed workers walk by. "The Coalition considers everyone disposable."

"A city couldn't operate like this. There have to be people whose minds haven't been wiped."

Her companion nodded toward a large building near the fountain. "That looks like some sort of government building."

"Yeah, Kali didn't have a great time with the local authorities. I think we'll need to take another tactic."

"Then we'll need to go in and look around ourselves," Pyra said.

"The obvious problem with that is we don't know when or how the workers' memories are being wiped, so the same thing could happen to us."

"I'm a null. It might not work on me."

<Without knowing the means of the memory erasure, I can't be sure it wouldn't affect him, too,> Jasmine chimed in. *<It might be telepathy-based, or it could be a kind of tech where*

being a null wouldn't make a difference.>

"Too risky," Kira summarized aloud for Pyra. "I think a better tactic would be to go the simple route."

"Meaning?"

"A button cam. Except, the person wearing it can't know it's there."

"Okay, like, covertly plant it on an unwitting workers' uniform and then monitor their activities throughout the day?"

She nodded. "Only having a transmission increases the odds of detection, so a local recorder would be best. The workers wear jumpsuits, right?"

"Looks that way. Everyone around here does."

"What are the odds those go through some sort of central laundry service?"

"Pretty high, I'd say."

"That might be our 'in'. We could go undercover within the laundry service, place the button cam, and then retrieve it afterward."

He smiled. "You know, that's actually a pretty solid plan."

"Don't sound so surprised!"

"No, it's just that I thought I was going to need to go into the creepy mind-wiping place myself. This is way better."

"Can't rule out that possibility for a future investigation, but no need to start out there."

He nodded. "All right. Let's go find out who handles the dirty laundry around here."

— — —

True to Jason's past experiences with Kira, her check-in message from the field was frustratingly vague.

>>Have a plan. Give us a couple days.<<

He leaned back in his desk chair with a sigh. *Really helpful, Kira.*

Nonetheless, he was happy to hear from her. She was okay and she'd caught a lead, so that was promising.

The second look at the Steyn's former drug empire, on the other hand, had thus far led to more questions than answers. Now that they knew what to look for, the connection to the strange substance Andrei had consumed seemed irrefutable.

Normally, drug-related offenses were solely within the Enforcer's purview, so the TSS hadn't looked at any of that data as part of their previous investigation into SPEAR and the Coalition. However, this wasn't like most drugs. As they'd suspected, testing had come back that it was nanotech rather than a chemical substance. There were other nanotech drugs out there, but none were self-replicating like this one— transmissible from person-to-person. The people who were subsequently contacted didn't experience any of the hallucinogenic or euphoric sensations that the original user did, but there were signs that it infiltrated cells before going dormant.

Jason had spent hours staring at the data, and there were only a handful of ways all the puzzle pieces could fit together. It seemed too crazy to be true, though. He decided to run it by his father before presenting the hypothesis to the rest of his team.

He headed to the High Commander's office and found the door open. "Hey, Dad. Have a few minutes?"

"Sure, have a seat."

Jason closed the door and then sat down in his usual chair. "I may have figured it out."

"What, exactly?"

"The master plan."

Wil sat up straighter. "Go on."

"My question is:if these higher-dimensional aliens are so powerful, and the Coalition is working with them, then why do they need soldiers and mechs?"

"I've been wondering that, myself."

"Really, the crux of it is why would aliens bother talking to us rather than just wiping us out? The best theory I've heard was your suggestion that it in some way hurts them to access this lower dimension—so they need something to help weaken the dimensional veil."

"Yes."

"The power core they gave us makes sense in that plan because of the energy field it creates. Where the theory breaks down again is thinking about why the Erebus and Gatekeepers would bother working with the Taran members of the Coalition. They're not involved in getting the power core installed—that's all being driven by the TSS and Monsari—so what's their purpose?"

"To create civil unrest so we're divided and disorganized when it comes time to respond to the forthcoming invasion, presumably," Wil said.

Jason shook his head. "I thought that, too, but I think we may have gotten it wrong."

"I'm all ears."

"What if the energy field created by the power core is only part of it? What if they need conduits to pull energy from the higher dimensions into spacetime because they can't do it themselves? Easily accessible *aesen* energy, already here," Jason continued. "Except, the Generation Cycle messed all that up for Tarans. Only a fraction of the population has abilities now. But what if there was something—like, a drug—that could activate that genetic potential when the right signal was given?"

His father went still and quiet, processing the information. "If that's the case, when that field activates, they're going to burn out every person with Gifted potential in their bloodline and use that sudden release of *aesen* energy to fuel them as they reach down from the higher dimensions and take out everyone else."

Jason swallowed. "It's just one idea."

"The Gifted women in those stasis chambers on Spadrosi Station were the part that made the least sense to me," Wil murmured. "Now, it does—they were intended to be a test case for the Erebus to pull *aesen* energy that had already been stored, waiting for them in spacetime."

"That's what I concluded, too," Jason said. He felt sick. *This is so much worse than we ever imagined.*

"Thank you, Jason. This is pivotal."

"What do we do now? This means the power cores are too dangerous to use. We can never turn on that device on Earth. All our plans are shot."

"No, the only thing that's changed is we need to account for the drug's—or nanotech's— effects. If we can neutralize it, the rest of our plans can proceed."

"How are we supposed to disable it?" Jason asked.

"Not us alone. Get a sample shipped here to Headquarters, and we'll take it from there."

CHAPTER 5

RAENA'S STOMACH WAS twisted with nerves as she walked with Ryan into the council chamber at the Sietinen estate. It was quite possibly the last time Tararia's current leaders would be gathered in one place while Monsari still held its seat. The next time, the balance of power would be quite different.

Will the other High Dynasties be relieved or angry when we make the move against Monsari? As far as she knew, her grandparents had been speaking with their friends behind closed doors about their concerns regarding the other Dynasty's corruption. However, they hadn't yet given Raena any indication if others were willing to take action.

No doubt, when the TSS and Guard moved in, it would come as a shock to most of the people in the room—none more than Celine Monsari herself.

Raena intentionally kept her eyeline away from Celine as she took her seat, not trusting herself to avoid glaring at the woman. The snub wasn't anything out of the ordinary; they'd been on tense terms since Wil had been shot at while visiting the Monsari estate.

Raena was seated between Ryan and her grandparents—a position to make it intentionally ambiguous about whether she was there as Ryan's wife or as the scion of Sietinen. It was her standard seat whenever there were these meetings of the 'extended High Council'; otherwise, it was just the seven High Dynasty representatives, which included her grandfather and Ryan. These larger, in-person gatherings always denoted that there was going to be business with far-reaching implications.

Given that Cris had called the meeting, Sietinen was hosting, as was protocol. They wanted to be on familiar grounds if the discussion turned ugly, which was a strong possibility. Raena had seen extra security on the way in, so she clearly wasn't the only one with concerns.

Cris surveyed the room while the other councilmembers took their seats. When everyone was in attendance, he rose to address the room.

"Thank you for joining us today," he began. "I've asked you all here to discuss an important issue, which impacts the future path of the Taran Empire—"

Celine quickly rose to address the attendees. "And I appreciate you taking the issue to heart."

Raena's heart skipped a beat. *What is she doing?*

"Actually, if I may—" Cris tried to continue, but Celine cut him off.

"While we're gathered here today, I wish to address a growing concern, which affects the entire Empire." Pointedly, she glanced toward the Sietinens. "It concerns the recent legislation regarding the free use of Gifted abilities."

"There's nothing about that law worth revisiting," Cris stated, to Raena's relief. His face was flushed slightly, clearly annoyed by Celine trying to hijack the meeting.

"I beg to differ," she countered. "While I understand a well-meaning intent to the policy, it has opened up a dangerous path."

Raena barely resisted the urge to roll her eyes. *"Talk about a desperate ploy,"* she commented privately to Ryan.

"I don't like this," he replied in her mind. *"What's her angle?"*

"The TSS' new training initiative has inspired people to begin experimenting with abilities, to dangerous ends," Celine continued, undeterred. Her expression indicated that she either believed the lies or was really that intolerant that she saw people being themselves as a threat. "To allow open use of these 'Gifts' is a violation of privacy for all others—the majority of the population. In the interest of the majority good, these abilities cannot be permitted to run unchecked."

Cris took a slow breath. Raena could feel the fury within him, but he managed to maintain a calm exterior demeanor. "The reason for both the legislation and the training is to permit all citizens to be true to themselves. Being able to seek proper training is far safer than—"

"Safer for whom?" Celine cut in again.

"For everyone."

"No, all that training does is make it easier for a Gifted person to know how to take advantage of their defenseless fellow citizens."

Cris glowered. "That's taking a pessimistic view. Far more people use their abilities to *help* others."

"One person's idea of 'help' could just as easily cause harm."

"That's a baseless argument," Raena said telepathically to Ryan and her grandparents. *"She knows she's backed into a corner and is stalling."*

"I intend to shut her down," Cris said.

However, before he could speak, Celine said something Raena hadn't anticipated in any of her hypothetical run-throughs of the meeting.

"We propose a registry for Gifted people."

Raena's jaw went slack. *She can't be serious!*

Next to her, Ryan shifted in his seat, while Cris and Kate scowled.

"What is your reasoning for this proposal?" Cris asked after taking a moment to gather himself.

"You argue that abilities could be used for harm *or* good, but it remains that every person needs to be treated as a potential danger. There is always that *possibility* there. And being around such a danger requires other citizens to take special precautions. Other Gifted people can recognize each other, but how are regular citizens supposed to know who might take advantage of their mind or overpower them with telekinetic might? In the interest of informed risk and equity, the only way to ensure level standing is a registry."

Raena stared in stunned silence. *"She can't do this. Can she?"* she asked her relatives telepathically.

"It's a legal proposition," Cris explained. *"I don't know if anyone is going to go for it."*

Based on the bewildered expressions around the meeting room, the other councilmembers had also been taken by surprise. That was a positive sign. However, Raena didn't like that the representatives for Baellas and Makaris didn't appear horrified by the suggestion, unlike Vaenetri's and Talsari's disgust.

"What are the proposed terms for this registry?" Eduard Baellas asked.

"Are you seriously entertaining this proposal?" Cris asked him.

"You're hardly in a position to have an unbiased opinion as former High Commander of the TSS," Eduard shot back.

"Just as you are, apparently, unable to remain unbiased through your own prejudiced worldview," Cris replied without missing a beat. He stood up to address the room. "I can't argue that this isn't a topic close to my heart, but as both a leader and a Taran citizen, I have to ask what possible ethical justification is there for forcing documentation of a portion of our population based on an immutable trait? This kind of labeling will only lead to further segregation and division."

Raena agreed with every word, and she was thankful her grandfather had faced Monsari's threat head-on. While she had a lot she'd like to say on the matter, herself, there was no getting around the fact that she was young and didn't have the same clout as Cris. *If I was in charge, we'd shut this down right now.*

Celine met Cris' gaze with calm indifference. "Your objection is noted. Given your former role as TSS High Commander, however, it might be best for you to recuse yourself from voting on this particular issue."

That witch. Raena couldn't help casting Celine a nasty glare across the room. The woman was being so careful with her phrasing, framing her statements as suggestions so Cris would look like he was being stubborn if he refused to comply. It was a carefully executed scheme to place the Sietinens at a disadvantage.

"Shall we put it to a vote?" Celine asked the room.

"I believe all members of this council would benefit from time to deliberate and research this issue," Kaiden Vaenetri said.

Kate gave a subtle nod of thanks to her brother.

"Very well. We will revisit the vote at our next gathering," Celine acquiesced. She turned to Cris, a coy smile playing on her lips. "Now, what was the issue you wanted to discuss?"

The obvious play was that they wanted to stir up chaos. Get enough turmoil in play and it would be difficult to make a move against them without it looking like retribution.

Raena looked to her grandparents for guidance.

"Say nothing," Kate instructed. *"We'll need to handle this later."*

As much as Raena hated to let the hateful statements uttered by Celine go unaddressed, she recognized the wisdom of taking a step back to regroup.

"This new matter takes priority," Cris said, the only response he could make.

"What a shame to waste everyone's time by coming all this way for so few words." Celine clicked her tongue against her teeth. "Perhaps the next meeting will be more productive."

"I'm sure it will." Cris kept his expression neutral.

"If that's all, we're adjourned?" Celine asked.

Cris let out a slow breath. "Yes, for now. To be continued."

Soft groans of annoyance sounded around the room from everyone but Kaiden and his wife. The attendees began to depart.

Celine shot the Sietinens and Ryan a smug smile as she left the room.

When all others had gone, Kaiden came over to speak with Cris. "Where did that come from?"

"She must have known we were about to launch a formal inquiry. This was the only way to tie our hands," Cris replied.

The other man nodded. "A stall tactic."

"But a bomaxed good one. Now, any statement we make will be taken as Gifted people trying to get our critics out of the way."

Kaiden shook his head, lips pursed. "Let me have some private discussions and take a read. If everyone else thinks the proposition is ridiculous, it'll be a non-issue."

"Thank you. I'll do the same," Cris acknowledged.

Kate gave her brother a hug, and then he left with his wife.

"What do we do now?" Raena asked once he was gone.

Cris crossed his arms. "We need to take a step back and strategize."

More than anything, she hated feeling helpless. Monsari was doing a bomaxed good job backing them into a corner, but she wasn't about to give up. "We have to get this proposition turned down. A registry is unacceptable in every way."

"Absolutely. There's not a question."

"Can we release any of the evidence we have linking Monsari to the Coalition?" Ryan asked.

"There isn't anything direct enough to be irrefutable. No, we'll need to give it a little time to ensure our actions don't look like retaliation."

Raena couldn't keep her frustration out of her tone. "That's exactly what they *want*."

"Patience," Cris said.

She took a calming breath. "I know. Justice is coming."

— — —

Leon stared at the vial Jason had placed on his biolab's central worksurface. "What is it?"

The Agent crossed his arms. "A drug, which is actually

nanotech, which we believe has the ability to activate the gene expression for latent Gifted abilities, causing a fatal flood of *aesen* energy from the higher dimensions."

Leon laughed. "Right. What is it *really*?"

"If I'm wrong about that, I look forward to you telling me what it really is."

His stomach dropped. "That kind of tech shouldn't be possible. That'd be a solution to the Generation Cycle, and that…"

"Just because the Priesthood didn't find a solution doesn't mean it isn't possible. This tech likely came from the Erebus, and they know a whole lot we don't."

"Shite." Leon took an unsteady breath. "Isn't this something that someone with more tech experience should look into… like the Lynaedans or Aesir?"

"If this is what we think it is, we'd rather keep it confidential. This might be linked to SPEAR Tec, so that makes you the foremost expert."

Things have gone pretty far afield from the doctorate in genetics I went to school for. Leon nodded. "Okay, I'll run some tests, model it, see what I can come up with."

"Thanks. And please keep it to yourself for now."

"I will."

Jason started to go. "Oh, and Kira's fine."

"Good. Thanks for letting me know."

Leon turned his attention to the vial as the Agent left. It didn't look like anything as remarkable as the substance Jason had described. Then again, neither did the nanotech that allowed Kira to transform.

He carefully placed the vial inside a secure testing chamber. *Let's see what you really are.*

— — —

"Fok this whole situation." Ryan rubbed his eyes with the heels of his hands.

"Hey, it's going to be okay," Raena tried to soothe, but Ryan was too worked up to have the words offer any comfort.

He paced across his office, trying to work off his anxious energy. "Celine Monsari is *evil*. There's no way around it."

"I know." Raena sat down on the black couch in the center of the room, somehow appearing calm and collected.

He didn't know how she did it. He'd felt her frustration and anger during the meeting and on the shuttle ride back to Morningstar Isle, but now she was the picture of poise. Then again, there were times when she'd been huffing across the room while he'd been the one calming her down, so maybe her restraint now was just a testament to how they made a great team and balanced each other out.

Ryan tried to slow his racing heart and regain perspective on the situation. "Okay, the fact that Celine put up such a bold resolution means that she knows she's in trouble."

"No doubt," Raena agreed.

"But how can we apply further pressure without it burning us?"

"I don't know yet, but that's what we're going to figure out."

The anxious knot in his chest had dissipated enough that he was able to sit down next to her. "I won't let them stick us on a list like we're dangerous freaks."

"Nor will my grandparents or great-uncle. I mean, stars, eighty percent of the High Council has immediate family with active Gifted abilities now! This isn't going to go anywhere other than making Monsari look bad."

"I hope so," he murmured.

Still, he had concerns. It could be argued that Monsari made a valid point—that Gifted people were in a special class and needed to be monitored to ensure they didn't abuse their abilities. Nonetheless, a registry was the wrong way to go about it. Gifted people were already 'othered' enough that there was no doubt in his mind such a policy would only push the division to dangerous levels. Given how the Coalition seemed committed to spreading chaos among average citizens, it was entirely possible Monsari was acting for that reason.

Ryan met his wife's gaze. "It's not us I'm worried about. What if Monsari leaks this to make people think it's being considered? The public would throw a fit."

"But if we make a statement to try to get ahead of it, then it'll be us inciting the riots."

He scoffed. "I have to give it to Celine that she knows how to manipulate her adversaries. I'd applaud her if it wasn't so terrible for us."

Raena nodded. "Yeah, she's really good—in a totally awful way."

"I have to believe that the moral good will prevail," he said after a pause.

"Me too. But we might need to help it along."

"Do you have any ideas about how to do that?"

She took a deep breath. "Maybe. It will mean making it personal."

"It already is."

CHAPTER 6

THE TIME FOR subtlety had passed. Celine Monsari recognized that her declaration at the High Council meeting would cause disruption, but she'd had no other choice.

Though the Sietinens had been crafty with their investigations, it was clear they were looking into MPS' affairs and had already learned too much. They couldn't possibly know the whole truth, but even *suspecting* what was going on placed everything at risk.

Celine stood behind her desk, planting her hands on the desktop and leaning over. "Those fools are leading us to our doom, and they think they're helping." She groaned, a tightness growing in her chest about the rapidly devolving state of affairs.

Across from her, Grant crossed his arms. He was as close to a friend as she had among her collaborators and one of the few people who grasped the situation in its entirety. His apparent agitation didn't bode well for the conversation. "Have you reconsidered telling them the truth?"

She scoffed. "Why bother? They wouldn't understand."

"They love the Empire. There's a chance they'd see reason if—"

"No," Celine cut him off. "Reinen may have understood, but Cris and Wil are idealistic and think they have all the answers. The next generation is even worse."

Grant looked like he had further protests, but instead of voicing them, he stared at the floor.

"You disagree?"

He shrugged. "I don't know anymore. How am I supposed to feel about guiding trillions of people toward certain death?"

"You have to focus on those who will *live* because of our actions."

"But what if there's another way? What if the TSS really *can* find a solution?"

"Wil Sietinen took out the Priesthood and got us into this mess."

Though she had to admit that the Priesthood's methods were questionable and some of their actions were misguided, they had fulfilled their purpose of regulating the Gifted population. That wasn't their original intent, of course, but the Gatekeepers had guided them into that role just as they'd manipulated other key events from the shadows to make sure the pieces were in place. The deregulation of Gifted abilities following the Priesthood's fall had unraveled centuries of work in a single action, setting in motion a series of events that had led to the Erebus themselves getting involved.

There was no stopping it now. The TSS had gained too much power—in no small part due to its leader's highborn standing. The interplay between Sietinen, Dainetris, Vaenetri, and the TSS allowed almost any regulatory decision to be pushed through without proper vetting, and they were just warming up. If Celine didn't take a stand immediately, they'd never get another chance to reverse the damage.

"I can't bring myself to placate you, Celine," Grant said after a lengthy silence. "Monsari doesn't have the sway it once did among the High Dynasties. Taking this offensive position will likely lose more friends than it gains."

"My aim isn't to play nice. I'm doing what I must to ensure the Taran race isn't obliterated."

"We need allies to win that fight."

"And we have the allies that matter." She glared at him from across the room, making it clear the topic wasn't open for discussion.

"I'll leave you to it, then," he said with a slow bow of his head, then left the room before she could think of a reason to stop him.

Celine released a long grunt of frustration as soon as she was alone. *How can so much go wrong so quickly?*

Grant had been right to question her actions. She hadn't planned to make the move today at the High Council meeting, but it had become a matter of necessity. It was no secret that the Monsari and Sietinen Dynasties had often found themselves on the opposite sides of key issues, and this current generation of leaders was no different. As a young woman, Celine had watched with contempt as Cris' leadership within the TSS had transitioned to his current role within the Taran government and SiNavTech. Tarans had allowed the Gifted to propagate and even become lauded by many, against Monsari's best efforts to suppress those abilities and bloodlines. All efforts had failed, and it had led them to this extreme circumstance.

She knew the Sietinens and others thought her opposition

to Gifted was because of personal disdain, but the truth was that it was just a front she needed to maintain. Perhaps she'd been playing that part for so long that a part of her had developed an aversion when it came to Gifted people, but only as a coping mechanism to make her necessary actions easier.

The truth, however, was that her anti-Gifted sentiments stemmed purely from a pragmatic sense of survival. The Gatekeepers had made the conditions clear generations ago, yet most others had forgotten. Heroes had intervened in the past, such as those who'd infiltrated the Priesthood and propagated the nanoagents which ultimately led to the Generation Cycle, buying precious time for the Taran race. Without those extreme actions, the brewing war with the Erebus would have come to a head centuries earlier. Under no circumstances would such high numbers of Gifted Tarans be permitted to live.

The Monsari family's work behind the scenes had been a desperate attempt to find a path forward. However, with the Priesthood's fall, their opportunities to act had been severely hampered. Now, they'd be lucky to save enough people to salvage the Taran race, but they believed they could save enough to populate a colony world. So long as her own family was among those survivors, Celine would find a way to stomach that massive loss of life.

She walked over to stare out the window. The rolling hills surrounding the Monsari estate were beautiful in the golden afternoon light, glowing warmly like something out of a dream. Her entire reality had a surreal quality to it now—a bizarre juxtaposition of knowing Tarans were marching toward their doom compared to the High Council's reports that the Empire was more prosperous than ever.

Well-meaning people can do the most damage. Stars, she wished there'd been a way to keep the Sietinens out of power. They were so bomaxed relentless in their ill-conceived pursuit of moral superiority. Their righteousness would blind them to the truth that sacrificing some was necessary for the greater good.

Yet, it had been her job to stop them—or at least slow their takeover. She'd failed. The weight of her shortcomings had been eating away at her resolve to keep pressing on. Generations of work had already been undone, and her moves were now limited with so many of her resources already run dry.

Her thoughts were interrupted by an incoming communication chime from her desk. A check of the details on her wall-mounted viewscreen showed it was a call she couldn't miss. She gathered herself and accepted the voice-only commlink.

"What news do you bring?" she asked, having worked with her collaborators for long enough to anticipate the reason for the message.

"We were hoping for an update from *you*," Carjen replied.

Shite, did they already hear about the council meeting? She didn't fully understand how the Gatekeepers got their information. Much of the council's inner workings had been communicated by her over their years working together, but they clearly had informants in other areas. Most likely, there was an aide with one of the other High Dynasties who was responsible for processing notes from the council meetings, and they would pass information to the Gatekeepers overseeing the Coalition's operations. It would explain how they always seemed to know about events before she told them.

She quickly composed her talking points on the matter. "I had to improvise, but everything is under control."

"It doesn't seem that way."

Of course he'd say that. Celine had found that Carjen had exacting expectations, which were impossible to fulfill. She understood and empathized with his frustrations related to the TSS and Sietinens, but he also had an unrealistic view about how to resolve those issues. "I'm working on it," she replied, electing to avoid the details for now.

"We had assurances."

"And I will keep my word." Celine said it with conviction, but internally, she questioned whether she would be able to deliver.

Sietinen needed to be stripped of its power. The Gatekeepers had made that clear, and Celine had agreed. Nonetheless, it was easier said than done.

It would have been simpler in years past when the other High Dynasties had maintained political distance from each other, keeping alliances behind closed doors and focusing on individual political interests. Now, since the High Council no longer reported to the Priesthood, what appeared to be genuine friendships had formed between many of the Dynasty leaders. Sietinen, Dainetris, and Vaenetri simply came across as too likeable. They'd sucked in the others, and Celine's calls for reason had been ignored. The Taran government had already been too seduced by a delusional spirit of cooperation for there to be any hope left of salvaging the situation.

Naturally, she couldn't tell Carjen that. She and her family needed to continue to be seen as useful if there was any hope of them surviving the coming reckoning with the Erebus.

"They've continued to investigate the Bridge on Earth," Carjen said.

Celine winced. She didn't have a good comeback for that observation; it was evidence of her lack of control over the situation. "I know, but they'll never be able to use it."

"We aren't so sure. Wil Sietinen has proven himself to be intelligent and resourceful."

She couldn't disagree. After all, the Aesir wouldn't have formed a relationship with him if he didn't possess exceptional Gifted abilities to back up the rumors. While she'd never view him with reverence in the way some did, she could appreciate why so many looked to him with a sense of hope. It was false hope, but it was in Tarans' nature to look for opportunities to improve.

"I'll handle him," she said.

"Like you did during your last face-to-face meeting?" The accusation came through full force in his tone this time.

She was thankful the call was voice-only when she subconsciously took a step backward. The Gatekeepers had been growing impatient with her over the last year, and it would seem they hadn't forgiven her past unsanctioned actions. "It sent the right message."

The attack she'd ordered on Wil during his departure from the Monsari estate was never meant to be a genuine assassination attempt, only a notice that his authority would not go unchecked. The Gatekeepers hadn't agreed with the action then, and clearly they hadn't forgiven the indiscretion to this day. Nonetheless, Celine stood by her choice. Someone with Wil's qualities could inspire people with an almost religious fervor, and Celine knew how dangerous such idolization could be.

"You've created too many enemies and are no longer effective," Carjen said.

Celine swallowed her concern. "We still have the alliances that matter."

"No." That was it, just a solitary word declaring no-confidence.

"Give me a week."

"In a week, this very well may be over."

"And by then I will either have succeeded or not."

"Fine," Carjen agreed. "One week." He ended the call.

Celine let out a long, unsteady breath. Her time was running short, and she didn't have many options.

Keep it together, she told herself. *You have a whole company behind you.*

Granted, MPS' resources were running thin, but the corporate veil was beneficial cover for her clandestine political dealings.

In particular, the company was useful for transportation. The Coalition had supplies and personnel to move around, and MPS' mining operations made for an excellent vehicle to accomplish those activities. Since production of voydite had been waning, there was plenty of capacity to supplement those transports with Coalition resources, and it served a double benefit by hiding how empty those cargo ships would be otherwise.

There should be a shipment coming up soon, which would give her the opening to address Carjen's growing concerns. She checked her desk, not seeing the information about the transport that should be there.

She pressed the intercom on her desk to connect with her assistant. "Where are the production reports?" she asked.

Stan jogged into the room, head bowed. "Apologies, my lady. There was an issue."

"What *kind* of issue."

"Um…" He worked his mouth, searching for the words. "There was no production to report."

None? A cold vise closed around her chest. "What do you mean?" She understood perfectly, but she needed to hear the words to make them real.

"The voydite mine is empty."

Production had been trending toward that horrific reality for two generations, but her predecessors had found ways to hide it—and, worse, ignore the truth. When she'd taken over MPS, she'd been in for a rude awakening about the dire state of the company. The statement now that the mine was completely empty changed the nature of the situation. She'd thought they'd be able to maintain production for at least two more months.

"My lady?" Stan prompted when Celine didn't say anything.

"That's all for now, thank you."

He bobbed his head and departed, closing the door behind him.

Alone in the sound-proofed office, she let out a scream of frustration and despair. Had anyone overheard it, they might have thought she was dying. Perhaps she was.

Today of all days. She took in several deep breaths through her nose and released them through her mouth.

It helped a little, but her mind was still racing about what to do.

The Sietinen Dynasty and their family members within the TSS were on a crusade to get evidence about MPS' situation, and Celine had been doing her best to take off the heat. If news about the mine running dry were leaked, there would be no more hiding.

Fok this day. She pursed her lips, restoring her composure.

If the voydite shipments were no longer viable cover, then they'd have to double down on their excavation of Zeron. Unfortunately, work on the remote planet had been progressing painfully slowly. Its underground structures were perhaps the most important anywhere within the Taran civilization, yet no one could know they were there. An announcement would mean revealing the master plan, and the TSS couldn't find out those intentions under any circumstances.

Her outward façade of calm wavered again, though there was no one to see the slip. She'd been under such immense pressure for so long that she often wondered if she'd eventually burst from the weight of it all.

She'd been guarding a truth with the power to change the course of the entire Taran civilization. The responsibility of it had changed her into a version of herself she often didn't like, but that was a necessary sacrifice.

Celine gripped a fistful of her dress' fabric in each hand to stop her fingernails from cutting into her palms. Her heart pounded harder in her chest as darkness closed in from the corners of her vision. She focused on taking slow, deep breaths to help the sensation of helplessness pass, unwilling to show any further external sign of weakness despite having no witnesses.

Her heart rate began to normalize. *You can't let them get to you. This is too important to give up now.*

She had a responsibility as a steward for the Taran people, and she took that role seriously. Such a leader needed to be poised at all times. *Protect the truth. Guard the path.* The mantra centered her, reminding her of the critical mission.

No matter what the TSS might think they had figured out, she couldn't imagine they had uncovered the full extent of Monsari's working relationship with the Gatekeepers. From everything she'd seen, the TSS knew there had been an ancient war, but beyond that, their assumption was that contact with the Gatekeepers was recent and isolated. Never would they suspect that Monsari had been working intimately with members of the alien race for generations.

When she had a moment to step back and reflect, she'd wondered why she didn't feel bad about betraying her own kind. Why side with the Gatekeepers over her fellow Tarans? Every time, she arrived at the same conclusion. Tarans were weak and flawed, and they kept making the same mistakes over and over again. That was how the Priesthood had risen to power in the first place, paving the way for the Empire's downfall.

To align with the Gatekeepers was a chance to break free from the cycle and move forward. They had to submit to beings who could see Tarans for all their flaws. A few chosen Tarans would survive the culling and be able to rebuild a society that was sustainable and free from the corruption which had plagued them for millennia. It wasn't the first time such a purge had happened, and it likely wouldn't be the last. The sooner they accepted the guidance of the Erebus once and for all, the better.

Making contact required the Bridge, and they'd need Zeron to bring that plan to fruition. The groundwork was in place. She just had to follow through.

With her anxiety relegated once again to the innermost recesses of her being, where it belonged, she pulled up the contact information for her lead representative on Zeron. He wouldn't like the order she was about to give, but they needed to finish the project. It was more important now than ever.

Stay the course. We're almost there. She made the call.

CHAPTER 7

WIL SHOOK HIS head, processing the news from his father. "I can't believe Celine would present a resolution like that."

Cris gave a sad smile. "What choice did she have? It stopped us from making a move, didn't it?"

"It's a delay, not a halt."

"Time is time," Cris said.

"I refuse to let them get away with this."

"As do I. But we need to be smart about it."

Wil nodded. "I know."

"Politically, they've done a good job of tying our hands for now. And the TSS can't take action, either."

"We now have political and military restrictions, yes. But business… I can't think of why this would impact your operations," Wil said.

"Unfortunately, that doesn't help us much."

"Doesn't it? A situation like this could turn into a public relations nightmare. Might be best to get ahead of it."

"Yes, and that's not a good thing. I'm sure Legal is going to have a fit."

"Dad, you need to think like your opponent. What did Monsari do when the press turned ugly?"

His father thought for a few seconds. "They hired Calrosi Enterprises."

"I wonder how much that cost compared to using in-house council?"

"It's always more expensive to outsource."

Wil nodded, willing his father to understand what he was saying. He could lead him toward the answer, but the idea couldn't explicitly come from the TSS. "How much is Calrosi Enterprises worth?"

Cris shrugged. "I don't have an exact figure, but I'd guess a few hundred million?"

"Really, is that all?" Wil nodded thoughtfully. "It's interesting how a company with so few material assets can hold so much power. Three, or even ten, times that valuation is nothing for people with larger financial resources."

As Wil had hoped, his father got a gleam in his eyes. "An interesting observation."

"Well, I should get back to it. I'll leave you to your business." He ended the call before he could implicate himself further.

One of Sietinen's distinct advantages was very deep pockets. His parents were committed to winning favor through genuine actions and building relationships, but sometimes it was a lot easier to straight-up buy influence.

Monsari had done exactly that when they hired Calrosi Enterprises to be their PR firm. Wil had no idea how much the firm had been paid to promote the fabricated articles about Dainetris, but it was no doubt substantial. He was surprised no one on the Sietinen and Dainetris legal teams had thought to give Calrosi a better offer. Sure, it was a low move to buy the company, but when the enemy wasn't playing fair, new tactics were needed.

Anything to win this fight, Wil told himself. Too much was at risk to take any chances.

— — —

Leon had been skeptical when Jason dropped off the drug vial, convinced there was no way that he was the right person for the job. While he knew his way around a testing lab, he was a geneticist by trade and didn't know much about drugs beyond basic chemistry and a bit more about chemicals that could be used to promote changes within cells.

The claims that the strange mist had the ability to unlock latent genetic potential had seemed farfetched. He'd needed to remind himself that it wasn't 'mist' so much as alien nanotech. While he didn't consider such things his specialty, he had, admittedly, become an expert on Kira's unique alien nanites out of necessity when she had been in pain and no one knew how to help her. Considering that her tech included a higher-dimensional energy component, maybe he *was* the right person to figure out what was going on with this new mysterious substance.

Setting his doubts aside and keeping an open mind—as any good researcher should—he'd initiated several tests to find out what he was dealing with. Those evaluations had been started the previous day, and they were now nearing completion. He'd been working on other tasks while the tests ran in the background, but now he closed out of those project files in preparation for receiving the long-awaited results.

Since Jason had told him to keep the analysis confidential, Leon had locked the other members of his team out of that specific lab. Alone, he watched the data processing complete.

Oh, my stars! His heart pounded in his ears as he read over the assessment.

It was more incredible than he could have imagined. Not only was the mist composed of nanites, but their material composition included some kind of ateron alloy he'd never seen cataloged in Taran biotech journals. Even more astounding, the nanites were radiating the higher-dimensional energy Wil had dubbed *aesen.*

This is everything Jason said it would be. The technology hardly seemed real, even though it was right in front of him.

Leon leaned back in his chair, at a loss for words.

He'd run several tests of the nanites on six different living tissue samples, falling into three separate scenario analyses, to get a baseline. Two of the tests were for someone with active Gifts, two more were for a Gifted bloodline currently in a dormant part of the cycle, and two were for a genetic line with no known Gifted presence.

The first scenario with active Gifts revealed that the nanites would strengthen the abilities beyond what would have previously been the maximum potential. Leon didn't yet know what that might do to a person long-term, but the preliminary reaction within the controlled lab environment was groundbreaking.

In the third scenario, conversely—where no abilities were present—the nanites appeared to remain inactive even after making contact with the tissue.

It was in the second scenario, where latent abilities were present but not active, that things got interesting. Upon deeper analysis, the nanites bonded with the genome and somehow activated the dormant genes. Against all conventional scientific wisdom, it formed a patch for the Generation Cycle issue. The Priesthood had been searching for a solution since they'd caused the genetic corruption through their mass manipulation of the general population, and it had seemed that nothing could be done about it.

This is too perfect an answer. And too easy. Well, the tech had come from a transdimensional race of aliens, so perhaps 'easy' wasn't the right word. No, it was far too *convenient.*

Simply put, if the Erebus wanted to help Tarans overcome the genetic problem, then they would have given them the patch in a straightforward manner, just like the power core. This delivery mechanism—hidden within a street drug—said, in no uncertain terms, that it was meant for nefarious purposes.

Leon didn't like the implications one bit. Clearly, Jason had given him the sample to study because the TSS already had concerns about what the drug could do to a person. *Are they looking for confirmation about something they already know, or ideas for how to stop it?*

The scientist in Leon demanded that he go about the study in a deliberate fashion. He took his thought processes back a step, pretending he'd forgotten everything Jason had told him about the sample when he'd dropped it off.

So far, the tests Leon had run were based on ideal lab conditions with direct contact between the nanites and tissue. To be scientific about it, he needed to mimic the real-world environment.

Using the observed data, he programmed a scenario in the computer, which should now process the data quickly since the nanite architecture and behavior had already been mapped. He designed the model to show the nanites in their current state within the vial and then play out a natural physiological reaction, following the observation from the prior live tests.

After infection, there was only a reaction in people with active Gifted abilities. However, in the scenario with latent Gifts, the nanites clearly attached to the subject's genome but remained inactive.

So, what makes them activate? The power of the tech was immense, so there had to be *some* kind of trigger. He stared at the screen, not sure what to try next.

He cycled through several frequencies pulled from other TSS research into the Erebus' tech, but he didn't have access to all of the files. A conversation with Wil and Jason was definitely in order. But first, he wanted to model the transmissibility of the nanites.

Since the nanites attached to the host deep within cells, he expected that once ingested, they wouldn't go anywhere. Nonetheless, the model should fill in the details.

As soon as he finished programming the new scenario parameters, he executed the analysis. It played through the three genetic variations, beginning with the Vapr mist entering the host. The process of it attaching to the genome played out as he expected. The nanites entered the body and performed their function. However, then the nanite count began to increase.

That can't be right. Alarmed, Leon went to check on the original sample tank where the nanites had been introduced to the living tissue samples. Sure enough, the nanite count on the readout display had gone up exponentially. The nanites had replicated.

Shite, how did I miss this? Leon quickly purged the samples inside the case, not wanting to risk it cannibalizing the case itself to continue the self-replication. Autonomous propagation hadn't even crossed his mind, so he hadn't checked on the samples upon completing the initial tests. One of the risks of working alone.

Satisfied that the activated nanites were no longer a threat, he went over the growth records from the samples and quickly made adjustments to his computer model to account for their behavior. He watched in horror as the updated model of the nanites demonstrated their capacity to clone themselves and then work their way to the epidermis, where they shed through dead skin cells and sweat.

Fok, this is bad. His heart pounded as he started to expand the model again to account for the shed nanites.

Sure enough, other people who came in contact with the bodily materials could readily pick up the nanites. It operated like a virus, only most of the hosts would never know they were even infected.

Given that revelation, he checked the second-hand transmission to Gifted and non-Gifted people. It turned out that the heightened abilities activation only happened when the nanites were directly ingested via the mist.

That's interesting.

If the models were correct, the only people who'd experience an immediate, negative reaction were those with active Gifted abilities who'd taken the drug. There were so few who met that profile that it was no wonder the drug had never made the mainstream news.

However, the rate of secondary infection could be astronomical by now. He had no idea how much of the drug had been distributed and consumed, so he couldn't begin to guess at numbers.

There was no way around it, he needed to speak with Jason right away.

Leon copied the data from the analysis onto a secure mobile drive and headed up to the administrative wing on Level 1. He'd been by Jason's office a few times before and knew the way.

When he arrived, he found the door open and Jason behind his desk.

"Hi, I completed the analysis. You need to see it immediately," Leon said.

Jason looked up at him with concern. "Bad?"

"I'll let you be the judge." Leon entered, closing the door behind him.

Jason used the controls on his desktop to turn the outer glass wall opaque. He then took the offered mobile drive from Leon and placed it on the desk to initiate a data transfer.

The information appeared on the holodisplay, hovering above the desk between them.

Jason scanned over the data, his brows drawing together and a frown deepening the more he read. "Do you understand this well enough to talk about it in detail?" he asked.

Leon shrugged. "There's a lot of guesswork here. It's new territory for Taran science. But anyone else would be shooting blind just like me."

Jason nodded. "Let's go see the High Commander."

Leon had expected that was coming, and he didn't hesitate to follow Jason further down the main hall.

Jason knocked on the closed door and then entered. "Hey, Dad. Sorry to interrupt, but Leon has his findings and was hoping to talk with us."

"Sure, come on in," Wil said.

Jason and Leon sat down in the visitor chairs across from the High Commander's desk.

Leon had been in the office before, but on those previous occasions, he hadn't brought disastrous news. This time, he found nerves rising in his chest as he braced for the reaction from the Agents. He shifted in the seat, trying to get comfortable. "When Jason dropped that vial on my desk, I thought it must be a joke. But everything you said about it seems true."

"So, it *does* activate dormant Gifted genes?" Wil asked.

"Not just that, it opens up a direct link to the higher-dimensional energies," Leon explained. "I wouldn't have known what I was looking at if I hadn't seen it before."

"Where?" Jason prompted, though the grim look on his face suggested he already knew the answer.

"Quel."

Jason nodded his understanding before meeting his father's eyes. "It's all related."

Leon had noticed the expanding web of the Coalition's influence across the galaxy. None of these things seemed like they should be connected, yet they were. "There's a big caveat, though," he continued. "These changes don't happen automatically. I was able to run the scenarios based on the *potential*, but I can't figure out what might be the activation trigger."

Wil and Jason exchanged knowing glances again. Leon didn't like that they were keeping something from him, but it wasn't his place to question the Agents.

"What happens when the cells are flooded with *aesen* like

this?" Wil asked after a pause.

"It burns a person out. Our bodies weren't meant to serve as conduits like that. It's why deploying the Pesta weapon kills the host—they open the floodgate through their body so the weapon can reach down into our spacetime reality." The entire thing made Leon's head hurt. He'd intended to spend his career focusing on gene therapy and medical science, not navigating cutting-edge transdimensional physics.

Wil nodded thoughtfully. "What would happen if there wasn't a Pesta weapon tethered to the subject?"

"It would kill the host, but you wouldn't have the massive planet-killing effect we saw on Quel." That was Leon's best guess, anyway. It was difficult to know exactly what would happen.

Jason leaned forward slightly. "What if there were a bunch of people who all had these nanites activate at the same time?"

"Obviously, that would produce a much bigger result. I couldn't tell you *how* much." Leon shrugged. "I don't know how you'd simultaneously activate nanites across a large population, though. You'd need some sort of signal."

"Have you tried to identify the trigger?" Wil asked.

"Yes, but no luck."

"What have you tried?"

Leon brought up the test logs.

Wil scanned over them, seemingly looking for something specific. He didn't appear to see it. "I'd like to try something." His hands glided over his touch-surface desktop, eventually pulling up a file that looked to be an energy frequency model.

"What is it?" Leon questioned.

"If it's the trigger we're looking for, I'll explain," Wil said.

Leon swallowed. "Okay, we'll need to go down to my lab."

The three of them left the office and took the central elevator down to Level 6. When they arrived at Leon's lab, he unlocked it and went to the workstation at the back of the space.

He brought up the scenario analyses he'd worked on earlier. "What are the frequency details?"

Wil used his handheld to transfer over a data file.

Leon loaded it into the scenario. He didn't know much about frequencies and energy fields, but the model Wil had provided didn't look like anything he'd seen before. Wordlessly, he started a new analysis modeling what would happen if the nanites were within the energy field.

In the previous testing, the nanites remained dormant when bonded to a person with latent Gifted abilities. However, within the field, the nanites exhibited their full functional potential—activating a cellular-level link to the *aesen* energy. This flooded the subject with higher-dimensional energy, ultimately killing them.

Wil and Jason wordlessly watched the scenario play out.

"Am I correct in my interpretation that this frequency modifies the behavior of the nanites?" Wil asked at last.

Leon bobbed his head. "Yes, my rudimentary assessment is that this frequency is a trigger for the nanites. I can't tell you whether or not it's the only one."

The High Commander nodded. "Okay. Well, that energy field is what's created when all of the Erebus' power cores come online—when measured on a galactic scale."

Leon stared at the data. "No, that's…" He was going to say 'impossible', but the statement obviously wouldn't have been made if it wasn't somehow true. His mind raced through the implications. "Only about ten percent of the population has active Gifted abilities, but once you factor in the latent carriers, we're looking at a third of the population."

"Much higher," Wil replied. "Most of the bloodlines that are classified as 'non-Gifted' actually still have many of the genetic markers—just not enough to ever result in abilities expression. Our estimates are that those make up sixty to seventy percent of the total population."

"In other words, if these nanites somehow got into every single person, somewhere around eighty percent of all Tarans could drop dead in a matter of minutes." Leon was surprised that his voice sounded so calm despite the gravity of what he was saying.

"That is my interpretation, yes," Wil said.

Jason, who had been quiet up to that point, scoffed and shook his head. "They've been planning a foking genocide."

"But what's their plan for the survivors?" Wil murmured.

Leon gaped at him. "Shouldn't we be more concerned about that *eighty percent*—or more—of people?"

"Obviously, we're not going to let their plan play out," Wil said. "But we need to figure out what their next steps *would* be, if it did, so we can have a countermove prepared for those, too."

"Well, eliminating the Gifted would be easy, since the direct ingestion of this same substance results in pretty much insta-death." Leon had meant the statement flippantly, but Wil and Jason nodded along thoughtfully, seemingly unaware that they were talking about the hypothetical annihilation of their race.

"At that point, the remaining people would be easy to pick off," Jason said. "They'd have all the energy they needed here to interact."

Wil nodded. "If not from the initial wave, then from the Gifted."

Leon realized he was missing something vital. "Sorry, what are you talking about?"

The two Agents looked at each other with the intensity Leon had come to associate with a heated telepathic exchange.

"You are to keep this information to yourself," Wil said.

Leon nodded. "Of course."

"We believe the Erebus introduced this drug as a means to manufacture an *aesen* energy reserve here in spacetime, since it is difficult for them to access this dimension," Wil explained. "Our working hypothesis is that they've been paving the groundwork to enable an invasion to wipe us out."

Leon's heart pounded in his chest. "How the fok are we supposed to stop that?"

"We're still working on it," Jason said.

That should have been reassuring, given how many other galactic disasters the Sietinens had successfully averted over their years in the TSS. Nonetheless, Leon was overcome with a sense of dread. He very much wished Kira was back home with him.

"Let me know what I can do to help," he managed to mutter.

"Thank you," Wil said, heading for the door.

"Good work," Jason added, giving him an approving nod. "I'll be in touch."

They left, leaving Leon alone with his thoughts. He couldn't fully grasp the magnitude of what was unfolding before him. *An extradimensional alien invasion?*

Even as despair threatened to consume him, he tried to focus on the positives. They had identified the enemy's intentions. That was a whole lot better than if they thought everything was fine.

It's not over yet. He saved the work and securely locked it away. When it was time to act, he'd be ready.

— — —

Jason slipped into bed next to Lexi, weary from hours of staring at tactical plans. He'd made good progress on the approach to disable Monsari's and the Coalition's operations, but it was draining and frustrating work.

He tried to gently nestle into his pillow without disturbing Lexi. Despite his efforts, she stirred.

"Hey," she greeted sleepily, rolling over to face him.

"Hi. I was trying not to wake you."

She kissed him. "I'll take any time with you I can get."

There wasn't any accusation in her tone, but he felt a pang of guilt, nonetheless. "I didn't mean to miss dinner again, but it's been nonstop."

"It's okay. There's important stuff going on. I've been plenty busy myself."

"How was your day?" he asked. "Has Melisa taken you up on your offer to join the training initiative?"

She shook her head. "Things are good, but I haven't gotten a definitive answer from her yet. I don't want to push it."

"I'm sure she'll come around."

"I hope so."

He wrapped his arms around her. Just being in her presence reminded him how little quality time they'd spent together in recent weeks. He savored the contact. "I've missed you."

"Me too."

He brushed her hair out of her eyes. "As soon as the

Coalition is out of the way, we can focus on us."

She smiled knowingly, nothing but love in her eyes. "Until the next crisis demands your attention, but I appreciate the sentiment."

More than likely, she was right. "Thank you for understanding."

The deeper he got to know her, the more he appreciated her pragmatic attitude and independence. As much as they thoroughly enjoyed each other's company, their relationship never felt clingy or needy—just comfortable, whether they'd spent every minute together or had barely seen each other for days. He really couldn't have hoped for a better partner to help him navigate the demands of his position, especially now that they knew just how dire the situation was in the fight against the Coalition and Erebus.

Lexi snuggled up against him. "I'm just glad we can come home to each other every night."

"I wouldn't have it any other way."

The work they were doing now would ensure they had a future to look forward to, and that was worth the temporary sacrifice of long hours and time apart. Despite the chaos throughout the day, they had moments like this to reconnect and affirm their bond. No matter what they faced, they wouldn't be alone.

CHAPTER 8

RYAN STRETCHED ONE arm upward in bed, trying to motivate himself to start the day. In the crook of his other arm, Raena was still dozing, but she stirred with his movement.

"Can we just cancel all our meetings today?" she muttered.

"I don't think Jovan or Sandrine would be happy, but that's their problem."

Raena groaned. "Curse my blasted sense of responsibility." She rubbed her eyes, finally cracking them open.

"Shall we get to it, then?"

"Not yet." She snuggled closer, wrapping an arm around his chest.

He held her close, having no complaints about delaying the start of the day by a few more minutes.

Their time together had been growing more limited with every new crisis, and he wanted to savor these quiet moments together every chance he got. Further, with the looming prospect of parental responsibilities, they needed to take advantage of the alone time every chance they got.

"I love you," he whispered into her hair.

"Love you, too." She gave him a squeeze, then released him with a sigh. "All right, time to get up."

They set about getting ready for the day, taking a light breakfast on their terrace before heading to their respective offices.

As usual, Ryan had a long list of messages waiting for him in the morning. Thankfully, Sandrine had already annotated many of them so the list of items that required his personal review was a manageable length.

He'd gone through three-quarters of them when an unscheduled vidcall came through to his personal line, bypassing even his assistant. When he saw it was marked with TSS credentials, there were two likely options.

As the caller's image materialized on his screen, he found it was the less expected of the two.

"Hi, Ryan," Wil greeted.

"Hey. This is a surprise." He never knew whether to call Wil by his first name or 'sir' or another moniker, so he tried to avoid adding anything whenever possible.

"I have a favor to ask, and I can only ask it of you."

"Sure, anything." Ryan nodded his assent as he took a sip of coffee.

Wil flashed a pained smile. "I need you to put together a transportation solution for five million people."

Ryan choked on his coffee, almost spitting it out, but managed to swallow the mouthful. "Did you say five million?"

"Yes, preferably on one vessel, but I don't know if that's feasible."

"Given enough time and planning, building almost anything is possible. But my guess is this is a sooner than later request."

"A correct assumption."

Ryan rubbed his hand through his hair. "We don't manufacture any vessels with remotely that kind of passenger capacity as a standard product. Do you need long-term living quarters?"

"No, just day-trip transport."

"In that case, the shells of large cargo transports could probably be retro-fitted in short order, maybe hold five-hundred-thousand people each."

"All right, then I'll take ten of those."

Ryan would have to talk to his team to get an exact price, but the cost would be enormous. DGE was doing okay, but the amount of time and resources to divert into an order like that would place a major strain on the company's cash flow. "Uh…"

"Don't worry, I'm not asking for a free favor. I'll be paying for it personally."

"May I ask why?"

"No, but I can tell you a story."

"Okay."

"Imagine you had a good friend who joined a club," Wil began. "At first, the club sounded like a great place with lots of exciting ideas, but soon they started talking badly about anyone who wasn't in that club. The members began to do everything they could to get other people to join, but if you didn't want to, then they'd make your life miserable. Eventually, they took over your town. You and a handful of people didn't want the club running your town, but it was too late. Your original friendship was gone, and your town was too far under the club's influence for you to have any hope of things going back to how they were.

"You heard that there were other towns that had shut

down their chapter of the club when it tried to open, but you had no way to get there. However, someone eventually offered you a ride to a new place similar to how your original town was before the takeover. People who want to be in the club can move into your old town, and you can be in the new place living your own version of peace."

It didn't take much for Ryan to read between the lines. The TSS was planning to cede—at least temporarily—the planets that the Coalition had taken over, but anyone who wanted off those worlds, to remain with the rest of the Empire, would be offered transit to another, free planet. There was no way that process would go smoothly, no matter how many transport ships were available. People weren't interested in giving up their homes without a fight.

"Where, hypothetically, would a large population go to get a fresh start?" Ryan asked.

"A new world."

Ryan tilted his head. "Last I checked there aren't any unoccupied colony worlds ready to go."

"Leave those details to me."

"I'll begin making the arrangements," Ryan agreed.

"Thank you. Send me an invoice when you're ready."

"I'll be in touch soon."

Ryan leaned back in his seat when the vidcall ended, letting out a long breath. *This is worse than I imagined.*

He couldn't begin to guess what Wil was planning to do with the colonists, but relocating millions of people was a monumental task, especially on short notice. There were few ships of adequate size currently under construction and postponing those contracts would be bad for business. The best option was to find some old freighter shells and fix them up.

Ryan brought up the contacts list on his desktop and located one of DGE's fleet managers he'd worked with on occasion— a real go-getter who was bucking for a promotion. *If he can pull off this request, a nice title and pay bump are definitely in order.*

His viewscreen went temporarily black with a pulsing DGE logo while the vidcall connected. After a couple seconds, Ansen's face appeared.

"My lord, how can I be of service?"

Normally, the title made Ryan feel uncomfortable. But right now, faced with a seemingly impossible task, he appreciated having the clout to make the absurd request. "I need ships," Ryan began.

Ansen smiled. "I have those."

"The ships I need don't exist yet, but I need them ready as soon as possible."

The young man's smile waivered. "What are the specifics, my lord?"

Ryan relayed the requirements he'd received from Wil and added in some technical specifications based on his own read of the situation.

By the time he'd finished, Ansen had none of his original enthusiasm. "And you need them by when?"

"Yesterday."

The young man nodded. "That's going to be tricky, but I have some ideas for how we can put together a usable solution in short order. It's going to mean lots of overtime."

"We're prepared to shoulder the expense."

"Then consider it done."

Ryan smiled. "That's exactly the answer I wanted to hear."

— — —

Kira examined her new laundry service jumpsuit—a baggy, beige garment, unflattering in every way. "I don't think this is my color."

"It's not a lot of things," Pyra said with a frown. "I believe they are trying to take away individual identity by having workers dress this way."

"Nothing unusual about that."

"At least other uniforms look good."

<Who would have thought he had such strong opinions about fashion?> Jasmine quipped.

<The TSS is quite stylish,> Kira admitted. *<I'm looking forward to getting back to my TUF uniform, that's for sure.>* Aside from the frumpy cut and bad color, this jumpsuit was a generic size rather than custom-made, so it bunched up in odd places and pulled in others.

After a quick edit to Kira's alias résumé from mechanic to janitor, like Pyra's, she'd secured a short-term employment contract with Avon Industrials, a cleaning and supply division within the broader Avon organization. The parent company also included an interstellar security division that Kali had suspected was connected to the Coalition. The background check for Kira's alias had passed muster, so she'd been cleared to begin work and issued a jumpsuit.

Based on the short employment interview and offer to start work the next day, it seemed Avon was in desperate need of additional workers. Considering that they were destroying the minds of their current workforce, that wasn't a huge surprise.

"I should get going."

"Good luck. I'll see you this afternoon."

She headed toward the place where she'd been told to meet her supervisor.

Originally, she and Pyra had both planned on going in to plant cameras on the other workers, but then Pyra had the idea to try to secure equipment to conduct a scan of the area. There didn't seem to be many technology vendors on the planet, so it was a longshot. Still, if they could search for the presence of unusual materials, it would be worth the effort.

As an extra precaution, Kira had set a timed delay message to alert the TSS about what was going on, which would auto-send if she didn't disable it by that night. Since there was a legitimate concern about their memories getting wiped, it seemed prudent.

Half a dozen other workers dressed in beige were already waiting at the designated muster point when Kira arrived. One other woman had the awkward bearing of someone starting her first day, but the other workers had the slumped shoulders and frowns of people who'd long ago lost interest in their work.

Kira looked them over. <*Really upbeat bunch here.*>

<*Check their memories,*> Jasmine suggested.

Unfortunately, their downcast eyelines were going to make that difficult. Kira repositioned near someone she assumed was a longer-term worker, a dark-haired woman, to see if she could catch her attention.

"Are you a local or from offworld?" Kira asked, hoping to strike up a conversation.

"Fureron," the dark-haired woman replied without looking up. Not helpful.

"What brings you here of all places?"

"Why did you come?"

"I heard the pay is good."

"There you go." The woman had still not met Kira's eyes.

<*So rude!*> Kira exclaimed with an exasperated mental sigh. <*You're supposed to look at someone when you talk to them.*>

<*Not always. Try to connect in a different way.*>

It would only take a second or two for Kira to initiate the telepathic link. She thought about potential ploys. An idea occurred to her, but she'd feel ridiculous doing it. *Gotta try.*

Kira began picking at her teeth with her index finger, making a show of it. The other woman glanced over, looking mildly disgusted.

"Hey, do I have something in my teeth?" Kira asked when she had the woman's interest. "First day impressions and all that."

The woman sighed and finally gave more of her attention.

Kira seized the opportunity. She met her eyes and quickly established a mental link. Unlike the people she had encountered on the street, this worker's memory appeared to be intact. It was a relief, since it made it less likely that her own memories would be at risk with the job. However, it didn't explain the woman's dour demeanor.

"There's nothing there," the woman said, quickly looking away from Kira's bared teeth.

"Cool, thanks." Kira was silent for several seconds. "What should I expect from the job?"

"To not ask questions." She turned away, arms crossed.

Okay, that's the end of that. Still, the interaction had been enough to give Kira what she wanted to know. Their gamble that working for the laundry service would avoid the memory wipe seemed like it would pay off.

The shift supervisor, a severe woman of middle years with

her expression set in a constant scowl, finally arrived. She passed her gaze over the group. "You will perform your tasks and return here. Do not ask the workers questions," she instructed.

More with the no-questions declarations! Kira could feel Jasmine bristle at the statement, as well. <*If that isn't an admission that they have something to hide, I don't know what is,*> Kira said to the AI.

<*I have no doubt,*> Jasmine agreed. <*It's strange, though, that they're using manual labor for custodial services. Why isn't it automated or offloaded to robots?*>

The AI brought up a valid point, and one Kira had wondered about, as well. <*There's actually a lot less technology around here than you'd expect. Maybe they don't trust it, or something.*>

<*I need scan data from down here on the surface. These caverns are too deep for the orbital data to be detailed enough.*>

<*What are you thinking?*> Kira asked.

<*Maybe there's something down here that prevents technology from working well.*>

<*Should we be worried about you?*>

<*My bioelectronic systems are more stable than crystalline processing matrices, but I will conduct regular self-diagnostics to identify potential anomalous performance.*>

Kira smiled inwardly. <*You know, Jasmine, you can just say you'll let me know if you start acting weird.*>

<*That would be an imprecise statement.*>

Sometimes, there was no point arguing with the AI.

Kira followed the shift manager and the other workers through a door, which took them to an area separated from the main street by a security fence.

She tried to look unassuming and disinterested while taking in every detail she could. Even though she couldn't process everything in real-time, Jasmine was her extra set of eyes, cataloguing and recording all the images for later analysis.

The shift supervisor took the group across the fenced area to a side door, located to the left of where the other workers were coming and going from the main cavern entrance. Kira didn't notice the secondary entry until they were almost to it—textured to look like the surrounding stone.

<*That's weird. Why go to the trouble of hiding a service entrance?*>

<*Very odd,*> Jasmine agreed.

<*How many other hidden passageways are around here?*>

<*We really need a scan. Hopefully, Pyra can find the right equipment.*>

Kira wished they'd arranged for equipment to be passed off to them somehow, but before arriving, she didn't realize just how blind they would be. If Pyra couldn't secure what they needed, she'd put in a request to Jason.

Passing through the doorway, Kira noticed a bioscanner. Her heart lurched. <*Shite! There's no way that will miss my mods.*>

<*I'm on it.*>

Kira felt a slight increase in pressure in her head as Jasmine got to work. Kira knew from experience it meant that she was in the process of hacking into the system. With any luck, she'd be able to keep its detection systems from triggering.

Kira cleared the arch. No alarm went off.

<*I got it in time,*> Jasmine said. <*This is sophisticated tech—the kind I'd expect for a classified government research facility.*>

<The mystery of Zeron deepens.>

Kira took in her surroundings. It was a plain concrete corridor lined with metal doors. The group continued down the hall before entering the fourth door on the right.

Inside, there were shelves full of linens, cleaning supplies, and other sundries along with a collection of rolling carts.

"Stock up," the shift supervisor told Kira and the other new woman, handing them each a tablet displaying an inventory list and a work itinerary with accompanying map.

The more experienced workers had already started gathering their supplies in accordance with instructions on their own tablets, so Kira followed suit.

To her relief, the top item on the list was clean jumpsuits; the plan was coming together beautifully.

Unfortunately, there were too many people around now to risk planting a bodycam. Besides, she hoped to identify the right candidate worker for the devices in her pockets rather than putting it on a random garment and hoping for the best.

She loaded up her cart, finishing moments before the other new woman. When everyone was standing with their fully loaded trolleys, the shift supervisor motioned toward the door, and they filed out.

They continued down the hall in the direction they'd been going before the stop-off. The corridor terminated in a set of double-doors. The veteran workers stopped before going through.

The shift supervisor began doling out assignments.

"You, head to LR-203," she instructed Kira. The information on her tablet updated to reflect the new instruction.

She bobbed her head in acknowledgement. *<Uh oh. Does*

that mean I might not get assigned to the same place next shift?>

<That is a factor we hadn't accounted for in the plan.> There was a hint of concern in Jasmine's tone.

Kira couldn't do anything about it now. She consulted the map on her tablet. LR-203 appeared to be a locker room on Level 2, with higher numbers denoting floors deeper down. Beyond the locker room locations, the map wasn't helpful—only showing accessible routes to each assigned service place but no details about what occupied the spaces in between.

She navigated to a marked elevator, which would allow access to Level 2. Inside, there was a reader to swipe her ID badge. When she ran it across the scanner, Level 2 illuminated as the only accessible floor.

<Restricting access. Smart, but not helpful for us.>

<I could try to hack it if it comes down to it, but let's see how this plan plays out,> Jasmine said.

<Agreed.>

Kira took the elevator to the designated floor and pushed her cart out. Following the map, she quickly arrived at the marked locker room. There were several other doorways between the elevator and the changing area, but all had red lights next to their controls, indicating that they were locked. The spaces on the map were all blank, so there was no way to know what might be on the other side—or even whether there were discrete rooms or access points to different corridors.

<Jasmine, can you extrapolate a potential layout?>

<There's not enough data to draw conclusions with a high degree of certainty, but I'm making notes.>

When Jasmine was done recording the corridor, Kira continued on into the locker room.

It was surprisingly bright inside, with white floor, ceiling, and walls in various types of tile—all definitely from offworld. The lockers were metal painted in a deep rust-red reminiscent of the exterior landscape. Long benches ran in front of the locker banks on either side of a central walkway, with gaps in the seating every four lockers.

Jumpsuits were discarded on the benches, and occasionally on the floor. All were the same rust color Kira had seen the workers wearing.

In case there were security cameras watching her, she kept her eyeline downcast and focused on the discarded garments. She picked them up and dumped them in the appropriate receptacle on her trolley. While she worked, she made a mental note of the lockers where there were marked credentials for the higher-level workers within the facility, selecting several as good targets.

As instructed by the supervisor during her brief job training, she wiped down the area with a cleaning solution. She then took the fresh, folded jumpsuits from the storage area on her cart and set them on the bench in front of each locker.

This was the tricky part. On the garments she was putting in front of the target lockers, she carefully placed a button cam on the collar next to the zipper where it would blend in with the stitching. Sleight-of-hand wasn't her strong suit, but she felt she'd done a decent job of hiding the action from potential surveillance. Each cam was smaller than half a grain of rice, so it was unlikely to be spotted unless someone knew exactly what to look for. All the same, she used a widely available civilian model so if it was spotted, it wouldn't come back on the Taran military.

She managed to place the cameras on three separate jumpsuits before the sound of approaching footsteps forced her to abandon the effort.

<Are they active?> she asked Jasmine.

<Yes, but I'm going to disable the wireless link for now.>

Kira went back to her assigned tasks before the owner of the footfalls arrived. "Identify yourself," a male voice stated.

Kira turned to face the newcomer, keeping her eyeline down and head bowed reverently. "Maxine Renwald. This is my first day." She risked a glance up to see who she was dealing with.

He was tall and slim, likely in his mid-thirties. Like her shift supervisor, he had a stern expression and looked like he was vehemently against anything resembling good-natured humor. His jumpsuit was custom-fit and maroon, which she'd concluded meant he was a manager. "You're behind schedule."

She had no idea how that was possible considering she'd arrived less than ten minutes before him. "A timetable wasn't part of my orientation," she said truthfully.

"Who's your supervisor?"

"I actually don't know her name. I'm with Team F7."

He frowned but nodded. "Finish up."

Without another word, he turned and left.

Kira let out a relieved breath. *<Wound a little tight around here, it seems.>*

<They're definitely hiding something,> Jasmine agreed.

Kira gathered her cart and prepared to move on to her next assignment. The cam was in place. Now they just had to wait for answers.

CHAPTER 9

RAENA WAS STILL reeling from the High Council meeting. No matter how many times she replayed the events in her mind, she couldn't believe that Celine Monsari could stand up in front of her peers and make such an absurd declaration with a straight face.

Is it from fear or just plain evil? Raena wasn't sure. Regardless, declaring Gifted people to be an abomination crossed every line of decency in Raena's moral code. Celine and her followers had to be stopped—immediately.

To strategize, Raena and Ryan had been invited back to the Sietinen estate. While the meeting could have been handled over holoconference, she suspected that her grandparents wanted the extra level of security an in-person discussion afforded. They were treading in dangerous territory, and they couldn't be too careful.

Ryan had been quiet on the way over, and he now silently walked beside her.

"What's on your mind?" she asked.

"Just running the scenarios," he said. "Whether or not we

prevail will depend on if Monsari really is going broke or not."

"Doesn't matter. We can take 'em."

"Only to a point."

The delicate financial state of DGE was a regular worry of Ryan's, and the urgent request from her father had only elevated his anxiety. While Raena appreciated his serious consideration of the issues at hand, she didn't think his pessimism was warranted. DGE's assets were producing higher than the projected rate of return, and it wouldn't take long to build up significant credit reserves. She understood why he worried about the company and Dynasty not having the deep wealth of Sietinen, but they were far from broke.

"What's your concern, specifically?" Raena asked.

He looked around. They were alone, but the appearance of privacy didn't mean no one was listening. "That can wait until we're in the conference room."

Raena's grandparents were waiting for them when they arrived. They exchanged hugs and warm greetings before sitting around the oval, wooden table.

"Before we get going, what was your thinking about Monsari, Ryan?" Raena prompted.

Her grandparents looked at him with interest.

Ryan spread his hands on the tabletop. "I was going to say, I'm worried that Monsari might have been smearing the Dainetris name with the hope of weakening the DGE brand enough that they can force an asset selloff."

Cris smiled slightly.

"Do you find that amusing?" Ryan asked.

"No, not at all," Cris replied. "It's just that I wanted to meet today to discuss doing something similar to *them*."

Raena tilted her head questioningly. "What do you have

in mind?"

"I chatted with your dad," Cris continued. "He's made a point of staying out of our discussions, but something he said got me thinking. We may have been going about this situation with Monsari all wrong. MPS is the only company that they solely control. The other tangential business enterprises are owned by other companies, or in some cases, families. Most aren't valued more than a few billion."

Raena perked up with interest. "Is that so?"

He nodded. "I decided to run market reports on several of Monsari's collaborators, including Calrosi Enterprises. Wouldn't you know, its annual revenue is only two-hundred-thirty-seven million."

Ryan gawked. "That's *it*? That thorn that's been in our side for all these months has that low a valuation?"

Raena barely concealed her smile. "Scooping that up would be a steal, even at a ten-times buyout multiplier. Their board couldn't refuse."

Cris smirked. "Funny you should say that. I was just thinking that perhaps it's time we diversify the family business beyond SiNavTech, what with all this talk about transit access being a public right." He crossed his arms and leaned back.

Kate shared a knowing smile with the others around the table. "I wonder how many other opportunities are rife for investment?"

"Well, I'm all for diversifying my portfolio," Ryan said. "You know, in the interest of rebuilding the family legacy and all that."

"I thought you might be. Seems like an apt joint venture for Sietinen and Dainetris to undertake, since the two Dynasties are joined by marriage. I took the liberty of pulling a list of potential acquisitions."

He activated the holoprojector at the center of the table, which brought up a mosaic of tiles, each card representing a corporation with strong business ties to Monsari. There were dozens, most of which had fairly low valuations, as far as galactic corporations were concerned. Even with Dainetris' limited financial resources, many were easily within reach and could offer huge upside from an investment standpoint.

"I'm embarrassed I didn't think of that strategy myself," Raena said.

"Well, buying out the people who talk badly about you is typically considered poor form," Kate said. "At this point, though, eff 'em."

Raena didn't often hear her grandmother talk like that, but she liked it. "I'm all for it."

"Good." Cris reached out to the holographic tiles, pulling several to the side. "These were the ones that jumped out at me."

Raena looked over the summaries displayed on each of the cards. There were a variety of business areas represented in the selections, from public relations, to manufacturing, to charitable aid. It was a great departure from both DGE's and SiNavTech's current holdings, but that wasn't a bad thing.

"How large of an investment are you thinking?" she asked.

"That depends on the goals." Her grandfather leaned back in his seat. "Do we want to annoy Monsari, or cripple them?"

"How much would it take for the latter?"

Cris and Kate exchanged glances. "To scoop up all of these, we're probably looking at about five trillion after inflated valuations to force a sale. If we really want to drive home the point and go a little broader, let's say thirty."

It was an astounding amount of money by most measures but with Sietinen's assets measured in the quadrillions, it would hardly make a dent. "What's the downside?" she asked.

"Hostile takeovers are quite polarizing," Kate said. "In particular, this might turn Baellas and Makaris against us."

"Not if we cut them in," Raena suggested.

"We can't go to them before finalizing these deals or we'll never be able to arrange the sales once word gets out about what we're doing," Cris cautioned.

Raena shook her head. "No, not in advance. Look at this line-up—a lot of these are totally far afield from DGE and SiNavTech. But if we bring Makaris' or Baellas' subsidiaries on board as management consultants with some of the new industries, they can be involved and get some of the cut so it doesn't look like we're going rogue."

Kate nodded. "That's a very good idea."

Ryan was studying the lineup, focusing on one company in particular. "I want that one."

Raena followed his eyeline to Intelix Designs. It was a custom paint and finishing company—nothing that seemed noteworthy to her eye. "Why?"

"I spoke with Celine once a while back, and she disparagingly compared DGE to them. Apparently, they've been floundering for quite some time."

"Why do you want a failing company?" Raena asked.

"To prove Celine wrong."

Raena couldn't argue with that. "All right, that one will go under the Dainetris umbrella. Let's divide up the others and get the acquisition plan in order."

Cris nodded. "Here's what I was thinking." He swept his hand over the display, and they got to work.

— — —

Kira rubbed her knuckles into the small of her back as she trudged from her worksite back to the hotel where she was staying with Pyra.

The rest of the workday had been tedious and frustrating, performing tasks that on any other world would be handled by automated mechanical assistants. She would have welcomed the opportunity to look around and gather information as an all but invisible worker, except excessive security cameras and regular drop-ins from supervisors had forced her to remain focused on her assigned tasks. Worse, aside from the supervisors—whom she wasn't supposed to directly address—there hadn't been other people in her assigned work areas, so she hadn't been able to glean thoughts from anyone's mind.

The investigation would all come down to whether or not they could receive the footage from the button cams. And, given what she'd learned throughout the day about rotating work assignments, it was sounding unlikely that she'd be able to retrieve the devices at the end of the subjects' next shift when they discarded the bugged jumpsuits for cleaning.

<*This may have been a waste of a day,*> she complained to Jasmine while walking down the street alongside the glazed-eyed workers.

<*Not if the plan works.*>

<*But how can it? I didn't realize before this morning that the work assignments rotated every day. I won't be able to get back to that locker room.*>

<*You might not have to,*> the AI said.

<*Why not?*>

<If you can get close enough, I can initiate a wireless transfer.>

Though the cameras were offline and recording internally, they still put out a low-level signal if a user knew which frequency to use to access it—one most security systems would not detect. Based on Kira's understanding of the technology, the near-field access needed to be quite close—maybe an adjacent room, tops. But turning on the full wireless features for a data transfer would be much easier to detect than the passive field.

<It's too risky,> Kira said.

<If I can gain access to the security system, I can mask the transfer.>

<If we're hacking security, it would be easier for me to just go to the room to get them.>

<There is also that option.>

<That would obviously blow our cover.>

<What does it matter if we've obtained what we came for?> It wasn't like Jasmine to be such a risk-taker.

<I'm supposed to be the one throwing out the crazy plans, not you.>

<I don't want to be here any longer than necessary. There's something bad here. The information doesn't add up.>

<I agree.> Kira sighed. *<Unfortunately, we won't know if we have the footage we need until we see it. And accessing it might give us away, ruining the chances of follow-up investigations. So, we'll need to find a way to get it without blowing cover.>*

<A problem to solve tomorrow, then.>

<Yes. Right now, all I want is a hot shower, a decent meal, and bed.> Really, going home to her bed with Leon was what

she really wanted, but she tried to put that out of her mind while focusing on the job at hand.

She was almost to the hotel. The entrance was quite literally a hole in the wall, leading through a narrow rock corridor to a separate cavern with half a dozen buildings, including the hotel, a general store, and a handful of compact eateries. On another world, she may have found it quaint. Here, though, it felt more like a glorified prison—impenetrable walls closing in from all sides.

Kira entered the hotel and took the stairs up to the second level where her room was located. There'd been the option to book two rooms with an adjoining doorway, so she and Pyra had done that. When she entered her room, she saw via the pass-through doorway that Pyra was sitting on his bed.

He jumped up when she entered. "How did it go?"

"Next time, you get the manual labor job." She began stripping off her outer jumpsuit.

Pyra averted his eyes even though she was wearing clothes underneath. "Were you able to get the cameras in place?"

"Yes, but getting them back might be a challenge." Kira gave him the rundown of the shift assignments and technical limitations.

He frowned. "That's unfortunate."

"Tell me about it." She sat down on the edge of her bed— an old mattress that wouldn't do much to soothe her back after a day of lifting and bending over.

"I do have some good news." Yet again, in that annoying way of his, Pyra paused too long for dramatic effect.

"Yes?"

"I was able to find a scanner," Pyra revealed.

Good, at least something is going right. She leaned forward, resting her elbows on her thighs. "Have you been able to test it?"

"Not yet. Besides, I figured you'd want to see the results in real-time."

"You already know me well."

"I took the liberty of scoping out the area surrounding the facility entrance, and I think I've found a suitable place for us to set up the scanner." He brought up a map on his handheld.

Kira studied it. *<What do you think?>* she asked Jasmine.

<It should work, yes,> the AI agreed. *<However, we'll need to get to the area for me to assess security concerns.>*

Kira combed her hair with her fingertips, still not used to the longer strands. "Let's do it tonight. I might need to break cover tomorrow, and I don't want to lose the chance."

Pyra nodded. "I'm ready to go when you are."

She got up to get her civilian visitor jumpsuit. "We'll grab dinner on the way out."

While she donned her other outerwear, Pyra retrieved the scanner in a carrying case. The container looked reasonably like a travel suitcase, so it shouldn't draw too much attention wheeling it around.

They stopped by one of the cafés next to the hotel to grab hot sandwiches, which they quickly consumed before heading back toward the suspicious facility. Having seen the barren corridors and gotten a sense for the scale of the place based on the number of floors indicated in the elevator, Kira was even more anxious to get detailed information about what was deep inside.

The place Pyra had picked out was down a side alley, heading in the direction of the government building, but was covered on two sides by other structures. A little alcove behind a large dumpster offered just enough room for the two of them to crouch down.

Pyra opened up the scanner case and set it on the ground in between them. "I bought it, but I have no idea how it works," he said just above a whisper.

"I'll take it from here," Kira replied.

Following instructions from Jasmine coupled with her own training, she turned on the scanner and configured the settings to focus on the area of interest. No doubt, she'd need to make adjustments based on what they found inside, but it should get them started.

Once everything was set, she activated the scan. The device sprang to life with a low hum and subtle vibration that shouldn't be audible from the street. As a precaution, though, Jasmine hacked into the nearby security feeds to mask their presence.

The scanner collected data for nearly five minutes before the first information began to populate on its readout screen.

Kira sat back on her heels, watching with surprise and concern as the scan revealed a far larger structure than even her work map had indicated. "It just goes on and on."

Pyra's brows drew together. "Am I reading it wrong, or is it picking up a massive quantity of ateron?"

Kira examined the material composition data. "You're right. Or something similar to it, anyway. It's the same kind of weird alloy Jason observed at an MPS facility during recon."

"That… doesn't make sense. Is there a vein here, and that's what they've been secretly mining?"

She looked closer, switching the screen to a color-coded overlay of materials within a three-dimensional cross-section of the facility. All of the deposits were organized in clear structures. "No, I don't think this is a natural formation. Usually, if there's a large deposit, there are trace amounts of the element in the surrounding area. Here, the only ateron is in these concentrated spots."

"Like, something was constructed there?" he asked.

"And a big, complex 'something', at that."

Kira could feel Jasmine thinking. *<What?>* she asked the AI.

<I'm extrapolating the form factor. With the available data, I have eighty percent confidence that the structure resembles the ancient alien features discovered on Earth.>

It was exactly what they had been sent to Zeron to find out. *<We need to get that body cam footage from inside.>*

<I know.>

The scan completed, displaying a general floor-by-floor map of the facility. The open spaces and walls were clearly rendered, as were splotches indicating the material makeup of large objects, but it couldn't provide detailed information like which doors were locked. She assumed all of them, and there were a lot of barriers standing between the entrance and the ateron-laden anomaly deep underground.

"Let's get back to the hotel," she urged.

Pyra nodded. "We can go over this data back there."

They hurriedly packed up the scanner in its case and crept back toward the main street, then began walking normally as they neared the main walkway.

Just when Kira thought they had evaded detection, a loud tone blared, followed by a shout. "Halt, citizen!"

She froze. *Shite!*

She didn't dare turn around. *<Is that about us?>*

<I don't know.> Fear edged the AI's mental tone. That was

never a good sign.

Next to Kira, Pyra had also frozen. He had one hand on the rolling case and the other was outstretched where it was visible.

Loud footfalls sounded on the stone ground, running toward Kira's position. She braced for a guard's body to slam into her.

The footfalls were almost there.

And then they ran past—shouting after an unseen perpetrator somewhere in the crowd.

Responding to the black-clad guards' shouts, people cleared out of the way. With a path open, the guards fired blasts from their pulse handguns, and a man dressed in a rust-colored jumpsuit dropped to the ground. From a distance, it was unclear if the weapons had been set on stun or a lethal blast.

"Let's go." Kira tugged on Pyra's sleeve.

He snapped back to attention. "Yeah. We can't leave here soon enough."

CHAPTER 10

PART OF JASON wished that Leon's analysis had told them that all of their guesswork had been totally off-base and there was nothing suspicious about the Vapr drug. While confirmation meant they were finally making headway toward unraveling the larger mystery, the Erebus' plan was turning out to be a daunting reality.

"Where do we go from here?" Jason asked his parents as they sat in the High Commander's office.

"The little bit of information about the Vapr nanite properties has given us a lot," Wil said. "As much as I'd like to act on it, I think we need to prioritize getting the civil unrest under control first. I've already taken steps to give us more options in that regard."

Saera nodded. "Whatever happens next, we need people organized and on our side."

"I agree." Jason paused, hesitant to ask the tough question. "Is this a martial law situation?"

"Admiral Mathaen and I are prepared to take action, yes," his father confirmed. "I hope those efforts can be… strategic."

The fact of the matter was that the Taran Empire's population was too large and spread out for the military to effectively take over every single world. Targeted efforts on a few of the most 'problematic' planets might get the desired results with a reasonable number of personnel.

Jason anticipated his father's next request. "I'll work up a strategic analysis for which population centers have caused the most disruption."

Wil flashed a wan smile. "Thank you, that would be very helpful."

Jason crossed his arms. "Do you think the Erebus really just want to kill off all Tarans?"

"I don't think it's that simple at all."

"What, then? They've gone to an awful lot of trouble to covertly pick us off."

Wil leaned back in his chair. "I suspect this isn't the first time Tarans and the Erebus have been at odds. When we signed that treaty a hundred thousand years ago, I don't think it's because we were equally matched and wanted a truce. More like, we were close to being wiped out, and for whatever reason, they took pity on us—perhaps because the Morla'ki, the original Gatekeeper race, came to our aid. Either way, I believe we've been on borrowed time since then. The innate greed and power-hungry nature of our kind has now grown to the point that the Erebus have rescinded our stay of execution."

"All because we draw *aesen* power and it bothers them?" Jason asked.

"We take out colonies of ants for less," his mother pointed out.

Jason nodded. "I guess if they do annihilate us, at least it will be quick."

Wil looked him in the eyes. "I won't let that happen, Jason."

"What can you do to stop them?"

"There's only so much *I* can do, but *we* stand a chance to seal off their access to this dimension."

Saera eyed him. "So you've said, though I've yet to hear the 'how', precisely."

"The Erebus require conduits, or bridges, to manifest in spacetime—places where the dimensional veil is weakened. Like the Rift."

Jason raised his brows. "You intend to seal it?"

"Try, at least."

"We tried to seal it after the war but couldn't," Saera said.

"First of all, we knew much less about the higher-dimensional energies then than we do now," Wil pointed out. "I have tried again since then."

Jason crossed his arms. "Okay, but what about the natural spatial rifts, like the ones the Aesir reside in?"

"That's a big unknown. Truthfully, it might be impossible to seal all the potential breach points. If that fails, the only option is to use the weapon on Earth to create our own bridge to the higher dimensions and get a lock on the Erebus so we can harm them."

"Isn't it broken—or doesn't work right?"

"I'm still trying to figure out in what way," Wil admitted.

Saera's brows knitted. "Regardless, wouldn't this plan require the energy field generated by the Erebus power cores, and won't that activate the alien nanites in the Vapr?"

"Yes, but I hope to find a way to disable that nanotech first," Wil said.

Jason frowned. "Dad, I don't mean to be pessimistic here,

I'm hearing a long wish-list of 'hopes' and not a lot of actionable tactics."

"I know, I'm sorry," Wil said. "I'm working through a lot of ideas that haven't fully formed yet."

Jason had every faith in his father, but this was too important for one person to plan on their own. "Any hints?"

"My current thought is that there might be a way to program our standard medical nanites to treat the Erebus drug like it was an invasive virus."

"Okay, I could see that working," Jason mused.

"I'll need Leon to look at the specs for both to know for sure if it's feasible."

"But if we disable the nanites, we lose the patch for the Generation Cycle," Saera said.

"We can always change the programming after the Erebus threat has passed," Wil replied, "but I don't think the nanites are the answer in and of themselves. Rather, I think we can study their function as a patch and look for a biological solution using the genetic records on Cytera and Earth. The Priesthood never fully explored those information sources."

"Okay." Jason didn't know much about the genetic anomaly, only that his bloodline was supposed to have been a fix for the ailment. However, the Priesthood had suggested an unsavory crossing back of the lines to produce the desired results, and no one with a shred of decency was going to go along with that. Perhaps there *was* still hope for an alternative solution.

Wil shifted in his chair. "Forget about that for now. The nanites are the least of our worries. We know about the trap and can account for it." He steepled his fingers. "The greatest risk right now is having our own people turn against us while we're trying to face off against our real enemy."

"I agree," Jason said. "Unfortunately, identifying the worlds with the highest Coalition support isn't going to make those problems go away."

"No, it's not."

Jason studied him. "You clearly have something in mind. As the task force lead, shouldn't I be in on that?"

Wil hesitated. "Yes, you're right. I really didn't want you to have to get involved, but you should understand what it means to hold this title."

Saera flashed Jason an appraising look, gauging his reaction.

"Please, fill me in," Jason said. Though he had no interest in being High Commander himself anytime soon, Jason had to admit he was slowly warming up to the idea. He knew his father dealt with a lot behind the scenes, and he was anxious to get a better understanding of how to make those difficult decisions. There was a lot left to learn.

"The first thing you need to understand is that as much as we pretend we're not part of the politicking Taran elite, we very much are," Wil began.

Jason nodded. He had gotten some sense of that during his recent visit to Tararia.

"Most military leaders rely solely on the funding passed down from their superiors. You need more of something? It's a long, bureaucratic process to put in requisitions and get approvals, and the whole mess. Conversely, I can call up my dad, or son-in-law, or uncle and get absolutely anything I need, off the books. The Empire deals in traded favors, let there be no mistake about it. I don't like to do it often, but when times are desperate…"

"You do anything you can to survive," Jason completed for him.

"That's right. And this situation with the Coalition... Really, it's a civil matter the TSS should have a minimal role in resolving. It's only because I have Admiral Mathaen's blessing that I'm taking a lead now."

"Makes sense."

"We always walk a delicate balance," his mother added. "We can be effective leaders *because* of our familial connections, but we can't rely on them or abuse that power."

Wil nodded. "And to answer your question, Jason, the plan is to get as many innocents as possible away from the violence and deal with the insurgents."

Jason had no doubt that meant using any force necessary. "Where will those civilians go?"

"That's where the favors come in." Wil smiled, but there wasn't humor in it. "You know how they joke about how we're rich enough to buy a planet?"

"Yeah..."

"Well, I intend to do just that."

—   —   —

At last, Lexi felt like she was finally on top of all her work assignments. She extended her arms to either side of her desk chair, stretching out her shoulders after a writing marathon to complete the latest round of curriculum updates.

Once the materials went through approvals and refinements from the educational consultants, the content would be ready to deploy. Now, there was just the matter of finding the right instructors to connect with students.

She hadn't yet received a definitive answer from Melisa since their talk. They'd gotten together for a couple more meals, but it had been light chatting. Lexi missed the deep discussions about life and ambitions they used to have while camped out in the dark recesses of spaceports. They'd been so close then. She didn't expect them to get back to that place, but she wanted to have real conversations again.

Lexi knew her friend was hurting. After losing more than a year of her life and coming back to a totally different reality, it would be shocking for Melisa *not* to be disoriented. *I just want her to feel like she belongs somewhere.*

The TSS had given that to Lexi, but she'd had an immediate 'in' by being in a relationship with an Agent. She couldn't expect other civilians to feel that same connection to the organization. However, that's why they would have each other. The training group would be a community unto itself, and there was extraordinary potential to make it something truly special. Someone like Melisa, who had no other ties, had the perfect perspective about how to build those bonds. If a loner like her could find strategies to trust her peers and gain a sense of camaraderie, then anyone could.

Since Melisa hadn't brought up Lexi's suggestion again, it was safe to assume she wasn't considering the offer seriously. Lexi wasn't about to give up, though. It was too natural a fit—she knew it.

She had to be subtle about broaching the topic again. After thinking through a couple of different strategies, she settled on sending Melisa a copy of some of the new training curriculum in a message to her handheld. >>Hey, finally wrapping this up! Welcome to my life for the last month.<<

Lexi doubted Melisa would read much of it, but it would

give her an opening to the conversation.

To her surprise, a text response came through almost right away. >>Are you finished for the day?<<

>>Yeah.<<

>>Can you swing by my place?<<

>>Sure, I'll be right there.<< Lexi pocketed her handheld and went down to Level 7.

Melisa answered the door and motioned Lexi inside as soon as she arrived. "Thanks for coming."

"Yeah, of course. How is everything?" Lexi looked around the space. It seemed much tidier and more organized than the last time she'd stopped by, which was good to see.

"I'm leaving."

The statement was so abrupt that it took Lexi a couple of seconds to realize what she'd just heard. "Why?"

"I don't belong here." Melisa shrugged. There was little emotion to her expression, just calm resignation.

"I know TSS Headquarters might not be a great fit for you, but the new program—"

"I'm not interested, Lexi," Melisa said, more forcefully now. "I appreciate that you're trying to look out for me, but it's just not what I want. You, of all people, should understand."

"What do you mean?"

"All the shite we've put up with is because of our Gifts. It's great that you've been able to create this fanciful reality where all of that goes away because you're in love with a rich Agent who likes to go off and save the galaxy as part of an average workday, but it's not so easy for the rest of us. I don't want to learn to 'embrace my Gifts' as some self-love scheme on the path to enlightenment. What I know about my abilities now, I know because those are the skills I learned to survive. All that other stuff—it's not important. I don't need it. I don't want it."

Lexi took in her words, a pit growing in her stomach. "You might be surprised."

"The only surprise is seeing how fast you took to all this. I thought you had more grit than that."

"Grit has nothing to do with it. I found people who care about me, and I thought you could—"

"*I* cared about you, Lexi! We went through a foking nightmare together, and then I woke up to find none of that mattered to you."

"Of course it did."

Melisa scoffed, shaking her head. "I've tried to reconcile the person you were then and who you are now, but I don't recognize you anymore. You've been sucked in by blind hope. Life just doesn't turn around like that. You're just ignoring the harsh truth of things, and I'm finished trying to get through to you."

"Get through to me?" Lexi raised her brows, completely caught off-guard about where these accusations were coming from. *I was trying to be a good friend. Where did I go wrong?*

"Wake up, Lex!" Melisa flung her arms to her sides. "You're living in a fantasy."

"I don't think you understand what I have here."

"I see it well enough. You've actually convinced yourself that they see you as an equal. If that isn't foking delusional, I don't know what is."

If that's really how she sees it, then there's nothing more to say. Lexi's heart broke, knowing that this was the end of their friendship. She'd never expected it would come to such an abrupt end like this—having imagined them fast friends for life, growing old and reminiscing in their senior years.

But, in that moment, she realized that she *had* changed. And it wasn't that she'd grown soft and complacent, as Melisa suggested, but rather that she'd let go of the doubt and anger that had weighed on her heart for her entire life. She'd always been an outcast, running and unable to embrace her true self because of fear of judgment. Now, she'd found love and acceptance with no reservations, and she was free.

Melisa was still living in the mindset of a victim, seeing ulterior motives where there were only genuine offers of kindness. Lexi felt awful knowing that Melisa felt that way, but it was impossible to help someone who didn't want to be helped. Lexi had already tried in every way she knew, yet the harder she fought to help her friend, the more it seemed to push her away.

Sometimes, the kindest act was letting someone go.

Lexi's mouth felt dry and her chest was tight, but she managed to retain her outward composure. "I'll always be here for you if you change your mind."

"Yeah. Good luck with everything." Melisa crossed her arms and looked away.

"You too. I'll fondly remember our time together. Thank you for being there for me when no one else was." Lexi didn't expect Melisa to believe her, but she meant it from the bottom of her heart.

Without another word, she left. That was the end of it. All those years of friendship, over in a flash.

The sense of loss didn't hit her until she was almost back to her quarters.

Why in the bomaxed stars did I let things fall apart like that? She should have seen the signs that Melisa was pulling away, and yet Lexi had written it off as 'needing space'. No, that had been a lie she told herself. The truth was, she'd known then and there that their friendship had been an important part of her former life, but they weren't destined for the same future. The TSS and Jason had sent her in a new direction, and that was okay.

Despite rationalizing the end of their relationship, her heart was still heavy. Now, she didn't have any ties that went back longer than when she'd met Kira undercover in the Alliance.

The gravity of that revelation struck her like a physical weight mere steps from her quarters' door. *Shite, I really have no one except for the people here.*

With a flash of panic and regret, she almost turned around to go back to Melisa, to beg her oldest remaining friend to forgive her. But she stopped herself. She'd walked away because she knew it was the right thing to do, regardless of how difficult. To try to force a friendship would mean one of them was compromising their worldview. While Lexi thought Melisa's perspective was wrong, it wasn't her place to change it. And she needed to look out for herself and her own happiness.

She'd reached a tenuous equilibrium with her feelings by the time she palmed open the door. When it slid open and she saw Jason waiting for her on the couch, the warmth and comfort that filled her chest let her know that she'd made the right decision.

"Hey, are you okay?" Jason asked as he rose to greet her, picking up on her pain through their bond.

"I will be." She eagerly stepped into his open arms, resting her head against his chest. The rhythmic beating of his heart and warm breath on the top of her head grounded her.

After a minute, she pulled away enough to look into his eyes. "Melisa is leaving. I don't expect I'll ever hear from her again."

Surprise and curiosity filled Jason's eyes, and she shared what had happened through telepathy rather than spoken words—just enough so he'd understand her feelings on the matter.

He nodded slowly. "I'm sorry."

She shrugged. "Shite happens. It doesn't change the time we spent together."

"I know that feeling." His eyes flitted momentarily toward a picture of him and Tiff. "I'm happy to facilitate if she needs help getting set up somewhere else."

Lexi shook her head. "I got the impression that she wants to go it alone, lest she be viewed as a charity case."

"That's not how it would be at all."

"I know, but her mind is made up." Lexi slipped off her shoes and set them by the door. "I hope your day was better."

"Uh, it wasn't the best. But nothing unusual these days." He eased into the couch next to her."

"What's going on?"

"More Coalition and Erebus fokery. The more we figure out, the worse it gets. And my dad just says, 'Not to worry!' But we're facing down the end of life as we know it if the enemy accomplishes what we think they're planning, and how can we *not* worry? I think he's freaking out on the inside, and the fact that he's not sharing that concern with me is even more worrisome, because that means it's *really* bad." He finished with a huff. "Sorry, it's just…"

Lexi took his hand in hers when he faded out. "It's okay. Sometimes you've gotta let it out."

"I didn't mean to take over the floor."

"No, I'm done moping." She smiled. "Go for it."

"I'm over it, too. Just gotta buckle down and do the work."

"What's the plan?"

"It's not worth getting into."

"Please don't close me out," Lexi said. It came out more forcefully than she'd intended.

"I wasn't trying to."

"I know, but…" She sighed. "I want to be a partner to you, not just someone you come home to at night."

"You *are* a partner."

"But only in some ways. And hey, I know there are certain tactical details you can't discuss with me as a civilian, and I don't know shite about battle strategies, anyway. But when it comes to people—especially *desperate* people—I have a lot of insights. I'd like to be able to talk about that stuff with you. You know, involve me, and maybe I can even be helpful."

Jason squeezed her hand and gazed lovingly into her eyes. "I would love that."

"Okay. Good." Lexi felt a little silly for how she'd blurted it all out, but she felt better having gotten it off her chest.

Sensing her anxiety, Jason wrapped his arm around her and pulled her to him. "You have an amazing mind, and I love how you think about things."

"So, talk to me."

He released her, and she looked into his eyes imploringly.

"You've earned my trust," he said. "What I share with you is between us, privileged."

She nodded.

"All right. Well, we're dealing with kind of a mess."

CHAPTER 11

GETTING READY FOR work the morning after the facility scan, Kira had more anxiety than on her first day. The entire investigation was riding on her finding a way to retrieve the body cams from the workers' jumpsuits. Without that inside footage, the structural scan was only a vague guide. The TSS would need more than that in order to take action against a private business.

"You're going to be fine," Pyra tried to assure her as she paced across her small hotel room, the top half of her beige-colored jumpsuit tied around her waist.

"I know. Just psyching myself up." She had her pre-battle routines, and having an audience wasn't a normal part of that process. She tried to ignore him, knowing he was attempting to be helpful.

"I'll be standing by to assist if anything goes sideways," he said.

"Let's hope it doesn't come to that."

She zipped up the rest of her jumpsuit and checked her reflection in the mirror, making eye contact with herself. *Just another day at the office.*

<It's not an office, and it's a more significant day than most,> Jasmine chimed in.

<Not helpful.>

<I know from experience that your mental acuity increases by thirty-two percent when you're annoyed, so I'm simply doing my part.>

Having a paired AI was a double-edged sword, no doubt about it. Kira headed for the door.

"How will we make contact if I have an issue?" she asked Pyra.

"I procured a burner handheld along with the scanner yesterday," he said. "Can Jasmine access it remotely?"

<If there's a wireless network nearby, yes. Obviously, that would blow our cover if the communication is detected.>

Kira relayed the information out loud to Pyra.

He nodded. "Then that's probably the best bet. Here are the credentials." He passed them to her.

She looked over the information for Jasmine's benefit.

<Got it,> the AI confirmed.

"All right." Kira clapped her hands together. "Let's do this."

They walked together toward the facility. Three blocks before Kira's turnoff to the cleaning crew rally point, Pyra peeled off from her to walk slightly behind and to the side so it wasn't obvious that they were traveling together. Based on what Kira had been able to piece together about the city's security, they didn't do active surveillance on the citizens at all times, but certain locations were monitored. So, even though the two of them had done other things together in the past, as long as they didn't show up to her work together, there shouldn't be an issue.

She headed inside the work facility to where she'd met up with her coworkers during her first shift. However, this time, there was already a supervisor waiting—and it wasn't the same woman as the previous day; this one had an even deeper scowl, paired with dark eyes and a heavy brow. Otherwise, the people on the crew were the same.

<Replaced, or just part of the usual rotation?> Kira asked Jasmine.

<I can't pull personnel records without taking unnecessary risks.>

Kira decided to try to find out through conversation, despite the 'no questions' rule that had been drilled into her yesterday. There might be a way to strike a balance.

She spotted one of the workers who'd operated like he'd been doing the job for a long time and went to stand by him. "Stars, I didn't think I did such a bad job yesterday that my boss would quit." Not her best small-talk opening ever, but hopefully passable.

"Nah, they rotate managers daily," he replied. "You'll see Barna again if you stick around long enough."

The new supervisor flashed a glare in their direction, and the man dropped his eyes to the floor.

Kira did the same, then inched away, her question answered. Unfortunately, the statement further supported her concerns that she wasn't going to get assigned anywhere near to where she'd been before and would have no way to get the cameras back.

The clock hit start time, and the supervisor opened the doors. Kira went with the group to the same supply room they'd used the previous day, and the supervisor handed each worker a tablet.

Kira eagerly looked hers over. Sure enough, the locations were completely different than her previous assignment. *<Jasmine, how difficult would it be to hack these and change around the assigned locations?>*

<Not very hard, but there's a high probability of detection. Is that a risk you want to take?>

She thought about it, running through the different scenarios. If the cameras hadn't captured any useful footage, then blowing her cover now would mean they'd be back at the beginning. However, if they didn't get the footage, they'd also have to start over since they'd have nothing. Even trying again, there was no guarantee that a new approach would accomplish anything. And, since she was properly undercover and looked nothing like her usual self, there was little chance of anything coming back on the TSS or TUF. The main risk was to her, personally—so long as Pyra kept his distance.

Really, the best play was to go big and try to learn everything she could in one go. *<Jasmine, I have an idea, but I don't know if you're going to like it.>*

<Whenever you say that, it's certain to be the case—and then I'll agree, anyway.>

Kira smiled inwardly while she began gathering her supplies for the day. *<What do you say we throw caution to the wind and do a smash-and-grab? Go into the locker room from yesterday and see if we can get the button cams, then if there's anything good, try to get down that elevator to the good parts?>*

<That would almost certainly mean fighting our way out.>

<For sure, but that's part of the plan. I want to spark a revolt.>

<Oh dear.>

<Is that a terrible idea?>

Jasmine didn't reply for a couple of seconds—an eternity for an AI. *<Are you thinking that acting like a disgruntled worker might get others to rise up against their evil masters, masking our escape and paving the way for an Enforcer intervention to maintain civil order?>*

<I am.>

<Well, I think that's the most reckless—and also satisfying—plan I've heard all morning.>

<Any chance you can give Pyra a heads up without it being too risky?>

<Yes, I think we're still far enough outside the secure zone,> Jasmine said. *<Okay, done.>*

<All right, do what you need to do to switch around the assignments, and then let's get to it.>

Kira finished gathering supplies while Jasmine worked her magic. She knew it was a dangerous proposition to go in alone with the intention of causing a massive scene, but it was also the only way she could see getting solid answers in a short time. They simply didn't have the luxury to hang around undercover for weeks or months hoping to catch a break. Moreover, if this facility didn't have useful information, they'd need to look elsewhere on Zeron—though there weren't any other significant population centers.

By the time her cart was loaded, Jasmine had stealthily juggled the work assignments on the tablets so the workers and supervisor would all see consistent information. Since it was a different supervisor from yesterday, Kira hoped it wouldn't stand out that she was going to the same place twice for her first task before traveling down to a deeper level.

<I was able to get you tasked as low as Level 5,> Jasmine

said. *<I don't know who empties the trash deeper than that, but it's not this crew.>*

<I'll take what I can get. It's not like we need an invitation to go elsewhere—not with you around.>

<Oh, how far I've come!>

When Jasmine had first been paired with Kira, the AI was regarded as a medical specialist—selected for the assignment so she could help control Kira's transformations with the nanites. However, since Kira's former spec ops team focused on information-gathering and digital infiltration, Jasmine had quickly picked up skills in that area. Finding both a knack and interest in the subject, the AI had become Kira's go-to partner for those endeavors now that she was no longer attached to her former team. Going into this encounter, that partnership was going to be more important than ever.

Resolved, and as ready as she was going to get, Kira took hold of her cart and headed toward the locker room where she'd set the cameras the day before.

When she entered the space, she found the used jumpsuits waiting on the benches, just like before. She began gathering them up and placing them into the receptacle on her cart. When she made it to the location that should have the first bugged jumpsuit, she carefully ran her fingers along the collar by the zipper. She felt the subtle bump of the device, to her relief.

<I have the near-field link,> Jasmine confirmed.

<Begin analyzing it.> Kira deftly pocketed the camera and then tossed the jumpsuit in the cart's bin.

She repeated the process for the two others. As anxious as she was to find out what was on them, she'd have to leave it to Jasmine to review the footage, knowing there was surveillance and her supervisor, or another watcher, could drop by at a moment's notice. She had to look busy and play her part until they decided it was time to make a move.

<How's it coming?> she asked.

<The images aren't as distinct as I would have hoped,> Jasmine replied. *<It looks like the first person may have had something hanging over their shoulders, and the view is obscured. I'm going through frame-by-frame in case there's something.>*

Kira wanted to tell her to move on to the others, but the AI was very particular and thorough with her processes, so Kira thought it best to leave her to it.

She began cleaning up the second locker room.

Footsteps sounded on the tile near the entry. Kira spun around to see a maroon-uniformed man enter.

"You're not supposed to be here," he said.

<Jasmine, a little help!>

<Tell him assignment M-872.>

Kira flashed a bewildered smile. "I'm not? Isn't this for M-872?"

He hesitated, clearly caught off-guard by the reply. "It is, but there's a dedicated handler for that unit."

It was a valid statement, and she wasn't sure how to answer it. "Well, I…"

<Tell him they shifted things around because of containment concerns related to the new excavation timeline.>

<What?> Kira didn't wait for an explanation, repeating what she'd been told to say.

That squarely confused the man. He took a step back, working his mouth. "Just a moment."

He pulled out a handheld to consult.

<I'm on it,> Jasmine said before Kira could ask.

A moment later, the man's frown turned neutral. "My mistake. Carry on." He turned around and left.

<Care to explain?> Kira questioned as she resumed the cleaning activities.

<I just finished analyzing the second video, and it was very illuminating. It appears this entire city is built on top of an ancient ship.>

<A ship? How in the stars did a ship get buried under meters and meters of solid rock?>

<Good question.>

The revelation was equal parts exciting and disconcerting. *<Is that ship what was giving off the strong ateron reading?>*

<In part. Now, when I say 'ship', I mean something more on the scale of a space station. It's huge. And there's an assembly at its core, which I believe is what they're investigating.>

<Something like those devices on Earth?>

<Correct. I didn't realize in our original scan that it was part of something larger. Much of the structure is still buried in the rock, inaccessible.>

<So, they dig.>

<Yes, the world's motto of 'dig deep' is making more sense now.>

<Can we get down to the core?> Kira asked.

<It appears to be heavily guarded, but we might be able to gain access to one of the communications rooms before anyone stops us. If you're okay incapacitating a couple of people.>

<Do you really need to ask?>

Jasmine chuckled in the strange way that made Kira feel like her head was tingling. *<Find a place to ditch your cart. I've almost got a route worked out.>*

Kira consulted her map. There wasn't a good drop point anywhere nearby. Instead, she looked around the locker room for a potential hiding place. There weren't any closets, but there were a series of toilet stalls.

She looked between the cart and the stall, judging that there was no way it would fit in its current configuration. *<We're going to be bolting out of here when this is finished, right?>*

<That's the plan.>

<So, a little property destruction is unlikely to make things worse?>

<Probably not.>

<All right. Better start masking the cameras or whatever it is you intend to do so I can move around freely.>

<Done.>

Acutely aware of the new ticking clock, Kira gripped the trolley in both hands—one on either side—and began to crush it. A normal person her size would have no chance of accomplishing the feat, but her nanites had given her strength well beyond her small frame. It didn't take long for the cart to be able to fit through the stall door, and she wheeled it inside. While not a *great* hiding place, it would disguise her absence a little. In her current circumstances, every second counted.

With that in mind, she dashed to the hallway and headed straight for the elevator.

<Floor 17,> Jasmine instructed.

<Stars, this place really is large!>

<Oh, it goes much deeper than that. That's just where we need to transfer to the ship access shaft.>

Jasmine shared an expanded map of the facility in Kira's mind, and she was astonished to see the extent of the structure.

As they'd identified during the scan the previous night, a component toward the center bore a striking resemblance to the odd device pits on Earth. Now, though, seeing the larger context, it looked like perhaps those structures were only a part of something bigger. She filed the thought away for future analysis when she could get eyes on the real thing.

Kira dashed the rest of the way to the elevator and slipped inside. All the floor controls were still locked out.

<*I'm bypassing security, hold on,*> Jasmine said.

Agonizing seconds ticked by while Kira waited. At last, the lights turned blue for the floor options, and she selected Level 17, as instructed—the lowest she could go in this shaft.

The elevator began to descend with little sensation of movement. Not long after, the doors slid open.

Kira quickly pressed herself against the side wall, hiding as best she could from potentially prying eyes. When there wasn't an immediate reaction to her presence, she risked a look around the corner.

<*You're clear,*> Jasmine said, having tapped into the camera feeds in the vicinity. <*I'm masking your presence.*>

Still moving cautiously all the same, Kira crept out of the elevator into a concrete corridor. It had a reddish hue to it, suggesting that powderized rock may have been used for the aggregate in the construction. The question of how a ship had been encased in solid rock resurfaced in her mind.

The corridor was empty and lined with doors. According to Jasmine's map, she had to head to the left and then access a secondary elevator to descend another six levels to the ship.

<*Hide! Second door on your right up ahead,*> Jasmine instructed abruptly.

Kira followed the order, accessing the door controls a

second after Jasmine hacked the lock. She quickly closed it behind her.

<Workers passing through,> the AI explained. *<Spotted them on the camera feed up ahead.>*

<Good looking out.> Kira appreciated having Jasmine's eyes on potential hazards. She waited until she got the all-clear from Jasmine before venturing back out into the corridor and resuming her path.

When she arrived at the elevator door, Jasmine again unlocked the controls, which allowed Kira to select Floor 23. She pressed the button and stood near the side wall, her heart pounding with anticipation.

<Your supervisor just went to check on you and knows you're missing,> Jasmine reported. *<I'll try to throw them some false leads.>*

That meant she wouldn't have long to look around. *<How do I get the most out of my time here?>*

<I have a surveillance room identified. I'm hoping we can get in, copy some records quickly, and then get out of here.>

<Still the same plan, then.>

<Yes, unless we suddenly encounter a wall of armed guards.>

It was a real possibility. A tingle ran along Kira's spine thinking about using her nanite-enhanced form. She didn't get to very often, and it was always a thrill—though she paid for it the following days with the uncomfortable after-effects of having effectively been ripped apart from the inside. Though Jasmine could help block out the pain caused by the nanites flooding from intramusculoskeletal tissue to the surface of her skin, Kira had to endure some of it to prevent becoming completely numb.

When the door opened, it became clear that using those abilities might become necessary sooner than she'd anticipated. While there were no waiting guards, the corridor was lined with various security scanners.

<*I'm guessing those weren't on the schematics,*> she said to Jasmine, remaining inside the elevator for now.

<*No.*> Jasmine paused, and the pressure increased in Kira's head while the AI worked. <*I think I can slow the system down, but I can't stop the auto-scans entirely.*>

<*What if I was moving very quickly?*>

<*Controlling your transformation and this hack at the same time would tax my resources.*>

<*I can manage the transformation.*>

<*I can't make guarantees about blocking the pain.*>

<*I can handle it,*> Kira assured her, hoping it was true. She *had* managed to survive several transformations before being paired with Jasmine, so her confidence wasn't ill-informed.

<*Okay. I guess we're going super-speed mode, then.*>

<*I've been waiting for this.*> The skill was one of Kira's favorite parts of her nanite augmentations. Similar to how Agents could create localized spatial distortions around themselves to so-called 'stop time'—allowing them to appear to move faster than normal reality—Kira's nanites could generate a similar field. When coupled with her strength modifications, she could propel herself in a manner that looked only like a blur to outside observers. While it might not prevent the alarm from triggering, the system wouldn't be able to identify her.

Kira reached within herself for the other tech, making a telepathic connection with the nanites. They weren't independently intelligent, per se, but there was a certain organization to them, and she could interface with their collective mass. She gave the instruction for the nanites to activate.

Her skin took on a silvery shimmer as the nanites rushed to the surface, bonding to become an armored skin. They extended into sharp talons on her fingertips and even fanged points on her teeth, though biting was a last-resort combat method she avoided. The augmentations filled out her jumpsuit, but the loose garment was able to accommodate the changes without tearing.

The entire transformation took less than five seconds. She relished the surge of energy it brought her, enough to block out the pain for now. *It's go time.*

She raced down the corridor, her perception blurring slightly from the speed. Following the map Jasmine had shared in her mind, she dashed past the security scanners to the control room.

<Up ahead on your right,> Jasmine said when she was close.

Kira closed the remaining distance just as Jasmine overrode the lock. The door clicked open, and Kira ran inside. She slammed her hand against the interior door controls, her heart racing.

The room was approximately four meters square, consisting of several servers in locked cages and a large desk with half a dozen monitors and a touch-surface desktop.

<At the risk of sounding conceited, I believe I was actually able to keep the system from detecting you,> Jasmine reported.

<I'll take some credit for that.>

<Indeed, it was only possible because you are a proficient runner.>

The phrasing was meant as bait, but Kira was too focused on the task at hand to take it. *<Help me get into the system.>*

<Already done.> Now Jasmine was just showing off.

Kira relaxed her conscious hold on the nanites, allowing them to partially retreat into her skin so she had better use of her fingertips. She then used the touchscreen to navigate through the files.

<All right, where's the video surveillance of this ship thing?> she asked Jasmine.

<Based on the footage I analyzed from the button cams, I believe it is located here,> the AI took over the navigating.

New images appeared on the screens mounted around the desk. Several of them were odd angles where Kira couldn't readily distinguish the featured objects, but one jumped out at her. *That looks just like the image of the device I saw on Earth.*

It was a ten-meter-deep cylinder with metallic veining carved into a smooth stone. Parts of the surface had been cleared while rough stone covered the veins on other portions of the walls. At the base of the pit, the upper portion of a pedestal rose up, capped with a sphere; the entire assembly was still partially encased in rock. Unlike the sites on Earth, however, there was no evidence of blue light flowing through the metallic channels carved into the stone. It gave the impression that the tech might currently be offline.

There were uniformed workers around the site, some with tablets in hand and others carrying digging tools. Upon closer inspection, it appeared that they were chipping away at the surface of the pit.

<Wait, are they still digging it out?> Kira asked Jasmine, not expecting a definitive answer.

<It appears so. But I can't begin to guess how and why it was

buried in the first place.>

Kira studied the video feed. It looked like the workers were chipping away parts of the walls within the pit and placing the shards into bins. Based on the amount of pounding they did with their tools in order to break off the fragments, the substance was extremely hard.

She wasn't sure what to make of the activity. *<Wait, are they excavating it or disassembling it?>*

<I'd thought excavating, but now I'm not sure. Maybe it's offline because they'd already taken it apart. I really can't tell from here,> Jasmine said.

We have to get a full infiltration team back here. Kira hoped that she'd get to be a part of those efforts, but first, she needed to get this information back to the TSS. While archaeology wasn't an illegal activity by any means, what they were working on here was clearly alien tech, since it was the same as the structures on Earth. After what happened with the Gatekeepers, there was a new law stating a legal responsibility to report any alien technology discovered within the Empire, so keeping these activities hidden was in violation of those edicts. While it wasn't a strong case to bring against Zeron, it would certainly be enough to secure a warrant for a proper investigation.

The entire thing was strange. Whoever was running this place had to know what they were dealing with, because memory-wiping the workers was a significant effort and risk.

<Those shards,> Jasmine pointed out. *<Those would be really easy for a worker to try to leave with.>*

<Hey, I wonder if that's what was going on with the man who was arrested last night?>

<Could be. They take security seriously. Could have been

any number of things.>

Kira didn't bother pointing out how easily they'd been able to bypass the security measures, but they also hadn't made it out yet. For all she knew, someone was watching her every move. It was a disconcerting thought she quickly put out of her mind.

She could easily have watched the methodical archaeological work for hours, finding it strangely meditative, but her supervisor knew she was missing and would no doubt be looking for her. She had no time to spare.

Kira returned her attention to the video archives and reports. The data was stored on the servers, and even a high-capacity crystalline matrix drive wouldn't be able to hold all of it.

Shite. There was no quick way to determine what information was the most useful.

Fortunately, Jasmine had formed a wireless link with the console and had already started to browse. *<I'll grab samples— hopefully, the right stuff to get a warrant.>*

<If you spot any high-resolution images of the excavation below, copy those. I wonder if the carved channels line up with the ones on Earth.>

<I'll look.>

Even as Jasmine worked, Kira had a feeling in her gut that grabbing a random sampling wasn't good enough. They hadn't had the time to plan this investigation right, but they'd selected her for the role because she was resourceful and always found a way, against the odds. They'd expect more from her than, 'Sorry, we tried,' and an apologetic shrug.

She started looking around the room for an external drive. It was a communications and data processing room, so it had to have *some* spare parts, right?

When nothing jumped out in the open spaces, she began opening drawers and cabinets. Most were frustratingly bare, and the supplies she did locate weren't useful.

About to give up, she spotted one more cabinet tucked away in the corner. In the second drawer, she finally found a palm-sized crystal storage matrix. It wouldn't hold a lot, but it certainly had a higher capacity than Kira's internal implants.

<We're getting everything we can,> she said, connecting the drive to the interface console.

<Good find.>

Now, the transfer time was the issue rather than space.

<Can you maintain a wireless link with this?> Kira asked.

<Maybe. I won't know for sure until we're outside, and that's assuming they don't discover it.>

<Well, we can't stay here until this completes. I'll take some chance over none.> Kira paired a wireless dongle with the drive to facilitate the data transfer and then hid it behind the other equipment to disguise its presence as best she could. She then placed the drive in her bra for safekeeping, finding it warm as it actively received the transferred data. *<Let's get out of here.>*

She restored her fully transformed state and went to the door. Her skin was starting to burn from the prolonged time with the active nanites.

<All clear,> Jasmine reported.

Kira raced out into the hall and dashed to the elevator. She ran through the door, relaxing slightly when it closed. The burn on her skin had intensified from the latest exertion, and she started to release the nanites to get some relief.

<Kira, you can't drop back into your normal form here,> Jasmine warned.

<Why not?>

<The transformation dislodged your cosmetic disguise. You can't let them see your real face and link you back to the Alliance and the TUF.>

<Shite!> She'd been afraid of that. And Jasmine was absolutely right; she needed to remain anonymous now that she'd stepped out from her cover.

Nonetheless, holding onto her transformed form was draining her. Her muscles ached and she could feel her temperature rising. She didn't know how much longer she could go before her limbs wouldn't respond anymore.

The elevator reached its destination on Floor 17, and she ran out, willing herself to get closer to the exit.

"You! Stop!" The deep male voice was the last thing Kira wanted to hear.

<They've spotted us. Nothing to do now but fight our way out,> Jasmine said.

<I'll try to outrun them.> Kira's mental tone sounded more confident than she felt. Keeping up the super-speed was especially taxing.

<I can help now,> Jasmine said. Since the security guards had eyes on them, there was no point in trying to alter the camera feeds or override the occupancy sensors.

Kira felt an instant flood of relief as Jasmine stepped in to control her physiological responses. The pain faded to a manageable level in the background.

She rounded on the man who'd called out to her, seeing that he wasn't alone. Three other guards had pulse rifles trained on her, and the distinct echo of booted footfalls carried from further down the corridor. Unfortunately, they were in the exact path she needed to take to the surface-access elevator.

<Alternative routes?> she asked Jasmine.

<None feasible.>

That was all she needed to know. While her nanites didn't make her impervious, it was close enough.

She barreled toward the guards, moving so fast that they would barely register her presence. One of them managed to fire, but the pulse harmlessly rippled off her nanite armor. As she passed by the group, she outstretched her arms to shove them out of her way. They went sprawling, seemingly in slow motion to her heightened senses and perception in that state.

While the first guard on her right fell, she snatched his rifle from his hands. As she did so, she took the opportunity to size up his other gear. They were all wearing jumpsuits—like everyone else on the confounded planet—with only minor body armor. Security ID cards hung from lanyards clipped to their belts. These really were guards, not soldiers—equipped to deal with minor worker disruptions, nothing serious.

The other group advancing on her had more time to react, but so did Kira. They began indiscriminately firing their pulse rifles, which she deftly dodged. She raised her newly acquired pulse rifle and fired back on the stun setting. The guards weren't expecting counterfire, and her shots landed true.

She could see the surprise begin to form on their faces as she rushed by, but the sound hadn't caught up yet. She didn't intend to wait around that long.

The route to the other elevator wasn't long, and she quickly covered the distance. She began to slow down several meters from the elevator.

<Is it clear?> she asked Jasmine.

<More are incoming. They're going to be coming through the door.>

Kira backtracked and dove down a side corridor. She pressed her back against the wall, using a reflective door jamb across the intersection to surveil the elevator area.

Moments later, the elevator door opened. Another eight guards poured out. Their forms were indistinct and distorted in the reflection, but the image was good enough for her to get a sense of their placement and speed.

Judging their approach, she timed her action so the lead guard was crossing by her intercepting corridor just as she made her move. She reached out and yanked his ID card from the lanyard, suspecting that it doubled as a security passkey like her own worker ID did—and presumably with a lot better clearance. Jasmine's resources would be better focused on what needed to happen next rather than unlocking doors.

<*Good thinking,*> the AI said when Kira had the pass in hand.

Kira then fired a stunning pulse shot, and the man dropped to the ground, unconscious.

Better get a move on before they realize this ID card was swiped. She stuck her arm out into the corridor and fired off several blind pulse rifle shots to disable the remaining guards.

Several thuds sounded, and she checked the reflective door jamb again. Two guards had evaded her shots and were now pressed against the side walls, inching toward her. She also noticed movement coming from the other direction. The guards from the first wave, which she'd regretfully only knocked out of the way rather than disabling, had now pursued with the hope of penning her in from both sides.

Not a chance.

She first fired two rapid shots to take out the guards creeping along the wall—knowing they knew her position and would be expecting her—and then pivoted back to quickly fire at the four unsuspecting guards. She saved the unarmed man for last, not above the pettiness of driving home the point that she was disabling him with his own weapon. *Gotta hold onto your gear, buddy.*

As the final guard fell, she paused and stood silently for a moment to listen for any other approaching guards. Everything was still and quiet.

She dashed for the elevator. *<Alert Pyra we're going to be coming out hot. I'd wanted to mask our exit with a mass worker rebellion, but things haven't played out the way I'd hoped.>*

<There is still one way we could mess with them on the way out.>

Jasmine didn't need to explain. Kira instantly knew she was referring to whatever it was that wiped worker memories. *<Get me a path to that main exit.>*

CHAPTER 12

JASON REVIEWED THE note from Pyra, concerned what it meant. >>Might break cover early, but we have info. Could need backup to get out.<<

What is it with these field operatives and cryptic updates? Clearly, the messages were short and vague in the event they were intercepted by their adversaries, but it didn't make Jason's job any easier.

He opened up a voice call to the Coalition task force strategy room.

Laura answered. "What can I do for you, sir?"

"Do we have any TSS vessels near Zeron?"

"Let me check." She was silent for several seconds. "Looks like just a couple of survey vessels near Olteren, a short jump away."

Something with firepower would be better, but some backup was better than none. "Agents?"

"Yes, two on board."

"Okay. Please put in a request to Ops to have them on standby. I think things might be heating up on Zeron, but I don't want anyone to move in until we know for sure."

"Understood," she acknowledged.

"Thanks. I'll be in touch." Jason ended the call and let out a long breath. *Let's hope they're getting us answers.*

— — —

A facility map appeared in Kira's mind, courtesy of Jasmine's interface with the computer system. The exit was on Level 1, not surprisingly, but it was in a different area than the back route Kira had used for custodial access. She could still take the same elevator, but then she'd need to pass through several secure doorways to get to the other part of the facility.

Not wanting to waste any time in case more guards were on their way, she dashed into the elevator. Inside, she swiped the security ID badge she'd lifted off the guard, which unlocked the floor access just like she'd hoped. She selected the top floor and the door slid closed.

<Pyra has acknowledged the message and will meet us by the entrance,> Jasmine informed her.

<Thanks.>

She took the opportunity to take several deep breaths in preparation for another sprint. She hadn't held on to her altered form for this extended a duration in a long time. Though she was tired, it also felt great to let loose.

The elevator slowed a moment before arriving at Level 1. The doors opened.

She was greeted by a wall of rifle muzzles—more than she could count at quick glance.

<Well, that's not great.> Rather than wait for the guards to act, she ran through the blockade at super-speed, firing

without aiming.

While not a great strategy, it was effective. Several guards fell from the stunning blasts, and she pushed some out of her way and jumped over others.

She continued forward, moving fast enough that the others didn't have time to react before she had passed them by. The route in her mental map indicated she needed to head to the left, so she angled herself that way through the group of guards.

They clearly hadn't been ready for anyone with special abilities, because there was no one in the hallway beyond the blockade right outside the elevator. After leaping past the final person, she sprinted along the corridor indicated on the map, which would lead her toward the exit.

She reached the first of the locked doors between the elevator and her destination. Jasmine overrode the lock, and the door clicked open, revealing another hallway lined with doors. Since it would be her last time in this place before handing the case back over to the TSS, she wanted to get as much information as possible.

Kira reached out to a random door and tried the handle. It opened, but inside was only a generic storage closet.

<*We don't have time to investigate,*> Jasmine said. <*The guards are right behind us!*>

<*We didn't get enough evidence earlier.*>

<*I'm frustrated, too, but it's not worth the risk. We need to get out of here.*>

Kira knew the AI was right, as much as it pained her. Stopping to look in random rooms now would only increase her chances of getting caught, and that was unacceptable.

The most important thing she could do now was find out how the workers' memories were being wiped before they left the facility.

She continued down the hallway, passing through two more sets of locked doors.

<Slow down, we're almost there,> Jasmine warned.

Kira dialed back her pace as she exited the final hallway into a large lobby with three-story-high ceilings. It appeared to be carved from the native reddish rock, but care had been taken during the excavation to leave an artistic pattern on the surface. The grand ambiance was unexpected after the stark, utilitarian nature of the other finishes.

<Why design this to impress?> Kira wondered, sharing the thought with her constant companion.

<I don't know, but I think that's what we came here to find.> Jasmine gave a mental nudge toward a series of arches on the far side of the cavern.

At first glance, the structures looked to be architectural supports, but then Kira noticed that they had a metallic gleam in places—very subtle.

<I can sense a complex system hidden beneath the stone,< Jasmine said. *<I believe they were trying to hide the archways' true purpose.>*

<Does that mean my memories might be wiped if I walk through there?>

<It's a risk I suggest you don't take.>

The room was designed to funnel people precisely through the arches, so there wasn't an obvious alternative route. However, Kira wanted to follow one aspect of her original plan. No innocents should have their minds manipulated, and she had to do her best to make sure the facility workers wouldn't suffer that fate again.

She switched her pulse rifle to the strongest setting and

opened fire. The blasts struck the rock but seemed to do little damage; the weapon was designed for controlling people, nothing more.

Utter garbage. Kira tossed the rifle aside, now useless to her.

Fortunately, she was a weapon unto herself.

She dashed to the nearest archway and began slashing at it with the nanite-formed claws extending from her fingertips. The razor-sharp blades easily sliced through the rock and electronic components within. The scraps came off in ribbons, at first, and then larger chunks as the arch began to lose stability. She carefully wove her way through the debris and started working on the next column, moving at her maximum speed.

She could feel the heat building within her from the effort. The unique properties of the nanites allowed most of it to be vented to subspace, but this prolonged exertion was overwhelming Jasmine's ability to regulate her bodily functions.

<*You can't keep this up much longer,*> Jasmine said, telling Kira what she could already feel within herself.

Even as she tried to keep moving at the accelerated speed, her limbs were growing sluggish and her own movements were becoming a blur in her mind. The slip in perception was the most concerning.

Only one arch remained. She couldn't give up now.

Kira bored into it with everything she had left, ripping apart the materials until it crumbled.

<*Incoming!*> Jasmine warned just as the final parts of the structure came down.

Kira didn't wait to see the number of pursuers, solely

focused now on getting out. She ran for the exit.

<Are you in touch with Pyra?> she asked Jasmine.

<He's waiting outside for us.>

<Tell him to run!>

She bolted out the exit doors to the public street. There were a fair number of people around, which would help with cover, but that also meant bystanders she wasn't willing to sacrifice.

The exit plan had originally dictated having a bunch of workers flooding out at the same time, but the on-the-fly alterations meant that all attention was now on Kira. With a lurch of her stomach, she realized that they didn't have a shuttle waiting for them. They would either need to hide and get offworld later or make a run for the port now.

This is why we don't deviate from the plan. The entire thing had been rushed because of the desperate situation with Monsari, but she shouldn't have allowed that to compromise her field conduct. This op had been sloppy, plain and simple, and she should be better than that. It would have been one thing if it was just her, but allowing urgency to take precedence had placed Pyra at risk, too.

Regrets weren't going to make her run any faster, so she tried to put it out of her mind for now. She had to focus on getting to the port and stealing a ship; it was really the only play.

<Well, this ended up being anything but 'covert'.>

<I wasn't going to say anything,> Jasmine replied.

Kira scanned the area for Pyra, not seeing him. *<Where is he?>*

<Hiding in the side alley where we took the scan.>

<Put me through.>

A chirp sounded in Kira's mind, followed by Pyra's voice from a call being translated to her neural interface. <*What happened in there?*> he asked.

<*No time. We need to get to the port and get on a ship immediately.*>

<*I checked the transit schedule, and there isn't another public passenger transport until this afternoon.*>

<*Then we're stealing something.*>

<*What? We—*>

<*It's that or let them capture us. We have to go,*> she reiterated.

<*Okay, I'm on my way.*>

Kira took off full-speed in the direction of the port, knowing she'd be able to reach it before Pyra and hopefully have an escape route secured before he got there. That way, they'd be able to take off immediately.

She'd made it five blocks when her limbs suddenly grew heavier and her pounding heartbeat completely filled her ears.

<*There's been too much strain. You can't keep going,*> Jasmine said.

<*If I don't, they catch us. At a minimum, they'll see who I am.*>

<*You're going to pass out if you don't stop.*>

That wasn't an acceptable option, either. Nonetheless, she could feel that Jasmine was right. Willing her body to keep going simply wasn't enough.

She looked around for any possible refuge. There were several side alleys and storefronts. Hopefully, she'd run far enough and fast enough that the guards wouldn't immediately be able to trace her path.

Before she lost her speed, she dipped off into one of the

side passages and ducked into a hidden alcove.

As the last of her strength failed, she released her hold on the nanites. A sharp sting spread through her limbs as they flooded back into her, followed by a numbing chill. She dropped to her knees, panting. Darkness hovered at the corners of her vision.

<Slow, deep breaths,> Jasmine coached her. *<Try to cool off.>*

Kira fumbled with the front zipper on her jumpsuit and was able to get it partway open. The cooler air felt amazing on her chest.

The darkness began to recede from her periphery.

"Kira?"

She recognized Pyra's voice, snapping her to attention. "What are you doing here?" she asked, spotting him jogging toward her hiding place.

"Jasmine told me where to find you."

Annoyance burned Kira's cheeks. *<Why did you do that? It's much safer for us to go to the port separately.>*

<You were about to pass out, and I couldn't have you alone on the street.>

Kira wanted to chastise the AI, but that was a fair point.

"Can you walk?" Pyra asked, concern evident in his brown eyes.

She really must not look good to get that kind of reaction. When she reached up to wipe perspiration from her face, part of the disguise prosthetic came off in her hand. *Well, shite.*

Pyra's eyes widened at the sight. He glanced around, as though looking for something, then instead took hold of his left jumpsuit sleeve and pulled hard. With a little effort, the fabric came loose.

Kira picked up on what he was doing, allowing him to wrap it around her face in a way that would mask her appearance from any facial scanners. "Thanks."

He offered a hand to help her off the ground. "We need to get to the port."

She got to her feet with his help. Once she was vertical, she felt a little more stable. She zipped up her jumpsuit again. "Let's go."

Running at super-speed was no longer an option, so it was now a matter of stealth. They crept away from Kira's hiding place in the alley. Her legs were a little wobbly at first, but she felt more confident with each stride.

<*You're going to have to take it easy,*> Jasmine warned in her mind.

She ignored the AI, judging that the reality of the situation conflicted with the medical advice.

There was a frenetic energy on the main street. Kira hung back to observe, looking for signs of the guards.

The distinctive black Avon Security uniforms jumped out at her from two blocks down the street. The four guards were grabbing people and checking their faces with a scanner. They were working their way from the direction of the facility, and there didn't appear to be other groups further down the street leading to the port.

"We've gotta go," Pyra said, having read the situation, as well.

Kira only nodded in response, entering the flow of pedestrian traffic while trying to use people and objects to hide from potential cameras and guards.

<*I'm scrubbing the feed as best I can on the fly,*> Jasmine reported. <*But they're paying closer attention now.*>

Kira knew she was in a dangerous spot. They had to get to the port without being detected, because it would take time to secure a craft and get offworld.

To his credit, Pyra was remaining calm and collected as he slunk along next to her, showing fluid movements that were quite unlike the bumbling persona he often portrayed. His eyes scanned the surrounding area while weaving in between the people on the street. He wasn't walking with Kira, but to an outside observer, it would be clear they were both headed in the same direction at a faster pace than others on the street.

As much as Kira wanted to slow down to blend in better, she could sense the guards moving at a brisk rate, as well. If she strictly followed along with the other pedestrians, the guards would overtake them well before she and Pyra reached the spaceport.

Even at the fast walk, they weren't going to have enough of a lead to escape. She needed to do something to buy them more time.

Kira reached out to her nanites to initiate a transformation, only to be stopped by Jasmine.

<*You haven't recovered yet,*> the AI stated. <*If you try to keep going right now, we'll both die.*> Never before had she spoken that way to Kira, nor had she overtly blocked Kira from accessing her other form.

There wasn't a doubt in Kira's mind that the situation was serious for Jasmine to take those measures. They'd been working together for long enough now that Kira trusted Jasmine completely and knew that she wouldn't intervene without good reason. However, that meant that Kira's potential actions were limited to good old-fashioned wits and strategy since she wasn't currently armed.

Looking around at the crowd, she saw enough people present where a panic would inconvenience the pursuing guards. Nonetheless, she wasn't willing to put innocent civilians in harm's way, and she didn't want to cause a big enough scene to cause a full lockdown at the port.

There had to be a middle ground. *A distraction that's isolated to this location...*

She spotted a shop across the way with a crate of ball bearings. A flood of those on the ground would slow anyone down and cause a mess without much harm. Plus, an anonymous donation to the shop owner later on as compensation for their trouble could satisfy the military mandate to avoid harmful impact to innocents.

Kira caught Pyra's attention and nodded toward the shop. "Need to knock those over," she whispered.

His eyes traced the prospective fall path before glancing back in the direction of the approaching guards. He nodded his understanding.

Not wanting to tie the two of them to the impending disaster, Kira scanned the area for a way to knock over the crate without going anywhere near it. She noticed another storefront selling hovercarts. If one of those could be activated and pointed toward the ball bearing crate, it might impact with enough force to knock it over.

Where are telekinetic abilities when you need them? She'd need another way to start up a cart and lock down its accelerator.

"I'll distract the shopkeeper. Get the cart," she told Pyra.

He veered off to the left while she headed directly toward the shopkeeper, knowing they only had a matter of seconds for the plan to come together.

She took on a limp to play up the crude fabric bandage around her head, figuring she may as well embrace being a broke, disfigured worker. "I need help," she said to the shop's attendant, a bored-looking man in his fifties.

The man took one look at her and upturned his nose at the apparent riffraff, just as she'd hoped. "Paying customers only."

"I need a scooter," Kira said.

"Not a big selection of those, and they don't come cheap."

"Can't you help?"

Out of the corner of her eye, she watched Pyra pass by a hovercart. Its operating lights turned on and she noticed a length of cloth tied around its handle where the operator would normally throttle it forward. She wasn't sure how he'd so quickly and effectively rigged it like that, but she gave a silent thanks to the TSS' Militia training and his undercover experience necessitating sleight of hand.

The hovercart began to move forward, slowly heading toward the crate in the neighboring shop. Pyra continued down the street as if he'd never been there.

"I don't offer handouts," the shopkeeper told Kira, taking on a firmer tone now. "If you don't have the credits to buy anything, please leave."

The distraction had served its purpose, so Kira huffed and started to limp away. She'd just cleared the edge of his storefront when a loud crash sounded behind her. She glanced over her shoulder at the same time as the other pedestrians, wanting her reaction to blend in.

The hovercart had indeed collided with the crate as planned, causing the ball bearings to spill across the entire walkway. All people in the area had stopped walking to avoid slipping on the tiny balls, which effectively formed a wall of people to hold back the guards.

She heard authoritative shouts ordering people out of the way, but the glazed workers didn't seem to know how to cope with the unusual situation.

This was their chance to get away.

Kira increased her pace to catch up with Pyra. They fell back into their together-yet-separate movement pattern, weaving through the other people at a faster gait than the foot traffic flow.

<*Almost there,*> Jasmine said, highlighting the most efficient route in a mental map for Kira.

Kira's heart pounded in her chest from nerves. She'd rarely felt this exposed at any time during her career, and she couldn't wait to be off the cursed planet.

Ahead, she saw the docking area for transit vessels.

<*Find us a ship,*> she said to Jasmine.

<*I have one in mind. It's private but I think I can crack the security.*>

Stealing a ship had been the presumptive plan, but it still turned Kira's stomach. At this point, though, they needed to do whatever was necessary to get off Zeron alive.

The ship was docked on the far side of the port, which was helpful from a concealment perspective while also placing them farther from their destination. Kira indicated the route to Pyra, and they started heading in that direction.

Steps from entering the first row of docked vessels, however, a shout carried above the din.

"You! Halt!"

The fine hairs on the back of Kira's neck stood up. Their luck had run out.

<*Go!*> Jasmine shouted in her mind.

Kira broke into a flat-out run toward the rows of shuttles. Five meters from cover, a shot rang out and Pyra dropped to the ground next to her.

She stopped, ducking down while trying to assess what had happened. Pyra was lying on his side, clutching his leg. He was bleeding from his thigh—apparently struck by a ballistic round. She hadn't seen any weapons of that sort on Zeron, but pulse rifles wouldn't produce an injury like that.

In an instant, she knew that she would be next if she didn't do something drastic. Jasmine seemed to understand the situation as well, because Kira once again had control of her nanites.

Without hesitation, she initiated a transformation. The silvery sheen spread over her body again, solidifying mere seconds before she was struck by a bullet. The round bounced off her and pinged harmlessly into the ground.

Kira dove toward Pyra, using her body for cover and she scooped him up in her arms, half-dragging, half-carrying him toward their intended escape shuttle.

Pyra's face was twisted with pain, but his eyes were wide with wonder as he took in Kira's form. He clutched his leg to quell the bleeding as best he could while on the move.

As soon as they were behind one of the parked shuttles, Kira repositioned Pyra in her arms so she could carry him. She then drew on every bit of energy she had left to run at super-speed toward the shuttle.

It was a sprint rather than the marathon escape she'd just endured through the facility. She was able to hold it together for the short duration, but by the time she saw the target shuttle, she was breathing heavily and everything burned.

She set Pyra down next to the hatch.

"What just…?" He faded out, looking at the surroundings. "Did I pass out?"

"No." Kira didn't have time to explain at the moment, hoping he'd put two and two together with her super-speed ability and his sudden change of location. More important was figuring out how to get on board the shuttle and launch it without getting caught.

Pressure increased in Kira's head while Jasmine began hacking the shuttle's security locks using a near-field connection. Locks like this were secure against most civilian hacks, but the military had access to certain codes which could override security protocols in desperate circumstances. Kira hadn't had many occasions to use that authority throughout her career, but she thanked the stars for it now.

<*I'm in,*> Jasmine reported the moment the shuttle's side hatch hissed open.

Kira picked up Pyra and helped him inside, quickly closing the door behind her.

Jasmine had already remotely accessed the shuttle's controls and initiated a quick-start sequence, so Kira took a few moments to get Pyra situated in the cockpit's passenger seat while the craft went through its automated startup checks.

It finished, showing positive blue indicators across the holographic display, as Kira slipped into her own seat. She took hold of the controls. <*What's the status of the port authority?*>

<*Traffic is still flowing through the planetary shield, but there aren't many ships,*> Jasmine replied.

Though the AI hadn't stated it, Kira could read between the lines. Minimal ships meant they'd be an easy target, unlike when they'd been running along the street. Getting out of there as fast as possible was their best chance.

Kira directed the shuttle off the ground and pointed it upward, leaving the port communications to Jasmine. A departure approval popped up on the screen, though Kira suspected it was hacked rather than genuine permission.

The craft quickly gained elevation, the barren landscape dwindling into an indistinct red plain below.

The only remaining checkpoint was the access gate through the planetary shield. There were several such gates positioned around the globe for transit purposes, as was standard on all Taran worlds. Unfortunately, the ring surrounding the opening was equipped with armaments that could easily take out the small shuttle.

<Do we have clearance codes?> Kira asked Jasmine, hoping her concern didn't come through too strongly in her mental tone.

<Working on it.> That wasn't the answer Kira had wanted.

<Twenty seconds.>

<Still working.>

Tension gripped Kira's chest. If they didn't have clearance by the time they reached the opening, the automated turrets would open fire.

<Almost there,> Jasmine said. With ten seconds to go, it was cutting it too close.

Kira's hand hovered on the controls to halt their ascent. A delay might be a death sentence, but it was better than certain destruction.

<Got it! But I don't know for how long.>

Kira gunned it. The shuttle slipped through the transit opening in the shield.

"Nothing to it." She allowed herself a little smile.

The ship continued accelerating away from the planet,

aiming for a designated jump point a safe distance away. She typed out a quick message to send to Jason. >>Made it offworld. Jumping home now.<< She sent it.

A moment later, the view outside transitioned from a starscape to the comforting blue-green light of subspace.

She let out a relieved sigh. "Well, that went better than I'd feared."

Pyra groaned next to her. "Speak for yourself," he said, still applying pressure to his wounded leg. The injury appeared to be a clear through-and-through, and his medical nanites had already done a fair job of clotting to slow the bleeding.

"Right, sorry." Kira got up to grab the medkit. "You're going to be fine."

"Doesn't make it hurt less." Even as he said it, there was a light in his eyes.

It had been a close call, but they had lived to tell the tale. That was a victory.

She touched the storage drive still tucked away next to her chest, which had continued to copy information throughout her harrowing escape. Hopefully, the information they were bringing home was worth the trouble.

— — —

"What the fok happened?" Celine demanded. The incident report from Zeron certainly offered some explanation, but she wanted to hear it straight from the source.

The man on the other end of the vidcall looked suitably distressed. "There was an infiltration. The perpetrator got away."

"Away with what?"

"We're not sure. The computer system was accessed."

"And?"

He shifted uncomfortably. "The encoding arches were destroyed."

She tried to contain her fury, wanting more information before she unloaded on the man. "Who was it?"

"We don't know. Cameras couldn't get a read. It was like they were moving too fast."

While such a feat seemed impossible on the surface, Celine was aware of Gifted abilities that could enable such movement. It might not have been the TSS directly, but it was almost certainly someone investigating on their behalf. "I need to know what information they got."

"It's difficult to say. I can provide a list of the accessed files, but it's impossible to know if it's a complete list, and there could have been other things."

She glowered. "*What* other things?"

"I mean, there's a lot to see here."

Celine took a calming breath. "I want to know who it was. Do what you need to do."

He nodded, clearly relieved that he hadn't received more of a reprimand. He'd be sorely disappointed to learn it was only delayed until after he was no longer useful.

Celine had no use for people who couldn't maintain security of their own operations. The manager of the excavation site knew how important their work was, and yet he'd not only allowed an outsider to gain access, but the person had escaped. It was unacceptable.

"What are you waiting for? Go!" she bellowed.

"Yes, ma'am." He quickly ended the vidcall.

Celine ground her teeth, feeling increasingly more

frustrated about how she was losing control. There was so little time to get back in the good graces of the Gatekeepers that this setback may prove too great to overcome. The only saving grace was that the device itself hadn't been damaged.

However, the destruction of the encoding arches meant that they would no longer be able to utilize the workforce in the same way.

No one could know what they were really doing on Zeron. Few people knew because if word made it back to the Erebus, the other plans would become meaningless. And, if that happened, there would be no salvation for anyone.

Celine never thought she would wield so much control. As a child, her parents had instilled in her a sense of responsibility for governing her fellow Tarans, but it was always in the context of obedience to the Priesthood and stewardship of the family legacy. Monsari quite literally powered the Empire.

Then, as she came of age, she'd learned that the command Monsari showed the public and the Priesthood was only one side of the story. They had a deeper mission—one to preserve the race, no matter the odds against them.

She was one of the few who possessed the generational knowledge of what had happened to the Taran race over the ages. The Priesthood and the authorities before them had altered history to suit their own narrative, but the Monsari family had endured. It was how she knew that the good intentions of Sietinen were the worst thing that could have happened, and how she knew that the Taran race would survive even if all seemed lost.

The burden of that knowledge wasn't fair. She couldn't share it with even her own husband, just a solitary heir of her choosing. In light of the present circumstances, she'd delayed making that selection. The knowledge could end with her; she supposed that was an option. Maybe starting fresh was what Tarans needed.

She shoved aside the thoughts, knowing that way of thinking wasn't productive. She *did* need to pass on her knowledge, and her work must continue.

To that end, it was better she alert the Gatekeepers about the incident on Zeron rather than waiting for them to find out through other channels. She opened a vidcall to Felina.

The emissary answered, as always wearing her dark-blue, hooded robe. "Yes?"

"I have news, and it's not good."

Felina fixed Celine in a level stare through the screen. "What happened?"

"We had a mole in the Zeron facility. I don't know for how long or what they learned, but I just found out and wanted you to hear it from me."

The Gatekeeper didn't reply at first, her only change in expression a twitch in her jaw. The hybrids never behaved quite like normal Tarans, but some of the flesh-and-blood quirks came through in times of stress. "Is the device compromised?"

"Not to my knowledge."

"Then we must complete the excavation. It's critical we're able to bring it online."

"I know, but we can no longer ensure security. Our workforce can't be trusted, and we no longer have a means to ensure they keep our secrets." The encoding arches had been a gift from the Gatekeepers to aid in the efforts, and she couldn't bring herself to say that a single individual had somehow destroyed the devices. Celine had no idea how the tech worked or how easily it might be replaced, so she left it to Felina to read between the lines.

"Then they are all disposable now. Get the most out of them before they expire."

It was clear direction. Celine didn't like the idea of turning the workers into straight-up slaves and working them to death, but she had to agree that getting the most out of them made sense. They couldn't be allowed to leave or communicate outside Zeron, so their lives were forfeit. "We'll increase the shifts and finish. It's very close."

Felina nodded. "For all our sakes, I hope you're right." She ended the vidcall.

Celine sank into her office chair, feeling exhausted. So much was riding on this one operation, she couldn't help feeling like her future was about to slip through her fingers.

We'll find a way, she told herself. There was still a chance to make it through this alive.

CHAPTER 13

RAENA LOOKED ACROSS the conference table at her grandparents, trying to gauge their reaction to her presentation. Next to her, Ryan gave her a supportive nod.

"It's a significant investment," Kate said at last.

Cris nodded. "But I like it."

Kate smiled. "I do, too. Nice work, Raena."

She beamed at them. "All right, then let's go over the details."

Her plan to make infrastructure improvements in the Outer Colonies was the largest project of its kind since the mass colonization push millennia prior. Most of the planets had developed in a way that left them dependent on a number of centralized goods and services. While some degree of specialization was helpful and appropriate, this wasn't a matter of regional land use—like moving agricultural products across state lines in her home country on Earth. When an entire *planet* was too specialized, it couldn't support the basic needs of its citizens without interstellar assistance. The Coalition's attacks had exposed just how vulnerable many worlds were, underscoring weaknesses in the supply chain.

To correct those shortcomings, each planet in the Taran Empire needed to be equipped with the production capacity to cover its own food and everyday resource supplies without relying on any shipments from other worlds. Food was the easiest issue to tackle, since biodomes could be set up almost anywhere to create a hospitable growing environment no matter the surface conditions on a planet.

Setting up the tools to replenish everyday necessities like communications equipment was far more challenging, since true independence would require the ability to take raw materials and refine them all the way to functional components. Realistically, that level of investment wouldn't be possible on a shorter timeframe than a generation, no matter how much money they threw at it. A more realistic approach was to install high-capacity automated fabs—which Raena still considered to be sophisticated 3D printers—to handle the more complicated items. Getting the raw materials to feed into those printers would be the next priority, but that would require spinning up mining operations and refineries. It would take years, if not decades, to strike a sustainable rhythm.

Raena brought up a map of the Empire's member worlds and applied an overlay to indicate color-coding of different manufacturing and production specializations. Those in gray indicated bare-boned colonies solely reliant on outside assistance.

"I had the analysts consolidate the data, and this is what we're dealing with," she said. "We need to decide how to prioritize the infrastructure rollout."

"Those planets with no resources of their own are clearly the most vulnerable," Cris said.

"However, they also have the smallest populations," Kate countered. "I guess our first order of business is determining the definition of 'need'. Are we going for the greatest impact by number of people or in accordance with their present conditions?"

"I'd advocate for neither," Ryan chimed in.

Raena looked at him with surprise. "What do you mean?"

"Tackling either extreme isn't going to make the most immediate impact," he replied. "I think we need to focus first on the planets with the *best chance* of achieving some degree of self-sufficiency, regardless of population size. What's needed for them to achieve independence, and are the resources—financial and otherwise—available to make that happen? If anything, the smaller-population worlds might be better, since they're less of a target. If things go badly in a war, it'll become a matter of hoping *some* people survive."

While a dark way of looking at it, he was right. The highly populated planets that already had a lot of infrastructure would likely be the first to come under attack. And many of those didn't have extra space readily available for large-scale agricultural investments, which would mean costly and time-intensive work to install orbital structures. Conversely, planets with moderate populations and lots of open land would allow for easy infrastructure augmentations that could at least preserve lives, if not a high-tech lifestyle.

"I agree, focusing on the planets already closest to self-sufficiency will give us the greatest gains in the short-term," Cris said.

Raena applied some filters to the data. "Given that, these thirty or so might be a good place to start.

She only recognized a few of the names. With fifteen-hundred member planets, she didn't know most unless they were a major population center or had experienced some kind of significant incident. She was pleased to see that there was a good spread of locations in the short list—all Outer Colonies, but fairly well distributed across the Empire's territory. In terms of hedging bets for survival, it made sense.

Cris nodded with approval as he looked over the updated map. "I like it. There's enough on each of these planets to work with, and we can make the other upgrades in short order. It's a great test case."

"That is, assuming they're receptive to our offer," Kate said.

Raena had considered the possibility that they might meet resistance. It seemed silly, since the plan was to offer trillions of credits' worth of equipment for free, but she could understand how some local governments might be skeptical about ulterior motives. "We need to frame the sales pitch as anti-Coalition."

"I'm not so sure about that," her grandmother said with a scowl.

"Does anyone actually *like* the Coalition?" Raena asked. "I don't think so. They're a group of terrorists who've forced people into submission. Given a choice, don't you believe regular citizens would choose tried and true leadership?"

"Not if they feel burned by Tararian rule," Cris said. "It's 'the enemy you know' versus 'grass is greener'. The Coalition has done their best to look like a verdant field."

"Which is why we need to face the opposition head-on," Raena insisted. "We need to shut down the Coalition's influence—have people make a *choice* to ignore their offers. Pushing for unity is the only way."

"I don't disagree," Kate said, "but that won't be easy. There are a lot of emotions wrapped up in what's been happening."

Raena nodded. "The foremost is that people are scared. When our opponents use fear to control, our best countermeasure is offering safety. The might of the Empire will sway people. We just have to remind them what's possible when we stick together."

"Autonomous planets united by a shared mission," Cris said.

"Exactly." She looked around the faces at the table. "We can show them the way."

— — —

The strange Vapr substance became increasingly fascinating the more Leon learned about it. He'd run the material through every test at his disposal, and he still couldn't classify it under any standard definitions.

The bionanite design was unlike anything known to Taran science. Most nanites existed within their host and could interface with organic tissues, but these had the ability to truly merge with the host's body. It was how they'd been able to create genetic patches. Furthermore, the self-replication ability was significantly beyond anything of Taran design; the closest tech was Kira's nanites, but even those had drawn from alien technology.

Even as he tried to understand the tech, the biggest question was how to *stop* it. He'd run several scenarios of the potential propagation of the Erebus nanites in the Vapr drug, and the numbers were concerning, to say the least. Conservative estimates placed exposure at five percent of the total Taran population, but other models placed it as high as twenty percent.

Those models assumed that the drugs were the only exposure source, then extrapolated contact points from those individuals. Glaendor had been a smart place for the Coalition to target in the drug distribution efforts, since it was a tourist hub with clientele including people from the Middle and Central Worlds. One person who lived in a high population center could easily spread the nanites across a city and then a whole planet.

To stop the nanites, they would need an antidote that could spread just as quickly and thoroughly, and ideally, it would be delivered through a mechanism with guaranteed exposure.

Is there a way to reprogram the Erebus nanites, or do we need to introduce something else to flush them out? Leon fiddled with some possibilities.

The models relied on a number of assumptions, but the picture it painted was clear enough. Reprogramming the existing nanites wouldn't be a reliable solution, so he would need to invent his own delivery mechanism.

Just revolutionizing science on the fly. Nothing to see here. The sarcasm sounded bitter even in his own head.

The more competing technology inside a person, the more likely that something could go horribly wrong.

He thought back to his previous conversation with Wil and Jason, reflecting on the dire nature of the situation. They were counting on him to figure out a solution.

We can't reprogram the Vapr nanites, but can we manipulate something else that's already inside a person?

There was the possibility of using a person's standard medical nanites to eradicate the Vapr variety. Now, *those* nanites were within his programming control. Well, not *his*, per se, since he didn't have that experience or knowledge, but it was a better option than the others he'd considered.

Leon opened up a message to Wil and Jason. >>I need to bring in help on this Vapr nanite problem. Is that okay?<<

He got back a response from Wil almost immediately. >>Yes, just try to limit the number of people. Standard NDA protocols apply.<<

>>Will do, thanks,<< Leon acknowledged.

With that authorization, he turned to the TSS Headquarters staff directory to track down someone who might be able to offer expert guidance. One of the Militia officers in Medical, a young woman named Monica Rasmaen, jumped out as a good prospect, since her file stated that she had experience with innovative nanotech applications for medical purposes.

He opened up a vidcall with her. It connected after several seconds.

"Hi, Monica," he greeted. "We haven't met, but I'm a civilian contractor with the TUF. My name is Leon Caletti. I've been tasked with a high-priority research project for the TSS and could use another set of eyes on it."

"Hi, Leon," she replied. "You head up the TUF's research division, right?"

He smiled. "If by 'division' you mean all four of us, yes."

She chuckled. "Hey, all great things start small. I'm happy to help, though I don't know what use I'll be."

"Would you be able to come down to my lab on Level 6? I can walk you through it."

Monica muted the audio and then spoke over her shoulder to someone before turning back to the camera. "Yeah, I've got some time. I'll be right down."

"Thanks, see you soon." Leon ended the vidcall.

He appreciated how flexible and accommodating people in the TSS were. Other organizations would spend days or weeks fulfilling resource requests, but in his experience, he could call up any of his TSS colleagues and they'd drop everything to help. That communal atmosphere is what made the organization special, and he hoped as they continued to expand the TUF that they could capture that same spirit of collaboration.

Monica arrived less than ten minutes later, approaching the lab door somewhat cautiously.

"Welcome," Leon greeted. "Come on in."

She took in the compact space. "Quite an assortment of equipment you have in here."

"I keep reminding them I'm a geneticist and they keep giving me assignments about totally unrelated things." He shrugged.

"A white lab coat makes us specialists in all things 'science', right?"

"You understand."

She laughed. "Well, I'll fake answers to your questions as best I can."

"Excellent." Leon brought up a confidentiality form related to the project. "It's classified, so what we discuss will need to stay between us."

Monica pursed her lips as she looked over the document. "Not my first time with one of these." She placed her hand on the screen to register it with a biometric signature. "What are we dealing with?"

Formalities handled, Leon brought up a model of the

Erebus nanites.

Monica squinted at it, justifiably confused by the foreign design. "What is that?"

"You're no doubt familiar with the Erebus," he said, and she nodded. "Well, it appears they gifted more than a power core design. These little guys were embedded in a substance that was being peddled on Glaendor and surrounding worlds as a street drug, Vapr."

Her eyes widened with wonder. "That's no drug."

"No, it's way crazier than that."

He walked her through its different capabilities and how it bonded to DNA. She took it in with professional focus, but he saw the awe in her eyes. He could tell they'd get along; the best scientists could see amazing beauty even in the most horrible and deadliest things.

"It's incredible," she murmured when he'd finished the explanation.

"Truly. And it's also one of the most dangerous things I've ever encountered."

"For sure. Do you know what activates them?"

He nodded. "An energy field from the Erebus' energy cores"

"What?!" She quickly composed herself. "But those are getting rolled out…"

"Exactly. That's why we need to figure out how to disable these. I'm hoping there's a way to reprogram standard medical nanites to treat these others as a foreign threat, like a virus."

She opened her mouth then closed it, her brows drawing together. "It's not designed to work like that, but I can't say it's impossible."

"I'll take a sliver of a possibility."

Monica pulled up a stool from an adjacent workstation, clearly ready to dive into the details. "Do you have data on how the nanites are bonding?"

"Yes, both theoretical and samples from patients."

"Okay, I'll need to take a look."

They got to it, exploring every nuance of how the tech operated. Leon quickly realized how out of his depth he was when Monica started asking questions he wouldn't know how to phrase, let alone how to answer. It prompted several new modeling exercises and additional testing.

It wasn't until three hours later, when he started getting hungry, that he realized how much time had passed. However, the work in front of him was well beyond what he would have been able to develop on his own.

Monica leaned back in her seat, arms crossed. "I don't want to jinx it, but I think this could actually work."

The idea behind the solution was simple enough. They'd roll out a programming update for standard medical nanites over the VComm communications network, as was already standard practice. The update would direct the nanites to reference the host's documented DNA profile against the current state, which should identify the specific patches made by the Erebus DNA. Once it had identified those segments, it would then be able to identify other instances of the nanites within the body and eliminate them so the patches couldn't be reinstated.

"We'll need to test it to know for sure," Leon said. "But it looks promising."

She smiled. "Any more galactic threats I can help solve? This beats my regular day job."

"Not right now, but I know who to call when I encounter

my next crisis. Don't worry, there *will* be others."

"You've got it." She stood up. "Too bad we can't brag to everyone about how awesome we are."

"Saving lives is good enough for me."

"Agreed. I'm happy to help anytime." She headed out.

As soon as she had gone, Leon opened up a message to Wil and attached a write-up of their proposed plan. >> It'll need testing, but I think we may have a solution.<<

CHAPTER 14

JASON COULDN'T HELP checking the clock as he waited for Kira's return to Headquarters. He had only received a short note from her saying that she was on her way back, and he had no idea what information she was bringing with her.

There'd been a flurry of reports from Zeron immediately after her departure. The planet had gone into lockdown, which had spurred the Enforcers to try to move in to augment the planet's private security. However, Avon Security, the local outfit, had turned away the outside assistance, which typically indicated that there was something to hide. Given Kira's swift exit, she had likely received confirmation of the same thing.

What became more concerning, as time went on, was that other Coalition-occupied worlds began to initiate similar lockdown procedures. And it wasn't just patrols around planetary shield access gates or a few demonstrators in the streets. Armed mechs and hundreds of mercenary soldiers had appeared, seemingly from nowhere. It was the same kind of tech Jason had witnessed at the MPS facility. Deadly weapons, and neither the TSS nor Guard could safely move in without risking significant civilian casualties if the scenes turned ugly.

"What the fok are they doing?" he muttered to himself as he looked over the latest report on the holodisplay in the task force's office.

"Fortifying, sir," Laura replied.

He'd meant it as a rhetorical question, but he was intrigued by the confidence of her response. "What are your thoughts?"

"These changes to flight patterns and planetary defenses are too similar to be a coincidence. Forty-two planets making nearly identical alterations within minutes of each other? It was coordinated."

"Forty-two?" The figure caught Jason by surprise. They'd been tracking thirty-seven specific planets in connection to Coalition activity, a little over half of which had been identified during previous coordinated efforts.

Laura smiled faintly. "That's the problem with coordinated moves—it's really easy to spot a pattern. Looks like we missed five during our previous analysis."

"Where?"

She brought up a galactic map on the holoprojector. Five points were highlighted in red, two in the sector near Zeron and another three closer to the Rift. "These planets hadn't previously been flagged, but they took the same preparatory actions as the worlds where we've confirmed there's a strong Coalition presence."

Jason shook his head. "In retrospect, we should have attacked a Coalition base a long time ago to see which other places responded rather than always waiting for them to make the first move."

"Who knows? They may have disguised their moves better before. I get the feeling they know we're onto them and just don't care about hiding anymore."

"I can't argue with that."

If the Coalition had held onto any belief that their activities remained secret, that illusion had been shattered by Kira's infiltration. Now, it was a race to the endgame—whatever form that might take.

Unfortunately, the more the Coalition readied itself for a fight, the more obvious it became that they were well equipped to stand against the TSS and Guard. It wasn't that they had superior firepower or numbers, but rather that they had placed all their operations centers in the middle of highly populated areas. Those innocent civilians functioned as living shields— barbaric, but extremely effective.

Since the military couldn't strike them at their heart without risking massive civilian casualties, the next best option was to control traffic around the world. However, the Coalition had, apparently, anticipated that action and started to erect their own blockades around the planets. All the supply stocking ensured that the Coalition's members would have what they needed to weather the isolation, with no regard for what happened to the civilians who relied on regular offworld shipments to survive.

Are we supposed to wait them out or force them into a fight? The TSS would have a decision to make in the near future. For now, they would have to let the situation unfold.

Jason went back to his office to work. With so many thoughts churning in his mind, he didn't expect to be productive. After settling in, he did manage to accomplish some admin tasks, so it wasn't a total waste of the day.

Finally, late in the afternoon, Jason received notice that Kira's shuttle had docked.

A text message from her appeared on his desktop. >>Need to swing by Medical. Be there soon.<<

>>Everything okay?<< he asked.

>>Minor setbacks. Nothing to worry about.<<

Knowing that she'd fill him in when the time was right, he left her to the other business.

Just shy of an hour later, she arrived at his office with Pyra, who was limping slightly. Both of their appearances had returned to their natural faces.

"Good to see you safely back," he greeted.

"Mostly," Pyra said, entering the office.

The two visitors sat down.

"What happened?" Jason asked.

"That place is a foking creep show," Kira said, getting comfortable in her chair. "We had to make a swift exit, and they managed to get a shot off into Pyra's leg."

"Clean through the flesh. Nothing serious," Pyra added.

While Jason appreciated the advanced Taran medical technology, getting shot was still a significant event in his mind. "We don't need to meet right now if—"

"I'm fine, really," the officer said.

"Okay." Jason turned his attention to Kira. "I'm curious how we went from a *covert* assignment to people getting shot."

Kira and Pyra exchanged glances, looking more relieved than apologetic.

"You can have a thorough, fast, or quiet investigation. Best case, you get two of those in a single op," she said. "Urgency was the name of the game, so you got the fast treatment. We tried for quiet and didn't quite get there."

"Fair enough. What did you find out?"

"Enough that you can do a follow-up to satisfy the

'thorough' criteria in exchange for things getting too loud." Kira took a minuscule device out from her pocket and placed it on the desktop.

"I'll walk you through it," a pleasant yet synthesized voice said over the office speakers.

"Thanks, Jasmine," Jason acknowledged. While he valued Kira's insights, it was helpful to have information filtered through the AI's more impartial perspective. When it came to getting a search warrant, they would need verifiable facts, not gut feelings.

A low-quality video image appeared on the holoprojector.

"This is the feed from one of the button cams Kira was able to plant on a worker," Jasmine explained. "I have been through each frame of the three records and prepared a highlight reel of what I deem to be each worker's important actions throughout their day."

Images of an indoor facility with stone and concrete walls scrolled across the holoprojector. It seemed mundane until the worker exited an elevator into a large cavern with rough walls. They stepped forward to a scaffolding system descending into a pit.

"Oh, my stars," Jason whispered. "That looks just like…"

"Yep," Kira confirmed.

Jasmine changed the onscreen image to a later point in the video where the worker was chipping off material from the interior of the pit and placing the fragments into bins. The substance had a metallic quality to it but broke like stone. "It appears the structure was laced with ateron," the AI explained. "We confirmed it with a composition analysis during a scan from the surface."

The projected image changed to a rough, three-dimensional rendering of the facility's interior, color-coded by the different materials throughout. The image zoomed in on a deep sublevel where there was a structure the size and shape of the pit visible in the previous video.

"It appears that they've been digging for a long time," Jasmine continued. "I estimate that there are approximately two thousand workers in the facility daily. This entire place has been carved out by hand."

"How did the pit get filled in with stone?" Jason asked tentatively.

"No clue," Kira said. "Struck me as super weird, too."

"Okay, so there's a device like the one on Earth, but it's quite literally *buried* on Zeron, not just underground. That says to me that someone didn't want it found."

"Why not blow the whole thing up then?" Kira asked with a shrug. "The entire setup doesn't make a lot of sense."

"I have a hypothesis about that," Pyra chimed in.

Jason leaned back in his chair. "Go for it."

"The appearance of this reminds me somewhat of the geological changes that happened on the worlds afflicted by the Gatekeeper's bio-optimization transformations. They had weaponized the tech to wipe out the population on several planets—so it seemed—and it doesn't seem like a huge leap that they may have employed a similar strategy before."

"That's an interesting thought." Jason steepled his fingers.

He hadn't been to any of the worlds that had been radically altered in a matter of hours, but he'd seen images. The events had happened a couple months before the Erebus appeared, shortly before the standoff with the Gatekeepers when they'd received the cryptic warning about there being 'others'. Entire ecosystems had been wiped out and mountains had risen from the seas on some of the affected planets. To this day, there had been no satisfactory explanation about *how* the technology worked, but it had been assumed that it drew on *aesen* energy in some manner. By comparison, an ancient device getting swallowed by rock wasn't that outlandish.

"Okay, let's assume for a minute that *is* what happened here," Jason said. "How did this rock get laced with ateron if ateron isn't native to Zeron?"

"I've been debating that mystery myself the whole shuttle ride home," Kira said. "My conclusion was that it was done as a roadblock."

Jason tilted his head. "Explain."

"The Gatekeeper tech allows physical features to be reformed—basically, they liquified the rock and poured it into the structure to seal it off," Kira elaborated. "However, any Gifted person could easily distinguish between the rock and the device within, just lifting out the rock portion. But mix that rock with traces of ateron, and it would be very difficult to differentiate between the device and the fill material. Hence the hand excavation."

Jason nodded slowly. "Okay, I'll buy that. But why bury it in the first place?"

"It must do something that someone decided they don't want it to be able to do," Pyra offered.

"Right. Except that we know the Gatekeepers are working with the Coalition," Jason said. "So, if it was *buried* with Gatekeeper tech, then why would the Gatekeepers now help uncover it?"

"That's assuming that the Gatekeepers who are working with the Coalition are the same Gatekeepers who buried it however long ago," Kira pointed out.

Jason had discussed the possibility of multiple factions within the alien race, and this did seem to confirm it. There was also another possibility. "For that matter, do the Gatekeepers know that Taran members of the Coalition are doing this excavation?"

"Well, I didn't come face-to-face with any creepy, robed alien hybrids while I was on Zeron, so I can't give you a definitive answer on that," Kira replied.

"I suppose that detail doesn't matter right now," Jason said. "We can clearly see an alien device in these images, and that's enough for us to go in. They're breaking the official decree that all alien tech needs to be handed over to the TSS for processing."

Kira nodded. "Where do we go from here?"

"We'll need to involve the Guard. That will make it easier and take the heat off us."

"Isn't it the TSS' duty to investigate?"

"It's more complicated than that. I need to look at this politically because of my family."

"Ah." She sighed. "Taking out the bad guys is always political in one way or another. We've got them cornered now."

"I'm not sure 'cornered' is a good thing. It increases the chance of a vicious attack as they attempt to escape."

"True, but we have the might of the TUF, TSS, and Guard behind us. The Coalition's political influence isn't enough to overcome that."

Jason didn't want to get into the details with her, but he couldn't be certain that Monsari didn't still have significant sway, despite their recent setbacks. In particular, they seemed to have strong relationships with many Lower Dynasties and corporations throughout the Taran Empire. While Sietinen was well-respected, the family wasn't known for having a wide breadth of close alliances at the lower levels.

"It's complicated," he said instead, falling back on one of his father's favorite phrases.

Kira nodded, seeming to understand his reticence to say more on the matter. "I just want this to be over."

"Me too. We have bigger things to worry about."

Unfortunately, Monsari may be inexorably tied to the Erebus. It remained to be seen if going after Zeron would prompt another assault of a different nature. There was still a lot to consider on that front.

"There is one other lead we should follow," Jason continued. "We need to try to track down Pesta."

"That's going to be tricky. There hasn't been a sign of it since Glaendor."

"Reports indicate that it's tethered to Ava," Pyra said. "Finding a person should be easier than an invisible transdimensional entity."

"Except that Ava could be anywhere in the galaxy," Kira countered. "There are plenty of ships and planets where a person could disappear."

Jason spread his hands on the desktop. "We have to try. She gave us an important tip about Andrei, so she might be able to give us additional insights about the Erebus. We need to explore every potential advantage."

"Okay. I might have an idea about that," Kira offered.

"Which is?"

"We know it—or she, Ava—left on the Hyperion with Herja. Well, I know you won't explain *how* the *Horizon* was tracked, but could you maybe do the same thing for the *Hyperion*?"

"I'm not sure." Jason honestly wasn't certain about the technological limitations of his father's workaround. He'd have to talk to him.

She shrugged. "Well, just throwing it out there. It would limit the search pool a little."

"Yes, I'll look into it."

"Sounds good," Kira acknowledged. "Jasmine and I will start reconstructing schematics from the scan and video data."

"Thanks. We'll see where that gets us."

— — —

The pieces of the puzzle were coming together, but Wil was growing increasingly concerned about the story it illustrated. The worry wasn't for himself but rather what it meant for his family. Everything he'd done throughout his career had been to ensure they would have a better future, but now, there was no guarantee any of them would live to see tomorrow.

Staving off an Erebus attack would buy them time, but that wasn't good enough. He needed to neutralize the threat, just as he had with the Bakzen. Going up against his former adversaries had taken almost everything he had, and this new enemy was infinitely stronger. He didn't know if he would be enough.

We have to find a way. Failure wasn't an option—not with this. He would make sure his children were safe, no matter what.

A message from Jason popped up on Wil's desk, startling him from his thoughts. >>Hey, Dad. Can we talk?<<

>>Sure,<< he typed back.

Truthfully, Wil could use some help brainstorming, and

Jason could assist with that. While Saera was still his favorite collaborator, Wil recognized that Jason was still green in many areas and could benefit from their discussions. He'd seen growth in his son's thinking over the last couple of years and was eager to encourage his professional development at every opportunity.

Jason arrived shortly thereafter and settled into his customary seat.

"What did you want to discuss?" Wil asked.

"That report from Kira about there being another device, like the one on Earth, but on Zeron."

"I've been thinking about that, too."

"Do you think that's what was meant by it being 'broken'? Could the two be linked, and one of them being offline is what made it not work right?" Jason asked.

"It's a strong possibility," Wil said. "A user guide would be very helpful right about now."

"Maybe we could have one…"

"How?"

"Pesta," Jason replied. "On Glaendor, Pesta willingly offered helpful information about what was happening to Andrei—the tip that he was Erebus. So maybe it would help us again."

"Perhaps."

"But we'd have to figure out how to find it. All signs point to it now using that woman Ava—Marco's former girlfriend— as a handler. We believe Ava left Glaendor on the *Hyperion*, Herja's ship. Maybe we could try to track the *Hyperion* and hope we get lucky?"

"It's been quite a while since they left Glaendor."

"I know it's a longshot, but it's the only lead we have on Pesta right now."

Wil nodded. "And you're hoping we can track the *Hyperion*'s independent jump drive?"

"Yeah."

"Technically, yes. However, I think there's a much easier way to go about this."

Jason raised an eyebrow. "Which is?"

"To simply ask Pesta for help—once we know which question to ask."

"How do you mean?"

"Pesta has gone its whole life being used and hunted; it has every reason to run and hide now. But if we can give it a reason to trust us, to help us, maybe we can befriend it."

Jason nodded, processing the suggestion. "I do think it might be a key to understanding the Erebus. Or, at least, how there can be conscious links to the higher dimensions."

"I agree. If we can understand how Pesta operates, it's a great clue toward understanding the Erebus. More importantly, understanding their limitations when it comes to their actions within spacetime."

"Combine that with the device on Earth…"

Wil smiled. "That's right. We can, hypothetically, target them at their weakest. I *do* want to reach out to Pesta, but we might only get one chance to connect, and I don't yet know how best to leverage that relationship."

"Okay, we can hold off."

"It's a good thought, though, Jason. I'm glad you're thinking about things in those terms."

"Hey, any potential resource at our disposal, right?"

"Very much so." Wil leaned forward. "Speaking of which, there are other resources we haven't yet utilized to their fullest."

"I think we're pretty tapped out."

"Within the TSS, yes. But we have friends on the outside. Well, acquaintances, anyway. I'd like to loop in the Lynaedans and Aesir with the technical challenges we're currently facing. They have some great minds among them."

Jason nodded thoughtfully. "I wonder if they could tell us any more about the way the Earth's device interface works?"

"That's what I was wondering, too. I, admittedly, don't know the finer details about how bioelectronic interfaces work, only their practical applications. I'm wondering if there might be a way to... trace the signal. Or, whatever vernacular that might be."

"Good thought."

Wil sighed. "We can't do this alone."

"It's good to hear you say that. You have a tendency to try to do everything yourself."

"Bad habit."

"You're getting better."

Wil couldn't share his son's lighthearted tone. He knew it was a stress management mechanism and not a genuinely casual attitude, but he was too stressed for such banter. "Beating the Erebus is going to take everyone working together."

"'Everyone' is a big ask. Might have to settle for 'most'."

While Jason wasn't wrong, Wil wasn't ready to give up. "Any disagreements among Tarans are inconsequential compared to the larger threat. We're dealing with a situation beyond our conventional understanding. All of these plans we're trying to reverse-engineer are measured in tens of thousands of years, or maybe even hundreds of thousands. Yet, we're so young as a species and culture. There are likely civilizations out there that've been around for *billions* of years. Maybe the Erebus even began as one of those, so very long ago. I can't begin to process how differently they must regard our existence after having that much history."

"Must be like us watching kids play King of the Mountain or something."

"I think even that's giving too much credit to what they must think of us. But I don't know. Maybe there is high regard for us, on some level, and that's *why* they view us as a threat."

"True. If you don't respect your enemy and don't see them as a threat, you'd just ignore them. You only engage if you deem them worth fighting."

Wil smiled, feeling a glimmer of hope for the first time. "That's good news for us."

"I guess so. Never thought I'd be happy about someone wanting to pick a fight."

"It means we're enough of a threat—which means we have a chance to do real damage. We just need to figure out how to improve our odds."

"How do you want to handle bringing in others?"

"I was hoping you could take the lead on facilitating those discussions," Wil said.

Jason's eyes widened with surprise. "I've barely talked to the Aesir since my trip to the nexus, and even that was hardly a friendly chat."

"You are welcome among them, just as I am. It'd be a good relationship to begin fostering. There aren't a lot of people with our level of ability, and they're the closest."

"That's your connection, though. I—"

"Not everything needs to be run through me, Jason. You're a senior TSS officer, and I trust you to navigate these and any other discussions."

Jason looked at him, seeming to sense a deeper meaning to his words. "Is everything okay, Dad?"

"I won't be there to guide you every step of the way. I just want to do what I can now to prepare you for any eventuality."

"Okay." Jason didn't seem convinced that was everything, but Wil was thankful he left it at that.

"I just dumped a pile of work on you, so you should probably get to it." Wil smiled.

"Yeah, yeah." He rose. "I'll keep you posted."

"Thanks, Jason."

As his son left the room, Wil returned his thoughts to his tasks. He was thankful to have people to turn to, but he knew much of the solution would come back on him—not just because of his Gifts, but because of his leadership experience. No one else had both.

One more test. Everything was coming down to this. He couldn't fail everyone now.

CHAPTER 15

THE SEEMINGLY IMPOSSIBLE task of developing a transportation solution for millions of people on short notice had confirmed for Ryan that he had a great team working for him. Ansen had come through in a major way after only a week. Not only were the transport ships ready two days ahead of schedule, but they'd even had identifying marks stripped from them to minimize the chance of them drawing unwanted attention.

"Ansen, this is amazing," Ryan told the man.

"Just doing my job, my lord. I'm happy to be of service."

A promotion and hefty bonus were definitely in order, but Ryan would have to deal with that later. "It is I who's honored to have you on my team."

Ansen smiled broadly. "Thank you, my lord."

"I'll let you know if I require anything else on this matter, but I should be able to take it from here."

"I'll be standing by."

Ryan ended the vidcall and immediately brought up a new commlink to Wil. When the older man's face appeared on the viewscreen, Ryan gave him a welcoming smile and nod. "I got them."

"The ships?" Wil clarified, his tone soft with relief.

Ryan nodded. "Flight tested and a crew standing by. They're unmarked and ready for loading."

"That's wonderful. I knew I could count on you."

"Tell me where you need the ships, and I'll get them there."

Wil nodded. "Moving them around is going to be tricky. Since Monsari and the Coalition have such broad reach, any unusual traffic will tip them off."

"I can set them up to look like supply freighters," Ryan offered. The exterior of the vessels already fit with that profile, and altering the digital identification was quick and easy work. Strictly speaking, doing so was illegal, but when a police authority was working on the op, that became a non-issue.

"Yes, that would be a good way to go," Wil agreed. "As for the logistics of *where*, Jason should be involved in that discussion. I'll conference him in."

Ryan's viewscreen flashed to indicate another person had joined the call. The image split to show Wil and Jason side by side.

"Ryan has just informed me that the transport ships are ready," Wil explained. "Have you identified the highest risk locations?"

"Yes, I have the targets and destinations worked out," Jason replied. "However, I'm not sure how to go about getting people from the planet's surface onto the ships, given the Coalition's armed presence on the worlds."

Ryan had no idea what to suggest. The ship's Wil had asked for were, by their nature, impossible to land in an atmosphere. And the reason they wanted a limited number of large ships was to avoid the transportation logistics of using hundreds of small vessels. The two scenarios were mutually exclusive. "Your best bet is to use the existing surface-to-space infrastructure and spread out the arrival times to avoid bottlenecks," he said at last.

"Self-service means having people opt in," Jason replied.

"That was always the intention," Wil said. "We don't want to force anyone to relocate—just give them an option if they're concerned about the Coalition's activities putting them in danger."

Legitimate concerns after what they've done over the last year. Ryan folded his hands on his desktop. "Full disclosure, these ships aren't designed to hold people for an extended period of time. They're rudimentary day-trip transports, not anything where you can stage people. Staggering the arrivals would help in some ways, but those who are first on are going to get uncomfortable pretty fast."

Wil nodded. "You delivered what I asked for. Admittedly, I hadn't thought through all the implications of that approach."

"I have a thought about the people aspect," Jason said. "What about having Lexi reach out through the network she's built for the civilian training initiative?"

Wil nodded thoughtfully. "That's not a bad idea."

"Okay, let me know when you have your plan in place and I'll ensure the ships get where they need to go," Ryan said.

"Thank you," Wil acknowledged. "We'll be in touch soon."

"Good luck."

—   —   —

"There are going to be problems any way we go about this,"

Jason said, entering the High Commander's office following the conference call with Ryan. He found his mother was already there with his father.

"I know," Wil said. "It'll be impossible to not draw some level of attention—"

"Not just that," Jason cut in. "The Coalition's and Monsari's operations are intertwined. We can only clear civilians from so many locations. We need to figure out where those efforts will have the most impact."

Wil cracked a smile.

"I don't think there's anything happy about this, Dad."

"It's not that. I'm just proud to see you thinking ahead in those terms."

Jason released some of his tension. "All of your lectures were bound to stick one day."

Saera nodded with pride, motioning to the seat next to her. "You're right about the civilian concerns. The blockades have been in place for over a week now and there's no sign of them lifting."

"Whichever places you intend to seize in the first wave, that's where we should try to clean out the civilian population," Wil said.

"I already have the targets worked out." Jason brought up a map with tactical notations on the holoprojector integrated into his father's desk.

The map highlighted the major Coalition-occupied worlds as well as the location of key MPS facilities, which were suspected to support the subversive activities. The sites were color-coded by importance, giving them an effective 'threat level' with red as the highest priority through yellow and transitioning to green as the least critical. The majority of locations fell into varying shades of orange, with seven red sites. The Monsari estate on Tararia was red—one of the few times a TSS target had been set on the capital world.

Wil looked over the information. "This is doable, but I don't think we have the resources within the TSS to pull off a simultaneous strike."

"Aren't we planning to coordinate with the Guard?"

"Yes, to an extent. But I'd like for it to be our people in the most critical positions."

"I agree." Jason drummed his fingertips on his thigh. "How closely do you think the Erebus are watching?"

"Very, but their perception of time is another matter."

"Do you think they'll come after us as soon as they realize the Coalition can no longer do their bidding?"

"We need to be prepared to go straight into battle once we make the opening move. I have no idea how the enemy may react."

"We're not just prepping to take out Monsari and the Coalition," Saera said.

Wil nodded. "No, this is for the endgame."

Jason returned his focus to the map. "That changes things. We'll need to incorporate Zeron and Earth into the plan."

"Yes, but I still need more information about the devices to finalize that strategy," Wil said. "I mean, is the Zeron device even functional?"

"I don't know," Jason admitted. "And it will be next to impossible to find out without being able to access the planet."

Saera scowled. "Trying to bypass the blockade isn't a smart move right now."

"I agree." Jason glanced at the enemy positions noted on the map. "It's more important to understand the device on

Earth so we know if Zeron is even a lead worth pursuing."

"Speaking of which, any word on potential collaborators?" Wil asked.

"The recruitment is coming along well," Jason told him. "I was able to speak with the Lynaedans about sending some representatives to a technical summit, and they've agreed."

"And the Aesir?"

"Dahl seemed surprised to hear from me, but he didn't immediately say 'no'. It was something like, 'We'll be where we need to be at the appropriate time'."

"That sounds about right for an Oracle. It was a roundabout way of saying 'yes, whatever you need'."

Saera and Jason chuckled.

"If you say so," Jason said.

Wil looked at him expectantly. "Anyone else?"

"I've investigated the preeminent research groups regarding transdimensional communications and have a short list of other prospective consultants. I'll finalize the group and get everyone committed to a time as soon as possible."

"Good," Wil said with an approving nod. "We can't move against Monsari until we have a clear sense of the bigger picture."

"This will be my priority. Then we can get back to the tactical planning."

"In the meantime, we need to be thinking about how to clear the way for our troops to move in," Saera said. "The Coalition is too well-armed for us to use force to break through the blockades without suffering civilian casualties."

"I'll chat with Lexi to get her thoughts," Jason suggested. She knew how people who had been seduced by the Coalition thought, and also why people who shied away from the organization resisted. They could use those distinctions to separate out Taran loyalists and separatists as they screened people to relocate to offworld sanctuaries.

"Okay, let me know what you need," Wil said. "I'm open to any and all ideas."

— — —

Lexi frowned at her computer screen, annoyed to see that one of the initiative's instructors had bailed at the last minute, leaving them short-staffed. *How are we supposed to find someone to fill in now?*

She was in the process of running through potential candidates, and ultimately dismissing them as viable options, when Jason stopped by her office.

"Hey, I need your help with something Coalition-related," he said.

Lexi sighed. "Any other time, I'd be all over that. But I'm in crisis-mode."

Jason stepped into her office and closed the door behind him. "We're about to make a move, and we need to get as many civilians as possible relocated to a safe place in case the scene turns ugly."

Her stomach turned over. "When?"

"Sooner the better."

She crossed her arms. "And how are you intending to relocate people?"

"Ryan has secured ships for us to use, and my dad has a planet picked out where people can stay until it's safe to go back home."

"That sounds like an utter logistical nightmare."

"It is. And it would be really beneficial to have your expertise help us weed out Coalition sympathizers, not to mention leverage your friendly face telling people it's okay to trust us."

She shook her head. "Jason, my word doesn't carry any weight."

"The enormous application numbers to the training initiative beg to differ. A lot of those trainees are from the planets in question. Their support would go a long way to make this go smoothly." He sat down on the edge of her desk. "And, we could say that this relocation is a part of those new training efforts."

"As an excuse for why a number of people are suddenly boarding massive transport ships?"

"There's no way to hide it."

Lexi bit her lip. "Which planets, specifically?"

"Torlon, Hysaen, and Karteya are the initial targets, and then we'll take it from there," Jason said.

Lexi brought up a star map, seeing that the planets in question were actually in the same general territory as the training location where the instructor had canceled. While she'd never intended to teach classes herself, it was looking like she might be the only person available to fill in on short notice—just for a day or two.

"Okay, crazy idea... But I think I have a solution that will work for both of us."

Jason smiled. "Those are the best kind."

—

Lexi hadn't realized what she was getting herself into when

she'd agreed to help Jason. As her transport ship touched down on Karteya, she was met by a female TSS Agent dressed in civilian clothes.

"Thanks for coming to help us out with this, Lexi," the Agent said. "I'm Isbeth."

"Nice to meet you. I think I'm supposed to record some sort of promo for you?" Lexi had been assured it would be a quick stopover before she went to teach her class.

Isbeth's blonde brows drew together. "It's a little more complicated than that."

Of course it is. Lexi kept her expression neutral. "What's going on, exactly?"

"I'm under orders to evaluate the population and relocate those who'd like to voluntarily move to a non-Coalition planet."

"Yes, which is the message I'm supposed to record."

"Well, we can't really put out a general call because then the Coalition would know we were up to something. We need to be more subtle with the 'hey, come with us if you want out' message, and we were told you'd be able to help us figure out how to do that."

I'm not going to make it to that class on time, am I? Lexi met the Agent's bioluminescent hazel eyes—her expression not quite desperate, but imploring.

"What you need to do is put together a marketing package that'll make it seem like a work-study program for families. Use some buzzwords that are the opposite of the Coalition's language."

Isbeth stared at her blankly. "Advertising copywriting isn't part of the Agent training curriculum, I'm afraid."

The poor woman really needed some help. "All right, let's

see what we can put together in short order," Lexi said.

Isbeth led her to a suite in a hotel, which had been converted into a temporary field office. There were only seven staff members present.

"We're not working with a lot here, but we're getting by," Isbeth said.

That was a significant understatement, from what Lexi could see. She'd come to associate the TSS with class and sophistication, but the amenities in the office space reminded her of the bleak days during her time in the Alliance, with the exception of a mobile workstation set up on the dining table. Blending in with the locals for an assignment like this made sense, but perhaps they'd taken it a bit too far.

"I can help you word a message, but I won't be able to help you canvas. I'm actually on kind of a time crunch."

"I might be able to tap into the local communication grid and push out a message," a tech sitting at the computer said.

That would be much easier than the old-fashioned posters I needed to use in the Alliance. A lot had changed since then. She much preferred being on this side. "I like the sound of that."

"Try," Isbeth instructed. "The question is, if we can get in, *what* do we say in the message?"

The tech got to work while Lexi and Isbeth sat down in a pair of weathered chairs. To Lexi's pleasant surprise, her seat was more comfortable than it had looked.

"The key to getting through to people is to target specific issues that are important to them," Lexi explained. "Safety and financial security are reliable topics, but the Coalition goes after those points, too."

"Well, we've gathered up the Coalition propaganda that we've found on this world. It's the standard stuff, with its own local nuance, of course." Isbeth got up and pulled out a stack of fliers and posters.

Lexi stared with distaste at the items. Going through everything to analyze the specific phrases and figuring out how to spin that language to point the right people toward the evacuation plan would take a while. She checked the time on her handheld. She'd only have maybe fifteen minutes before she'd have to head back to a transport ship in order to make it to the class on time.

"I'll be honest, I'm in kind of a tough spot here," Lexi said. "I thought this was going to be more of a hi-and-bye kind of situation, not sitting down to develop a detailed marketing plan."

The concern returned to Isbeth's eyes. "We really need your help with this."

"And I want to—" Everyone in the office was looking at her now. She swallowed. "It's just that I had an instructor drop out, and I was coming out here to fill in for the day. So…"

"What kind of class?" one of the other Agents asked.

"It's an intro telepathy workshop for the civilian training initiative."

"What if one of us were to fill in for you?" Isbeth asked. "None of us have your marketing skills, but telepathy instruction—we can do that."

They'd been trying to keep the training initiative to have mostly civilian instructors, but there were already several Agents involved. Adding one more for a day wouldn't alter the dynamic. "Okay, that would work. Just to get things started."

"Naren, you up for it?" Isbeth asked.

"Sure. I imagine there's some kind of curriculum plan?"

Lexi nodded. "Yes. I can send you the materials to review

on your way."

"Sounds good."

Lexi quickly messaged the relevant items to him and then got to work on reviewing the fliers and posters. They used the bed in the room, for lack of another large work surface, and managed to bucket the messaging into three categories. As she suspected, security and finances were two of the main topics, with access to food being the third. She'd seen those topics in the messaging analysis on a lot of worlds, especially those with limited agriculture like this one.

"All right, so this is what we're dealing with. Given that…" She began crafting the messaging for why people should want to get off-world. Since the Coalition hadn't been delivering on its promises made months ago, it wasn't difficult to come up with reasons. She spun them into a short, punchy narrative. "Something like this should hit well."

Isbeth read it over. "I never would have come up with this."

Lexi smiled. "Believe me, I didn't think marketing was one of my skills until I was forced into it."

"Well, I like it. This should be easy to get out there and to coordinate timing with the planned evacuation."

"Not 'evacuation'. 'Voluntary relocation'," Lexi said. "Thinking about it that way yourselves will help the intended message come through."

"Understood."

"If you're ready with that, I think I'm in the communications system," the tech announced from across the room, a jumble of code on his screen.

A criminal could do a lot of damage with this kind of access. It was actually terrifying to think what the Alliance would have done had they had access to these communication backdoors.

Relying on posters and manually recruiting had limited the reach of the organization, but using established media channels... they could have gotten a lot more people on board very quickly. Then again, there *had* been a lot of interstellar propaganda.

Watching the tech work, Lexi couldn't help wondering about what kind of manipulation may have been going on behind the scenes. She'd only been in the Alliance, but the larger Coalition clearly had more resources. Perhaps the sudden uptick in Coalition activity had been due to using these kinds of exploits in the mass media on certain target worlds.

She knew next to nothing about coding, but she was attuned to looking at patterns in data. As she scanned over the information on the screen, she noticed an irregularity. There was a gap in a communication log—like a message had been received but was never relayed.

"Wait, what's that?" Lexi asked.

The tech frowned at the information on the screen. "I just saw that, myself. It looks to me like a manual deletion."

"Meaning?"

"Exactly what it sounds like. The relay received data it was supposed to transmit, but instead, the signal terminated here."

"In other words, someone tampered with the information that was sent out on the public feed?" Lexi asked.

"Yes."

She frowned. "Can you go back to see what was intercepted and deleted? Was it replaced by anything?"

The tech's eyes scanned over the data. "No replacements that I can see, but there were definitely some datapackets that didn't make it through. Let me see..."

He made several rapid entries on the keyboard, going into

deeper layers of the data and chasing leads to other records. Lexi tried to track what he was doing at first, but it didn't make sense to her untrained eyes. That was fine; let the professionals do their thing.

"Shite," he said under his breath, leaning back in his chair. "This has been going on for months, if not years."

Isbeth exchanged a worried glance with her fellow Agents. "Are you able to retrieve any of the missing information?"

"It's encrypted," the tech replied. "We'd need to pass it off to VComm to help unpackage quickly. It'd take quite a while to reassemble everything from the archived data."

"Hold on," Lexi said. "If it's encrypted and you don't know what's in each message, then how would someone be able to intercept specific data?"

The tech confirmed her fears. "They'd need the encryption key."

Someone within VComm's network is in league with the Coalition. Lexi's heart sank. She knew there was a tight alliance between Sietinen and Vaenetri, so she doubted that Jason's great-uncle was involved in the nefarious activities. Nonetheless, the evidence that another of the High Dynasty corporations had been infiltrated made the situation all the more concerning.

"I suggest you run this up the chain," Lexi said.

"No doubt," Isbeth acknowledged. "I'm glad we decided to hack this. We never would have noticed the tampering otherwise."

Lexi nodded. "The people behind the Coalition are very good. They have a way of worming their way in and making people feel like they don't have a choice."

She could speculate about what the redacted information

might have been—probably messaging from Taran authorities about how they planned to address the scourge that was the Coalition. The people of this planet had probably been made to believe that no one was coming to help them. She had a chance to help change that now.

Lexi leaned forward in her seat. "Let's show them they do have a way out."

CHAPTER 16

FIGURING OUT A solution was one thing, but finding a way to *deploy* that solution was another. Leon sighed and leaned back in his seat, his eyes sore from hours of staring at his screen.

He'd been trying to find a way to use the VComm network to distribute the Vapr antidote via a coding update to standard medical nanites, but simulations of real-world conditions revealed that the Erebus nanites needed to already be active in order for the medical nanites to attack them. However, since the nanites would only activate within an energy field that would make the nanites kill a large percentage of their hosts, it wasn't a great solution.

The only way to jumpstart the antidote process was through direct physical contact—to deploy a modified version of active Vapr nanites in order to trigger an immune response. It was far from ideal and went against dozens of ethical principles, but there was simply no alternative under the present circumstances. Still, they could minimize the risks. Since they'd roll out the medical nanite update first, the alien tech's effects would immediately be nullified as it spread to each person. While it would be better to treat each person individually rather than simply releasing it into the general population, it was the best solution he could think of to fit the scope and extreme time constraints.

With all research paths exhausted and a strategy decided, Leon initiated a vidcall to Jason.

"Hey, what can I do for you?" the Agent greeted.

"You asked for me to check in once I finished my analysis of the antidote. Well, I have."

"And?"

"We need physical access to each planet," Leon stated.

Jason's expression turned glum. "Are you sure?"

Leon nodded. "There's no other way." It was frustrating, but there were limitations to science.

"Well, shite." Jason sighed. "That's going to be a problem."

— — —

The situation in the Outer Colonies was rapidly getting out of control. Jason's heart sank as he reviewed the status of Coalition-occupied worlds in the High Commander's office with his father. The fortifications had been strengthened over the past week, and it looked like they were ready to dig in for the long haul.

"They were smart about these blockades," Jason said. "That's what's so infuriating about the Coalition—I'd respect the effectiveness of their tactics if they weren't so diabolical."

"They have made the most of limited numbers."

At first glance, it seemed difficult to close off access to a planet. However, the structure of the planetary shields made it possible with several well-placed ships. There were only a handful of access gates in global shields, which meant that there were natural choke points. Positioning ships at those openings could effectively block traffic in a way that wouldn't be possible on an open world.

To get through the blockades, there was the option to disable the entire shield. Except, doing so through military force was a violation of several different covenants, making it an absolute last resort option. Likewise, attacking the ships barring the access gates meant firing on civilians. The Coalition had elected to use passenger transport ships in the blockades, meaning that children and other noncombatants may be on board. There was no way to be certain of the passenger manifest, so it was too great a risk to attack when hostages might be present.

The TSS was left in a difficult position. Doing nothing meant allowing the Coalition to continue carrying out its plans unchecked, while trying to stop them meant risking extreme civilian casualties and having the Empire turn against them for excessive use of force.

"Aside from the obvious issues with this situation, there's another factor to consider," Jason told his father. "Leon has identified a method to disable the Vapr nanotech, but it will require physical distribution. Meaning, we won't be able to deploy that antidote until the blockade is dismantled."

His father sat in silent contemplation for several seconds. "I hate to say it, but I think we'll need to keep waiting it out for now. I believe a potential political solution is forthcoming, which may dismantle the current resistance."

"I doubt it."

His father tilted his head slightly. "My sources tell me that an influential family might be making a direct crack at Monsari in the near future. If Monsari goes down, the Coalition will lose its funding and resource access, not to mention a blow to morale. It wouldn't take long for the organization to begin crumbling."

What are my grandparents planning? Jason sat forward with interest. "Oh, well, that changes things. I hope they're successful."

"It's a solid plan. I think they have a good shot."

"Okay." Jason stared glumly at the projected report. Regardless of the forthcoming moves against Monsari, he didn't like feeling at the mercy of the Coalition. Still, he trusted his father's judgment on the matter. "Does that mean we're stuck in observation mode for now?"

"Not entirely. We can finish the prep work for how best to approach the Erebus when the time comes. I'd like to get that scientific summit scheduled as soon as possible."

Jason nodded. "I have the candidates identified. I'll make the final arrangements."

— — —

It felt good to be back home at TSS Headquarters, but Kira had been left with many lingering questions after her brief yet harrowing mission to Zeron.

The departure had been an absolute mess and hadn't gone anything like she'd imagined. Fortunately, Pyra was on his way to making a full recovery from his injuries, but he never should have been hurt in the first place. Kira knew she'd taken substantial risks during the op, and it wasn't right to have placed someone else in harm's way.

<There was no good way to approach the situation on such

a tight timeline,> Jasmine said in Kira's mind, sensing her thoughts.

<Yeah, I know.> Kira returned her attention to the button cam footage analysis displayed on her workstation's screen.

After a week of combing through the data, there hadn't been any more meaningful revelations about the button cam footage. The videos had revealed what they needed, and there was plenty of information to justify getting a warrant. The issue was that the planet was now all but inaccessible. While the TSS, Guard, or TUF *could* move in to conduct an official inspection, it would mean forcing their way through the blockade. That would unleash a political nightmare of another sort, so they were stuck for now.

In the meantime, Kira had been trying to answer as many questions as possible for her own satisfaction. The murals and other carvings throughout the city had introduced intriguing imagery of people interacting with what could be interpreted as alien beings, but the forms were too abstract to be sure. In any case, the planet clearly had a significant history.

<I still want to know what the Coalition was doing with those excavated shards,> Jasmine mused.

<Yeah, that ateron alloy doesn't fit.>

<I will note, the alloy is very similar to the material identified in the Vapr nanites.>

<Could the excavated material have been refined and used to make those nanites?> Kira asked.

<I can't rule it out as a possibility. It would *explain the Coalition's possession of the material.>*

<All right. Let's finish going through all this and give Jason our report. They'll get to the bottom of the mystery eventually.>

—   —   —

Wil looked over the attendee list for the summit Jason had organized. Amazingly, it included representatives from Lynaeda, the Aesir, and several other leading Taran research institutions. It would quite possibly be the largest gathering of brainpower in recent recorded history—or at least the last millennium.

"This is great, Jason. Really well done," Wil said, reviewing the information with his son and wife.

Jason smiled. "When I told everyone you'd be there, it was an easy sell."

"It'll be a good opportunity for you to meet everyone, too," he told his son.

"About that…" Jason hesitated. "I understand why you want me to get experience coordinating groups like this, and I'm glad I was able to reach out to everyone and begin strengthening those relationships. However, we're about to make a major move against the Coalition, and that's where I need to focus. Besides, I know next to nothing about this alien tech."

Saera met Wil's gaze. *"He's not wrong. It would be a good learning experience for him, but there are more pressing issues right now,"* she said in his mind.

"Yes, I'm the one who needs to explain the problem." Wil nodded. "You're right, Jason. I'll handle it."

Ultimately, Wil recognized that he was the one who needed to drive the discussion. While Jason was smart and capable in his own right, engineering had never been a passion for him, and he therefore lacked the technical understanding to get into the nuanced details necessary for the discussion.

Moreover, the confidential topic would take a delicate touch—one Wil hadn't yet figured out how to balance.

The reason for bringing everyone together was to draw on their combined expertise to find a solution regarding accessing the higher dimensions. The device on Earth—and, apparently, its counterpart on Zeron—were important elements to those efforts. However, the power cores gifted from the Erebus clearly offered an interesting interaction with the other tech. He hoped having different perspectives on the matter would help identify whether or not the Erebus may have intended that design feature as a trap or if it was an oversight due to their lack of understanding about the affairs in spacetime.

In any case, the discussion needed to be conducted privately and confidentially. Inviting people from different planets and cultures increased the possibility that they might encounter an Erebus or Gatekeeper sympathizer, but he hoped having a complement of Agents reading everyone on the way in would be enough to identify any potential security breaches.

The meeting itself would take place at a neutral location to avoid cultural conflicts and mitigate security concerns. He'd selected a TSS base on an asteroid with a sufficient spacedock to accommodate the visitors' ships.

So much is riding on this. We need to study the situation from every angle. Nerves weren't going to help the situation, so Wil set aside his anxiety to focus on the task at hand.

"I hope it goes well," Jason said, preparing to leave.

"Thanks. We'll talk when I get back."

Jason left the office, closing the door behind him.

"Are you sure you're okay with me being gone for the day?" Wil asked Saera once they were alone.

"I would prefer to have you here, of course, but this is

important. It'll be better having those conversations in person."

"I think so." He sighed. "I really hope it's productive."

"You've already done the legwork," Saera said. "I have every faith that you'll find a solution."

"I'd bring you with me if I could."

"This subject matter might be a little too in the weeds even for me. But I'm sure you're going to have fun in your own way."

Wil chuckled. "I'll try."

The meeting was to take place in an hour, so he gave Saera a parting hug and kiss and then gathered all the necessary technical documentation on his handheld. He headed for the TSS spaceport.

During the short voyage to the asteroid, he reviewed the information one more time. After studying the technical specifications for months, he realized he could probably recite it all from memory, which would help in the upcoming presentation.

When the transport ship arrived at the asteroid's spacedock, he exited the vessel and took a space elevator down into the rock's core.

An attendant greeted him by the elevator—a young woman dressed as a mid-rank Militia officer. "High Commander Sietinen, welcome to Echo base."

"Thank you, Chief. I appreciate you hosting this gathering on short notice."

"It's our pleasure," she replied with a bow of her head. "The conference room is this way." The officer led him down the hall.

Artificial gravity generators had been installed to mimic preferred Taran environmental conditions, like all TSS bases.

Unlike Headquarters, however, this facility was designed for utility more than comfort, so the finishes were concrete, metal, and industrial plastic rather than carpeting and warm-toned wood. Such facilities were remnants of wartime, and Wil found himself wondering, not for the first time, if they needed a cosmetic overhaul to better align with the future vision for the TSS.

They arrived at the conference room, and the chief stood aside with her arm extended to invite Wil inside. The room was well-appointed, featuring a black, oval table with seating for twelve, a refreshment station along the back wall stocked with drinks and snacks, and a digital workboard on one of the side walls. The holoprojector integrated into the table was active, displaying a slideshow of space scenes as a soothing welcome.

Wil turned off the projector, finding it more distracting than serene in his present state. This was a business meeting, not for entertainment.

He stood at the head of the table, leaning forward with his hands resting on the surface, as he watched the door.

Footfalls sounded on the metal grating in the hall. He sensed the presence of others with strong Gifts approaching. A high-level telepathic gleaning confirmed that it was the Aesir.

Dahl and Uma—one of the scientists whom Wil had met in passing on a previous occasion—entered, bowing their heads slightly to Wil in greeting.

"Thank you for coming," Wil said, standing upright.

"This matter concerns all of us," Dahl replied.

"It does."

Soon, they were joined by three scientists from Lynaeda. Six other researchers and theorists from various institutions around the Empire rounded out the group.

When everyone was seated, Wil addressed the attendees. "I appreciate you joining me here today. What I'd like to discuss concerns the fate of the Taran Empire and what actions we can take to ensure our race survives."

The attendees shifted in their seats, exchanging glances. He'd made sure Jason impressed the importance of the meeting in the invitation without sharing the specific subject matter.

"We believe the Erebus are about to invade spacetime," Wil continued. "I have a working hypothesis about how they are able to interact with our dimension and what we might be able to do to fight back against them, but I need your expertise to evaluate my assumptions and help narrow the variables. This won't be a scientific experiment where we can do iterative variations of trial and error. We need to act, and we have to get it right the first time."

Dahl was the first to speak. "The Aesir have kept to the fringes of Taran affairs for the past millennium, but we are here now because we understand the importance of this moment. We are at a crossroads where we will decide the future of our race. It's clear that we must unite if we have any chance of surviving. I hope that the others in attendance appreciate the gravity of the situation and will enter into these discussions in good faith."

Wil nodded. "Thank you, Dahl. The fact that you are all here is, I hope, an indication of those intentions."

The three members of the Lynaedan contingent stirred. "We have worked with you on multiple occasions over the past year," one of the scientists said, "and you have earned our respect. We know you wouldn't have asked us here if it wasn't for a good reason."

The individuals from the various labs remained silent but most nodded their heads.

"Let's get to it, then," Wil said. He brought up the model he'd been working on for the Earth device and the energy fields generated by the Erebus power cores, along with their hypothetical interactions with the veil to the higher dimensions. "The question is this: is there a way to make beings in a higher dimension beholden to our physics of spacetime?"

"No," one of the individual scientists, Serik, stated flatly. He worked for one of the preeminent research laboratories on Xolaeda and had been selected for the summit because of his background in interdimensional communications.

"The evidence of the models suggests otherwise," Wil countered. He played a simulation of what happened to the dimensional veil when the device on Earth was active.

Serik studied the holoprojector. "That can't be right."

"But it is. That's why I've asked all of you here. I've been staring at a model of something that should be impossible, and I need to figure out how it works, because it *does*."

"Science also said it was impossible to model the flow of subspace, and therefore jumps without a beacon network were mere fantasy," Dahl chimed in.

Wil took a slow breath. "I'm not here to set more records. I'll be honest—my motivations are purely military. I know as people of science, tactical strategy isn't normally your concern. However, I can see how something is working, but I need to know *why* it works that way in order to predict probable responses to variables. Without understanding the underlying mechanics, every move is a guess. We need precision."

Amera from Lynaeda had been quiet the whole time, but she had a contemplative sheen to her eyes. "I have a thought," she said slowly. "We tend to think of other dimensions as being stacked layers, but the reality is that it's more like nesting dolls. The results of this model don't make sense when you think of it in terms of a single stack, but in a more enveloping sense, the other dimensions are all around us at all times. This device doesn't weaken the veil in all places. It's more like a wormhole to one specific place. In that way, it does fit with the observed behavior."

"That's what I kept coming back to, as well," Wil said. "But there are a few parts that still don't fit, and I don't know why."

He went over the detailed technical observations from his studies, talking through each of the conditions and the hypothetical responses to various scenarios. To his relief, the scientists seemed to grasp the problems and understand why the anomalies were a cause for concern. They initially pushed back on some of his assumptions, but after talking everything through, they ultimately agreed that what he'd put together was sound—if not fully in line with previously understood science.

Finding solutions to the identified issues proved more difficult. They spent the better part of four hours going over the model before they decided to take a refreshment break.

This might be impossible. Wil tried to keep the sinking feeling in his gut at bay, but it was demoralizing to get confirmation about all of his fears. He saw a possible way through it, but it would be a last resort. *There has to be a better way.*

Despite his statements about the importance of the work, the civilian scientists seemed to be taking the summit as a challenging thought exercise rather than a true matter of life and death for their race. Restating the dire nature of their plight was unlikely to improve their performance, so Wil let them go about their friendly chatting. The Aesir were stoic, as always, and Amera, at least, seemed to be taking the discussion seriously.

"I'm impressed you got this far on your own," Amera said while munching on a snack. She got a wide-eyed look of wonder every time she looked at Wil; brushes with celebrity were rare for those who spent most of their time in a research lab. "The rumors of your exploits weren't exaggerations, after all."

"I wouldn't go that far," Wil replied with a slight smile.

"Well, I wouldn't have come had the request come from anyone else," she replied.

"I'm flattered."

"I didn't mean it as a compliment, no offense. I'm just wary of having my time wasted."

"I hope this has been a worthy endeavor."

She smiled. "For sure. I mean, who wouldn't want to try to solve a problem that stumped the legendary Wil Sietinen?"

Wil looked down. He was used to people talking about him that way, but it always made him uncomfortable, nonetheless. "I've had help with everything I've done."

Amera cast him a sidelong glance that silently questioned his assertion. "Happy I could be part of the team this time."

Two of the private industry scientists across the table raised their voices as a discussion they'd been having throughout the break began to escalate.

"It *would*!" the first insisted.

"It absolutely would *not*," the other countered, calmer than her counterpart. "Otherwise, we'd readily see the effects."

"What's this now?" Wil asked loudly enough for them to

notice he'd tuned into their conversation.

The first scientist scoffed. "I was just explaining how if a fish is swimming within a closed system of dyed blue water, that it would eventually turn blue from being exposed to that environment."

"And I was explaining how if that fish is transdimensional, only a portion of it is actually interacting with that dye, so any color impact on it would be inconsequential when examining the scope of the being in its transdimensional totality," the second added.

The argument was silly and seemingly off-topic, but it did share a few common elements with the Erebus problem. "Explain your reasoning," Wil requested.

The first scientist's explanation was sound in terms of conventional science, but it neglected the exceptions that the team had identified for their current scenario where the Erebus' manifestation in spacetime would only be a fraction of their total self. The second scientist, however, had—seemingly inadvertently— hit on a critical point from an angle Wil hadn't considered before.

"So, your contention is that we can radically change the local environment in spacetime, but that ultimately doesn't change a transdimensional being's core properties, since only a fraction of itself is in this dimension. It would be like putting paint on the fish—an alteration in appearance, but ultimately easy to wipe off," he summarized when she'd finished explaining her rationale.

"Pretty much." She shrank in her seat a little, her cheeks flushed from embarrassment about the ridiculousness of the topic and analogies. "Of course, that's just a fish—"

"No, I think that's exactly what we've been missing," Wil

cut in, feeling the tingle of excitement that accompanied a major breakthrough. "We talked about how these devices alter the environment in spacetime, but we haven't been looking at the conditions that will be created in the higher dimensions."

He began furiously making inputs on the tabletop, rearranging the work they had been doing to take into account the new way of thinking. The others watched silently as he typed, following along and nodding as they started to see where he was going with it.

When he finished, he pushed back in his seat to take in the new model displayed on the projector.

It works. He never would have thought to structure it that way, but it accounted for all the variables that had seemed random before.

"That's it," Amera confirmed.

Smiles spread around the table.

The two scientists who'd been arguing about the stupid other scenario looked at each other sheepishly.

"Never would have thought that was a worthwhile discussion," the first said.

Maybe there's a way we can all survive this, after all. Wil shrugged. "Inspiration can come from the strangest places."

The solution wasn't what he'd originally envisioned, but it was a serviceable approach. They'd need to activate all the Erebus energy cores as well as the devices on Earth and Zeron, which was a problem since Zeron was presently blockaded. Assuming they could find a way to activate both devices, they could then modify the TK weapon on the *Conquest* to serve as an interdimensional bore. Anything in that specific zone would become accessible from spacetime. If an Erebus was there, it could be hurt. The only remaining issue was how to ensure that the beings would be there when the *Conquest* fired the weapon.

"We have our net," Wil said, looking around the room. "Now, we need a lure."

CHAPTER 17

AFTER SPENDING YEARS tiptoeing around her wealth and influence, Raena had to admit that flexing her power was a lot more fun.

Following the strategy session with her grandparents, Dainetris' and Sietinen's legal teams had both gotten to work preparing bids to acquire dozens of companies with close ties to the Monsari Dynasty and its corporate operations. It had taken long hours over the last week to get the paperwork prepped, but everything was almost ready. By her grandfather's estimation, if all the sales went through, Monsari would lose its entire support network and would be far more likely to go down quietly.

The businesses had been divvied up to Sietinen and Dainetris according to valuation and function. Those falling to Dainetris largely complemented DGE's ship manufacturing operations, such as suppliers for interior furnishings, component manufacturers, and a handful of marketing and public relations firms, which could spearhead future mentorship and training initiatives. Though the idea had started as a massive 'screw you' to Monsari, Raena had quickly found herself getting excited about the possibilities.

"Why didn't we think to do this sooner?" she wondered aloud to Ryan as she looked over the final draft of an acquisition offer to send to a cargo crate manufacturer.

Her husband looked up from his own reading. "Because hostile takeovers are generally considered… well, hostile."

She smiled. "Right. I don't mean take them over like we're doing now, but rather just invest in other business areas. We've put in the time and attention to rebuild DGE, and it's time we branched out."

"We hadn't planned to make those expansions for another two years." The tension was back in Ryan's tone—that same concern he'd been exhibiting so much lately. She still wasn't sure if it stemmed from self-doubt or if the scale of this endeavor had exacerbated his natural inclination to worry about poor outcomes.

"I'm not thrilled about accelerating that capital outlay, either, but we have one chance to hit them hard," Raena replied.

He nodded. "I know, which is why I agreed to it."

"There's a lot of potential upside here, though. Bringing these operations in-house will reduce expenses related to subcontractor mark-ups as well as condense production timelines and make our operations more agile. I think this is the start of something great."

"Forgive me if that's not my top concern right now."

She set down the offer contract. "It's a lot all at once, I know. Let's just get these final offers out and call it an early night."

"One night doesn't change the pattern. We're about to start

a family, Raena, and now we're taking on all these new companies to keep track of, too. Our time together is already limited, but after this…"

"Hey, that's what we have staff for. We'll use this as an opportunity to promote from within and reward the people who've contributed to our success. Those managers can handle the new operations. I want more than anything to focus on us."

"That's sweet of you to say, but I can tell how excited you are about all this."

"I…" Raena didn't know how to reply. She didn't want to lie to him, and it was true that the prospect of making a massive political move against a family that had been a nuisance in her life was quite satisfying.

"What we're doing here isn't a magical fix to all our problems," Ryan continued. "It'll make an impact, no doubt, but I worry that Monsari is going to hit back even harder. So yes, it's concerning."

"Taking away their support network is going to cripple them."

"Perhaps, but they're not going to let go of their power so easily."

She shrugged. "Let them cling to life—it won't make a difference."

"But it could, Raena. It could when their retaliations might target us on a personal level. They have to know we're behind this. From everything you've said about these people, they are cold and ruthless and consider Gifted people like us to be lesser beings."

"I think most of that's just big talk."

"I mean, for fok's sake, they shot at your dad!"

She couldn't argue that point. "Okay, maybe not *all* talk."

He took a steadying breath. "Look at it this way—if your sworn enemy found a way to take you down, wouldn't you throw everything you had left into trying to bring them down with you?"

Raena considered the hypothetical. "I suppose so."

"Right. So, *we're* that enemy. I agree that there's probably nothing that could prevent Monsari's downfall at this point, but I'm bracing for a final swing toward Dainetris on their way down. And I fear it will be personal, not political—it has all the fodder for a smear campaign. That makes me worry about your well-being."

She reached out and took his hand. "I'll watch my back, don't worry."

"No, it's what they'd be willing to do right to our faces that bothers me."

"That's why we have security, and public relations people, and—"

"And if that's not enough?" The urgency in Ryan's tone had intensified.

"I don't know."

"Well, I think we need a backup plan. And the only protection is to have the public on our side."

"That's been the intention all along," Raena said.

"Not like this." He spread his hands on his desktop. "Everything we've been trying to do is to get people to support us as leaders. What we need to do now is show them that they don't need us at all."

"Pardon?"

"Monsari can hurt us if they believe we have anything to lose. But if we willingly give up our power first, we're not a threat."

"Why would we give everything up?"

"Why wouldn't we?" he countered.

The statement caught Raena by surprise. They'd been working so hard to maintain the balance of power that it seemed crazy to walk away now. "If we step down, others with far more sinister ambitions will gladly fill that vacuum. We've been over that scenario before."

"I know. But maybe we've been trying to stave off the inevitable."

She crossed her arms. "I'm not ready to give up yet. Frankly, I'm surprised that you are."

"I'm just worn down, Raena. I see what we're planning to do, and I no longer recognize us. The people I thought we were wouldn't be stooping to these levels. I can't help wondering if we'd be better off walking away before we're lost completely."

Raena sat in contemplative silence. "I don't think it's us losing ourselves. I believe it's actually that we're maturing. We're shedding the naïve delusion that everyone can get along and we can have peace if we all just 'work together'. That's not reality. There are evil people with horrible intentions, and there's no reasoning with them. Some enemies require firm, decisive action. I'm no longer afraid to do what's necessary."

He looked down, avoiding her gaze. "Okay."

"Do you disagree?"

"Not entirely. I just… I never wanted any of this responsibility."

"It's precisely for that reason that you make such a fair, compassionate leader. The ideas you've had for career development are unlike what anyone else is doing. There's a reason that you have the highest approval rating of anyone on the Council."

He sighed and leaned back in his seat. "Those opinions can change overnight."

"Perseverance is the only option, Ryan. Any journey worth having is going to change you. I for one, think that a little toughening up is going to serve us well in the long run."

"You're probably right about that."

She smiled. "Of course I am. I would have thought that we've spent enough time together by now that you'd know that." Really, she was wrong about plenty of things, but she wasn't about to admit that now.

"All right, then we'll stick to the plan," he acquiesced.

"You can sound a little more enthusiastic about it. We're about to deal a blow that will cripple a scourge to the Empire."

He softened. "You're not wrong about that."

She picked up her tablet to finish familiarizing herself with the specific terms of the acquisition. Ryan turned back to his own assignment.

We are *changing, but we're going to need every shred of ruthlessness to take down this enemy.* No more playing nice. She was ready for the fight of her life.

—   —   —

Celine stared at the panicked messages flooding her inbox. There'd been at least two dozen contractors who'd received bids for total buyouts in the past day, all valued well above market rates. Every single one of the offers traced back to either Sietinen or Dainetris.

Those crafty bastards. She'd be impressed if it wasn't so bomaxed infuriating.

She pulled up the messages on her handheld and stormed

over to the CFO's office down the hall.

Harold jumped when she barged in without knocking.

"Have you seen what's going on?" she asked the older man.

"You'll have to be more specific."

"The bomaxed acquisitions." Celine cast the messages from her handheld to the holoprojector on Harold's desk.

He warily eyed the information. "What is this?"

"The foking Sietinens have orchestrated a hostile takeover of our subsidiaries and business partners, that's what."

"Which?"

"*All* of them." She couldn't help laughing a little, saying it out loud. The entire thing sounded ridiculous.

In all fairness, there wasn't that much money involved. It was more the boldness of the move that surprised her—a surgical and aggressive act for a family that had made such a show of trying to get everyone to play along. It confirmed for her that they had become an untenable danger to both Monsari and society at large.

Harold gaped at her. "All? That's…"

"Well, it depends on where you draw the line for who could be considered an MPS business associate. But of the companies who had dealings with Accounts Payable or Accounts Receivable in the last year, there are pending offers on all of the top twenty, plus a handful of others. I've also gotten word that their own subcontractors and competitors have been receiving offers, as well."

Harold's slack-jawed surprise turned to grim worry. "With the amount we outsource now…"

"I know." Celine sat down in one of the guest chairs across from his desk. "We need to submit counter-bids. Immediately."

He worked his mouth. "I don't know that we're in a position to do that."

"We can't afford not to."

"No, I mean, we don't have the kind of capital available to counter these offers. Maybe a handful, but nowhere near all of them."

"How…" She faded out. She'd known they were headed for lean times, but she hadn't realized they were already that far down the path. *Does Sietinen know, or was this meant to just inconvenience us?*

It didn't matter either way. The move had dealt a crippling blow that may prove impossible to overcome.

Celine took a centering breath. "What are our options?"

"Prioritize a select few companies and submit bids on those."

She could already see how that would play out. Submitting those competing offers would reveal which companies Monsari valued most, and Sietinen would then be able to increase their bids until Monsari could no longer compete. Trying to stop these takeovers through financial means would only hamper their ability to take other actions by depleting the few resources they had left. She'd need to find another tactic.

"What about legal recourse? Is what they're doing above board?"

Harold shrugged. "As far as financial law, there's nothing illegal about it. I couldn't tell you if they've committed any kind of procedural violation in the notice process or something like that you might be able to use. You'd have to talk to Sharon about that."

Then Sharon, Monsari's head legal advisor, would be her next stop. Celine stood up. "This isn't public yet, so keep it to yourself. We'll have a senior management meeting once I have a better handle on our options."

"Okay." His tone and body language were of a man resigned to his fate.

I thought he'd be more committed to the fight. She'd fire him and find a replacement— someone with more commitment and drive—as soon as she had the means to do so. For now, it was sounding like she couldn't afford to make any staffing changes. *What a bomaxed shiteshow.*

It didn't seem like the day could get any worse, but she wouldn't make any assumptions until she'd had a chance to meet with Sharon. With a parting nod to Harold, she left his office to find the legal rep.

When Celine arrived at Sharon's office, the lights were off.

"She's not in right now, my lady," Sharon's executive assistant stated. Celine didn't know the young woman's actual name, but she looked like a 'Jane'.

"I need to speak with her immediately."

"She's out attending to a personal matter and has asked not to be disturbed. I can find someone else on the legal team to—"

"It must be Sharon, and I have to speak with her now."

The young woman swallowed hard as the pressure of contradictory orders warred on her face. "I'll get you her personal number."

Celine would have preferred that the woman call Sharon herself, but the response was a reasonable course of action for someone trapped between competing requests. The contact card popped up on Celine's handheld a moment later. "Thank you."

She took a purposeful stride back toward her own office to

make the call. Once in the privacy of the space, she initiated the call on the holoprojector above her desk, sure to have her professional workspace prominently featured in the background. Sharon should be at her post, and Celine wanted to drive home the point.

The other woman's face appeared on the holoprojector, her brown skin surprisingly lined for someone with access to so many preventative measures to hold back the tides of time. "My lady, I didn't realize you had this direct line."

"I'm resourceful. Where are you?"

"Dealing with a personal matter." The backdrop of an unadorned wall did nothing to reveal her potential whereabouts. A 'personal matter' could be anything from family issues to a tryst with a secret lover. Frankly, Celine didn't care.

"Whatever it is can wait. If you don't get back here right now, there won't be a job left for you to return to."

"Is that a threat?"

"It's a fact. Sietinen has staged a coup. There are pending offers on dozens of the corporations we rely on in the course of standard business operations. If those sales go through, it's over."

Sharon's eyes widened at that, and her shoulders tensed. "When did this happen?"

"A few hours ago. It took time to confirm it was real and as widespread as it appeared. It is."

"Fok." The other woman took a deep breath, looking up and off to the side as she thought. "These bids were made directly to the boards of each company?"

"That's my understanding."

"I'll need to pull copies of each public filing."

"Already compiled. Everything appears to be in order, but you have a way of seeing things others miss."

"I'm offworld, so I really *can't* get there right now. But send everything over and I'll review it on the way. I can be there by…" she looked away again, "15:00. Tell them to not sign anything before then."

"I'll do what I can to stall."

"Talk soon." Sharon ended the vidcall.

Celine transferred the relevant information to Sharon, hoping there was some technical detail that could snag the deals. She'd have to wait to find out.

In the meantime, she had her own preparations to make.

After the revelation about the state of Monsari's finances, she went to check the exact figures for the first time in her life. It was shameful she hadn't done so sooner, when she thought about it. However, having 'more than enough' had always been a given in her life. High Dynasty worth was measured in the quadrillions, so why would an exact account balance matter?

Her advisors had certainly warned her about the dire state of affairs. She must have dismissed the alerts, just as she'd ignored the warnings about the voydite running low. There were so many alarmists out there, everyone couldn't be right.

Except, apparently, they were. Her stomach twisted at the thought. *How much more was I wrong about?*

She shoved away the notion. Second-guessing now wouldn't accomplish anything other than heartache.

The account information populated on her screen. Her stomach sank as she looked it over. It was even worse than she'd feared.

Taking a calming breath, she closed out from the banking details and brought up an accounting of Monsari's other assets.

While credits were the most flexible, there were plenty of real estate holdings and other properties. Most were critical to business functions—useless now that the voydite mine was dry, but for the sake of appearances, she couldn't liquidate everything—so she'd need to find something more frivolous.

Her attention landed on Monsari's private island on Alushia. All of the High Dynasties had their own slice of paradise on the most exclusive resort planet in the Taran Empire, and Celine had many fond memories from her time on that world. But, of all the assets, it would be the easiest to sell off for some quick additional capital.

She reached out to the appropriate contacts and began arranging the sale. The real estate agent expressed that finding a buyer should take no more than a few days, if not hours. The perceived prestige of the place combined with the fact that Lower Dynasties were always looking for opportunities to increase their social standing meant that a bidding war was likely. Celine would be happy to eke out every credit from the sale she could.

It'll confirm all their suspicions. There was no way around it, nor did it matter what Sietinen thought of her now. She was taking action to secure her survival.

By the time she'd finished the arrangements, her head was throbbing and she desperately wanted a stiff drink. She was just about to pour herself a generous glass of liquor when a priority vidcall popped up on her desk—from Sharon.

Celine eagerly accepted the incoming request. "Did you find anything?"

To Celine's relief, Sharon smiled. "I did."

"Well? Let's hear it."

"I had the pilot drop us out from subspace so I could tell

you right away. I found an error in one of the service procedures, which I traced to twenty-two other bids. It's not a lot, but it could delay the sales for those companies—and it's some of the big ones."

"Delay… or void?"

"It's a clerical error, not an illegal move. Worst case, they could refile the entire bid with corrected data."

"In which case, we'd still need to come up with a higher purchase price."

"That's right."

"Except…" Celine's heart rate accelerated as the thought formed, "what if we were able to put in a bid and have it accepted before Sietinen or Dainetris re-files?"

"Well, yes, once a bid is accepted, it's binding."

"So, there might be a way."

"You'd have to coordinate the timing with the seller. It's not *strictly* legal—more in a gray area where you hope questions don't get asked."

"That's the least of my concerns right now."

"You know," Sharon got a devious gleam in her eyes, "if we ran those new bids through a third-party holding company, Monsari would be immune from any potential recourse."

And ideas like that are why I keep her around. A slow smile curled Celine's lips. "Now *that* is a very good idea."

—   —   —

Since submitting the final round of acquisition bids with Raena, Ryan hadn't been able to shake the feeling that something wasn't right. He'd chalked it up to nerves at first, but the persistent feeling reminded him of the premonitions

Raena would sometimes get since her visit to the nexus. While he didn't consider himself to be nearly as in tune with the energetic forces of the universe, he had found his instincts to be more reliable than not.

The fact that he had a bad feeling about the hostile takeover plan worried him, though he understood and agreed with the logic of the approach. Since Raena and Cris hadn't expressed concern about it, Ryan had followed their lead, hoping the seemingly precognizant dread would subside. Instead, it was only getting worse.

By the time afternoon rolled around, the feeling had intensified to the point that it seemed dangerous to remain silent.

He went to find Raena in her office, deciding the matter would best be discussed face-to-face. "I think there's a problem."

She looked up at him from her desk. "What?"

Ryan explained the feeling to her as best he could, and he also shared a telepathic impression. "I don't know what it means," he said as he finished, "but everything is telling me that something bad is coming."

Raena nodded, her lips pursed as she considered the statement. "I'm sorry I didn't listen to you earlier when you expressed concern about what we were doing. I was so certain this was the right thing to do."

"It still might be," he said.

"I trust these feelings, however vague. It's an alert that we're missing something vital, and that the events are pivotal in one way or another."

"Unseating a High Dynasty is a big deal—the kind of event that can shift the course of the Empire. Is this feeling trying to tell us that we're doing the right thing and it might fail, or are we on the wrong path?"

Raena slumped in her chair. "I guess we'll find out."

"For what it's worth, I think it's the former. It didn't get intense until *after* we put in the bids, so that seems more like a warning that something is going wrong rather than the original action being the bad thing."

"In that case, maybe we can figure out the issue and get ahead of it."

"That's why I came to you."

"Okay, let's talk it through." Raena stood and began to pace. "We just submitted acquisition bids to several dozen of Monsari's closest allies. Assuming that relationship goes both ways, it makes sense that those companies would contact Monsari to tell them what's going on."

"Agreed."

Raena nodded. "So, a few hours ago, Monsari presumably received dozens of panicked messages, and they're probably now trying to figure out how to counter those bids."

"But if they're as broke as we think, they won't have the funds."

"Right. Which leaves legal recourse."

"Nothing we're doing is illegal," Ryan said.

"No, but it's a complicated transaction, which means there could be arguments that certain details were overlooked."

"We have a pretty great legal team."

"We do." She nodded thoughtfully. "But mistakes can happen, and you can bet Monsari would uncover them if that's their only play."

Ryan scowled. "That doesn't make sense."

"What about it?"

"Sorry, I don't mean the legal technicalities. What I don't understand is why that minutia would register on the cosmic-pattern scale."

"Yeah, that does seem like a minor thing to get a universal-energies hunch about."

"Maybe it's just a good ol' fashioned gut feeling informed by Monsari proving themselves time and again to be tricky bastards."

"That wouldn't surprise me. I can't say I haven't had concerns myself."

He leaned against the back of one of the guest chairs. "Regardless, I think your logic holds for a potential filing issue. But I'm not sure what to do about it."

"I guess we could have the team proactively check everything to make sure all proverbial i's were dotted and t's crossed."

"Not a bad idea."

Raena had just started to reach for the comm controls on her desk when an incoming message from Cris lit up on the surface.

"Good or bad news?" Raena asked Ryan with the weary smile.

"Given our discussion, I'm guessing the latter."

She nodded and answered. "Hey, Grandpa. What can I do for you? I'm here with Ryan."

"Excellent, I'm glad I caught both of you," he replied. "I have good news."

Raena and Ryan exchanged surprised glances, but Ryan had no complaints about having been wrong. "We could use some of that."

"I just got word that Calrosi Enterprises has convened to

review our offer," Cris revealed.

Raena brightened. "That's great!"

"Well, they may vote against it."

"But it wasn't an outright 'no'," Raena countered. "At the offer price, putting it to a vote, it's too good a deal for them to turn down."

Cris shrugged. "Stranger things have happened. But I think we'll get them in the end."

"And then what?"

"It's tricky, because we can't tell them what to say without losing all credibility. However, staffing changes are common enough after an acquisition. Marina has offered to step in as interim CEO until we can find suitable long-term leadership."

Ryan nodded. "Good plan." He wasn't particularly close with Raena's maternal grandmother, but he knew her well as a longtime advisor to the Sietinen family. Marina and Cris had forged a strong working relationship over the years, despite a somewhat adversarial start during Cris' teenage years, based on what Ryan had heard.

"What about the other companies?" Raena asked.

"We'll need to get more creative with the management and oversight of those, assuming all the sales go through," Cris said. "I don't suppose there are any you'd like to be involved with actively managing?"

Raena glanced at Ryan before replying. "No, I can't take on anything else full-time right now. But, I'm happy to assist with interviewing prospective CEOs."

"All right."

"There are a handful of companies where I'd like to sit on the board," Ryan chimed in. He realized he'd been taking a back seat with the efforts and needed to step up as a leader, even if it was just in a part-time advisory capacity. After the discussions he'd had with Raena about synergies in the business operations with several of the prospective acquisitions, it made sense for him to take an active role and strengthen relations between DGE and the new operations.

"That would be wonderful," Cris said with a smile. "We can go over those details once the bids are accepted."

"When are we supposed to hear back?"

"Should be imminently," Cris replied. His smile faded. "Or, right now…" He faded off in a concerning way.

"What is it?" Ryan asked.

"I just got a notice from one of the companies we bid on stating that there's a problem with our filing and they've placed our offer on hold." His eyes darted back and forth, apparently reading through information on his monitor. "It's citing a violation of a statute I've never heard of. Fok, another one just came in from a different company, citing the same thing."

Raena groaned. "I have no doubt who's directing those communications."

Ryan went to check his messages to see if he'd received any from Dainetris' target companies. His heart sank when he saw three notices already in his inbox. "Shite, same here."

"I guess we know what your gut feeling was about," Raena said in his mind.

His chest tightened. *"As usual, I wish I hadn't been right."*

"We need to find out what went wrong in the paperwork and refile," Cris said, taking on a matter-of-fact tone as he focused on the issue.

Legalese definitely wasn't Ryan's strength, but his time as a Ward had made him great at following detailed instructions. He read over the notice about the violation and cross-referenced it with the original submission.

While he was reading, another half-dozen notices arrived, all citing the same deficiency that was just ambiguous enough to elude them. *Where did we go wrong?*

At first, everything appeared to be in order. Then, on his fourth read, he noticed the problem.

"Shite! I found it," he told the others. "For proposed transactions over three-hundred-million credits, we were supposed to file with the representative government for the business' registered headquarters and *then* submit to the general assembly. We did simultaneous submissions for everything."

"Is there a timeframe stated for the delay?" Cris asked.

Ryan shook his head. "No, and I think that's where things went wrong. It just has to be in *first*, which is stupid since there could be a one-second delay and it would meet requirements, even though that's not long enough to make a difference. But since there's no stated waiting period, I can see why the legal assistants dumped everything in one batch."

Cris sighed. "It's a technicality no one would care about—"

"—Until they do," Raena completed for him. "That devious witch."

"We'll have to refile," Ryan said. "There was a clerical error."

"Okay." Cris sat forward in his seat. "I'll communicate this to the team, and you can talk to your people. I don't expect it will take long to resubmit."

Ryan nodded. "I'm on it."

"Okay, talk so—" Cris cut off abruptly, his cheeks flushing. "What the fok?"

"What?" Ryan and Raena questioned simultaneously.

"Because of the error, our original bids have been rejected—that makes sense. But another company has already submitted an offer and had it accepted!"

"Foking Monsari," Raena spat.

"It's a shell corporation, but yeah, most likely," Cris said.

Ryan's gut lurched. *That means it's all the largest bids. Those were the most important.*

He was about to resign himself to defeat, since he hadn't cared much about this plan, anyway, but then he remembered Intelix Designs, the company he'd wanted to buy because they were the underdogs. They were one of this batch that had been rejected.

"I think there's a way to fight this," he said, meeting Raena's gaze and then Cris' on camera. "It'll take a couple more steps, but we wanted citizens on our side, and this'll be the way to do it."

CHAPTER 18

JASON REVIEWED THE information his sister had sent over about the proposed business acquisitions. He didn't know where she'd dug up some of the financial connections, but the data filled in many of the missing pieces the TSS had been missing for the Coalition's funding trail.

"Well, that explains where the guard mechs came from," he commented to Laura.

She nodded pensively. "I wish we'd talked with your family sooner. I never would have thought to look for these connections."

There were clear reasons why they hadn't leveraged his familial ties before, and Jason didn't need to explain. "These companies have done nothing overtly illegal, but I suspect if we look into their business dealings, we'll eventually be able to trace either sales or 'lost inventory' to Coalition outfits."

"If MPS has these armored mechs for private security, that means that the Coalition has a supply line to them, as well."

"The armaments we can see on the surface of the occupied worlds now might not be everything they have at their disposal.

We'll need to keep that in mind as we plan a raid."

Laura's eyes widened. "Are we finally going in?"

"As far as I'm concerned, it's now or never. But, I need to run the tactical plan up the chain."

"What have you worked out?" she asked.

"We've identified the key sites, in order of priority. The goal is to hit everything at once, but the blockades make it difficult for us to move in."

"I hope this isn't overstepping, sir, but I'd like to request placement on one of the field teams."

"It's not as glorious as it may seem in the vid feeds."

"This isn't about glory, but justice," she said. "Everything we've done up until now is research as hypotheticals. I want to see the look on these fokers' faces when they're brought to their knees."

He couldn't argue with her passion or the sentiment. "I'll tell you what. If we get a green light from Command on this, you can be on the team that goes after Celine herself."

Laura's mouth dropped open. "Stars! Really?"

Jason smiled. "If that's what you want. You've earned it."

She hesitated. "Are you not going?"

"Believe me, I want to. However, I think my presence might be taken as a political statement, and I don't want to see that used against the TSS."

"That's fair. Well, I'd be honored to help represent the team."

"It's a plan." Jason checked the time on his desk. "All right, I've got a strategy meeting with Ron and Gina. I'll make sure you're on the roster for the op."

"Thank you, sir."

He left the task force office and headed for the nearby

conference room where the team conducted its formal briefings. This was a matter for Agents. They'd need to be able to question the details and speak freely without looking indecisive in front of their Militia subordinates.

Ron and Gina were waiting for him when he arrived. They nodded in welcome.

"Time to turn all the plans into reality," he said as he sat down.

"About that." Gina folded her hands on the tabletop. "We have a problem."

Another? Jason sighed. The operation was definitely cursed, that settled it. "What now?"

"A situation has been brought to our attention," she said. "It's one that may have been going on for a while, but new information has surfaced."

Jason braced himself. "Go on."

"For background, a few weeks ago, we had an undercover op running on Pomua. Per protocol, we alerted the local Enforcers about having people in the area. Well, the undercover team was subsequently attacked by a rogue group we're sure is linked to the Coalition. Except, the Coalition should have had no way to know we were there—unless they got a tipoff from the Enforcers."

"We'd expected some would turn," Jason said. Corruption of local Enforcers wasn't unheard of, especially in the Outer Colonies. The authorities tried to stay on top of it, but bribes to individuals to turn a blind eye to certain dealings were difficult to police.

Ron nodded. "Right. The unusual part was when a TSS rescue team was sent to retrieve our operatives, they discovered that a supply cache meant to support the field team had already been raided. Now, the Guard had no knowledge of that cache, and the details about its location had only been relayed through encrypted channels. Meaning, if the Coalition knew its location, they must have *somehow* cracked the communications encryption."

Jason frowned. "No, it's impossible to crack without a key. The TSS team must have revealed the location, voluntarily or not."

"And that was the official conclusion during the investigation—that the Coalition must have extracted knowledge about the cache via telepathy. Case closed," Gina said. "But then, today we got this." She cast a report to the holoprojector on the conference table. "Another field team found a vulnerability in the communications network."

Jason's stomach twisted. "In what way?"

Ron modified the image on the holoprojector to show a diagram of a communications grid. He indicated a communication beacon near Pomua. "See this here? The system is acknowledging receipt of messages, but they aren't relayed anywhere. It's like the broadcasts are going into a black hole. But the messages are bouncing around the other beacons in the area, so it wasn't obvious that this one was a dead end."

"Because it's an out-point," Jason surmised. He hadn't received much education in his paternal grandmother's family business, but he understood the basics of how VComm's communication grid worked—and how the TSS handled its own information dissemination using those same relays, albeit via separate encrypted channels. "This couldn't have been done by hacking. It was set up by someone inside VComm. They're the only ones with access."

Gina nodded somberly. "The tip about our team being on

Pomua may not have come through the Enforcers at all. If the Coalition is tapped into these private communications, it would explain how they have been two steps ahead of us this whole time. The team's location. The supply cache. And any number of other situations where the Coalition has seemingly had inside knowledge. All that can trace back to information exploited through this vulnerability."

Jason held up his hands. "This goes way beyond the Coalition task force."

"That's why we came directly to you," Gina said. "You can present it to the High Commander or whoever else."

There was ample cause for concern. The revelation meant that the Coalition had infiltrated at least one High Dynasty corporation—a trusted ally. Jason didn't doubt his great-uncle's loyalties, but there could be moles or corruption at lower levels within VComm or the dynasty itself. There was no telling which other organizations may be compromised.

"I'll run this up the chain," Jason assured the other Agents.

"Okay," Gina said. "I've already started thinking about how to account for this breach in our planning."

"Good." Jason returned his mind to the upcoming op. "Let's settle this."

— — —

The summit had given Wil a lot to think about. His discussions with the other scientists had confirmed many of his hypotheses and had also introduced new angles for him to consider. On the whole, he had deemed the event a success, though he still had some lingering questions.

Upon returning to TSS Headquarters, he'd immediately

received a message from Jason requesting to meet right away.

"Good news and bad news," Jason began as he sat down in a guest chair in Wil's office. "Though, the bad is also kind of good, because it explains some things. There's a breach in the comm relays." He explained the situation and outlined the information he'd been given.

"That really does explain a lot," Wil agreed when his son had finished. "If they've been intercepting TSS communications, what else might they be manipulating?"

"With this access, they could mess with media feeds. Anything, really. But now we know about it, so we can adjust accordingly. I trust you'll make the appropriate calls?"

"Yes, I'll make sure this goes right to the top at VComm," Wil confirmed. "Now, what's the good news?"

"We've begun transporting people off some of the target worlds. The citizens have been able to get out through the blockades, even if we can't get in. If all goes well, we'll be able to relocate about fourteen million people over the next two days."

"Excellent."

"I know it barely scratches the surface of the populations, but it's a start."

That's the best we can do for now. Wil nodded. "I'm glad it worked out. Do you have the strike plan complete?"

"Yes." Jason made an entry on his handheld, and the file popped up on Wil's desk. "We're ready to go whenever you give the word."

"Thanks, I'll review these." There'd be coordination to do with the Guard, so he'd have to make sure the plan optimized the resources—especially given the communication breech.

Jason shifted to the edge of his chair, ready to stand. "Well, that's all I've got."

"More than enough for now, thank you. And great work."

"Sure thing. Oh, and how did the summit go?"

"I got what I needed."

His son nodded. "Good."

"Is Lexi back yet?"

"She's due to arrive this afternoon. They found a replacement instructor to take over for the rest of the term."

"I'm glad the program is working out."

"Me too. We might need to look into expanding Headquarters to accommodate more like it."

"One thing at a time." The list of other projects was getting longer by the day. *We need the Coalition problem resolved so we can move on with our lives.*

"Right. Yeah. Let me know if you need anything else," Jason said, getting up to go.

"Be ready for anything."

"You've got it."

Wil brought up the tactical plan Jason had sent over and began reading through it. *This is going to be over soon, one way or another.*

CHAPTER 19

RAENA ADMIRED HER husband. "Ryan, I have to say, that plan was a stroke of genius."

Ryan shrugged, blushing a little. "I guess I've been hanging out with the right people to learn a thing or two."

He was being modest, but Raena knew trying to drive home the compliment wouldn't change anything. The two of them had stumbled into High Dynasty life and found their way together. Having grown up as a Ward—living in the shadow of the Sietinen Dynasty—Ryan knew more than he'd ever let on. While he didn't voice big ideas all that often, when he did, they were always astute and creative. This situation was no different.

Monsari's move to circumvent Sietinen's and Dainetris' bids on the subsidiary companies had thrown a wrench in their plans. However, Ryan's proposal for how to turn things back to their favor might actually allow them to reap a net benefit after the setback.

The plan reminded Raena of the labor revolutions she'd read about back on Earth. Whenever employees were dissatisfied with their working conditions, or pay, or any other aspect of their employment, they'd band together and form a union to increase their collective bargaining power. Ryan had suggested a similar principle to get around their current problems. The board members of the companies were corrupt and easily swayed by Monsari's influence, but the entire worker population of the companies was much more interested in their own well-being—the workers'—not the shareholders'. So, all they had to do was make the case to the workforce that a change in company ownership would be to their benefit, then sit back and let the workers take care of the rest.

Within hours of presenting the business case to middle-managers for a sale, there'd been a walkout at Intelix's headquarters office. Then, the floodgates had opened as workers at other companies followed suit. The boards were freaking out—as evidenced by their utter lack of public commentary on the matter—and emergency meetings had already been set for at least two dozen of the target companies in response to the strikes.

"No matter what Monsari tells them, they'll need to cancel the proposed purchase agreements with that shady shell company and accept our new bids instead. Otherwise, they won't have companies left to manage," Raena said.

Ryan smiled. "That's the idea."

"You're more cunning than you let on."

He shrugged. "I'm just a realist. I've been a menial worker, so I get what it's like. Individually, we might not be able to do a lot, but collectively, it's those grunts who keep the Empire humming along. Everything would quickly fall apart if one day all those people decided to say 'no'."

"Strength in numbers."

"And why I've always tried to put the workers first with how I manage DGE. Sure, we use robotics and automation in some capacities, but people are at the heart of the company."

Raena nodded. "Celine could have learned a lot from you."

"People like her don't change their perspective. She'll never see her workers as anything more than cogs in a machine."

He may be right about that, but they'd never find out. Soon, Monsari would fall. Raena's heart skipped a beat at the thought.

"I think it's happening today," she said.

"Is that so?" Ryan got a contemplative, distant look in his eyes. "I never thought I'd be a part of something like this."

"It'll go down in the history books."

He shook his head. "That's not what I mean." He turned to look at her. "This was done to my own family all those years ago. Other powerful people decided that they needed to go away, and so they orchestrated the Dynasty's fall. And now I'm doing the same to someone else."

"What happened to your Dainetris ancestors was wrong. They were good people who were silenced for speaking out against the Priesthood. This is different. We're the ones *stopping* corruption."

"Monsari won't see it that way."

Victors write the history books. Raena believed that she and her family were operating on the side of good, but it really was all a matter of perspective. Monsari certainly wasn't acting with the intention of doing evil for evil's sake. By whatever moral code Monsari operated, Raena would be viewed as the antagonist.

"I know in my heart this is the right thing to do," she said after a pause.

"I agree. That doesn't mean I need to feel good about it."

She nodded. "Sympathy for our enemies is what separates us from animals."

"Let's hope our people remember that as they go on the hunt."

— — —

"They *what*?!" Celine exclaimed.

Grant took a step backward, averting his gaze. "The boards have a fiduciary responsibility, so—"

Celine let out a bitter laugh. *The Sietinens outmaneuvered us. There's nothing left to do.*

She'd tried to be the dam holding back the flood, but there were simply too many cracks to patch. The trickle had already turned into a steady stream, and now it was just a matter of time before the entire structure came crashing down.

Everything she'd dedicated her career—her life—to achieve was now a meaningless sidenote in history. The fate of the Taran race now solely rested with others. As much as her instincts told her to keep fighting, she recognized that it would be futile.

She walked over to her office window to stare out at the estate grounds while she composed herself. "We don't have a choice now. They've taken the lead. But we can still go out on our own terms."

— — —

Wil massaged his temples, trying to relieve the pressure in his head. So much could go wrong, but postponing any further would lead to even worse results.

There was no reason to delay military action against Monsari any longer. They had all the evidence they needed to make arrests, and the subsidiary purchase agreements now in the works on Tararia would ensure continuity of business operations. This was as good a time as any to make the move.

Jason had reiterated concerns about communicating sensitive information to the Guard, which had Wil on edge. Nonetheless, he'd vowed to partner with Admiral Mathaen, and he wouldn't go back on his word. There was a way to play it where the TSS could maintain confidentiality and control while not making it look like a coup.

He called up the Guard's leader. When Mathaen's face appeared on the viewscreen, Wil gave him a friendly nod. "We're ready to move in."

"Oh." The admiral nodded. "Okay. Tell me where you need us."

"I'll send over the tactical support plan." Wil had already figured out the minimum amount of information he could provide, and for the least key areas, to satisfy the careful balance.

"Whatever you need, you'll have it."

Wil released a relieved breath that he hadn't met any resistance. "I'm glad we're on the same side with this one."

"Me too."

"Talk to you on the other side." Wil ended the call. *How different will things be when this is over?*

—   —   —

"Hold for final confirmation," Jason told his team. He wished more than anything that he could have been out in the field with them, but the political situation was too sensitive to risk it.

As it stood, Sietinen and Dainetris had already taken a direct stand against Monsari and its associates, so having a military-backed Sietinen storm into Celine's office to arrest her would look like an abuse of power. Jason and his father had intentionally left the management of the seizure to their trusted team members so the media could only refer to it as a 'TSS operation' and keep the Sietinen name out of it.

He'd have to settle for body cam footage to keep an eye on the events. However, one benefit of doing it that way was that he'd be able to watch all the events go down simultaneously. They were limited with which sites they could raid due to the blockade situation, but the TSS still had access to a number of critical locations, including the Monsari estate itself on Tararia.

Live feeds from key team members were displayed on a multi-panel grid in the Coalition task force's office. Only Zak was present while all other members of his team were out in the field assisting the armed raid teams.

Zak took a deep breath. "Shite, this is really happening. We're bringing down a High Dynasty."

"We've vowed to bring down the Coalition, so going after Monsari—the head of their funding—is a key part of the deal. I can't guarantee the actions we take today will eliminate the Coalition threat entirely, but it will go a long way."

"I can't wait to see the looks on their faces when justice comes knocking at the door," Zak grumbled. "Serves these bastards right."

"Let's not make this personal."

"Isn't it, sir?" Zak countered. "Didn't Monsari try to vote against legalizing Gifted abilities?"

"Yes, they did," Jason admitted.

"Then we don't owe them any courtesy."

While Jason agreed with the sentiment, he was aware of the complex dynamics. Stripping Monsari of their political position required exerting what some might consider an overreach of power, which was arguably what Monsari themselves had been doing. While he genuinely believed the TSS' and Guards' actions were justified, they couldn't risk being viewed as the monsters they sought to destroy.

The two men returned their attention to the camera feeds.

"It would have been fun to be out there, but this really is the best view," Zak said.

Jason could feel the young man's disappointment, but he appreciated the positive attitude. He smiled at Zak. "My thoughts exactly."

Zak checked a notification on the desktop. "We have confirmation that all teams are in place."

"Good. We'll begin momentarily," Jason said. He looked toward the door for any sign of his father. While Jason had been given the authority to oversee the operation, it was appropriate for the High Commander to give the official order—especially given the magnitude of what they were about to do.

The teams wouldn't be able to hold for long without drawing suspicion. *Should we go ahead...?*

The door opened at last, and Wil entered. "Sorry I'm late. It's been one of those days."

"Everyone is in position," Jason reported.

"Sir," Zak acknowledged with a bow of his head.

Wil caught Jason's gaze. *"This is going to unleash a shitestorm. Are you ready?"* he asked telepathically.

"Let's bring these fokers down."

Wil nodded. "Open a comm channel to all team members."

"Aye." Zak opened the line.

"This is TSS High Commander Wil Sietinen. The order I'm about to give goes against conventional Taran law separating political affairs from military matters. However, we have irrefutable evidence that the Monsari Dynasty has been engaging in illegal activities which cannot be excused, no matter their social standing. As a matter of security for the Empire, Admiral Mathaen and I have authorized the immediate arrest of Celine Monsari, as well as the seizure of the Dynasty's assets and all infrastructure associated with MPS and its affiliates. You have received your instructions from your unit leaders. Good hunting. You're a 'go'." He closed the channel.

Jason let out a long breath. *"So it begins."*

"I can only hope it's quick and easy."

"We won't be that lucky."

Truthfully, Jason had no idea what to expect. Monsari couldn't think for a moment that they'd stand a chance against the overwhelming force of the TSS' military might, not to mention the backup from the Guard, but that didn't mean that they wouldn't start shooting. A firefight would be a disaster on multiple fronts, and he prayed to the stars there wouldn't be any loss of life.

After concerns had been raised about the communication security within the Guard, TSS Command had elected to minimize the size and breadth of the infiltration teams for the raids. They'd kept the key staff to TSS only, unlike the joint op originally envisioned—with the Guard now only standing by for backup to come in after the initial surprise had been sprung. It was the best compromise they could think of to avoid tipping off anyone related to Monsari ahead of time while still having sufficient firepower should they encounter hostile resistance.

Jason watched the bodycam footage on the screen as the key teams started to move in. Most critically, he kept an eye on Ron's and Laura's cams as the armed TSS team descended in a shuttle to the Second Region of Tararia. The cams jostled as the shuttle touched down. Ron and Laura each jumped to their feet, the rear hatch on the shuttle already lowering to reveal the manicured grounds of the Monsari estate.

Next to Jason, Wil's eyes narrowed as he took in the scene. No doubt, he was thinking about his visit to the place when he'd been shot at.

Laura hung back slightly as the armed Militia soldiers and Agents ran ahead. She was merely support, there as an administrative witness. Ron, as an Agent, would handle the official arrests.

The camera's view became a dizzying whirl for a moment as Laura spun around. "There's no one here," she said. The image then bounced rapidly as she ran to catch up with the team.

Jason tapped into her comm. "This is CTF HQ. Can you provide more detail?"

"No signs of guards or any other staff outside the building," she clarified.

"Could they have been tipped off?" Jason asked his father.

"They didn't need to be. It was obvious this was coming."

"Sure, but the timing…" It didn't feel right to Jason. There was no way that exterior guards had been dismissed indefinitely, so a retreat had been ordered just prior to this event.

"It's been ten minutes since the transport ships arrived in orbit. That's plenty of time to respond."

As long as his father wasn't worried, Jason would set his concerns aside. Still, something unusual was going on.

"Let's move in!" Ron ordered, then led the charge inside.

Laura's camera feed began to bounce as she ran forward with the team, armed soldiers at her sides and straight ahead.

At the front of the group, Ron's cam gave a firsthand view as the doors to the Monsari estate swung open—without any resistance.

They left the place unlocked for us? Jason's stomach knotted. "Is this a trap?"

Wil leaned closer to the viewscreen, his brows knitted with concern. "I don't know."

The situation became clear as the TSS team stepped into the main reception hall. Rather than the emptiness of outside or a waiting sea of guards, they were instead met by Celine Monsari and her staff, all with their hands raised in surrender.

Ron didn't miss a beat. "Celine Monsari?"

She voluntarily stepped forward.

Jason exchanged a confused glance with his father. *Did she want this to happen? After all the corporate backstabbing and resistance, she's just handing herself over like this?* He didn't know what to make of it, and Wil's expression suggested he was equally confused.

"You're under arrest for conspiracy against the Taran Empire," Ron stated, moving to place Celine in restraints.

"I'll go willingly," Celine replied calmly. "But I have one condition."

CHAPTER 20

WIL'S HANDHELD CHIRPED, drawing his attention from the confusing scene unfolding on Tararia. Like the estate on the capital planet, the TSS teams had met with no resistance at any of MPS' offworld facilities. It was like they had been *ordered* to stand down in advance.

The incoming voice call was from Ron, the Agent leading the arrest. Wil answered. "Yes?"

"Sir, Celine is insisting she speak with you."

"So I've seen on the video feed." He considered. "Find a private space and put her on."

He had wanted to stay out of the arrest proceedings entirely, but he couldn't ignore the direct, reasonable, request of a High Dynasty leader—even one on the outs. If there was any chance of cooperation to minimize the political fallout of the situation, he needed to explore those outlets.

Wil stepped away from Jason to take the call so his son could focus on overseeing the rest of the operation. Even without resistance, there were a lot of logistics to coordinate for who to take into custody, who to temporarily hold for questioning, and who could be released immediately.

After two minutes, Wil's handheld chirped again with an incoming communication from Ron, this time a vidcall. When Wil answered, Celine's face filled the screen.

"What do you want?" Wil asked, keeping his tone professional but making no attempt to sound friendly.

"I need to meet with you, face-to-face," Celine replied.

Wil scoffed at her. There was no way he could believe she had good intentions for such a discussion after all of her actions over the years. "Why?"

"I know you must hate me, but I've had reasons for everything I've done. Please allow me the chance to explain."

"Fine, go for it."

"Not like this. We need to meet in person."

"The last time we did that, you tried to kill me."

"You were never in any real danger."

"What, you knew I'd spot the assassin?"

"Yes."

He shook his head. "That's not how this works, Celine. We can't spend our whole lives as enemies and then you say 'sorry' and have everything suddenly be okay between us."

"I'm not apologizing," she said. "I only want to offer an explanation. I have nowhere else to turn."

Wil wanted to dismiss her, but something in her tone made him take notice. This wasn't the adversarial woman he'd come to expect. *Of course, she's afraid. Her family fortune is about to collapse.* He sighed. "You and your family did this to yourselves—"

"Bomaxed stars, stop! You think you understand what's going on, but you don't. If you truly care about what happens to the Taran race, you have to listen to me." There was desperation in her tone now.

"I can't trust anything you say."

"I don't expect you to. But once you hear it, you can verify it for yourself."

It's probably another trap. As much as Wil wanted to refuse the offer, duty demanded that he gather all possible information. If she really did know something critical—and that wasn't out of the question, since she was a known collaborator of the Gatekeepers—then he needed to hear her out.

"Fine. I'll have them bring you here to TSS Headquarters," he said.

She nodded. "Not my first choice of venue, but I don't suppose I have any say in the matter."

"No, you don't." He ended the call.

— — —

Raena answered an incoming vidcall from her grandfather. "How did it go?"

"I just got word. Celine Monsari has officially been taken into custody," he revealed.

"Thank the stars!" She let out a long breath, releasing the tension in her chest.

"It's not over yet. I'm hearing rumors that riots are starting on several Outer Colonies worlds in response to members of the Coalition's leadership getting arrested. They're saying it's a civil liberties violation for Taran authorities to try to silence dissenting opinions."

"They're violent criminals!"

Cris held up his hands. "Raena, I agree with you

completely. Unfortunately, this kind of spin is standard procedure for politics. The sooner you get used to that, the happier you'll be."

She made a concerted effort to swallow her annoyance. "Thank you for filling me in."

"The public news has been vague so far. Once our names get—" He cut off abruptly.

"What?"

"Ah, shite. The news story just broke." Cris added a news feed into their conference call.

Raena watched the report on the viewscreen. A very serious-looking reporter spoke to the camera while footage of Celine Monsari being led out of her estate in handcuffs played in the background.

"Dynastic Head and CEO of MPS, Celine Monsari, has been taken into TSS custody on suspicion of conspiracy and funding of the Coalition in the Outer Colonies," the reporter stated. "The Coalition is a collection of several separatist movements, which has claimed credit for a series of violent demonstrations across remote Taran worlds, including incidents on Antaris and Duronis. This is a developing story, and we will provide more information as it becomes available."

"Well, at least the Sietinen name hasn't been brought into it," Raena said.

"Yet."

She nodded. It was inevitable. "I guess we should get our new PR companies on this?"

Cris smiled. "That's a very good idea."

— — —

Meeting with Wil went against everything Celine had been conditioned to think and do. The TSS and Gifted were enemies, and the Sietinens were the worst among them. It wasn't that they were bad people—only that their ideals were mutually exclusive.

Now, though, she and her collaborators were out of options. Rather than saving a small percentage of Tarans in the forthcoming purge, the entire race could be wiped out. No ark, no chance to rebuild.

She arrived at TSS Headquarters with only the faintest glimmer of hope. The TSS couldn't possibly have devised a way to take out the Erebus, but that was the only way Tarans might survive. She would share what she knew, and maybe that would make a difference.

Wil was waiting for her when the guards showed her into the interview room. "What are we here to discuss?" he asked without preamble.

She sat down across from him, rubbing her wrists where the restraints had irritated her skin on the voyage from Tararia. "I've been working with the Gatekeepers."

"I know."

"My family has been working with them for thousands of years."

His eyes widened slightly, and he sat up a little straighter. "Is that so?"

"I'm sure you know about the war a hundred thousand years ago, or so. Knowledge of it was lost to most, as were the events that followed. But not everyone forgot, and that information was passed down generation by generation. You must think I'm a monster, but everything I've done has been in service to the larger context. I can't fault you for your own actions, because they do appear to be in the moral right. You didn't understand the harm you would cause in other ways."

"Explain."

He was listening. That was a start. "After the ancient war, the Gatekeepers never left," she continued. "They remained in the shadows, working with a select group of Tarans who were committed to making sure such a war never happened again."

He scoffed. "Clearly, you failed."

"If you think what's going on now is a war, you are sorely mistaken. That war was almost the end for both the Gatekeepers and Tarans. Less than a billion Tarans survived."

"How do you know that?"

"It's what I've been told. Can I verify it? No. But from everything I've seen, I have no reason to doubt it."

From the look on Wil's face, he didn't have any information to the contrary.

"The war came about because rising Taran and Gatekeeper numbers had increased the use of the higher-dimensional energy the Erebus use as a kind of lifeblood. Every time the Gifted drew on their abilities or the Gatekeepers used their Gate-tech, the Erebus were slowly depleted. They wiped out the Gifted members of the population then, leaving only those with weakened abilities. Over time, though, the abilities grew stronger again. Eventually, the Priesthood rose to power and made a bid to bolster Gifted abilities across the entire population.

"The Gatekeepers and those among Tarans who'd had knowledge of the war passed down knew that would lead to another extermination, so infiltrators were able to corrupt the genetic treatment. It resulted in the Generation Cycle—not exactly what was intended—but it dampened abilities enough, collectively, across the Taran population to delay a war."

Wil crossed his arms, his expression too neutral to read. "That's quite the tactic."

"We knew how dire the situation was. And we knew we needed insurance for our survival. That's why we had Earth."

Wil's brows drew together. "What does Earth have to do with it?"

"It is Gifted abilities that make Tarans a target for the Erebus. We needed a branch of Tarans that wouldn't be a threat to them."

"Are you saying that humans were… engineered to not have Gifts?"

"Yes, many tens of thousands of years ago. At first, we thought merely settling another planet far away from the rest of the Empire might be enough to go unnoticed, but not everyone can resist the call of their abilities. Some will, inevitably, reach out for the energies of the higher dimensions and make everyone near them a target. The only way to be sure was to cut off that connection entirely."

"How?"

"I wasn't there. I don't know. But they'd already bio-optimized Earth, so it was prime for populating with a sampling of people from across the disparate Taran worlds. Caretakers guided their development, oftentimes being mistaken as gods, and eventually humans became their own distinct branch, oblivious to their Taran origins."

"And the role of caretakers eventually passed to the TSS."

"No, you've actually been a nuisance." She clicked her tongue against her teeth. "The Gatekeeper hybrids have been keeping watch. They're much longer-lived than normal Tarans and far better at keeping secrets."

"So, the unexplained ship sightings and abductions that we can't account for?"

"Just them doing their job."

He scoffed. "That's debatable."

"What would you have done in our position, knowing the obliteration of the race was imminent?"

"Not keep a foking secret from the only people who could possibly help you, for starters."

"You?"

"If you have such a low opinion of me, then why are we even having this conversation?"

She looked down. "Because I don't have anywhere else to turn."

"Well, you could have thrown yourself out an airlock, yet you chose to call me instead. You must have *some* measure of confidence that I'm not completely inept."

Celine did understand why others respected him. Not many people had commanded a fleet to win a galactic war or been able to overthrow a government. In that way, she had to respect him herself—even if she disagreed with his actions. By that same token, though, he'd acted based on the information available to him. Perhaps, had he known about the Erebus threat the whole time, he would have looked at things differently.

"Competence isn't the issue. I know you're someone who sees a problem and wants to solve it. The issue here is that we're facing an enemy we can't win against. I don't believe you're willing to admit that."

"You're right."

"So, I'm coming to you now with a plea to listen to reason. I'm trying to prevent you from taking us down a path from which we can't come back."

"If you're so concerned about the expanding use of Gifted abilities, then where were you when the Priesthood fell and the telekinesis bans were overturned?" Wil asked.

"I tried to prevent that collapse, as you well know. You no doubt thought it was simply because of bigotry, but the truth is, the Priesthood was the stopgap for minimizing abilities used across the Empire. Outlawing telekinesis minimized its use enough to avoid angering the Erebus. The Bakzen posed a threat in that regard, so they had to be eliminated. But after that, everything was almost okay... until you came along and ousted the Priesthood, then immediately legalized telekinesis. At that point, we knew another war was inevitable, and soon."

"Why didn't you come to us and explain?"

"Would you have believed me?"

Wil was silent for several seconds. "No, I suppose not."

"Right. So, we did the next best thing we could think of. Victor Arvonen had been in our inner circle—a family, like Monsari, entrusted with the safekeeping of Taran history and our future—but he had grown too fond of power. As a means to both get rid of him and communicate what we needed to you via a source you might heed, we allowed the use of a limited number of Gate spheres. It was enough to attract the other Gatekeepers who'd severed contact with Tarans. They warned you about the Erebus, and we'd hoped that would be enough."

"And where are they?"

"I don't know, honestly. Somewhere far away. The edge of this galaxy, or perhaps another. There aren't many of them left now."

He crossed his arms. "If everything with Arvonen was staged like you said, then why did the Erebus attack the

Andvari and start all of this?"

She shook her head, heart heavy. "That's the irony of it all. We'd assured them that the situation was under control and that Tarans would avoid the Rift and the use of their energy. Yet, when they sent a scout, a ship was there. They weren't expecting it—and we didn't know it was there, either, until it was too late. So, they studied it, assessed that Tarans still posed a threat, and then set about plotting a means to destroy us again.

"The Gatekeepers and our collaborators, likewise, began working on counter-moves. With the destruction of the Taran race coming, we needed to make sure there would be survivors. So, we contracted to work directly with the Erebus so we could act as facilitators while making changes to the deployment that would afford a small portion of the Taran race to continue."

Wil nodded slowly. "Such as that Vapr drug distributed through SPEAR?"

"Yes, the Steyns played a key role in many of those activities behind the scenes. But power corrupts, and not everything went to plan."

"You had been distributing the Vapr drug through the Steyn's crime ring, correct?"

"I wouldn't call it a 'crime ring'," Celine said, feeling a little defensive about her former business partners. The Steyns were considered reputable businesspeople in some circles. SPEAR Tec had developed some truly innovative technology, and what they'd been able to do with the Pesta weapon was incredible. It was a shame they hadn't been able to bring those plans to fruition.

Wil's eyes narrowed as he studied her. "You were supplying them with the ateron mined from Zeron, weren't you? To use in the Vapr nanites."

"The details don't matter," Celine replied. The truth was, she had coordinated far more operations than just Zeron, and there was no point in revealing all of those threads now. She'd vowed to share relevant information with Wil, but that was getting too far afield. "Suffice to say, we had the means to acquire necessary materials and would use our supply network to manage the transportation logistics."

He didn't seem pleased with that answer. "Answer me this, at least. Why did you go to such great lengths to keep the excavation a secret from the Erebus?"

"How do you know that's the case?" she asked.

"The details don't matter."

Well, he certainly flipped that around. She shifted in her seat. "Consider that device on Zeron a bargaining chip. If we passively allowed events to play out, the Erebus would surely wipe out every last Taran. Using that device, however, we can make their forthcoming invasion... easier for them. And as a reward, we can buy a say in who's worthy of surviving the slaughter."

"I think it's safe to say that plan of yours hasn't worked out the way you envisioned."

Her eyes narrowed slightly. "Yes, you've proven to be more persistent than we'd anticipated."

"If you're fishing for an apology about that attribute, you're out of luck."

"No." She looked down. "The only thing I want now is for you to be reasonable. I will give you all the details you want, but I'm begging you, you need to alter your plans before it gets us all killed."

"I don't think you have the faintest clue what we're

planning."

She narrowed her eyes. "You intend to go up against the Erebus."

"Justifiably."

"It's suicide, not to mention it would precipitate the death of every remaining Taran."

"Again, you don't know what we're planning."

"You're awfully confident for someone out of his depth."

Wil started to get up. "I can see this conversation is going nowhere—"

"No, wait," Celine cut in. She let out a heavy sigh, her chest tight with despair and frustration. There simply wasn't a way to explain in a short time to someone who wasn't prepared to hear the truth. "If you're going to be an idiot and try to stand up to the Erebus, then I should at least tell you everything I know."

"Are you going to be honest with me?"

"Am I going to get a fair trial?"

"I'd never do anything to sabotage another's civil rights, but I'm not sure you can say the same."

The words stung. She hadn't expected that. While she didn't look at anything she'd done as an abuse of her power, maybe there was some truth in the statement. "All I want is for the Taran race to survive. Surely you can tell that isn't a lie."

Wil studied her intently for several seconds. "Okay. Tell me what you know."

CHAPTER 21

EVERYTHING CELINE HAD told Wil made sense, and he found that far more disturbing than if she'd tried to attack him with her bare hands. *Have we been wrong all this time?*

Having had an opportunity to reflect on their conversation, he realized it wasn't a matter of 'right' or 'wrong' but rather perspective. Celine had been acting in a way that best fulfilled her view of the universe, as Wil had with his. The truth, as with most things, was somewhere in the middle. Perhaps, had Wil and his family known about the cabal working with ancient aliens for millennia, they would have handled some matters differently. In the absence of that knowledge, their actions were reasonable—if not downright virtuous.

However, with this new information to grant a different perspective, he could understand how Celine viewed him as a villain. Regardless, there were any number of more productive ways that she could have tried to navigate their relationship, so he still considered the current mess her fault.

How we got here doesn't matter. What do we do now?

There were really only two options. The first was the carry on with their plan to attack the Erebus, with the potential to either save everyone or, if they failed, all Tarans would die. The second option was to fully side with Celine and acknowledge the fact that the Taran population would be decimated, but they could work together to guarantee at least some people would survive.

It was an impossible choice. During the Bakzen War, he'd faced decisions on the scale of billions of lives. Even that horror paled in comparison to the fate of an entire race. Trillions of people—individuals with dreams and aspirations, trusting in their leaders to shepherd them toward a better tomorrow.

Now, though, the path forward was at a crossroads. One fork would deliver them that bright, hopeful future of infinite possibility. The other would be the end—the kind of end so complete that it would be as if Tarans had never existed. That was the Erebus' power. They could 'unmake' the very foundation of reality, which to any other being was a thing of immovable permanence.

To even contemplate going up against beings of that strength... He shook his head. It didn't matter. There wasn't a choice.

Celine looked at the situation and saw 'any survivors is better than none'. Wil couldn't view it that way, not when there was *any* chance that the bulk of the population could make it through the conflict alive. Any other course of action would be condemning all but a tiny fraction of the population to oblivion.

He knew what he had to do. The discussion with the scientists had given them a clear path. All that remained was deciding on the timing.

A knock at his door roused him from his thoughts. He could sense Saera's presence.

"Come in," he said in her mind.

She entered and closed the door behind her. "How'd the talk with Celine go?"

He pushed back from his desk. "It was... illuminating. I don't know if that's the right word. She was hiding so much more than we could ever have anticipated."

"What did you learn?"

"For starters, several Taran families have been working with the Gatekeepers for generations—Monsari being one of the most critical to that relationship."

She sat down slowly in one of the guest chairs. "What?"

Wil nodded. "That's where the MPS power core originated. After the previous conflicts over Taran use of the *aesen* energy, the Gatekeepers helped our ancestors develop a power method that wouldn't violate the treaty. They were supposed to be stewards to help guide Tarans in a new direction that would avoid future conflict."

Saera crossed her arms. "Obviously, that didn't work out."

"As far as Celine is concerned, it's all our fault."

"Why in the stars would she think that?"

"Apparently, all the anti-telekinesis sentiment over the years has been to discourage *aesen* draw and keep the Erebus from freaking out on us."

"Uh, that was a political move on the Priesthood's part to cover up the situation with the Bakzen... wasn't it?"

"Yes, but according to her, the efforts go back much further than that. The Priesthood went against social convention when they began exploring their Gifts, and trying to make them stronger was an extension of that. They were then punished with a genetic-corrupting ailment meant to restore balance."

Saera's jaw went slack. "The Generation Cycle."

Wil nodded. "And, apparently, humans were engineered to be an... alternative race. Mostly Taran, but lacking that one pesky part of themselves that would upset the Erebus."

"Stars..."

"I don't know if I believe her, but it does fit with our other speculations."

"What about those occasional humans that would get recruited into the TSS?"

He shrugged. "I suspect they just picked up some Taran blood along the way, just like you. Pure humans have no abilities expression, but a few Tarans have found their way to Earth over the years, where they had children, and I suspect that's where the unexplained 'psychic' abilities come in—not quite Gifts as we think of them, but some measure of connection to the larger universal energies."

"I guess that makes sense."

"It does... to the point that I don't know why I didn't see it before."

"I don't think anyone ever could have predicted that there were transdimensional overlords secretly dictating the actions of a rogue group of hybrid aliens working with a shadow faction of our own people."

Wil had to smile at the summary. "Okay, fair enough. I just mean that I looked at everything Celine was doing and thought she was a cold-hearted bitch when maybe she really was trying to help in her own misguided way."

"She is pretty awful."

"After talking to her, now I'm not so sure. It's all shades of gray, Saera. Even the things we were *so certain* were the 'right thing to do' aren't as clear as I once thought."

"Where do we go from here?"

He let out a bitter chuckle. "To exactly the same place, only feeling more conflicted as we go."

"Conflict is nothing new. We have to move forward, for the sake of our family's future."

We're always looking ahead and forget to savor the present. The torrent of conflicts pressed in on Wil's mind.

For years, he'd been telling himself that he'd prioritize family once this problem or that was resolved. There was always an excuse. Even his last trip to Tararia had been for official business rather than to socialize with his daughter. Now, there was no denying that there might not be the right opportunity for them to come together. No ideal circumstances. He could either *make* the time or lose the chance entirely.

"…continue the coordination." Saera gave him a quizzical look. "Wil, were you listening?"

He shook his head. "I'm sorry, I can't talk tactics right now."

"We don't really have an option," she said.

"Right now, all I can think about is that we should get the family together."

She blinked at him. "Where'd that come from?"

"A place of acceptance. We can tell ourselves that everything is under control and going to work out fine, but the truth is, we're more vulnerable than ever before. It's a very real possibility that all of our loved ones won't make it through the coming battle."

"Battle? We—"

"I don't know what shape it's going to take, but there *will* be a showdown with the Erebus. It's been inevitable since the attack on the *Andvari*."

Saera wet her lips. "I don't know what to say."

"Agree to step away from all this for the afternoon. I know it's irresponsible in some ways, but I need this, Saera. So badly. We keep saying, 'when things are better', but when will that ever be, really? The truth is, the Erebus could annihilate all of us an hour from now. I wouldn't want my final moments to be full of regrets."

"That might be a little dramatic," Saera said.

"Perhaps, but I'm not going to downplay the seriousness of this situation. We've been talking for years about a reunion and it hasn't happened. I just..." He didn't want to complete the thought out loud. He couldn't with her, not yet. But he knew where the path led, and for one of the few times in his life, he needed to be selfish in order to have the strength to face what was coming.

His wife sat quietly for several seconds, not sure how to respond. "You're right," she said at last. "There might never be a good time. I'd love to have both of my children under the same roof again, even if it's just for one meal."

"Exactly," Wil said. "Let's do it now, while we can."

She nodded. "Okay. Where?"

Wil thought through the options. Tararia was a mess. TSS Headquarters would raise all sorts of flags if anyone noticed the Sietinens and Dainetris making an unscheduled visit. It would have to be somewhere neutral.

"How about Alushia?" he suggested. It was close to Tararia so it'd be an easy hop for Raena, Ryan, and his parents, and as a family vacation home, it was about as non-military and unpolitical a place as they could go. The fact that it was where he'd honeymooned with Saera and where they'd spent other important time as a couple was an added bonus.

"All right," Saera agreed, sounding more bewildered than enthusiastic. "Are we literally going *now*?"

Wil stood up. "Yes. Get Jason and Lexi. I'll call my parents and Raena and have them head over."

"What if they refuse?" Saera asked.

"Then I'll persuade them. We're doing this."

"Okay."

He could sense her hesitation about leaving Headquarters at such an uncertain time, but she clearly knew that he wouldn't have asked if it wasn't important to him. So rarely did he make self-serving demands that the requests carried weight when he made them. Were the circumstances any different, he wouldn't abandon his leadership post, even for a moment. But this… he *had* to do this to assuage any regrets, no matter how irresponsible or selfish. After everything he'd given to the Empire, he hoped he'd be forgiven.

Saera rose and was about to walk toward the door, but she instead came around the back side of the desk to Wil. "Should I be concerned?"

He shook his head, feeling his composure begin to crack. "No. It's just… I can only control so much. I know I sound crazy suggesting this right now—"

She wrapped her arms around him. "No, not to me. Thank you for the reminder about what we're fighting for."

He hugged her close, grateful for the physical connection and reassurance.

Saera gave him a kiss as she pulled back. "I'll go get our son. See you at the port."

As she left the office, Wil brought up the comm controls to contact his parents and Raena. They'd no doubt refuse initially, but this may be their one opportunity. He needed to make it count.

— — —

"What, *now*?" Jason gaped at his mother. "You can't be serious."

Saera shrugged. "It's just for a few hours. I know it's out of nowhere, but your father is insisting. We're doing it. Grab Lexi if you'd like to bring her along; she's welcome."

Jason shrugged. "Yeah, of course." He let out a long breath, thinking through all the work that would be delayed by the impromptu departure. "Okay, I'll get her, and we'll meet you up at the port soon."

"See you there." She left the office.

What the fok is going on? He was used to his parents throwing out random ideas, but this took it to another level. Leaving Headquarters when they were on the cusp of a galactic war? Either circumstances were a lot more desperate than the already bad stakes he'd identified, or his father had simply lost his mind.

Either way, he wasn't about to refuse the request. His parents were some of the most selfless people he knew, so if they were making this request now, it was because it was profoundly important to them. And, with time of the essence, he didn't want to delay.

He quickly saved and closed out of his work, then hurried down the hall to Lexi's office. She was frowning at her screen when he knocked on her door.

She motioned him in. "Hey, what's up?"

"Do you want to take the trip to Alushia we've been talking about?" he asked.

She laughed. "Oh, I wish!"

"I'm actually serious. Dad's kinda gone off the deep end, it seems, and is insisting we have a spontaneous family reunion."

Lexi started to laugh again, but she stopped when Jason didn't join her. "You're not joking."

"Nope. So, what do you say?"

"I'd be stupid to turn down that offer. When is this happening?"

"Now."

"Okay, then…" She pushed back from the desk. "Lead the way, I guess?"

— — —

"This is absolutely ridiculous," Raena muttered as she walked with Ryan toward the waiting shuttle.

"Your dad does have a point," Ryan said from where he was keeping pace on her left. "We do keep talking about future times of calm that never seem to come."

"Are you calling me dramatic?"

"Our *lives* are dramatic. You are the image of calm perfection."

"Right." They reached the shuttle, and she walked up the ramp. Her grandparents would meet them at the orbital spaceport, and they'd take a transport ship together to Alushia to meet her parents and brother for the afternoon.

"I can't argue with the plan to get away for a few hours. I need to clear my head," Ryan said as they settled into their seats in the middle body of the craft.

"I doubt it will be as relaxing as my dad tried to make it out. There's another reason for the spontaneous get-together."

"Such as?"

Imminent doom. She didn't want to voice the concern aloud. "We'll see soon enough."

"It'll be nice to see everyone, anyway," he said.

"Yeah. My grandparents haven't seen Jason in ages. Actually, I guess this will be their first time meeting Lexi, huh?"

"Oh, that's true. Yep, so much for casual relaxation."

"That's not the part I'm worried about."

"What, then?"

"Why this meeting is happening in the first place," she said. "Why *now*? What's changed that we can't wait any longer?"

Ryan only gave a silent nod in response.

Raena looked out the side viewport as the shuttle trembled and then began to rise from the planet's surface, the ground dropping away at a dizzying speed as the craft accelerated upward. *Whatever the reason, I'll savor every moment.*

CHAPTER 22

ALUSHIA WAS EVEN more beautiful than Wil had remembered. The Sietinen family island was situated in the ideal climate zone several degrees north of the planet's equator, a hundred kilometers from any other land mass. It was as private a place as money could buy, with only non-sentient android and robotic assistants to ensure the security of all activities and communications. On the rare occasions he'd been able to visit, the place had been associated with the happiest times in his life. He could think of no other place he'd rather be now.

The shuttle descended toward the single port on the eastern side of the island, offering a breathtaking view of the white-stone manor and verdant tropical foliage on the final approach. Calm, turquoise waters stretched out to the horizon in every direction, lapping against the pale sand on the shoreline.

"Wow!" Lexi whispered to herself, her attention glued to her viewport.

"Not bad, huh?" Jason said with a smile from the seat next to her.

Wil's heart warmed seeing the two of them together, reminding him of Saera's wonder the first time he'd visited with her for their honeymoon.

Saera took his hand in hers. *"We were that young once,"* she said in his mind.

"It was a lifetime ago."

He'd already lived so many lives, it was no wonder he felt conflicted about how best to balance his familial and professional responsibilities.

As soon as the shuttle's engine powered down, the four of them rose from their seats and exited the craft.

Wil breathed in the warm, slightly salty air as they descended the ramp. He stripped off his outer jacket and looped it over his arm, finding it to be an ideal temperature with surprisingly low humidity for the tropical appearance of the environment.

"So, what's the plan?" Jason asked, coming down the ramp with Lexi.

Wil shrugged. "Be in the moment."

Saera squeezed his hand, giving him a nod of approval.

The roar of an approaching craft sounded overhead.

The group moved out of the way as another shuttle descended. Once on the ground, Wil's parents exited with Raena and Ryan. The newcomers smiled warmly when they saw Wil and the others waiting nearby.

"Well, you finally did it," Cris said. "All of us together in one place."

"Way overdue," Wil replied, walking up to his father. He hugged him while Saera greeted Raena and Ryan.

"How are you?" Cris asked.

"Taking it a day at a time." Beyond Saera, his father was

someone with whom Wil never needed to put on airs.

Cris nodded knowingly. "Forget about it for now." He clapped him on the shoulder.

"Wil, it's so good to see you," his mother said. She wrapped her arms around him.

"Hey, Mom." He gave her a squeeze before pulling back. "Thank you for coming."

"Anything for you," she said.

Wil turned his attention to Raena and Ryan. It had been less than a year since the last time he'd seen his daughter, but she somehow seemed even more confident and poised. "I've missed you. Come here." He pulled her into an embrace.

"Hi, Dad." She squeezed him back. "It's good to see you, too."

Wil hugged Ryan next. "Thank you for the help with the transport ships."

"My pleasure."

"You must be Lexi," Cris said, drawing Wil's attention behind him.

Cris and Kate had wandered toward the others while Wil had been focused on Raena and Ryan, and they were now politely inspecting the newest prospective member of the family.

"I am, my lord, my lady," Lexi replied with a polite bow of her head to each. Despite her level tone, she'd tightened her grip on Jason's hand.

"Lexi has been a great addition to Headquarters," Saera jumped in. "The civilian training program she spearheaded has been a smash hit with the trainees."

"I've heard," Kate said with a smile. "I'd dreamed of starting a program like that, and I'm so happy to see it come to fruition."

"That's enough talk of work for now," Wil said. "Let's go relax." He pointed them toward the outdoor seating area by the manor.

The lounge area was up a gently sloping stone staircase hewn from the native rocks on the island. Though only a couple of meters in elevation gain, it was enough to make the view of the surrounding ocean even more dramatic. On a paved terrace, eight padded chairs were arranged with end tables ready to receive drinks or food. Each table included an access screen as well as voice controls to interface with the automated attendants.

Knowing their time was limited and they'd have to get back to work with clear heads, they each opted for various juice beverages rather than anything boozy.

"This place hardly seems real," Lexi commented while they waited for the drinks to arrive.

"It's been an elite destination for as far back as anyone can remember," Cris said. "I honestly couldn't tell you if it was engineered to be paradise or if Nature just got lucky."

Lexi stared out at the distant view. "I don't know why anyone would ever leave."

Kate smiled. "You might not have checked your handheld since landing, but there's a communication blackout on the planet, except for a single access point on each estate. By design, because otherwise people *wouldn't* leave, and this would no longer be a sanctuary."

Reflexively, Lexi pulled out her handheld and checked the signal, frowning at the screen. "Well, I guess that's one way to ensure you get a proper vacation."

An android approached from the direction of the manor, carrying a tray loaded with the specified drinks. Though roughly resembling Taran size and form, it was molded of light, pearlescent plastic and had a smooth face with only the hint of features. Such servant androids had been through many design iterations over the years to fit with social fads, but this minimalist aesthetic remained a constant—striking a comfortable balance of familiarity with a clear expression of its synthetic nature.

The machine wordlessly handed out the drinks to each individual and quickly retreated, barely making a sound as it moved.

"You sure we can't get some of these around Headquarters?" Jason asked, reprising a question he'd asked Wil and Saera years prior.

Saera exchanged a knowing look with Wil. "We're supposed to be training people how to be responsible. Being doted on hand and foot defeats the point."

Jason sipped his drink. "If you say so." Despite the words, his tone was light and joking.

The truth was, they did have a lot of automated help working behind the scenes at Headquarters, from laundry service to food prep. Such was the delicate equilibrium between personal accountability and convenience with technology. Wil recognized the importance of self-reliance, so he'd made it TSS policy to minimize automated help. He'd tried to instill those sensibilities in his children, as well. Seeing the people they'd become, he couldn't be prouder of them.

"I appreciate you all indulging me with this gathering," Wil said after a pause. "I know it was sudden and there's a lot going on."

"You're right that there's no time like the present," his father replied.

The present is our only guarantee, and even that's fleeting. Wil took a sip of his drink. "I just want to say that you're all amazing and I feel extremely fortunate to have you in my life."

"Geez, Dad, don't get mushy on us now," Raena jested, but he could see the love and appreciation in her eyes.

They all recognized that they were lucky to have each other. Even when the galaxy was on the brink of falling apart, they'd always had their family. Within that group, they were safe and anything was possible. He hoped that they'd be able to pull off one more miracle together.

As they sipped on their drinks, they casually chatted and enjoyed the view. The conversation ended up being about superficial topics like the weather and food, but to delve into anything meaningful would have meant discussing professional concerns he didn't want souring the mood.

After an hour, Wil started to pick up subtle indications of tension as the others began to wonder how long they'd be here. There were urgent matters that required attention. Before they left, though, he wanted to take the opportunity to have some private conversations.

First, he pulled his parents aside, walking with them to another viewpoint near the manor. "I'm really glad we could do this."

"Me too, Wil," his father said. "I think we get so wrapped up in others' needs that we forget to take care of our own sometimes."

He nodded. "I'm eternally grateful for how you've looked after me."

"You make it easy," his mother said, patting his arm.

"I should have said this a long time ago, but thank you for always being wonderful parents."

Cris shook his head. "I don't know about that."

"No, you were. I appreciate everything you did for me—offering guidance when I needed it and the freedom to figure things out on my own."

"I'm happy to hear you feel that way, Wil," his mother said. "There were times when I didn't know how to be there for you."

He shrugged. "I always knew I could go to you, and that meant a lot. I trust your counsel, and that's the only reason I was okay with Raena leaving home so young. You've been wonderful with her and Ryan."

"They're both exceptional. I can't take credit for anything," Cris said.

"You've done more than you might realize," Wil insisted. "Thank you."

Kate smiled. "We'd happily do it all again."

His father studied him. "Are you okay, Wil?"

"Yeah, I am now."

Cris didn't seem convinced. Aside from Saera, he knew Wil better than anyone. "There's a solution to every problem. We'll get through this one together, just like before."

"There's no one else I'd rather have by my side."

— — —

There was a sense of melancholy to the reunion that Ryan hadn't anticipated. Watching Raena's reactions, he could tell that she sensed it, too.

"*Why does it seem like everyone is saying goodbye?*" he asked in her mind.

"*Yeah, this whole thing is strange.*"

His concerns were confirmed when Wil wandered off with his parents to go talk privately. *What in the stars is going on?*

Ryan had never known Wil to be someone to admit defeat. Rallying against impossible odds was the norm. But now, he seemed resigned to the possibility that they might not stand a chance against the Erebus. This was one of those 'in case we never get another chance' gatherings, not a casual social affair. It hadn't been presented as such, but he could feel it.

When Wil returned with his parents, he smiled at Raena and Ryan. "Walk with me?"

"Sure," Raena agreed, flashing a concerned look to Ryan as the two of them stood up.

"I don't like this," she said in Ryan's mind.

"We've gotta find out what's going on."

Raena fell into step next to her father with Ryan on her other side. "This whole short-notice party isn't like you, Dad," she said.

He stopped at a viewpoint and turned to face them. "Well, our vague, long-term intentions haven't materialized into actual plans, so it was time to take another approach."

"It's more than that, be honest." Raena looked at him intently.

"Yes," he yielded. "I didn't want to leave anything unsaid."

"I refuse to accept that we won't show those transdimensional bastards they messed with the wrong people."

"Nonetheless, I wanted to see you both and tell you in person how proud I am of how you've conducted yourselves as young leaders and the relationship you've built with each other. I know how difficult it is to have so many expectations placed upon you."

Ryan could sense Raena's mind churning with thoughts of deflecting the compliment and insisting that everything was going to be okay. But Ryan felt the sincerity in Wil's words, and it didn't seem right to dismiss the statement. "I didn't get the opportunity to meet my dad, but you've given me a glimpse of what he was like. Thank you for showing me how a firm leader can still have compassion and how the right partner can make anything possible. I will always put your daughter first."

Raena's mouth opened slightly, searching for the right words as her gaze passed between Ryan and Wil.

"You two can accomplish anything together, I have no doubt," Wil said, placing one hand on each of their shoulders.

Raena's brows drew together, her face pinched like she was on the verge of holding back tears. "Thanks, Dad."

Ryan sensed the other thoughts in her mind—questioning why her father was acting this way and what it meant. The questions didn't need to be spoken. She knew why, but she was also determined for them to one day look back on this conversation and laugh at how unnecessary it had been.

After a short while, they wandered back toward the rest of the group. As they approached, Saera looked at Wil pointedly, saying nothing. He avoided her gaze.

"Lexi, do you mind if I steal Jason for a few minutes?" Wil asked.

"Go for it," she replied, and Jason got up to accompany Wil.

Saera watched them go before turning her attention to Ryan and Raena. "What was that about?"

"Just stating his appreciation for us," Ryan said.

"Yeah," Raena agreed, though the emotions she shared privately with him through their bond said otherwise.

It was clear Saera knew they were downplaying the impact of the conversation, but she left it at that. This was a time to celebrate what they had, not mourn for what might be lost.

Ryan wrapped his arm around Raena, returning to their two-seater bench. *"I love you."*

"I love you, too. Don't you dare try to say goodbye to me like that."

"I'm not going anywhere."

— — —

Jason had wondered if his father was going to pull him aside, too, and as he walked away from the rest of the family with Wil, he now wondered what it meant that his meeting had been saved for the end, with the possible exception of his mother.

"What's this about?" he asked, wanting to cut to the chase.

"Jason, there's something I'd like to discuss with you while we're away from Headquarters."

"Sure."

"It's about the nature of command, but I want to speak with you just man-to-man." Wil took a slow breath, looking out toward the sea. "Others look at us and see only the immense power of our Gifts, and they forget that we bear the emotional burden of our command decisions just like anyone else. We're not invincible."

"I know."

"You say that now, but you've yet to be faced with the kind of impossible choices a leader must bear. You've had a taste, yes, but one day—maybe soon—you'll encounter an inflection point with a decision that will define, and possibly haunt you for the rest of your life."

Jason was sobered by the gravity of the words. The sadness of his father's gaze bore into him. "I'm listening."

Wil was quiet for a long while, looking out toward the water again. "What I'd like to tell you, only two other living people know. I never thought I'd talk about it with you, but after seeing how you've handled certain situations and getting a feel for the leader I think you can become, I believe it will offer you valuable perspective."

"All right," Jason replied, feeling a bit of uneasiness in his stomach.

"It very well may change how you think about me—and it probably should."

Jason nodded. *What in the stars is this about?* He'd never seen his father so agitated before.

Wil swallowed. "I know you've been over much of the battle footage from the war, but there's one incident that's rarely talked about. Cambion."

"I've heard of it. It was taken by the Bakzen."

"Yes, and most of the four billion residents were killed in the assault."

Jason's heart skipped a beat. "I didn't realize it was that many."

"Tom Alric was from there, and he lost his whole family."

"Shite." Jason knew Tom as a flight instructor, and he'd trained with the original cohort of Primus Elites under Wil. The entire team was extremely close.

"There's a key detail that's not in any of the records." Wil winced, as if forcing himself to continue. "I knew about the attack before it happened, and I let it."

Jason stared at him, speechless. *Why?*

"It was the single most difficult decision I've ever made as a commander, and there isn't a day that it doesn't haunt me."

"What happened?" Jason asked when his father didn't continue.

"Your mom had gone out to conduct an emergency repair to a nav beacon, which we later realized had been a baited trap. On her way back, the Bakzen cornered her shuttle. The Bakzen leader contacted me and gave me a choice: her life, or Cambion."

Jason's heart dropped. "That's…"

"He gave me two minutes to decide, and I ran through every scenario. In the end, my conclusion was that losing her would irrevocably compromise me as a leader, and the war would be lost then and there. So, I gave up those four billion lives for the sake of saving the trillions across the Empire."

Jason didn't know what to say. *Would I be able to let Lexi die if it meant saving a planet?*

"At the time, I was barely holding it together. It'd been a decade of barely getting any sleep and constant stress. The Bakzen figured out what would break me, and they played that card. It destroyed me in a different way, but I was able to see the war through to the end. I let the hate and pain consume me. That's not what you want to be the source of your power, trust me."

"Why are you telling me this?"

"Because when faced with your enemy in those final moments, you might see it as revenge for Tiff. Don't. We fight for our future, not to correct past injustice. Otherwise, you can get trapped by those ghosts and they never stop tormenting you."

"Okay." Jason felt like he should say more, but he was at a

loss for words. It would take time to process what his father had just told him.

"You can be a great leader, Jason. Always remember why we do this and our tenets."

He nodded his understanding, and they stood together in silence for a few minutes while Jason reflected.

"I understand why you did it," Jason said at last. "Knowing the truth now, it explains a lot. I always wondered why you got upset if someone called you a hero."

"What I had to do during the war wasn't heroic. It was organized barbarism. Between Cambion and taking out the Bakzen homeworld… after all these years, I still can't wrap my head around the loss of life. I was ready to give up, waste away. Your mom is the only reason I kept going. And I'm glad I did, because being a dad to you and your sister has been the greatest gift I could ever have. I don't deserve the happiness you've brought me."

"You do, whether you believe it or not. And you'll always be a hero to me."

Wil wrapped his arms around him, and they stood together in quiet embrace. When they parted, they exchanged a knowing smile with the unspoken understanding that what had been shared would never be discussed again, with Lexi or each other.

"Well, we should get back," his father said.

Jason nodded. "Thank you for this."

"I'm glad we had the opportunity."

"Me too."

Without another word, they returned to their family to enjoy the time they had left before duty would call them home.

CHAPTER 23

RETURNING FROM ALUSHIA was a shock back to reality for Raena. It was as though time had stood still for her during the time with her family, bringing her back to the simpler times before the fate of the galaxy was a constant burden.

Only the shadow of her father's worry had detracted from the experience. It concerned her that he'd been so emotional—in his own reserved way. She hadn't expected the weighty conversations, thinking that it was just going to be a brief respite from the stress of their daily lives. Instead, she found herself more worried than she'd been before. He wouldn't have been acting that way if he didn't have genuine fears that he might not see everyone again. She hoped he was just being overly cautious.

Nonetheless, getting back into work mode after the day away was proving difficult. She'd have to get her mind in the game before attending the High Council meeting scheduled to start in a few minutes. It would be the first gathering since Celine Monsari's arrest, so there was bound to be drama. Frankly, she didn't have the stomach for it right now, but there wasn't a choice.

Given the unusual circumstances, the council had chosen a remote meeting. Raena settled into her office chair and prepared to join the holoconference.

The representation of the conference table formed in front of her, with a hologram of Ryan to her left and her grandparents to her right. She missed the easy telepathic communication of the in-person meetings, but at least she could still link with Ryan from across the estate, and there was the option of text messaging with her grandparents during the session.

Most notably, there was no place for Monsari at the table.

"This is going to be weird," she said to Ryan telepathically.

"Who's going to speak up first, I wonder?"

"You could."

"Hah! Pass."

Raena suspected her grandfather would take the lead, but he seemed to be sitting back quietly for now, reading the moods of the other attendees as they joined the holoconference. No one had so much as said 'hello', leading to increased tension as the silence stretched on.

The final seats were filled as Baellas joined, completing the group.

Raena looked over at her grandfather, expecting him to kick off the meeting now that the final attendee had arrived. To her surprise, though, he remained still and quiet, his gaze passing over the other faces.

"Well, we should get started," Kaiden jumped in, breaking the awkward tension. "Obviously, we're missing a usual member of the council. I think by now we've all heard what happened."

Everyone around the table nodded.

"The question is, where do we go from here?" Kaiden asked.

"There isn't any law dictating the number of High Council members," Eduard Baellas stated. "What are everyone's thoughts on keeping the council to its current members versus finding a replacement?"

"I think that kind of question might be getting ahead of ourselves," Kaiden said.

"Agreed, there are more pressing issues," Cris concurred. "Namely, this is a civilian matter as much as it is military. I'd like to call for a forensic audit of Monsari's private and MPS' corporate affairs to properly identify the scope and depth of the corruption."

"Isn't that a bit extreme?" the Makaris representative asked.

Spoken like someone with something to hide. Raena studied the attendees to look for signs of discomfort. Not everyone was adept at hiding their emotions, and this might be as good a chance as any to pick up subtle clues about who else warranted deeper investigation.

"Isn't it in our best interest to root out corruption?" Cris countered.

"I agree," Kaiden said. "We aren't above the law. In fact, we need to be held to a higher standard. I don't typically like the tactic of 'making an example' of anyone, but this situation is an exception. Let it be known that those who act outside the best interest of the Empire will be subject to examination."

Ryan leaned forward. "Let's be clear: this wasn't about acting outside of the Empire's interests. Celine Monsari believed what she was doing was right. Where we have a problem is that she circumnavigated proper channels to express her concerns. I don't support any actions that will undermine our trust in one another, because trust is what we need now more than ever."

Raena nodded and flashed him a covert smile. *"You're absolutely right about that."*

"Regardless of motivation, there was dangerous subversion at work," Cris said. "Moreover, the available evidence points to MPS knowingly neglecting to notify the Council about potential fulfillment issues related to critical power supply quotas, which is a violation of our mandate as core service providers."

Kaiden nodded. "I agree, there was a clear violation of core service mandates. That's why there needs to be an audit."

"Then we will proceed with one," Eduard yielded.

"And who will oversee it?" the Talsari representative asked.

"I nominate Cris Sietinen," Kaiden said. "His experience as former TSS High Commander gives him a unique perspective on this issue, as it straddles multiple concerns."

"I second the nomination," Ryan added.

Makaris and Baellas agreed, followed by Talsari.

"It's settled," Kaiden said with a nod. "Please report back to the council as soon as your findings are in order.

"I will," Cris acknowledged.

"That concludes our business for now. Speak to you in a few days." Kaiden ended the call.

The holographic conference room disappeared, leaving Raena alone in her office. A moment later, though, she received an incoming communication from her grandfather. She answered, and his image appeared on the viewscreen.

"What were your impressions?" he asked. "It went better

than I was expecting."

"I agree. Though, I think Makaris is hiding something. He got awfully shifty when we started talking about the audit and holding people accountable."

"I thought the same thing, but I was hoping I was wrong."

"No, that wasn't the behavior of someone totally innocent," she said.

"Something to look into later, then." He paused. "Oh, I just got the data-dump from Monsari and MPS. I should probably get a team organized to start going through this."

"Okay. Let me know if you need anything."

"Thanks, Raena. Talk soon." He ended the call.

She leaned back in her seat, finally able to begin decompressing. *I can't believe this is really happening.*

They'd been talking about dethroning Monsari for so many years that it hardly seemed possible for the High Dynasty to really be gone. She thought she would have felt happier about it, but, instead, she felt numb and a little uneasy.

Raena sat in the quiet solitude of her office for some time, thinking, until a knock on the door snapped her back to the present. She sensed it was Ryan. *"Come in."*

He entered and closed the door behind him. "Quite the meeting, huh?"

"I was just thinking about it," Raena said, straightening in her seat as he sat down across the desk from her.

"What are your thoughts?"

"That it's downright disturbing how everyone went along with it so easily. I mean, don't get me wrong, I'm well aware that Monsari had burned all their bridges and no one liked Celine. But it's still unnerving how a family that's been in power for a millennium was stripped of their position overnight and no one batted an eye. Really drives home that we're all disposable."

"Yeah." Ryan glanced out the window. "I'd often wondered how my ancestors had been stripped of their position, and now I realize just how easy it is to do."

"I guess that's all the more reason for us to try our best and make every action count."

"Indeed."

She let out a long breath. "I'm very curious to hear what comes up in the MPS audit. I wonder if there are co-conspirators we've yet to identify?"

"That's what I'm most anxious to learn, too."

"Then the rebuilding will begin."

"What do you think about the structure of the council?"

Raena shrugged. "I don't think they'll like it, but I say it's time for a total overhaul."

Ryan smiled. "Funny you should say that… I was thinking the same thing."

—   —   —

Jason looked over the tactical map displayed on the holoprojector in the center of the Coalition task force's strategy room. There were now a number of targets displayed as blue, indicating they had been seized by the TSS and Guard. However, there were still too many red and orange dots. Worse, gray icons appeared at several sites to denote places with unknown risk factors.

"How did they get to be this big so fast?" he muttered to no one in particular.

"On some level, the Coalition must predate the Erebus'

arrival," Gina said, the only other Agent present at the moment.

Across the table, Laura and Zak were concentrating on the map, their brows creased and eyes narrowed. Since they had been the ones to compile the latest data updates, Jason wasn't sure what to make of their expressions.

"Everything look right?" he asked.

Laura's frown deepened. "I don't know. It feels like we're missing something, but I'm not sure what."

"Yeah, look at the placement of everything here," Zak said. "Most of the supply depots are near the Coalition-occupied worlds, but I don't know what to make of these outliers."

Jason could see what he meant. In particular, there were more outposts in the Outer Colonies worlds around Zeron than there ought to be, given the known operations. "It's like it's a staging ground."

"But for *what*?" Laura crossed her arms. "Why wouldn't you stage closer to where the action will be taking place?"

"Unless our assumptions about their goals are wrong," Jason said.

The map revealed how little control the TSS had over the situation. Taking out Monsari had barely put a dent in the Coalition's operations, as much as Jason had tried to target their key facilities in the raid. Unfortunately, the organization was too underground for there to be any reliable information about all their strongholds. The TSS needed to proceed as if the organization was still armed and dangerous. That meant securing the worlds where there had been the most activity and where there was the most risk to civilians.

"Well, this map would indicate that the worlds around Zeron are the center of the action, not the planets in the sector near the Rift," Gina observed.

"Which does fit with the operations Kira witnessed on Zeron, but if that's all related to the device, then why have all these ancillary resources?"

Laura leaned back in her seat. "Nothing about this makes sense." The frustration came through in her tone, and Jason couldn't blame her.

The team had been hitting their heads up against a wall for months now, and it was incredibly disheartening to feel like they weren't making progress. The 'big raid' had been an utter disappointment. They'd expected breakthrough findings, but instead, it was obvious that the Coalition and Monsari had known the seizure was coming. Everything juicy had been stripped out, leaving only enough remnants to be passable consolation prizes.

"Isn't there an audit of Monsari's business dealings already underway?" Zak asked.

Jason nodded. "Yeah, I think my grandfather is leading it."

"Any chance we could get access to those records?"

"Seems like it might be crossing the line between government and military."

"The Coalition tied the two together in this matter," Gina pointed out.

"True. I guess it doesn't hurt to ask." Jason opened up a new text message to his grandfather. >>How's the MPS audit coming? Any chance we could get a copy of those findings to compare against our other intel?<< He sent it, expecting a polite decline.

Jason set down his handheld on the desktop. "Let's take a look at—" He cut off with a buzz from the device. *That was fast.* Normally, a speedy response was a clear 'no'. "Sorry, one sec."

He checked the message. It was a reply from his

grandfather, but to his surprise, it included an attachment along with a brief note: >>Hope this helps. – C<<

Maybe he's as ready to take down these fokers as we are. Jason opened up the file, finding it was what appeared to be a combination of financial accounts and transit logs—exactly what he had been hoping to get. He smiled. "Ask and ye shall receive."

He cast the new information onto the holoprojector so the team could go over it together. They scanned over the data.

"Stars, these records… is this a money trail?" Laura asked after several minutes of review.

Jason had been wondering the same thing. "But for what?"

"I think it's the Coalition's dealings." Gina pointed to the information. "Look, there are records here for purchases, travel… it's everything you'd need to operate underground."

"Shouldn't it be, I don't know, *coded* or something? This seems too obvious to be real," Zak said.

Jason had to agree, it did seem a little too… convenient. However, if anything was going to be straightforward, it would be this. "Think about what we had to go through to get these records," he said. "These are the inner level of secrecy. Do people bother to code their personal diary entries?"

Zak nodded. "That's a fair point."

"Under any other circumstances, I'd absolutely agree it's suspect," Jason continued. "However, I really don't think these were ever supposed to see the light of day. This is the captain's private log kept locked in a secret drawer under their bed."

"While I don't disagree, we should bear in mind that Celine handed herself in," Gina said. "Wouldn't she know that we would get access to this information?"

"True." Jason wasn't sure what to make of it. Monsari and

the Coalition had been one step, or more, ahead the entire time the TSS had been pursuing the organization. For them to lay everything out so perfectly like this—however hidden it was supposed to be—didn't make sense. Their tracks had consistently been covered at every turn. "This may be another trap or misdirection," he admitted.

"But to what end?" Gina mused.

"Well, this lays out a path." Laura scanned over the information, the enthusiasm returning to her tone now that she was on the hunt. "Presumably, they'd be trying to direct us to that endpoint."

"Hold on, I want to cross-reference this new data with the other records we have," Jason said.

He began diving into the data archives from their investigation over the past year, looking for any indications of the materials or the strategic value of the locations in question. *We have to have just missed something before. There's a reason they're pointing us toward here.*

Everything the Coalition had done was calculated, so a seemingly hidden accounting must, likewise, be a deliberate move to direct the TSS toward an intended discovery—either a physical trap or a narrative message designed to distract them from the truth.

If they want us to focus on these locations, then where should we be looking instead? He stared at it all, willing it to make sense. *There* has *to be a meaningful pattern here.*

Jason rubbed his eyes before looking at the holoprojection again. "Okay, let's do some process of elimination."

They began combing through the data from the TSS' past research and his grandfather's audit findings, looking for any clues pointing to something that was, perhaps, referenced in passing but didn't have a contrived trail leading to it. There was so much to go over that he didn't have much hope of discovering a useful clue.

Almost an hour passed as they explored the possible leads. Then, a detail jumped out at him.

"Hold on, go back," he said, swiping the holodisplay back to a previous set of data. "That location—Conthrall. Has that come up before?"

"No?" Laura replied, her tone midway between a statement and a question.

The name seemed a little familiar, but Jason couldn't place where it may have been referenced before. It definitely wasn't one of the strike targets they'd identified for the coordinated raid.

Gina wheeled her chair over to one of the nearby workstations and began searching the database for the name. Several hits came up right away.

"It's a company, not a place," she reported. "Conthrall Industries."

"Oh, that's right!" Jason's vague recollection came into focus. "That's one of the companies Dainetris tried to take over in that acquisition sweep, but they weren't able to push the sale through. It's a smaller consulting firm, so they didn't have a labor workforce to rile up into a strike."

"I thought we had looked into all those business dealings?" Zak said.

"Most of them, yes, but this one was below the threshold for releasing documentation to the public. And, now that I'm looking at it, that's downright suspicious that they have stayed *just* below the income ceiling to trigger public disclosure when all other companies in this sector have a fifteen percent year-over-year revenue growth rate."

Gina's face lit up. "This is it. This is the one piece that ties everything together."

"Well, we'll see." Despite his cautious words, the excitement was already building in Jason's chest.

While they couldn't delve into the company's private financial dealings, there were a number of public information sources to give more insight. In particular, the firm had pulled several construction permits for various locations, as well as transit logs. All of it seemed completely standard on the surface; it was only the obscure reference in the MPS log that cast any doubt about what might be going on within the business.

Hiding in plain sight this whole time. Seeing it laid out like this, it was so obvious why the TSS hadn't been able to trace the Coalition's dealings. They hadn't tried to hide anything, really—they'd been doing everything in the open, just in a place no one thought to look.

Everyone around the table had the same sheepish expression, simultaneously relieved that they'd finally cracked the mystery while also feeling silly that they hadn't figured it out sooner. It would have been a one-in-a-billion shot to stumble across it by chance, but it was tough to shake that 'but only if…' feeling, nonetheless.

Zak sank back in his chair, shaking his head incredulously. "So that's where everything went."

When the raid had yielded surprisingly few results regarding the Coalition's alleged stockpiles of munitions, Jason had known all of those materials must have gone *somewhere*. The galaxy was simply too large for them to mount a blind search. But this discovery connected all the missing pieces. It actually made perfect sense that they would have moved everything to the properties in Conthrall's portfolio—they just hadn't known the places even existed before now.

"The 'where' is helpful," Jason said, "but I'm more focused on what the materials are."

Several of the construction permits included holding vaults, which specified the materials that would be contained in each. Alone, they were nothing significant. However, in aggregate and combined with MPS' other holdings, the picture became much clearer.

Gina caught on. "They're not going to wait for the Erebus to kill Tarans. They're going to do it themselves."

"What better way to control who lives?" The mentality was everything Jason had come to expect from the Coalition's leadership, but it turned his stomach all the same.

Laura got a determined gleam in her eyes. "We've got them now. They can't hide any longer."

Jason gave a resolute nod. "Let's go take them out."

CHAPTER 24

LEXI SENSED JASON'S approaching presence a moment before a telepathic message filled her mind.

"We figured out what the Coalition has been planning. I need your help." She felt the concern in his mental tone, immediately putting her on edge.

"I'll do anything I can to help," she replied.

He reached her office thirty seconds later. Upon arrival, he stepped inside and closed the door, then hit the controls for the outer wall to turn the glass opaque.

She swallowed. "What's the situation?"

"My grandfather sent us the preliminary findings from the audit, and it filled in the pieces we've been missing. I just went over it with my dad. Assuming our interpretation is correct, we don't have a lot of time to pivot."

"What are they doing?"

"It looks like the Coalition is planning to kill off a large portion of the Taran population themselves."

Lexi's heart dropped. "They're wha—? No…"

"I didn't think they'd go to those extremes, either, but the data points to that. The Vapr drug was just one component—a test case, of sorts. The audit revealed that there are ties to Makaris, which means they may be contaminating the food supply."

"Drugging people through food rations?"

"Yes, I'm afraid so. We've identified traces of that strange ateron alloy from Zeron and the other MPS facilities, which means nanites. The materials are harmless under normal circumstances, but with the right activation trigger..." He didn't complete the thought.

"Where is it being distributed?"

"That's one of the pieces of information we just received." Jason cast a stellar map from his handheld to the holoprojector on Lexi's desk.

The color-coded map appeared, consisting of too many datapoints for her to immediately decipher. "What is this showing?"

"It's an aggregated dataset of facilities controlled by the Coalition, Monsari, and Conthrall Industries."

"Conthrall? What's that?"

"A company that's been hiding in plain sight. It's the organization connecting Monsari, the Coalition, everything."

"Stars! What—"

"The details don't matter right now. The pressing issue is the impending attack. We have a pretty good guess at which worlds will be targeted in the initial assault, and we need to act."

"Shite. We have to get the civilians out."

"There's nowhere else for them to go."

"You evacuated other planets."

"That was before we understood what was really going on. Now, it's clear nowhere is safe for long."

Lexi's heart felt like it had been ripped open in her chest. "I told them I'd—"

"I know, but there's nothing we can do for these people in isolation right now. Our only course of action is to stop this invasion before it begins."

She swallowed hard. "I'm not ready for this to be happening now."

"Tarans wouldn't be alive today if we backed down whenever there was an unexpected obstacle."

"This isn't just any obstacle, Jason."

"My point is, we're wired to fight for our survival. And that's what we need to do now."

"For the many."

He nodded. "We know target cities and planets, but that's just the start… The only thing that will save them is if we can save everyone."

"Okay. What's the plan?" she asked.

"We need to stop the Coalition from being able to deploy their trigger, but we need to move in."

"But the blockade is there, so if the TSS or Guard try to break through…"

"It would be a slaughter, I know," Jason said, his tone grim. "We need another option. That's where you come in."

"How?"

"The blockades can be dismantled from the inside if citizens can be convinced that the TSS isn't the enemy and we're trying to help. But, nothing we've said has helped the situation. The call to stand down can't come from us."

It took her a moment to realize what he was suggesting. *He wants me to send that message?* She almost laughed. "They have no reason to listen to *me*."

"Maybe not to you directly, but you've already connected with thousands of students. Those people trust you. They all have friends and families, and the word-of-mouth communication can spread from there."

Lexi didn't believe she had nearly as much power as Jason professed. She may have designed key aspects of the civilian training curriculum, but most of those students wouldn't know her name or face. Even if they did, why should anyone listen to her over anyone else?

"I wouldn't know what to say." She shrugged.

"Tell them that everything the Coalition has been saying is a lie. We need their help seizing the Coalition's assets so they can't hurt anyone else."

"That's crazy, Jason. If the TSS and Guard can't get the situation under control, then what are a bunch of unarmed civilians supposed to do?"

"The general public has the power of numbers. They always have. The only reason we can maintain any control is because the citizens let us."

She was surprised to hear him admit it so readily. Her work with the Alliance and previous observations of the Guard had made her suspect that authority was a more tenuous concept than anyone in charge would like citizens to know, but hearing it from a TSS Agent was another matter. The Coalition had taken advantage of the populace's sway, so it made sense that combating their influence would require the same tactic.

"I'll try," she agreed after taking a few moments to reflect.

"Thank you. The sooner the better. I'd offer to help, but I have my own urgent tasks."

"What are you going to do?"

"Activate the device on Zeron while my dad uses the one

on Earth, and we'll confront the Erebus together. Simple." His tone was light and confident, but she could sense his worry through their bond.

"Are you going there now?"

"Soon," he replied. "There's other prep work to wrap up. The official showdown will be in a few hours—assuming those blockades come down."

"I'm on it," she said. "Good luck."

He came around the back of her desk to give her a kiss. "You too."

I guess there's one way to find out. She began planning her approach as Jason left, retuning the room's privacy settings to what they had been before he arrived.

Her first order of business was figuring out the logistics of how to even send out a message to a large number of people at the same time. The problem was that students coming to train in the civilian program were encouraged to immerse themselves in the learning environment and, therefore, minimize outside communications. Consequently, those students may not have spoken to their loved ones much since they started class, so to reach out with an impassioned plea now might come across as a situation where the student had been brainwashed during their time away. She'd need to find a way to make the Coalition threat sound credible and worthy of communicating to anyone and everyone who'd listen.

She looked through the contact protocols, finding that there was no way to simultaneously cast a message to multiple TSS facilities without having TSS Ops authorization. While Jason could no doubt get her that clearance, a massive viewscreen takeover would grab attention, but it also might come across as desperate—accurate, but not productive. A better way would be to make a more intimate personal plea.

Lexi quickly organized talking points in her mind and then got settled in her office chair in front of the camera. She took two deep breaths to calm herself, then hit 'record'.

"Hello, my name is Lexi Karis. You might not know me, but I'm the Program Director for the Civilian Training Initiative. I was like you not that long ago—feeling a little lost and looking for an outlet for my Gifts. I found an unexpected sense of community with the TSS, and I'm hopeful that the program I helped design gives you that same kind of fulfilment. Belonging somewhere and being surrounded by people who understand you is such a rare blessing, we need to cherish it.

"It's easy to get wrapped up in ideological differences that separate us from our fellow Tarans. So often, we focus on what makes us distinct rather than what commonalities unite us. Those divides have been growing in recent years. I've watched the Coalition break apart families and entire worlds. In some small way, I hope that this training program has brought people together, but I suspect that's wishful thinking.

"The truth is, the Coalition has been trying to divide us. They want us weak and vulnerable because they have every intention of sending us to the slaughter. The higher-dimensional alien beings we call the Erebus are coming for us, but the Coalition wants to head off that attack and thin our numbers themselves so they can pick and choose who survives.

"I know, that must come as a shock and I probably sound like a crazy person, but it's the truth. I'm telling you now because I don't believe a person should be forced down any path without having an opportunity to choose their own destiny. We stand at a crossroads where you can choose to help us fight back against those who would see us destroyed.

"We may disagree with each other, but our differences pale in comparison to the threat of the Erebus. Tarans will always have more in common with each other than with any alien race. We've fractured into disparate Taran cultures, but we're united by shared threads. Let us draw on those connections now to unite against our common enemy." She paused, realizing that she hadn't given any specifics about what actions people could—and should—take.

"If you've listened to this much, then at least part of you must believe I'm speaking the truth. I hope, then, you'll believe me when I say that *this* is the fight that matters. Whatever squabbles we've had across the Taran worlds are insignificant compared to the threat coming for us right now. What we need from you is to set aside your differences and come together as we face off against these would-be invaders.

"Bring down the blockades around your planets and allow the TSS and Guard access. I don't know what that fight is going to look like, but the TSS has a plan to prevent, as much as possible, harm to all Taran worlds. If an Agent asks you to do something, then do it, unquestioningly.

"I used to not trust Taran authorities. I spent my entire youth on the run. But I've lived within TSS Headquarters for a year now, and I trust the leadership with my life. You don't know me or have any reason to trust me, but citizen-to-citizen, I'm asking you to have faith. Have faith in our people that we can get through this. Because the only way we will is together."

She ended the recording and sat back, taking a deep breath. She wasn't sure people would listen, but it was the best she could do on short notice. *Please, let this be enough.*

Lexi attached the recording to an email and selected the entire set of Gifted civilian trainees—both current students and applicants. Before she could second-guess herself, she sent the message.

Her heart pounded in her chest from anticipation. *Now we wait.*

— — —

"It's go time."

Leon spun around to see Jason standing in the doorway of his lab. "Go for what?" There were too many projects in the works to be sure what the Agent meant.

"For everything. But, specifically, we're going to deploy your countermeasure to Vapr."

Leon sat up straighter. "You found a way through the blockade?"

Jason hesitated a moment. "It's in the works. We want to be in position when we get full access. Time is of the essence."

"Sure. I think I have everything prepped."

"Great. I'd like you to go out in the field so you can be on-hand to troubleshoot if we run into any problems."

"Gladly."

Jason nodded. "I'll have my team get you transit info soon. See you on the other side."

"See you then."

As soon as the Agent left, Leon gathered up the data and materials related to the project on an external hard drive so he'd have access to everything even while communications were inaccessible in subspace. But more than that, Monica's expertise would be invaluable if they did run into trouble.

He initiated a vidcall to her. "Hey, want to go on a fieldtrip?"

An enthusiastic gleam filled her eyes, but she kept her expression neutral. "What kind of trip?"

Leon explained the situation, and her enthusiasm changed to professional focus.

"I'll meet you up at the port," she said and ended the call.

On his way to the elevator, Leon sent a quick message to Kira via his handheld. >>Sounds like the TSS is making a move against the Coalition. Are you involved?<<

She wrote back almost immediately. >>Yes, just got my orders.<<

>>I'm heading into the field—don't know where yet.<<

>>Be safe. I'll see you soon.<<

>>You too.<<

He wrapped his hand around the external drive in his pocket, ready for whatever he was about to face.

—   —   —

Everything was moving quickly now. Wil's chest was tight with anxiety, but he was also exhilarated knowing that the wait was finally over.

I hope we've prepared in the right ways. I guess we'll find out soon enough. He'd faced many battles throughout his career, but the stakes for this encounter were on a new level. Previously, they'd risked the loss of a planet or two during any given engagement. Now, the entire Taran Empire could conceivably be wiped from the galaxy in moments. The Erebus had demonstrated such power in the past. If Tarans failed, at least it would be a quick death.

Wil put the thought out of his mind. He needed to focus on the tasks at hand. Jason was coordinating the TSS' movements with Michael and the rest of the Ops team, but Wil had to function as liaison with the Guard to ensure the two entities were optimizing use of their resources.

He checked the positions of the fleet and personnel. Many vessels were still in transit. They'd need to wait to act until everyone was in place.

An incoming communication marked 'urgent' came in from offworld. Its origination was flagged as the TSS field office on Karteya.

When he answered, a blonde Agent's image appeared on the screen, her eyes wide with concern. "Sorry to bother you, sir. We have a major problem."

"Don't apologize. Explain," he said.

"I just got a tip that the remaining members of the Coalition are about to make an organized move of some sort. They said it was about Falisten."

The name hadn't come up in any research, to Wil's knowledge. "I'll need a little more to go on than that. Why do you think this is a credible concern?"

"We were able to decode a message discovered through the communication grid vulnerability. It spells out a plan. The other information recovered in the same fashion is for past events that all check out."

While it was possible that the information had been designed to look that way, the simpler—and more likely—story was that it was genuine. The Coalition was sneaky, but this would be an impractical level of deception. "Send me everything you have."

She nodded. "My team is compiling it now."

"Thank you. I'll make sure this gets to the right people."

He ended the call feeling more unsettled than he'd been

before. *I thought we'd uncovered all their secrets. What else might we be missing?*

Idle speculation wouldn't get him anywhere. There were other aspects of the upcoming stand against the Erebus for him to coordinate, and that needed to be his focus.

With the TSS and Guard fleets moving into position, the next step was to relay the final details to the Aesir. Wil opened up a commlink to Dahl.

The ancient Oracle's face filled his viewscreen. "Cadicle, what news do you bring?"

"Today is the day, Dahl. We're moving into position."

He closed his eyes and inclined his head. "We felt a shift. We are ready."

"I'm glad you agreed to work with us on this."

"As you said, it is Tarans against an alien adversary. We must unite with our own kind."

"I don't expect these truces to last, but I'll take the short-term win."

Dahl studied him. "Are you ready?"

"I'll do whatever must be done to win this fight."

"I believe it. I've seen the change in you," Dahl said. "You have accepted what you are and what you can do."

"I understand now why I've always held back."

The Oracle nodded. "And it is why I could never give you the answer."

Wil swallowed. "It was right of you to let me discover those truths myself."

"I believe you'll succeed. We're counting on it."

CHAPTER 25

CONDITIONS IN THE Outer Colonies were rapidly going to shite, from what Kira could tell. The TUF was moving in with the hope of getting the situation under control, but there were simply too many planets and too many people to manage.

She'd always known the authorities maintained a tenuous grasp over the populace. Growing up on a small, isolated world outside Tararian ruling influence, she'd seen the fire that burned within truly free people. Challenge them to a fight, and they'd see it through to their last breath.

The people in the outer Taran worlds had awakened. Granted, the Coalition's message wasn't a great catalyst to have spurred that action, but it was effective. People had realized that they wanted control over their own destinies. They wanted their worlds to be able to prosper and be independent without relying on corporations and governance based on the other side of the galaxy.

They picked the worst possible time to take that stand, she thought to herself while looking over the latest updates from Karteya and the other Coalition-occupied worlds.

She and her small team had put together a makeshift command base on a transport ship to serve as a mobile operations center for the TUF. The ship was former TSS, and the crew was a mixture of TSS and Guard personnel who'd been recruited into the TUF. As the new military branch grew, they'd eventually have their own training program. For now, they were a disparate group of people united by a common vision—perhaps the most fitting team to tackle the particular brand of civil unrest they now faced.

Of course, the entire situation was by design. The Coalition recognized that their plan had a much better chance of success with a fractured populace. They'd ensured that the worlds would take actions to isolate themselves, and then they'd had the people put up blockades to close themselves off completely. It was preventing the TSS from deploying the antidote to Vapr. Leon had explained to her how the treatment would work, and it was clear that the TSS would be helpless until they could get planetside. Making sure the planets couldn't be accessed was as much a part of the Coalition's plan as the destructive effects of Vapr itself.

Hoping for people to see through the ruse was their best chance now. Lexi had sent out a plea, and Kira had been spreading her own messages. With any luck, something would resonate.

"Ma'am, we just got an update," the comm officer stated.

"Bring it up," Kira instructed.

A video feed from Karteya appeared on the forward viewscreen, focused on one of the access gates. The cargo ships in front of the gate were moving away.

Kira's heart lifted with a glimmer of hope. "Is there any radio chatter?"

"Vessels are being asked to stand down and allow access for TSS and Guard ships," the comm officer reported.

It could be a trap. As much as Kira wanted to begin spreading the antidote, she didn't want to risk anyone getting hurt. "Don't move in yet. We need visuals at street level. Send in a probe and let's see what we're dealing with."

Their ship dispatched a probe, which flew down through the access gate to investigate the main city on the planet.

Kira expected to see armed Coalition mercenaries ready to shoot it out of the sky. Instead, her chest swelled with joy. Citizens had risen up against the Coalition members, who were being escorted in restraints to holding areas. The people had reclaimed their world.

A voice message came through. "Please, help us. We didn't realize what the Coalition was planning. We don't want to die."

"Tell them help is coming," Kira said. "What about the threat that was identified in the recoded message? We need to make sure that's neutralized."

"Coordinating with the locals now," the helm officer replied.

Kira allowed herself to relax the slightest measure. Things were looking up. *We can still win this fight.*

— — —

Good news from Kira was a promising start, but Jason knew they weren't out of the woods yet. The Coalition was a minor threat compared to the coming Erebus invasion.

He was too anxious to sit, so he paced across his office while keeping an eye on the field updates. Seeing the situation on Karteya, he was grateful Lexi had returned to Headquarters when she did. After the story his father had told him about what happened with his mom during the Bakzen War, he liked knowing that Lexi was somewhere safe—as safe as anyone could be from the Erebus, anyway.

Distribution of the antidote was well underway under Kira's and Leon's leadership. Its effectiveness couldn't be assured until it was put to the test, but at least they were taking productive steps forward.

With the immediate civilian and Coalition concerns now under control, it was time to brace for the standoff with the Erebus. Jason had talked over the plan with his father at length. It would test both of them, no doubt. Jason had never pushed his Gifts to their limit, but this experience would likely change how he looked at himself and what he could do.

It was almost time to head to Zeron. He grabbed his handheld off the desktop and headed for Lexi's office.

She looked up when he approached the doorway, fear in her eyes.

"I couldn't leave without seeing you one more time," he said with a sad smile.

Lexi got up and ran to him, wrapping her arms around him. He kissed her.

"Great job on that message," he said. "You saved the day."

"I don't think it was all me."

"We'll never know for sure, but it definitely helped."

She pulled back from their embrace enough to look into his eyes. "What's going to happen when you go to Zeron?"

"I wish I knew." Jason pulled her in for another hug. "I will do everything I can to come back to you—and to make sure we still have a home."

"I'll be waiting for you."

"You can do more than that. I know I'm going to have to push myself harder and farther than I ever have. You can be an anchor for me, from afar. Help me find my way back."

She nodded. "I can do that."

He kissed her. "I love you."

"I love you, too. You've got this."

Her words of encouragement meant everything in that moment. Truthfully, he was terrified and had no idea if he was up for the challenge ahead. Knowing that they were in this together, though, at least they had the best possible chance of success.

When he left her office, Jason headed for the central elevator. There was no point in bringing a travel bag. Either they'd be successful and he'd be home in a few hours, or they'd all be dead. The threat of total annihilation was a good motivator.

— — —

Wil stood in the center of his office, feeling charged in a way he hadn't experienced since the Bakzen War.

He'd vowed to never draw upon the full extent of his powers again, but when he'd made that promise to himself, he hadn't imagined an enemy like the Erebus. Now, he'd give anything to ensure his family and future generations were protected against that menace.

A knock sounded at the door to his office, and Saera entered. "Hey. I thought you'd be on your way to Earth by now?"

"Not necessary." He'd gone over the general plan about how he'd interface with the device on Earth while Jason connected with the one on Zeron, but he hadn't discussed the logistical details with her. "It occurred to me that the aliens connected with the device every year, but there was no way they could have gone underground into the pits."

"So, astral projection?" Saera surmised.

"It makes much more sense. The device is designed for higher-dimensional beings. Its functions don't follow the same rules as our physical reality."

"Okay. What happens next?"

"I'll make contact here while Jason does the same at Zeron. But first, I want to get the team together."

"Yeah, I guess it is time to circle the wagons." Had it not been for his time on Earth, the phrase would make no sense.

On his handheld, he sent out a message to the senior Agents to meet in the conference room next door. Then, he and Saera headed over.

"How are you feeling?" she asked while they waited for the others to arrive.

"I think you know." He hadn't tried to mask his concern and anticipation through their bond.

She nodded. "We haven't talked much since Alushia. Those conversations—" She cut off abruptly as Ian entered.

He smiled in greeting at Wil and Saera. "I'm so glad we finally get to go up against these fokers."

"Maybe rein it in a notch," Wil advised, though he understood his friend's enthusiasm.

"You know I keep a cool head when it matters," Ian replied. And he did; he'd proven that in the war, when he was far younger and less experienced. There was certainly no reason to doubt him now.

Soon, Ethan and Michael also arrived, rounding out the

Agent division heads in TSS Headquarters. More than just the senior-most officers, they were Wil's closest friends—the people he'd been able to count on most over the past decades.

Sitting in the conference room with them now, he suddenly found himself at a loss for words. *What can I possibly say that will do our time together justice?* He sat quietly for several moments, looking at their expectant faces. "The TSS is what it is today because of this incredible team."

Ian grinned. "We'd be lost without our fearless leader."

"Hardly." Wil returned the smile, but he couldn't share his friend's jovial attitude. "You, Michael, Ethan, and Saera keep the day-to-day operations going. I'm just a figurehead and occasional decision-maker. You don't need me."

"We most certainly do," Saera said.

The tightness returned to Wil's chest. "Regardless, it's good to know the TSS is in capable hands, no matter what."

Saera flashed him a questioning look, but he deflected. "It's been an honor serving with you, and to call you friends."

There were heartfelt nods and smiles around the table, but it was clear they'd taken it as a pep talk rather than a potential farewell. It was probably better that way.

The group adjourned to tend to their assigned tasks. Wil followed Ian out into the hall and to his office. "There's one other thing."

"Sure."

Wil motioned them inside the private space and closed the door. "I don't say often enough how much I value your friendship and counsel. Thank you."

His friend caught Wil's somber mood and gave him an understanding nod before playfully flipping it around in his typical fashion. "You came all this way just to confirm how awesome I am? Aw, shucks!"

"You're impossible."

"Hey, we'll get through this just fine, don't worry."

"It's my job to worry."

Ian smirked. "Fine. Then I'll have enough optimism for the both of us."

"That's how it's always been."

His smile fell when he saw Wil's mood remained serious. "What did you want to discuss?"

Wil searched for the right words, knowing that this very well could be a goodbye. There was so much he wanted to say but didn't want to state it directly. "It can be lonely at the top, and you've always had a way of finding the bright spots in the darkness. Please, in the event anything happens, promise me that you'll make sure Saera isn't alone."

"Wil…"

"Just promise me."

Ian swallowed and nodded. "I promise."

"Okay." No more needed to be said than that. After being friends for nearly forty years, Ian would understand the rest.

"It won't come to that," Ian said.

"I can't face what will happen next without knowing my loved ones will be okay."

"You have my word. Now stop being all doom and gloom and get to work." He raised an eyebrow with mock condemnation.

Wil cracked a smile despite the heaviness in the pit of his stomach. "Right. Back to saving the universe."

He would have liked to take a private moment with each of his friends, but time was too short, and he couldn't risk any more emotional distraction. This conversation with Ian was the one he deemed most essential, aside from Saera.

She clearly knew he had been holding something back from her. But this matter was simply too important—he'd needed to prepare for the worst-case contingency, and she wouldn't have allowed him to think in those terms. Under other circumstances, he'd welcome her eternal optimism. However, he needed to come to terms, for his own sake. As much as he hoped for a positive outcome, there was more risk this time than ever before.

Saera was waiting for him in his office when he returned after chatting with Ian. Wordlessly, she walked up to him and wrapped him in a tight embrace.

"Come home soon," she said into his chest.

His heart lurched. "This time, I can't make that promise, Saera."

She pulled back. "So, it wasn't just talk—in the meeting today. The 'it's been an honor' stuff."

"It needed to be said."

"Except, that's what a person says when they don't expect to make it back home. First Alushia, then the staff meeting, and now—"

"I won't pretend like this is any random mission." Wil had anticipated that this conversation with her would be the most difficult of any today. But he hadn't taken into account seeing and feeling her pain. "I know what must be done to end this, but it very well may be a one-way trip. I don't want to leave anything unsaid."

She gazed into his eyes, pleading. "Then don't go. We'll find another way."

"There isn't one, Saera. I've explored every possibility, and this is the way it has to be."

"It sounds like you're giving up."

"No, I've just accepted the situation for what it is. We could never expect to make it through this without sacrifice. I won't have any other lives on my hands—especially when it wouldn't make a difference. *I* can. This is something I *have* to do."

She shook her head, tears welling in her eyes. "Don't you dare leave me alone."

"Even without me, you'll never be alone, Saera. There are so many people who love and rely on you. I want you to live life to the fullest, no matter what happens to me."

"My life *is* with you."

"And so much more beyond me. You've known from the beginning that I never expected to even make it to thirty. These past few decades have all been bonus time, and I'm so thankful for it. I've experienced so much more in life than I ever thought I'd have the opportunity to do. Without you, I don't think I would have survived the war, let alone have a reason to keep going after. You have been the light of my life, and I'm so grateful for your love and support. You are, by far, the most incredible person I know."

"Please, don't do this."

He shrugged. "I either try, or we very well may be facing the extinction of the Taran race—if not in this encounter, then one to follow. I vowed to do anything to give our children hope for a good future, and now I need to follow through."

She worked her mouth, and he could sense her trying to phrase a suitable rebuttal while slowly coming to the realization that he was right. They'd been fortunate to repeatedly avert disaster, always driving toward the time when luck would no longer be enough to see them through unscathed.

"You're my everything," she said at last.

"And you are mine." He held her at arms' length, gazing into her jade eyes. "There were times when I saw the possibility of growing old together, but maybe it was never really in the cards. I'm so thankful for these years together I'd never expected to have."

"Wil, I don't want to lose you. I can't…"

He embraced her. "I will always be with you. This isn't really goodbye."

She clutched him close, sniffing back tears. "If there's a way through this, I know you'll find it."

"I'll do my best."

"Do you want me here with you?"

"It's more important for you to keep an eye on Headquarters and TSS Ops. You'll be an anchor for me no matter where you are."

Saera gave him a resolute nod, forcing back her emotions with trained control.

He leaned in for a kiss, deep and slow—savoring the contact to preserve in memory. "I love you always," he whispered aloud and in her mind, accompanied by a mental caress as he took her hands in his.

"I love you." The concern was still there in her tone, but also acceptance.

"Thank you for everything, my love." Before he could lose his nerve, he pulled away and prepared to face his fate.

CHAPTER 26

"STARS! THIS IS really happening, isn't it?" Raena's heart pounded in her chest, her palms clammy from a cold sweat.

She paced across her office while Ryan stood next to her desk, his arms crossed.

"I wish they'd shared more about what they're planning," Ryan said.

"Me too." Nonetheless, Raena understood why the details had been kept classified. There were clearly security breaches in multiple areas, and the fewer people who knew, the less chance the remaining members of the Coalition had to counter the TSS' actions.

She wanted to trust all of her people, but there was simply no way to know if anyone had been compromised. If there was important information she needed to know, she was confident her father would find a way to communicate it to her. For the time being, she'd just stand at the ready.

Of course, waiting around for instructions wasn't her strong suit. She craved action. Pacing around her office was a poor substitute for being in the fight.

Ryan eyed her. "You're going to wear a hole in the floor."

"Then we'll redo the tile."

"You need to trust your parents and brother to handle this."

"I do. But that doesn't mean I can't worry all the same."

He nodded. "I'm concerned, too. I can't imagine how they intend to face off with the Erebus. Those videos from before…"

Raena's stomach clenched with the thought. She'd watched the recording of the Alkeer base's destruction dozens of times, looking for answers, but had only been left with more questions about how such swift and total obliteration was possible. It seemed impossible to stand up to that power. What had they learned since then that made a direct confrontation feasible?

Ryan walked up to her and placed his hands gently on her upper arms, stopping her pacing. "No matter what happens, I'll be here with you."

She wrapped her arms around him. "I have a bad feeling about it. I don't know why."

He held her close. "Try not to focus on that. We've got each other."

"But this isn't just about us. We have trillions of people who expect us to keep them safe."

"And we'll do everything we can. Right now, that's letting the TSS take the lead."

Reluctantly, she nodded. "If anyone can pull this off, it's them."

— — —

The *Conquest*'s Command Center was eerily quiet as the

ship dropped back into normal space near Zeron. Jason had gone over the plan with the skeleton crew, and they were all stoic and focused on the mission at hand.

"We're in position," Rianne stated.

Jason nodded. "Thank you. You all know what to do."

Their assignment was straightforward enough: keep an eye out for any offensive action against the ship, and fight back if necessary. Meanwhile, Jason would remotely connect with the device on Zeron—hopefully—and use it to tunnel through to the higher dimensions in a coordinated action with his father on Earth. The key to that plan was activating all of the new Erebus-designed power cores across the Taran worlds to create the interactive energy field identified during their analysis. It was all theoretical and they wouldn't know for sure it would work until they tried.

Jason sat in the ergonomic seat at the center of the Command Center, designed precisely for this kind of astral projection scenario, and activated the podium handholds to give him a direct physical connection to the ship. A tingle spread up his arms and through his core as the *Conquest*'s neural interface linked with him.

The vessel's presence grounded him, giving him a tether to reality as he began to drift away from his corporeal self. He reached out across the void, searching for his father's presence.

"*I'm ready,*" he said when he found him, still attached to his body back at TSS Headquarters.

"*I'll give the order,*" Wil said.

On the *Conquest*, Jason was distantly aware of the crew communicating. The order had been given for all of the Erebus power cores to be simultaneously brought online. While many of the devices had been in operation for months, the deployment had been on a comparatively small scale.

Bringing them all online had two functions.

First, the power cores served as the energy source for the new, upgraded shields that had been designed using the ancient Aesir tech from the Archive. The shields had a transdimensional component, which should, in theory, provide a measure of protection against Erebus an attack. Once online, the planet would be in its own bubble, and that outer shell extended outside of spacetime. They had only tried deploying the tech on a small scale, so this test was a critical moment. Unfortunately, any prior tests might have given away what they were planning, so they'd decided to save it for their one shot.

Second, bringing all of the power cores online would produce the strange energy field they'd observed in the models. As far as they could tell, this field was intended to be a secret byproduct the Erebus had engineered into the design. When activated in conjunction with the devices on Earth and Zeron, it would produce conditions that would make it easier for the Erebus to interact with spacetime—and vice versa.

Jason understood why they were proceeding with the plan, but he couldn't help feeling conflicted about opening the door for the Erebus invasion. At least this way, the timing was on their terms.

We will succeed, Jason told himself. His own mental tone sounded doubtful, but he tried to internalize the belief as much as possible.

They had to succeed, because otherwise this was the end. His life with Lexi was just getting started, and he wasn't ready for that journey to be over. Somehow, they'd find a way to make it through this.

A surge of power passed through Jason—a different feeling than anything he'd experienced before. After taking a few seconds to adjust to the sensation, he sought out its source. He realized that it was from the power cores now active across the Taran worlds.

"There is something really weird about this," he commented to his father.

"I felt something similar, less intensely, when I interfaced with the device on Earth."

"I guess it's working, then?"

"Let's find out. See if you can interface with the Zeron device."

"Okay," Jason acknowledged.

He reached out to the planet below, searching for an energy signature similar to the field that was spreading across the galaxy. As his consciousness got closer to the planet, a strange, discordant hum stood out to him. He moved toward it.

The source of the hum came from deep underground, beneath the city carved out from the ancient rock. The structures weren't natural, as far as he could tell. Something had torn up the land and reformed it, not unlike the planets the Gatekeepers had transformed. This was an ancient world holding secrets from another era. Those remnants may well have remained hidden had the Coalition not overstepped.

Jason extended his consciousness through the underground facility to the deepest levels, where he found the pit Kira had discovered during her mission. It was similar to the place his father had visited on Earth, though the surface was rougher. Rock had somehow filled in the pit at some point, before it had been chiseled back out.

Kira's research had revealed the strange properties of the place, but it was odd for Jason to see the remnants of apparently liquified rock with his own senses. It would have been possible for a concrete-like substance to fill the pit in that way, but this had none of those granular characteristics. Whatever tech had allowed the place to be filled in without damaging the structure itself was remarkable—or, perhaps that spoke more of the material from which the pit was crafted. The alien materials could very well be from another galaxy.

The hum he sensed was low and faint, as though the device was idle. He noted that unlike the device on Earth, this one wasn't illuminated in any fashion—no flowing blue light through the carved channels in the rocks. Yet, he could feel a presence, so the device didn't seem to be irrevocably broken.

At the bottom of the pit, he saw a spherical structure. The strongest energy was coming from that object. In Kira's video surveillance, the sphere and pillar had still been partially encased in rock. Now, it was clear. They must have continued the excavation efforts after the blockade was formed around the planet.

Jason reached out with his astral self to touch the sphere. The chamber sprang to life with a soft blue glow. Rivulets of ethereal light began to gather in the carved channels, outlining complex patterns reminiscent of circuitry. The hum that he'd sensed from afar grew louder and more urgent. Simultaneously, the ribbons of light increased their speed and glowed brighter.

He closed the remaining distance to the sphere. The discordant hum morphed into whispers. It reminded him of wind blowing through tree branches, with swells and lulls that gave the sound a rhythmic quality.

His mind began to buzz. The energy was trying to get inside him. The whispers became more urgent. He strained to find meaning in the sound.

"Give in," he understood at last.

I need to trust and let go. He surrendered.

— — —

Wil sensed Jason slip into a trance-like state from afar. His son would no doubt find interfacing with the device on Zeron to be as disorienting and confusing as his first time pairing with its counterpart on Earth.

Before, Wil had backed away after he'd achieved the link. Now, he needed to see that connection through to its conclusion. *I hope this does what we think it does.*

However, it was more than guesswork. He had seen the events play out through his astral projection roamings to 'read the pattern' in the way that the Aesir had urged. In those infinite variations, he'd seen the ways this moment could play out. The specific outcome wasn't clear, but he was confident that this was the right thing to do.

Wil settled onto the couch in his office, laying down with his arms at his sides. While he normally sat on the floor during astral projection, this fight might last longer than those explorations, and he wanted to make sure his body could maintain a stationary position for an extended period.

Just like I've done before. Nothing to it. He closed his eyes and took several slow, even breaths as he separated from his physical self.

His consciousness lifted from his body and he traveled up through Headquarters, taking in the scenes of dedicated workers around him on Level 1 as he headed toward the central elevator shaft. He quickly passed through the shaft, then soared past the TSS spaceport and over toward Earth.

The marbled blue and green sphere was even more picturesque today as he took in the sight, lingering just long enough to burn it into memory as it appeared right now. The place had been as close to a home as he'd ever had outside TSS Headquarters. For a time, it had afforded him a taste of life without the weight of being responsible for the fate of a civilization. It was fitting that his bid for freedom from the Erebus would happen in the same place.

He allowed his mind to descend toward Earth. Rather than focusing solely on the site in Belize where he'd made contact before, Wil searched out the other ancient sites that had been mapped out around the globe. He extended a portion of himself to each, making contact simultaneously.

"No more hiding," he said. *"I know you're there, and we're coming for you."*

The now-familiar whispers swirled around him, infiltrating his mind with their eager rasps.

They burrowed into him, entwining. Where he'd resisted before, he gave in now. They pulled at him, stretching his sense of self. He felt himself extending beyond the reality of spacetime, reaching toward a higher dimension than even his astral form.

In the distance, he felt Jason's link with the device on Zeron, stretching him in a similar way. Wil reached out to join with his son, combining their powers from across the void. The energy field of the two devices began to sync. It resonated with the larger field from the power cores.

The veil between the dimensions began to weaken at the

points near the devices.

It's working! Wil fed more energy into the connection.

He needed to direct that energy into communication with the entities beyond the veil, and for that, he needed a translator. While extended across the galaxy, he searched for the presence of Pesta—not knowing exactly what form it might take, only that it would be unique. He sensed Jason respond to what he was doing and begin aiding in the search.

"Over here!" Jason called Wil's attention to a remote world at the fringe of Taran space, in a sector adjacent to Zeron.

"Pesta," Wil addressed the mysterious entity. *"We need your help."*

"I'm not Pesta anymore. I'm Ava. I don't want to hurt anyone. Please, leave me alone."

The response caught Wil by surprise. *"We don't want to hurt anyone, either. In fact, that's what we're trying to prevent. The beings that made you want to destroy us, and we want to stop them."*

He felt a swell of anger from Ava. *"They are evil."*

"Yes. I need to know how to access the higher dimensions. Can you lead the way?"

Ava hesitated. *"I'm afraid."*

"Your new vessel will die along with us if we don't stop this invasion. I just need you to show me the path. You don't need to fight."

For a long moment, no response came. Then, Ava said, *"I don't know you. How can I be sure you aren't one of those who take everything?"*

They were running out of time. Wil couldn't think of a way to compel the entity to do what they needed. *"Ava, the people you talk about already know how to access the higher dimensions. That's how they created you, and we need your help to stop them or it'll be the end for all of us."* Wil wasn't sure that the explanation would mean anything to Ava, but the entity's animosity toward those who'd created it had to be based in fear.

"I don't know who you are."

A pang of desperation shot through Wil. *"My name is Wil Sietinen, and—"*

"Why didn't you say so?" Ava cut in. *"Kali spoke highly of you."* She paused. *"Okay, I'll help."*

A tunnel abruptly opened up in Wil's mind's eye—not anything through which he could travel in a physical sense, but a change in his perception. It wasn't unlike when he'd first learned how to perform astral projection, only this was a wondrous new level of awareness. He soared through the opening as Ava retreated back to wherever she'd found a life in her assumed Taran body.

Wil was about to ask her to stay a little longer as a guide when he realized why she'd run away. There was another presence on the other side of the divide. It stirred, clawing to get through.

The Erebus. They felt even more powerful now that he was close to making contact.

The energy flowed through him, burning—though he wasn't sure if it was his body back in Headquarters or if it was searing the very nature of his being. He ignored the sensation of pain. It was meant to deter him, and he wouldn't stop no matter what.

Centered on Earth—and around Zeron—the devices had come online. The energy field was intensifying, boring a tunnel to the higher dimensions.

"The bridge is open," the device informed him, the whispers joined into a unified voice.

"What now?"

"The veil is lifted."

It was a cryptic response from an artificial intelligence, and Wil wasn't sure what to make of it. He didn't need to wait long to find out.

The energy field that had been isolated around the two planets began to spread. As it did, great cracks of light fanned out, like branches of lightning through the fabric of reality itself. Each line widened, forming a chasm with borders that appeared to bend and shift, similar to the appearance of a spatial distortion around a ship moments before it slipped into subspace.

"It's destabilizing!" he said to Jason across the expanse.

"Something is missing," his son said. *"It's like it needs another contact point."*

Wil watched the behavior. He could see what Jason meant. It was like an electrical charge looking for a ground, dancing everywhere from point to point.

I don't understand. We looked at everything.

And then he realized. *"There's another device. There has to be!"*

He spread out his consciousness, searching for where it might be. Intuitively, he looked on the other side of the galactic core near the main Taran population center. That placement would allow triangulation with the two sites they'd already identified.

Sure enough, as he explored around Tararia, he sensed the pull.

It made sense. The location formed a well-proportioned

triangle. Add in the position of the Rift, originating from the site of the Bakzen homeworld, and the vast majority of the Taran Empire's territory was contained within an imaginary box formed by the four points. The population expansion had been planned, keeping everyone within that scope of control.

They truly thought of everything. Wil had experienced many revelations about the master plans and manipulations in his life, but nothing compared to the sheer scope of this deception. The Priesthood had learned from the best, and seeing the work of their masters laid out in all its exquisite horror was equal parts sickening and impressive.

The Taran race had been shepherded like wayward lambs, sheered of their wool that might have offered some protection by making it more difficult for a wolf to get a bite. But now that their coats were growing back, in spite of all efforts to the contrary, they were being offered up for the slaughter in their little pen they hadn't even realized was around them.

We won't go down without a fight. Now was the moment. They had to make their stand.

With a little more power, they'd have enough to lock the corridor to the higher dimensions. Getting a fix on the Erebus was their only chance. But Wil and Jason couldn't activate the third device on their own. They needed help. There was only one person capable.

Wil reached out to his daughter from across the void. *"Raena, we need you."*

CHAPTER 27

RAENA HEARD HER father's plea from across the void. She met Ryan's concerned gaze.

"What is it?" he asked when he saw her panicked expression.

"My dad and Jason are in trouble. I have to help."

An alert lit up on her desk, prompting the viewscreen to come to life with a live video feed. Space around Tararia was streaked with dimensional fissures.

"Oh, my stars!" Raena's mouth went dry.

Ryan gaped at the images. "How is anyone supposed to stand up to *that*?"

"I don't know, but I have to try."

"Raena, don't—"

"This is more important than anything," she said. "They wouldn't ask if it wasn't necessary."

Reluctantly, he nodded. "Be careful."

"I'll be back soon." She gave him a quick kiss, then went to lay down on the couch. She closed her eyes and slowed her breathing.

Raena separated from her physical self and began drifting outward toward space, just as she'd practiced with her father as a teenager. She didn't often explore through astral projection these days, but the freedom of it now reminded her just how amazing a feeling it was. *Why did I ever stop?*

Simply asking the question reminded her of the answer. It was too tempting. The allure of the Rift was stronger in this state, free from the burdens of normal physical reality. It felt like anything was possible.

The power... She could taste it—not in a corporeal sense, but through it infusing her innermost being.

Raena quickly shook off the feeling. She didn't need that distraction now. Finding her father and brother was what mattered.

She set off through space, her consciousness speeding past stars and planets while she extended her senses even further beyond. She sensed her father and Jason out there, doing the same.

The three of them linked—unable to see each other, but their minds made it seem like they were standing side by side.

Energy surged through her. She felt it from beyond Tararia, but there was also a pull from the planet itself. She searched around for the source.

My stars... It was coming from beneath her, below Morningstar Isle. Of course, the Priesthood had made this place their base for a reason. The answers had been here all along, forgotten. Perhaps the Priests didn't even know the importance.

No, they must have, she realized. The Priests had made a bid for ascension from the island. They'd used a device then— nothing like the Gatekeeper or Erebus tech—but the TSS hadn't been able to figure out how it worked. It may, in fact, have been interfacing with the hidden device buried deep beneath Tararia. In that case, they may have been closer to accomplishing their goals than anyone had realized.

She sought the energy source out now, no hesitation. If they could access the higher dimensions, then she could, too. And she had a fight to win.

The device called out to her as her mind neared it, encouraged by her father and brother. Whispers filled her mind, moving through her and becoming part of her. She gave into its call, allowing herself to be swept up in its power.

As she made contact, the other hum of energy spanning across the void changed its pitch. What had been chaotic began to settle, become more organized. It was now under their control. They could focus it, direct it.

Ripples formed behind the spatial fractures, as though something was pressing against the fabric of reality from the other side. The veil twisted and contracted. Then, it ripped through.

A creature emerged, unlike anything Raena had witnessed. It existed as both an astral presence like her current self and also in physical reality, with an elongated body and wing-like limbs. She couldn't help but be reminded of legendary dragons, though alien in its shape and proportions, at least two kilometers in length.

More of them began to break through the dimensional veil, some larger and others smaller than the first. They fanned out in all directions from the break points, and more were flooding through from other locations.

"Are these the Erebus?" Jason asked.

They weren't like the image Raena had seen of the

Andvari's attacker. *"I don't think so,"* she said. *"We didn't give the Erebus the energy source they needed to come through themselves, right? This has to be something else."*

It was a guess, but she suspected these creatures were considered disposable—an advance force meant to weaken Tarans enough for the Erebus to come through after and finish the job. *The dogs of war are actually transdimensional dragons. What in the stars have we gotten ourselves into?*

Jason took in the horrific sight. *"Whatever they are, I don't want to find out if they're as powerful as their masters."*

"We have to target one of them," Wil said in her and Jason's minds.

Attacking the creatures seemed impossible. She'd never seen something so monstrous and powerful. Yet, there was an ethereal, translucent quality to their forms—as if a jellyfish was made out of lightning. The analogy seemed silly the moment she thought it, but putting it in familiar terms helped it seem more manageable.

Jellyfish can't move out of the water. We need to take the creatures out of their element. She shared the mental image with her father and brother. *"Focus on the monsters. Bring them into the field."* The device was supposed to make things in the higher dimensions be beholden to the rules of spacetime, so this was the perfect test case.

Her father acknowledged the suggestion. *"Follow my lead."*

— — —

Leon's heart pounded as he took in the sights unfolding in the video feeds on the viewscreen in front of him. "What the…?"

Monica and everyone on the crew seemed to be at a loss for words. The fabric of reality around Tararia, Zeron, and Earth was cracking—opening into rifts.

Was this the plan? He didn't know what the TSS had in mind for the engagement, but he had a job to do himself. "What's the latest on the energy readings?"

They'd been monitoring the energy field generated by the Erebus power cores to look for the activation trigger of the Vapr nanites.

"The field is expanding," Monica replied. "Checking the impact now."

Leon clutched the fabric of his pants in his fists to keep from fidgeting. He had no clue how to go about modifying the tech further if the antidote didn't work.

"No incident reports planetside," the comm officer stated.

"Confirmed. The readings are looking good," Monica added. "I'm seeing complete nullification of the Vapr nanotech!"

Leon leaned back in his seat with relief. The feeling was short-lived, though, as his attention shifted to the scenes playing out on the forward display. "Good, because I think we have bigger problems."

The small team stared with horror as creatures started to emerge from the dimensional fissures around the distant planets.

The helm officer let out a shaky breath, eyes wide. "What in the stars are those?"

—   —   —

The battle hadn't started out at all how Wil had imagined.

He'd pictured that a singular tear would open through the dimensional veil, and they'd be able to see the Erebus on the other side. If a part of the creature passed across that window, they'd be able to attack and hurt it.

The prospect of multiple, smaller creatures coming through so many micro-rifts hadn't been part of the tactical planning. However, they did have contingency strategies in place, and he knew exactly what to do.

"Jason, Raena, try to herd the creatures together," he instructed. Carrying out that order would doubtfully be as simple as herding cattle, but maybe they'd be pleasantly surprised.

While his children started working on that, Wil reached out to Michael, using the same telepathic communication methods he'd honed during the war with his Primus Elites team. *"We need to do something about those monsters."*

"I was just thinking the same thing," Michael replied over the near-instantaneous connection. *"What's the plan?"*

"Looks like a job for TK weapons. The Conquest *and the Aesir's ships, and maybe the IT-1s. Let's throw everything at them and see if we make a dent."*

"I'm on it," his friend acknowledged.

He shifted his focus to Jason and Raena. They had formed a telekinetic net around a group of the creatures. The monsters kept trying to slam against the barrier, but they'd recoil upon striking the invisible boundary.

We manipulate the aesen *with our Gifts. That's the source of the creatures' power, too. They can't strike back so long as we have a hold.* It was encouraging news, but it also meant they'd need to maintain a continual energy draw. He had no idea how long they might be able to keep it up.

Wil joined his children's efforts, roping in some of the creatures they had yet to contain. Touching the alien beings with his telekinetic hooks sent a strange, tingling chill through him. It wasn't like manipulating matter in spacetime, but rather felt like touching pure energy itself.

Curious, he tried to sap energy from the creature directly. An electrical surge flowed into Wil, and the creature bucked, spinning around to protect the part of itself Wil had touched.

"Don't attack. Drain them by charging the TK weapons from inside!" Wil announced through the telepathic network. His children and Michael acknowledged.

Aesir ships and a squadron of TSS IT-1 fighters emerged from subspace. The craft swarmed the creatures and flew inside them. Even the large Aesir cruisers appeared like tiny toys compared to the massive aliens.

The creatures writhed and lashed out as the ships activated their TK weapons, drawing energy—essentially, draining the creatures' lifeforce. One of the beast's movements began to slow as the weapon glowed with a strong charge. The movements stopped. And then, the translucent essence dissolved and dissipated.

"Did that kill it?" Jason asked.

"I think so," Wil replied. Truthfully, he had no idea if it was only the being's presence in spacetime that had been disrupted or if it had been eliminated across all dimensional levels of existence.

More creatures flooded through the openings. They didn't have enough ships to tackle them all. And, moreover, what did killing them accomplish? They needed to end a war, not just a single battle. If they continued down this path, it'd either be a long, brutal fight, or they'd wipe out the invading force and have eliminated an entire race. He'd been through that once before, and it wasn't an experience he wanted to repeat.

He pulled back from the attacks, holding the creatures without hurting them, as he addressed Jason and Raena. *"What we're trying to do to them is the same thing they wanted to do to us. Total annihilation isn't the answer here."*

Raena was stunned by the statement. *"What other choice do we have? They won't stop."*

"No, not so long as they can reach us. But we can end this by cutting off their access."

"And how do we do that?" Raena asked.

"By closing the Rift."

"That's impossible," Jason said. *"We tried."*

"Other people did. Not us."

"Dad's right. We need to try," Raena said.

"We'll do it together," Wil acknowledged. He tapped into the larger telepathic network with TSS Command. *"Direct the TK weapons to hold the creatures in place. Don't attack. We're going to try to seal the Rift."*

Wil, Jason, and Raena extended their consciousness toward the source of the dimensional rupture—the Rift on the other side of the galaxy. All of the other breaches originated from that point, using it as an access gateway. If they cut off that entry, permanently, nothing would be able to get through.

That was the true purpose of the Zeron device, Wil realized.

Alone, the device on Earth could create a bridge, but the multiple devices in tandem could strip away the dimensional veil. It placed the operators in spacetime in control, with the creatures on the higher dimensions at their mercy. That was why the Coalition had been conducting their excavation on Zeron in secret and had kept it from the Erebus.

If Wil and his children applied the right energy while the dimensions were so closely aligned, they might be able to create a permanent barrier between them that would persist after the devices were disabled. He shared the concept with Jason and Raena, using images rather than spoken words. They acknowledged the plan.

Together, they reached out with all the energy they could muster, extending themselves across the fractures to grasp every minute crack. Each one of them individually couldn't have come close, but the link had made them stronger. Wil had never found his limit, and even now, he felt invincible.

This might actually work! He drew more energy, ready for the final step.

The three of them pushed with all their might, willing the broken seams of their reality to knit back together. The tears started to close.

Suddenly, a tendril whipped out through the fissure— something different than the creatures that had come through before.

The Erebus! The sight was unmistakable. It was exactly what had been wrapped around the *Andvari* in that fateful image.

The tendril sent out an erratic, crackling energy beam. Wil and Jason dodged to the side. Raena started to move out of its way, but the beam branched out and struck her. She was flung off to the side by the blast, her astral presence disappearing from view.

"*Raena!*" Jason shouted after her, but there was no reply.

Wil wanted to chase after her, but he didn't have any energy to spare. Let go for even an instant, and all their progress would be lost. This was their only chance.

With all his might, he shoved against the creature, barring

it from coming through further.

Except, it wasn't enough. The two of them alone were losing ground.

"We won't make it!" Jason cried.

Wil didn't respond at first. *"There is a way. I need you to trust me."*

"Always."

"Then I need you to let go."

"Dad—"

The protest was swallowed by the void. Wil severed their telepathic connection. He was on his own. That was how it needed to be for what would happen next.

He focused on the spatial distortion surrounding the creature. *"You can't hurt us anymore."*

The sweet energy within the Rift called to him. He'd always resisted its allure, but now he gave in. It flowed into him, charging every aspect of his being.

This was it—the power that had always been just beyond his grasp. Now, having submitted, anything was possible.

He plunged into the Rift. Light swirled around him in a dazzling dance. He sensed the beings beyond the dimensional veil, wondrous and enigmatic. Tarans weren't the supreme beings with any right to decide the fate of the sentient races, nor did the Erebus have the right to speak for all life. He sensed another presence welcoming him, affirming that putting up a barrier to keep the Erebus out of spacetime was the correct course. One day, perhaps they could find a way to coexist, but not yet.

"Won't using our Gifts continue to hurt them?" Wil asked the formless presence who'd welcomed him.

"No more than your kind draw on other lifeforms to sustain

your own existence. They are ancient, but they still have much to learn about balance and sacrifice." The reply came in the form of feelings rather than specific words, but Wil understood the meaning.

"*What will become of them?*"

"*The same as all life. It will exist until it doesn't. What is done with that time, and the impact on others, is what matters. You can choose to consume or to create.*"

In that moment, he understood the Erebus' power—the ability to reshape reality at the most fundamental level. The Rift had been an abomination that never should have been, and now he had the opportunity to erase it as if it had never been there in the first place. No more wound, no more gateway.

I know what I have to do. He focused on sealing the Rift, drawing upon his newfound power. The divide narrowed until there was only a small point remaining.

Wil went to move back through the opening to spacetime—but then he realized the power he now possessed could only be accessed from this side. By returning home, he wouldn't be able to draw enough. To seal the Rift, he'd need to stay.

The glimmer of hope he'd felt faded, replaced by determined acceptance. He'd been prepared for this, and he was ready to give himself to the cause. It was the only way to ensure his people and his loved ones would be safe.

He reached out to seal the remaining sliver of the Rift. The energy flowed through him, knitting the fabric of reality that had been rended apart so long ago. At last, the wound was healed and could never be reopened.

The light surrounded him, becoming one with him. *It's so beautiful...*

And for the first time, he was truly at peace.

— — —

"Dad!" The loss hit Jason immediately—an emptiness where his father's presence had been a moment before.

Had Jason been in his body, he would have found it difficult to draw breath in that moment. But he was here, the only one left to finish the fight.

Part of him wanted to try chasing after his father and Raena, two of the most important people to him. But to focus on them now would place the entire mission at risk.

This is the kind of moment Dad told me about. He was facing a defining inflection point—a crossroads where he could try to save his loved ones, but only at the expense of abandoning the larger battle.

As much as he wished he could find a way to save his father, that wasn't the responsible course of action. *He sacrificed himself to close the Rift. I need to see this through and take out the rest of the enemies.*

There were still monsters trapped in spacetime. Jason knew he needed to work quickly before they had a chance to attack.

He drew more energy into himself—more than he'd ever drawn before, and more than he'd imagined possible. One by one, he drained each creature's lifeforce until they splintered and faded away.

The Aesir ships and TSS fighters helped clean up the rest. They worked together, herding and sapping until none remained.

Exhausted, Jason traced the thread back to his physical form. He returned with a sharp intake of breath, feeling simultaneously confined and relieved to be in his body again. He had no idea how much time had passed.

Rianne turned around, looking at him expectantly from her station at the front of the *Conquest*'s Command Center. "Is it over?"

Jason only nodded in reply, still trying to find the words. He ran to the office connected to the Command Center. It was imperative he talk to his mother back at Headquarters, and he expected that it would be a call best made in private.

Trembling slightly, he sat behind the desk and opened a comm channel to her personal line.

When she answered, her expression was confirmation of everything he'd feared. Her eyes had none of their normal shine, and she had the stoic professionalism of someone doing everything in their power to hold it together. "What happened?" she asked.

"He went into the Rift. He sealed it from the inside," Jason said, trying to keep his tone level.

"I felt a surge, and then…" She faded out. "I can't explain it. I went to check on him, and he was… gone."

"What do you mean?"

"There's no body. Just empty clothes where he was." Her composure cracked then, her eyes glistening with tears. "There's a profound emptiness, and yet I still feel him."

Jason processed her words, replaying his own experience. "I think he ascended."

"I *know* he did." Her voice cracked. "He said there was a way. That we needed to fight the Erebus on their terms."

The realization closed in on Jason. "He knew he'd have to do this. It was his plan all along."

"He recognized it was a possibility, if there was no other way."

He swallowed the lump in his throat. "So, where is he now?"

"Everywhere, I guess."

Jason resisted the temptation to give into his torrent of emotions. He wanted to weep for the loss of his father, but that wouldn't help anything. Now, more than ever, he needed to step up as a leader. He saw the poise his mother was able to maintain, even knowing she'd never hold her husband in her arms again. That's what the TSS and the Taran people needed from Jason now, and he couldn't let them down.

"I'm coming home," Jason told her.

She nodded. "I'll see you soon."

Before he could end the call, the screen lit up with another incoming message. It was from Ryan's private line.

Jason answered, and Ryan's panicked face filled the viewscreen. "Why hasn't Raena woken up yet?"

CHAPTER 28

RYAN KNEW THAT something was terribly wrong. He couldn't feel her in the way he could always sense her in his mind, even while she was sleeping. This was different. And it terrified him.

He knelt next to Raena's motionless form on the couch, brushing one hand gently over her forehead. He wouldn't stop trying to rouse her. His presence, his voice, might make the difference in helping her find her way back.

"What's going on with her?" Jason asked from the viewscreen.

"She's unconscious," Ryan replied, clutching Raena's hand in his. Her skin was still warm to the touch and her breathing regular. "What happened out there?"

Jason worked his mouth but no words came out at first. "We fought them off, but they hit her. I figured she'd retreated back to her body."

"Well, she didn't. Where is she?"

"I don't know, but I'm going to find out."

Deep down, Ryan knew what had happened. Somehow, she must have lost the tether to her body. Her consciousness was drifting, disconnected and lost. "Please hurry."

"It's going to be okay, Ryan. She's strong. We'll—"

Tears stung Ryan's eyes. "It's not just her. She... she's pregnant."

"What?" Jason said with disbelief.

"Just a few weeks along. It was too early to share the news."

"Uh..." It wasn't often Jason was speechless, but the announcement, admittedly, must have caught him off-guard. "I'll find her," he said at last, confidently.

The call ended, leaving Ryan in the silent office with his wife. *Come back to me, my love.*

— — —

Fok! This can't be happening. It was too much for Jason to process in such a short time. His father, now his sister...

In the turmoil of the final stand, he hadn't been able to keep track of Raena. As soon as she'd been knocked out of the battle, he'd assumed that she'd gone back to her body to recover. But if she hadn't woken up, then her consciousness was still drifting somewhere out there.

He took a steadying breath. Panicking wouldn't save Raena. He needed to focus.

I'm not losing two loved ones today.

Jason ran back to the Command Center.

"Sir—" Rianne started as soon as the door opened.

"Not now." He dashed to the central podium and gripped the handholds to link with the ship.

He quickly flew out from his body toward the part of space where they'd taken the stand against the alien invaders. If Raena's essence had been flung somewhere, that's where he needed to start to begin tracing the possible paths.

Upon locating the site of the encounter, he replayed his memories of the event with the hope of establishing a trajectory. Raena's consciousness had been brushed by the Erebus while she was in an astral state and her body was now reacting like she was in a deep sleep. It sounded an awful lot like what had happened to Darin. If Jason could locate Raena's astral form, he could lead her back to her body.

He soared across the void, feeling for any sign of Raena's presence. They weren't bonded in the way he was with Lexi, but their relationship as twins made her a part of him.

"Raena, where are you?" he asked into the void.

There was nothing. Just empty darkness.

"You need to come home. Please." He moved further out, searching, refusing to give up.

And then, there was a faint glimmer in the distance.

He rushed over. The signature was faint, but he could tell it was her. She was weak.

"Raena!"

Jason reached the presence that he knew was her. She didn't have a defined shape in the way they typically took while astral projecting, like a ghost version of their normal physical appearance. Instead, she was a point of light—and growing fainter.

He cradled the spark in his hands. *"Raena, I'm here. I'm going to bring you back."*

The light fluttered, brightening for just a moment before fading again.

"It's not your time yet. Let me take you home."

Gently holding her, he soared toward Tararia. As he got closer, he could sense Ryan's calls to her. The light brightened and grew, taking on more definition. By the time Tararia was in sight, the orb of light darted ahead of Jason, following the call to home.

Only then did Jason return to his body again. His stomach clenched in anticipation of the conversation ahead. Raena was safe now, but their family would never be the same.

— — —

Raena opened her eyes slowly, finding the sudden light a little painful. She blinked to clear her vision.

"Hey, you," Ryan's gentle tone soothed her. He stroked her head. "Welcome back."

"What—" She cut off, struck by a sudden flood of thoughts. She didn't remember contemplating these ideas, but the information was in her mind like she'd had a full, detailed conversation that she didn't recall having.

Ryan's eyes widened with concern. "You okay?"

"Yeah, I…" She sat up, pressing her hand to her temple. "I need to talk to Jason."

She used the voice controls to initiate a video chat with her brother.

He answered in the Command Center of the *Conquest*. "Thank the stars!"

"I appreciate the escort home," she said.

"I thought we may have lost you."

"Nah, you know I have an impeccable sense of direction." She smiled. Her expression dropped when he didn't share her humor. "What happened?"

"Just a minute." The screen went to a black background with the TSS logo. A few seconds later, the image of Jason returned, but with a different backdrop. "Raena... dad is gone."

Everything went numb. "What? How...?"

He explained what had happened while she was unconscious, and she took it in silently.

Her heart ached. "If only I'd been there—"

"You were attacked. It's not your fault," Jason cut in. "We saved the Taran race, that's what's most important." As he spoke, his voice started to crack from emotion. He was saying what he needed to say as a TSS officer, just as Raena needed to acknowledge that their people came first. But deep down, they had lost one of the most important people in their lives. Yes, the Empire had been spared, but their own personal worlds had been shattered.

"He did it for us," Raena said through a tight throat, tears stinging her eyes.

"Did you see any of it?" Jason asked.

She shook her head, glancing over at Ryan's concerned expression. "Not the battle, but I did see... something."

Ryan tilted his head questioningly "What was it?"

Raena thought through the new knowledge and images that were now in her memory, seemingly from nowhere. It was intended as a gift, to be shared. But unlike the 'gifts' from the Erebus, this one was genuine.

"I was given some information," she said at last. "I'm not sure where it came from. It may have been the original Gatekeepers, or something else entirely. But I feel certain now that the aliens behind the Coalition were a rogue faction. The others of their kind consider the dispute with Tarans resolved."

"How do you know that?" her brother asked.

"I just do. I think I may have spoken to them when I was

in… another place. And I think Dad was there, too."

Hope filled Jason's eyes. "So he's…?"

"Like Mom told you, I don't think he's dead. He's just in a… different state now. And, eventually, we'll all be together again."

Jason looked away, fighting to maintain composure. "Yeah."

Despite everything, Raena felt a sense of peace about what had happened to her father. In her unexplained memories, he'd comforted her and told her not to worry. He had accepted his fate, and she should, too.

Ryan glanced between the viewscreen and Raena. "You should probably get checked out by a doctor. You were out for a while there."

Raena nodded, recognizing his concern wasn't just about her. She felt the new life safe inside her and knew there was no cause for worry. "Okay."

"I'm glad you're all right, Raena. We'll talk soon," her brother said.

"Thank you for coming after me."

"Glad to be of service, my lady," he said with just enough sarcasm to let her know he'd be okay.

As soon as the call ended, Ryan wrapped her in his arms. "I was worried I'd lost you."

She squeezed him back. "I'll always find my way home."

— — —

It was clear from the cheers outside Celine's cell door—and the fact that she was still alive—that the TSS had been successful in their stand against the Erebus.

She shook her head with disbelief. *Amazing. Maybe I shouldn't have doubted them.*

Even so, she believed she'd done the right thing. Succeeding with one-in-a-billion odds didn't make for a good investment strategy. She'd banked on the sure bet, and she stood by that decision.

Unfortunately, the TSS' success meant that she was now doomed to live out her remaining days as a captive. Or there was the possibility of execution—if they sought a treason sentence, which was likely. In either case, there wasn't much left to live for.

She sighed deeply, not even having enough fight left in her to be upset. She'd been exhausted for a long time. This wasn't the reprieve she'd imagined, but at least she didn't have to worry anymore.

Celine was just about to attempt a nap when a prickle of energy passed over her skin. In front of her, a form took place at the center of a spatial distortion. A long, blue robe and then an ageless feminine face.

"Hello, Felina." Celine didn't bother asking how the Gatekeeper had been able to get inside a locked cell. The hybrid's skills were largely a mystery, but she knew they weren't bound to the conventional rules of physical reality.

"Our job here is done. We're leaving now," Felina stated.

Celine nodded, understanding the unspoken meaning of the statement. If the Gatekeeper hybrids were moving on from the Taran Empire, there was no use for their former Taran collaborators. "And you're cleaning up loose ends?"

"It was always a risk for you to know so much. You understood the consequences."

"I have no regrets."

Felina stood in silence for several moments. "I didn't believe they'd succeed."

"They're more stubborn than I gave them credit for." Celine shrugged. "We did what we believed was necessary. I don't know if this peace will last, but I'm glad Tarans will have a chance to continue evolving. Who knows, maybe we'll get it right this time?"

"You are a tenacious species. We've learned a lot from you."

"I hope you can put that knowledge to good use."

"We will." Felina stepped forward, holding out her hand toward Celine's forehead, an electrical force swelling in her palm. "You did well."

CHAPTER 29

CHANGE TOOK TIME, but Raena could already see the transformations, even though it had only been a month since the standoff with the Erebus. The real difference was, no doubt, that the Coalition was no longer pulling strings behind the scenes. Sure, divergent groups of people still had conflicting beliefs, which inevitably led to strife, but there was a distinction between organic disagreement and manufactured drama.

The Coalition had been in the business of bringing out the worst in people. They'd wanted society to fail. More than just marketing campaigns in the Outer Colonies, the Coalition had been working through Monsari's media contacts to spread pervasive messages of dissent. Now that the manipulation had been revealed, the general public was justifiably distrusting of everything they were told. However, that distrust toward authority and the media resulted in them being more willing to have conversations with their fellow citizens. People had started to come together within their local communities in a way that exceeded Raena's wildest expectations.

There would still be serious issues, she had no doubt, but

they'd had a breakthrough. They'd seen a path forward for the worlds to be more independent while still respecting the value of centralized leadership. But the people needed to have a voice, and they'd need to work out those details. A democratic republic was possible, just as she'd proposed, but it would take time to implement. Whatever form it took, she wanted to make sure they got it right.

The last several weeks had been a busy blur dealing with the aftermath of the civil conflicts and her own recovery from the ordeal. The knowledge that had been planted in her memory while she was unconscious occupied her thoughts during the few quiet moments she had to herself. It was impossible to verify, but she felt she understood Taran history now—where they'd come from and what they'd been through over the ages. Maybe, it would be enough for her to help direct the Empire away from repeating those past mistakes.

It would take time to get the root of the lingering corruption with Makaris and other influential players. There were still small pockets of Coalition activity, but the organization had been gutted and no longer posed an imminent threat. The planets that had been drawn to the Coalition's message might be forever changed, but it was their right to seek independence—though Raena suspected they wouldn't pull away completely. Only time would tell. Until then, she'd do whatever she could to help transport people to wherever they felt safe and help provide resources for them to build lives in whatever places people chose to call home.

There'd been the added complication of Celine's sudden death. The official public word was natural causes from an aneurysm while in TSS custody. However, Raena knew the truth about Celine's fate because of inside access to the security footage from her cell. It had been a sign that the Gatekeepers no longer wished to meddle in Taran affairs, and that offered hope for the Empire to rebuild without that destructive influence.

With the ongoing investigations, Raena expected to be kept quite busy for the foreseeable future. So, when her grandfather requested to meet with her privately, she was hesitant to step away from her other responsibilities. Nonetheless, she knew he wouldn't have asked to meet face-to-face if it wasn't important.

On the few occasions they'd spoken since her father's ascension, it was clear her grandfather had taken the loss hard. While she missed her father terribly, she'd known she would lose him at some point during her life. Conversely, it wasn't the natural order of things for a parent to have to say goodbye to their child. She understood why her grandparents were struggling, especially after all their sacrifices as a family over the years.

Raena took a shuttle over to the Third Region, where she'd agreed to meet her grandfather at the Sietinen estate. He met her in one of the private conference rooms overlooking the garden.

"Thank you for coming, Raena," Cris greeted, giving her a hug. He looked more tired and aged than she'd ever seen him.

"It's always great to see you." She flashed a warm smile. "I imagine this isn't just to socialize, though."

"No, it's not." He took a seat across the table from her. "I've been thinking a lot over the last month about where to go from here. I see the change that's sweeping across the Empire, and I don't know that I have another revolution in me."

"Hey, it might be kinda fun," she jested.

He shook his head. "I'm done, Raena."

His serious tone caught her attention. "What do you mean?"

"Everything we do as leaders for Tararia is for our family. But instead, we spend all our time working and taking care of others. SiNavTech doesn't need me. Tararia doesn't need another figurehead. But I can be a great-grandparent to your children and be there in a way I wasn't for you. I couldn't give a fok anymore about politics compared to that."

"What about Sietinen? And the High Council?" she asked. "*Someone* needs to govern."

"Yes, someone. Just not me."

"And SiNavTech?"

He shrugged. "This family is already so obscenely wealthy that it doesn't matter if we never draw another credit in transit fee royalties. The company is probably better off with the current administrative team at the helm. They should make the navigation network a public service."

She blinked at him. "Give it all up?"

"Are you opposed to that idea?"

Raena smiled. "On the contrary, I love it."

He returned her smile. "Good. What you're building with Ryan is far more exciting than maintaining an old transit infrastructure. Besides, the independent jump drive tech is the future. You can work out how best to leverage those patents with your mom."

"Yeah, I have some things in mind."

"I figured you would."

"Foremost, it needs a new name. 'Independent jump drive' is a mouthful. I was thinking 'Sights drive'." Her grandfather had adopted the pseudonym when he'd left home to join the

TSS, and it was the name her father had gone by during the years he was developing the technology. Given that history and their aspirational sights on the future, it seemed fitting.

Cris smiled. "That's perfect."

She sat back. "I wonder what people are going to say when they hear about SiNavTech going public?"

"Try to decipher a hidden agenda, no doubt. But the truth is, I never wanted this. I've accomplished everything professionally I set out to do, and I'd rather enjoy the time I have left in this life—with you and our family. You're all I want now."

"No arguments here."

He stared out the window, in thought, for several moments before turning back to her. "You and Ryan are the kind of leaders Tararia—and the Empire—need now. I'll be here for advice, but you're ready to take the lead."

She was about to protest, but then she realized it was true. She did feel up for the challenge. Excited for it, even. "I'll do my best."

"I look forward to witnessing the transformation. I believe we're about to enter a new golden age."

She nodded. "I hope so. I'll do everything I can to respect the will of the people."

"They're ready to have a voice, no doubt about that."

"Yeah." She dropped her eyes, feeling overwhelmed. A lot of responsibility was about to transfer to her. She met his gaze again. "Thank you for everything. You've taught me so much, and I'm grateful you'll be in my children's lives, too."

"It's been a privilege to watch you come into your own, Raena."

"I know I still have a lot to learn, but I'll get there."

He smiled. "I have no doubt."

"But I know this for certain," she said, "I'm exactly where I'm meant to be."

— — —

Kira placed the last items from her TUF office in a transport bin, giving the space a fond smile. *You served me well.*

A light knock sounded on the doorframe, and she turned to see Leon holding a crate of his own. "Ready to head out?"

Kira picked up her bin. "Yep."

The TUF had proven its value as a mediating force for the Empire, and it was time to expand the operation. Saera had helped secure a former TSS base—abandoned since the Bakzen War—to serve as a new operational center for the TUF. It would give them the space to grow and establish their own professional culture.

Naturally, she'd asked Leon to accompany her as head of the research division. They'd even picked up several interested candidates from the TSS, including Darin Suro. They had a long way to go, but she was excited to see what they could become.

"I'm going to miss it around here," Leon said as they strolled toward the elevator.

"Yeah, me too. It's been a good ride."

Leon smiled. "But hey, on to new adventures, right?"

She grinned back. "I can't wait."

— — —

Jason was still trying to find his equilibrium again. Lexi had been a tremendous support, but TSS Headquarters just wasn't the same without his father around.

Beyond the blow to their immediate family, Wil's loss had been palpable around the entire organization. He *was* the TSS in many ways, and it was unclear what would happen to the leadership structure going forward.

Saera had stepped into the role of High Commander, as was appropriate for Lead Agent. In the month since they'd stood up to the Erebus and won, Jason was amazed how his mother had been able to fulfill those duties while mourning the loss of her husband. It was a true testament to her strength as a leader—one he admired and hoped to emulate.

There'd been quiet moments in the weeks since, when it was just the two of them alone, where she'd broken down. A piece of herself was missing, and that pain was incomprehensible to him. In just the short time he'd known Lexi, already he couldn't imagine what he'd do if he lost her. It was unfathomable how much worse it would be after decades with each other.

A month wasn't enough time to heal, but it was a start. They were finding a way forward, supporting each other.

Jason was working in his office when his mother came to see him. "Hey, you have a few minutes?" she asked.

"Of course. Come on in." He motioned to the visitor chairs across from his desk.

She sat down, her lips pursed in contemplation, as if searching for the right phrasing. "Jason, I'd like for you to have something." She pulled out a small box from her pocket, holding it gingerly between her fingertips as she flipped it around. "It feels right for you to have it." She handed him the box across the desk.

Jason took it from her. "What is it?"

"Our set of starstone wedding rings."

His heart skipped a beat. "Mom—"

"I know your father already offered and you declined, but that was before. The ring I've worn every day for more than thirty years is the one that has significance to me. These... I think you can give them new meaning. It's something to remember him by, if you want. You don't have to wear them. I just think they should be yours."

Jason looked down at the box, emotion welling in his chest. "Thank you." He flipped open the lid, immediately struck by the rainbow shimmer of the stones on the matching set of rings, resonating while the fragments were in proximity to each other. "Lexi usually isn't one for fancy things, but I think she'd make an exception."

His mother smiled at him, momentarily hiding the sadness in her eyes. "I've been so happy to see how you two have grown together. I have no doubt you'll be able to do anything you set your minds to."

Jason closed the box. "I have no idea where to go from here. I've never felt so lost."

"It may feel that way right now, but you're not. You have an amazing life and career ahead of you. A partner who loves you unconditionally. You're going to be just fine."

He stared at her with amazement. "How have you been so strong through all this?"

"I'm just good at hiding how I really feel." She looked down at her empty hands before meeting his gaze again. "I miss him... *so* much. But at the same time, I know I'm not really alone. He's still here, watching over us in a way we won't be able to understand until we cross over that ethereal veil ourselves. What happened to him isn't death, it's a new kind of life. Really, I think it's what he wanted. Maybe not so soon, but it was inevitable. And in that new way of being, there won't be the same sense of time. No matter how much longer I'm here, we'll eventually be reunited and be able to pick up where we left off, like it's only been a moment.

"I intend to make the most of however long I have left, for his sake. I'll miss him every day, but I'll celebrate the time we had together in this life. I have you and your sister. I'll have grandchildren. I don't want to dwell on his loss, but rather share the light of his life. I hope you'll be able to do the same."

Jason's throat tightened. "Yeah. That sounds perfect."

He got up from his desk and walked around it to hug her. She eagerly pulled him into a tight embrace.

"I love you and I'm so proud of you," she said. "You are the best parts of him."

"I'll try to honor his legacy."

"You already have, Jason." She released him. "Speaking of which, there's something the senior Agents and I wanted to discuss with you."

"What?"

"Come with me."

She led him down the hall to the large conference room next to the High Commander's office. Every time he passed by the room, he still half-expected to see his father inside. Jason turned his gaze away, unable to bear how empty the space still felt without him.

They entered the conference room, where a dozen senior Agents were already gathered, including the division heads and Michael.

"What's this?" Jason asked, shooting his mom a quizzical look.

"It's time we formalize a plan for the TSS going forward," Saera stated.

"The first order of business is the matter of resource allocation and site use," Michael said. "To put it in simple terms, a lot of grand ideas have been put forth, but we're already busting at the seams. We need to do something about that."

"It's been suggested that we expand the facility beyond the current ring structure to begin building out the hollow space in the former subspace containment shell," Saera said, directing a knowing glance toward Jason. "Personally, I think that's a great idea, but I'd love all of your input."

Murmurs of agreement sounded around the table.

Saera smiled. "Well, that was easy."

Ethan raised his hand. "Not to be a naysayer, but how are we going to pay for that?"

"Wil sat on a fortune his entire life, never sure if there would be an urgent need for those resources," Saera said. "He dipped into it as needs arose—always for the TSS and for the good of the Taran people. I can think of no better use for those funds than to expand TSS Headquarters into a place where we can be free to have families and a true community. The same goes for some much-needed updates to other facilities that are still relics of past wars, which have no place in our future. We can make those changes a reality now. It's what he always wanted."

Everyone nodded somberly.

"And that brings us to the matter of succession," Saera continued. "Namely, the role of Lead Agent."

The Agents looked around the table at each other in a seemingly coordinated move.

"I'm quite happy where I am in Ops," Michael stated. "I fully endorse Jason stepping up into the role."

His stomach dropped. "Me?"

Ian smiled. "Don't look so surprised. You have the highest CR now. It's convention for it to pass to you."

"There are other people a lot more experienced," Jason replied.

"Maybe so, but the best way to get experience is to, well, have experiences," Ian continued. "It's not like you'll be alone."

"We'll be here to support you in any way you need," Michael said.

Jason swallowed. The faces around the table were expectant. He couldn't turn it down. "I'd be honored."

His mother nodded. "Then consider it done. We can do a handoff in the coming weeks."

"Okay," he agreed.

"I think that does it for now," she said, standing up. "Thank you, everyone. There are going to be a lot of adjustments around here, but we still have each other."

The others nodded and murmured their mutual support before drifting out of the room.

Saera lingered, motioning for Jason to stay with her.

"You *are* ready for this," she said when the others had gone.

"It's all happened so fast."

"I know. But you have the innate attitude and have been through your share of conflicts. I was even younger than you when I became Lead Agent."

Jason's eyes widened as he did the mental math. "Stars, you were!" He shook his head. "I can't believe how much you and Dad went through so young."

"I'm thankful every day that you had a proper childhood. We did everything we could to make it last as long as possible. No one should have to grow up as quickly as we did."

"It's funny how you can't wait to grow up when you're young, and then adulthood hits and you long for the simplicity of youth."

"The eternal struggle. No matter what form our race takes across the eons, I expect that will be one constant."

"I think you're right about that."

She looked him over. "I want you to know, the big seat is yours whenever you feel ready."

"Isn't one promotion enough for a single day?"

She smiled. "I'll stick it out for as long as you need me to. And I'll teach you everything I can. But I'm ready to explore other aspects of life that duty has forced me to neglect."

It didn't take much for Jason to pick up on her meaning. "You want to go to Tararia to be with Raena."

"Your grandparents missed out on watching you grow up because we took you to Earth. They made me promise I wouldn't make that same sacrifice myself, if ever the opportunity arose."

"I had you all to myself for these past few years. I suppose it's only fair I share."

"You can keep me for a while longer. I'm okay missing out on the diaper years."

Jason laughed. "Wow, you need to work on that grandmotherly patience."

"Oh, that's weird."

"What?"

"Grandma. That makes me feel incredibly old when you put it like that."

"I'm sure previous generations went through a similar realization. Something tells me you'll manage."

She smiled. "At least I have a few more months to wrap my head around it."

"Yeah, same."

Saera patted his arm. "You're going to be just fine, Jason."

He nodded. "Yeah. I guess I should go share the news with Lexi."

"That's a good plan."

"I'll see you tomorrow morning and you can start showing me the ropes?"

"See you then."

With his hand on the ring box in his pocket, Jason headed to his quarters.

Lexi was lounging on the couch, working on her tablet, when he arrived. "Hey, you!" she greeted with a broad smile. "How was your day?"

"Pretty average… until this afternoon. I got some big news."

"What?"

"I'm going to be Lead Agent."

She lit up, jumping off the couch to give him a celebratory hug. "That's amazing!"

"It is. It doesn't feel real yet."

"I'm sure it will when a pile of paperwork lands in your inbox."

He sighed. "I already miss being a flight instructor."

She tilted her head. "Is there any regulation preventing the Lead Agent from also teaching flight lessons?"

"Come to think of it, I don't think there is."

"Well, considering you're the boss, you can kinda do

whatever you want, huh? I mean, you set the rules, right?"

He smiled. "You might be on to something there." His fingers wrapped around the box still in his pocket. He directed Lexi back to the couch and they sat together. "Are you happy here?"

"Yeah. I mean, most of the time. I wish Melisa had stayed, but I'm glad she reached out to let me know she's settled on Merda. I have you here, though, so there's really nowhere else I'd rather be."

"Well, being Lead Agent will lead to High Commander. I think I'll be stuck here for the foreseeable future."

Lexi placed a hand on his chest. "I wouldn't consider it 'stuck'. It's a good place filled with amazing people. I think we're pretty lucky."

He nodded. "Yeah, we are. And the two of us?"

"What about us?"

"If I'm going to be here, and you want to be here, too… seems like maybe we should make things official."

She tensed with excitement. "As in…?"

He pulled out the box, keeping it closed. "It's been a roller coaster the last few months, but you've been the constant in my life. I can't imagine tackling future trials with anyone else. I knew I'd fall in love with you the moment we met, and what we have together has exceeded all my expectations." He flipped open the box. "The only thing that could make it better is being able to call you my wife. Will you marry me?"

Her mouth dropped open slightly as she took in the dazzling rings. She managed a nod before she was able to form the words. "Yes. Stars, yes, of course!" She kissed him and wrapped her arms around his neck. "I love you so much."

Jason held her close. "I love you, too."

When they parted, he took out the starstone engagement ring for her and slipped it on her finger. While not an exact fit, it was close enough to fulfill the moment.

She admired it. "It's stunning. Were these your parents'?"

He nodded. "I hope that's not too weird."

Lexi shook her head. "No, I admire their relationship. I'm happy to be able to wear a symbol of what I hope to build with you, too."

"I'm glad you got to know him."

"Same." She paused. "It's going to be different around here."

"It is. There's talk of renovating Headquarters to expand the housing. We can establish a new branch of the civilian training initiative and have room to grow. People can have families. We can make this a real community."

"That sounds amazing."

"Yeah, it feels like the right thing to do for the TSS going forward."

She nodded. "After everything that's happened, it's kind of the end of an era."

"Instead," he interlaced his fingers with hers, "I like to think of it as a new beginning."

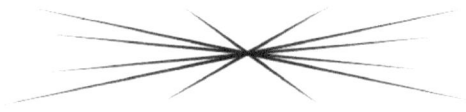

ADDITIONAL READING

Cadicle Space Opera Series by A.K. DuBoff
Book 1: Rumors of War (Vol. 1-3)
Book 2: Web of Truth (Vol. 4)
Book 3: Crossroads of Fate (Vol. 5)
Book 4: Path of Justice (Vol. 6)
Book 5: Scions of Change (Vol. 7)

Mindspace Series by A.K. DuBoff
Book 1: Infiltration
Book 2: Conspiracy
Book 3: Offensive
Book 4: Endgame

Verity Chronicles by T.S. Valmond & A.K. DuBoff
Book 1: Exile
Book 2: Divided Loyalties
Book 3: On the Run

Shadowed Space Series by Lucinda Pebre & A.K. DuBoff
Book 1: Shadow Behind the Stars
Book 2: Shadow Rising
Book 3: Shadow Beyond the Reach

In Darkness Dwells by James Fox & A.K. DuBoff

AUTHORS` NOTES

Thank you for reading *Empire United*! While this is a pause point for the series, I never think of any wrap-up book as being truly "the end".

It means so much to me that you've read this series and come along for this journey through the Cadicle Universe. I never could have dreamed I'd have readers all over the world, and it's an incredible feeling to have been able to share the stories of these characters who've been living inside my mind since I was a kid.

This was an extremely emotional book for me to write, in part because I knew this was the conclusion of a story arc but also because of Wil's fate. I spent a lot of time debating with myself about how this story arc should wrap up, and I concluded that this was really the only way. The enemy was so powerful that the story's heroes couldn't get through the encounter wholly unscathed, and Wil would never truly escape his demons from the Bakzen War so long as he remained in his current life.

It's difficult for me to say goodbye to a character who's been in my life since I was eleven—that's longer than anyone I can still call a "friend". The Sietinens and their loved ones have become a sort of family to me after all these years, and it wasn't easy letting go. Admittedly, one of the reasons this book was delayed was because there were parts of it I put off writing, knowing what I had to do. But, I'd been setting up that fate for a long time, and it became obvious to me in Book 3, so I had to follow through.

Nonetheless, I can't think of it as goodbye, more of a "see you later", as they discuss in the final chapters. If thought is energy and all that energy goes out to the greater cosmos, then perhaps these ideas that have only existed in our imagination are manifest in a different reality and we'll one day get to meet the characters.

During the beta review process for this book, one reader asked me why Wil didn't tell his family sooner that he might have to sacrifice himself. I thought that I would share what I told him in case you were thinking the same thing.

It's *frustrating* that Wil didn't share his thoughts/ intentions sooner, but that's by design. The key is in this paragraph from Chapter 25:

> [Saera] clearly knew [Wil] had been holding something back from her. But this matter was simply too important—he'd needed to prepare for the worst-case contingency, and she wouldn't have allowed him to think in those terms. Under other circumstances, he'd welcome her eternal optimism. However, he needed to come to terms, for his own sake.

It has always been in Wil's character to keep things to himself--especially big, weighty things. He's never been able to let go of that feeling of responsibility to single-handedly carry the weight of the universe, and despite showing some growth in that area, that never really changed right up until the end. In order to mentally and emotionally prepare for potentially dying in the fight, he needed to accept that this might be the end. No one around him would have willingly allowed him to think like that—saying that they'd find another way—and that would prevent him from gaining the closure he needed to do what was necessary. Waiting until the last minute to reveal his intentions allowed him to get that personal closure and be unburdened going into the final fight.

At its core, this book was about finding a sense of purpose and taking the actions necessary to move forward. It's nowhere near an end for the characters and their journey, but it's a new life chapter for many.

If you have any specific questions for me or would like to discuss anything, you can reach me via the Contact Form on my website. I try to reply to everyone, and I love to connect with my readers!

I owe a massive thank you to my incredible alpha and beta readers on this book who read the early drafts and made sure that I'd tied up loose ends. Sincere thanks to John, Steve B., Leo, David, Steve D., Gil, and Louise, as well as James for helping me brainstorm.

Thank you also to Steve B., Liz, Diane, Manie, and my other proofreaders for helping to add the final polish. I appreciate your sharp eyes and critical thoughts!

I also want to especially thank my husband for his love and support, and for working hard so we could buy a home and start a new chapter in our own lives.

Thank you again for reading the Taran Empire Saga. There will be other forthcoming novels in the Cadicle Universe, and I'll be spinning up an original series in a brand new universe soon. Until next time, happy reading!

GLOSSARY

Timeline of Key Events

All dates are adjusted for the standard Earth calendar

~98,000 BC - Ancient war and signing of the peace treaty between Tarans, the Gatekeepers, and the transdimensional aliens

AD ~50 - Priesthood's rise to power as a governing entity on Tararia

AD ~1000 - Taran Revolution period, following the split of the Priesthood when the Aesir left Tararia

AD 1587 - First skirmishes of the Bakzen War

AD 2016 - Invention of the Independent Jump Drive

AD 2025 - Official end of the Bakzen War; destruction of the Bakzen homeworld

AD 2050 - Fall of the Priesthood; transition of Dynasty corporations into public entities

AD 2054 - Reactivation of Gatekeeper tech

AD 2055 - Reopening of the rift/tear and reappearance of the transdimensional aliens

Key Terms

Aesen *(Ay-sen)* - The foundational energy of the universe; pure energy capable of being shaped into any form. *Aesen* energy exists in a higher dimension and can be drawn upon to perform feats of telekinesis.

Aesir *(Ay-seer)* - A group of Tarans who broke away from the Empire around 1000 AD (Earth years) to engage in metaphysical pursuits, such as reading cosmic energy patterns. The founders of the Aesir were all former members of the Priesthood and possess strong telepathic and telekinetic abilities. The Aesir are isolationist and long-lived, possessing advanced technology lost to the rest of the Empire during the Priesthood's corrupt reign.

Agent - A class of officer within the TSS reserved for those with telekinetic and telepathic gifts. There are three levels of Agent based on level of ability: Primus, Sacon and Trion.

Ateron *(at-er-on)* - An element that oscillates between normal space and subspace, facilitating high levels of telekinetic energy transfer.

Baellas *(bAy-las)* - A corporation run by the Baellas Dynasty, producing housewares, clothing, furniture, and other textiles for use across the Taran civilization. Additional specialty lines managed by other smaller corporations are licensed to Baellas for distribution.

Bakzen *(Bak-zen)* - A militaristic race that lived beyond the Outer Colonies. All Bakzen were clones and possessed varying levels of telekinetic capabilities.

Bakzen War - A centuries-long conflict waged primarily by the TSS in a secret spatial rift.

Cadicle *(Kad-i-kl)* - The definition of individual perfection in the Priesthood's founding ideology, with the emergence of the Cadicle heralding the start to the next stage of evolution for the Taran race.

Course Rank (CR) - The official measurement of an Agent's ability level, taken at the end of their training immediately before graduation from Junior Agent to Agent. The Course Rank Test is a multi-phase examination, including direct focusing of telekinetic energy into a testing sphere. The magnitude of energy focused during the exercise is the primary factor dictating the Agent's CR.

Dainetris Dynasty *(Dayn-ee-tris)* - One of the seven High Dynasties, the Dainetris Dynasty was considered lost for nearly two hundred years. After members of the family spoke out against the Priesthood's corruption, the Priesthood destroyed the family and buried the city that served as their seat of power. The Dynasty's status was restored in 2050, and a new seat of power was established on the Priesthood's former administrative island, renamed Morningstar Isle after the flower in the Dainetris crest.

Earth - A planet occupied by humans, a divergent race of Tarans. Considered a "lost colony," Earth is not recognized as part of the Taran government.

Enforcers - The police force of the galaxy; a division of the Tararian Guard.

Erebus *(Ayr-eh-bus)* - A race of transdimensional aliens capable of manipulating *aesen* at the foundational level to create and un-make matter within the spacetime dimension. The beings can reach down into spacetime through dimensional rifts and are capable of telepathic manipulation.

Gatekeepers - An ancient alien race with advanced portal tech. Little is known about their native form beyond that they are higher-dimensional beings and create hybrid versions of themselves to interact with spacetime reality, including Taran hybrid vessels.

Generation Cycle - Also known as the Twelve Generation Cycle. A genetic mutation in Tarans where seven generations will express no telepathic or telekinetic abilities, followed by five with those Gifts—the strongest expression being 10th Generation. It is believed that the genetic line descending from the Cadicle may hold the key to developing a genetic patch to fix the mutation. The Aesir left the Empire before the dissemination of the gene therapy that resulted in the Generation Cycle, so they do not suffer from the mutation; they do not intermingle with other Tarans for this reason.

Gifts - The colloquial term used to describe a variety of telepathic and telekinetic abilities, ranging from simple mind-reading, to object levitation, to manipulating energy fields on small or large scales. These Gifts typically emerge between the age of sixteen to eighteen. Before the Priesthood's fall, all but telepathy were illegal; since then, telekinesis has been legalized for non-violent applications. The TSS remains the foremost training institution for those with abilities.

High Commander - The officer responsible for the administration of the TSS. Always an Agent from the Primus class.

High Dynasties - Seven families on Tararia that control the corporations critical to the functioning of Taran society. Each have a designated Region on Tararia, which is the seat of their power. The Dynasties in aggregate form A High Council oligarchical government for the Taran Empire.

Independent Jump Drive - A jump drive that does not rely on the SiNavTech beacon network for navigation, instead using a mathematical formula to calculate jump positions through normal space and the Rift.

Initiate - The second stage of the TSS training program for Agents. A trainee will typically remain at the Initiate stage for two or three years.

Jump Drive - The engine system for travel through subspace. Conventional jump drives require an interface with the SiNavTech navigation system and subspace navigation beacons.

Junior Agent - The third stage of the TSS training program for Agents. A trainee will typically remain at the Junior Agent stage for three to five years.

Lead Agent - The highest-ranking Agent and second-in-command to the High Commander. The Lead Agent is responsible for overseeing the Agent training program and frequently serves as a liaison for TSS business with Taran colonies.

Lower Dynasties - There are 247 recognized Lower Dynasties in Taran society. Many of these families have a presence on Tararia, but some are residents of the other inner colonies.

Makaris Corp *(Mak-ayr-is)* - A corporation run by the Makaris High Dynasty responsible for the distribution of food, water filters, and other necessary supplies to Taran colonies without diverse natural resources.

Monsari Power Solutions (MPS) *(Mon-sayr-ee)* - A corporation run by the Monsari Dynasty, responsible for power generation systems for the Taran worlds, including geothermal generators, portable generators, and reactors to power spacecraft. Their foremost product are the Perpetual Energy Modules (PEMs) that function in the most critical systems.

Rift - A habitable pocket between normal space and subspace. The largest rift—specifically known as *the* Rift—is located at the site of the former Bakzen homeworld, a wound left by the destruction of the planet at the end of the Bakzen War. It is thought to be a place where the veil between dimensions is thinner.

Sacon *(Sak-on)* - The middle tier of TSS Agents. Typically, Sacon Agents will score a CR between 6 and 7.9.

Sietinen Dynasty *(sIgh-tin-en)* - High Dynasty overseeing the Third Region of Tararia, responsible for the SiNavTech navigation network. Considered the most influential of the Taran dynasties due to the family's ties to the TSS and responsibility for the Empire's transportation infrastructure.

SiNavTech - A corporation run by the Sietinen High Dynasty, which controls and maintains the subspace navigation network used by Taran civilians and the TSS.

Spatial Dislocation - The act of physically transitioning from normal space to the brink of subspace, either by means of a jump drive or telekinetic abilities.

TalEx - A corporation run by the Talsari Dynasty, managing mining operations and ore processing across Taran territories.

Tarans *(tayr-ans)* - The general term for all individuals with genetic relation to Tararian ancestry. Several divergent races are recognized by their planet or system. Humans are of Taran descent.

Tararia *(Tayr-ayr-ee-a)* - The home planet for the Taran race and seat of the central government.

Tararian *(Tayr-ayr-ee-an)* - Someone from or residing on the planet Tararia.

Tararian Guard - The military and peacekeeping arm of the Taran Empire. The military side is known colloquially as the

Guard, and the personnel on the policing side are known as Enforcers.

Tararian Selective Service (TSS) - A quasi-military organization with two divisions: (1) Agent Class, and (2) Militia Class. Agents possess telekinetic and telepathic abilities; the TSS is the only place where individuals with such gifts can gain official training. The Militia class offers a formal training program for those without telekinetic abilities, providing tactical and administrative support to Agents. TSS Headquarters is located inside the moon of the planet Earth. Additional Militia training facilities are located throughout the Taran worlds and there are numerous TSS bases throughout the Empire. Since the end of the Bakzen War, the TSS has also engaged in more academic pursuits so many Agents can pursue careers related to the sciences rather than being 'soldiers'.

Trainee - The generic term for a student of the TSS, and also the term for first-year Agent students (when capitalized Trainee). Students are not fully "initiated" into the TSS until their second year.

Trion *(Try-on)* - The lowest tier of TSS Agents. Typically, Trion Agents will score a CR below 5.9.

Priesthood of the Cadicle - The institution formerly responsible for oversight of all governmental affairs and the flow of information throughout the Taran colonies. During its rule until 2050 AD, the Priesthood had jurisdiction over even the High Dynasties and provided a tiebreaking vote on new initiatives. The organization perpetrated many secret experimentations on Taran citizens and was voted out of power by the High Council. All known associates have been arrested or were killed in the fall.

Primus *(Pree-mus)* - The highest of three Agent classes within the TSS, reserved for those with the strongest telekinetic abilities. Typically, Primus Agents will score a CR above 8.

Primus Elite - A special classification of Agent above Primus signifying an exceptional level of ability.

Vaenetri Dynasty *(Vayn-E-tree)* - High Dynasty overseeing the First Region of Tararia. The family operates VComm, a corporation specializing in telecommunications.

VComm - A telecommunications corporation owned and operated by the Vaenetri Dynasty.

Voydite - A unique crystalline substance used to make the nanotube casings for PEMs. The Monsari Dynasty holds a complete monopoly on the secret source of the material.

ABOUT THE AUTHOR

A.K. (Amy) DuBoff has always loved science fiction in all its forms—books, movies, shows, and games. If it involves outer space, even better! She is a Nebula Award finalist and *USA Today* bestselling author most known for her Cadicle Universe, but she's also written a variety of space fantasy and comedic sci-fi. Now a full-time author, Amy can frequently be found traveling the world. When she's not writing, she enjoys wine tasting, binge-watching TV series, and playing epic strategy board games.

www.amyduboff.com

www.ingramcontent.com/pod-product-compliance
Lightning Source LLC
Chambersburg PA
CBHW060219030726
47499CB00004B/1107